TROUBLING THE ASHES

a novel by **Shirley A. Aaron**

Woodson Knowles Publishing Group

108 S 8th Street

Opelika, AL 36801

Aaron, Shirley A.

Troubling the Ashes / by Shirley A. Aaron.—1st ed.

Summary: Marley Jane Steele and her family are living through the aftermath of the desegregation of schools in the 60s, which resulted in a school being burned to the ground in a small, rural Alabama town, divided by racism.

p. cm.

ISBN: 978-0-9905675-8-5 (paperback)

First Edition

1. Alabama—History—Fiction. 2. United States—Civil Rights—Fiction. 3. Lee v Macon County Board—Law and legislation—History. 4. Segregation in education—United States—History. 5. Family—Fiction. 6. Murder—Fiction. 7. Racism—African-Americans—Fiction.

c2016   [Fic]

Cover design by Iris Saya Miller

Cover image of the two young girls is used by permission of Leslie G. Leak and Serlanda S. Todd.

Dedicated To:

Fred Gray, Civil Rights Attorney
and
Plaintiffs of Lee v. Macon County Board of Education

In Memory Of:

Judge Frank M. Johnson
and
Robert B. Anderson

"For an angel went down at a certain season into the pool, and troubled the water: whatsoever then first after the troubling of the water stepped in was made whole..."

— John 5:4

Chapter 1

December, 1963, was the last youthful, ordinary time that I can remember before my perception of the world around me changed forever. It would be my last month of innocence before a new year began, the last month of my almost total unawareness of what was happening so close to home.

Looking back over the decades of my life makes me realize how unaware I was of the overt racism that existed less than fifty miles from where I lived. Until that time, I was essentially untouched by the evil forces that regarded racism and injustice as the normal and acceptable way of life. January, 1964, would change all of that. And it would change me, an ordinary young woman with an ordinary life.

* * * * * * *

It was December 18, and we couldn't wait to begin enjoying the Christmas break. None of us knew the conflict that was so near—yet so far—as we rushed out into the December cold, with dark clouds overhead. The clouds hung so low that they seemed to hover just over our heads, casting shadows around us. The wind whipped our scarves and bit our cheeks, as we bent into the teeth of the wind and walked rapidly down the steep sidewalk to the car.

The cold, cloudy Wednesday was the beginning of a two-week Christmas break from shorthand, typing, filing, and bookkeeping. We four girls pushed all of that from our heads before we opened the door of the school and thrust ourselves into unusually cold temperatures for the South.

In our hurry, we didn't make our usual comments about how downtown Opelika, Alabama, with its dips and hills, was dressed for Christmas. None of us bothered to wave at the Salvation Army volunteer who was ringing a bell over a red bucket. None of us wanted to walk down an extra steep sloping hill for a Coke at the drugstore, before heading home from Opelika Business School.

We'd made our inexpensive purchases for Christmas gifts to family and friends. Driving into school that morning, we'd exchanged silly gifts, laughing at the story behind each purchase. And, today meant that half of the school year was over. Only one semester left before we joined the adult world and got jobs. There wasn't a doubt that we'd get good jobs as secretaries or bookkeepers, with some of the best businesses within a hundred mile radius, in any direction, of Opelika. Businesses were aware that Opelika Business School was the best in what it did—preparing girls to become secretaries and bookkeepers.

The four of us were friends in high school and had graduated in May of that year. I never asked the others their reasons for choosing to attend business school instead of college. Auburn University was only ten minutes further south. Maybe, like me, their parents couldn't afford college, or, maybe, they just wanted to be a part of some business.

Another thing that we never discussed was the fact that I didn't have a driver's license. I was the only one who didn't drive. I never talked about the reason. So, I hitched a ride each day with my friends. Sometimes, I paid. Sometimes, I didn't. When I couldn't pay, no one mentioned it. By this time, I assumed that they understood and knew I was too proud to talk about it. About how poor I was.

* * * * * * *

Even if I had a driver's license, I couldn't have driven, because my parents owned only one car. My dad used it to go to work. It was all he could do to maintain one car and support four kids. Four of my older brothers and sisters no longer lived at home. Three were married and a brother, who was two years older than I, moved into an apartment with a friend. That left four of us at home—Zelda, Laura Faye, Johnny Lee, who was the baby, and myself, Marley Jane.

Daddy drove our old 1954 green beat-up Buick back and forth to work, praying each time he opened the door that the darn thing would crank. We didn't dare go on a trip that was further than Dadeville or Opelika. The tread on the tires was bare. If a tire blew, Daddy would buy a recapped one that'd been patched. Driving at my house was not a luxury or a pleasant Sunday ride into the country. When Daddy or Mama drove the old Buick, it was a necessity, with a prayer.

Forget a second car. My parents were barely able to pay my tuition to business school, and I was already dreading the return to school in January. Then, I'd have to pay tuition for the second semester, coming right behind Christmas. I hated the thought, because it meant that my two younger sisters and brother wouldn't have much for Christmas. It made me feel selfish and ashamed. My tuition would be my Christmas gift from my parents. I didn't mind that I wouldn't get another gift. It was enough. More than enough, considering that it deprived my brothers and sisters. Everyone was sacrificing for me. The only things that I could give in return were good grades and a certificate in May.

Although Opelika Business School was a two-year program, the four of us girls decided when we enrolled in August that we'd only stay one year. With the school's reputation, we'd be able to locate good jobs with a certificate. And I knew that I couldn't ask my parents to finance another year.

I never allowed myself to make plans to attend college. It'd never happen. When I was in high school, the guidance counselor didn't bother to talk to students about college, if he thought or knew their parents were unable to afford it. There was never any talk about grants or scholarships. I thought the only people who received scholarships were athletes, salutatorians, or valedictorians. Neither my parents nor I knew enough to ask questions. Ignorance is a sad thing and stops many people dead cold. With ignorance comes fear or shame. It can make a person a coward.

In some households, it was a given that the children would go to college. My parents hadn't graduated from high school, and my graduation from high school was a huge event for them. Already, I'd accomplished more than they'd been able to do.

Mama ran away from home at fifteen to marry Daddy, who was twenty-six. Late one cold night, she climbed out of her bedroom window to meet Daddy, who waited in an old Model T Ford on a dirt road near her house. My Granddaddy Baker, holding a shotgun between his legs, sat on a bucket by the side of the road in the late evenings for weeks, watching for my daddy to drive by so that he could "kill that son-of-a-bitch, Robert Claude Norrell."

The sheriff came by one afternoon and told Granddaddy Baker to go home, to stop waiting. "By now," he said, spitting tobacco juice to his left side, "yo' girl's done slept with him and ain't nothin you can do 'bout it. Jus' forget it. They're married now."

By the time Mama saw her parents again, she was pregnant with my oldest sister Janet. But that didn't mean my grandparents got over the marriage. They never liked or forgave my daddy. Even as a young girl, I'd see the contempt on their faces when anyone talked about him in their presence. They always believed my mama was too good for my daddy and that he came from trash.

* * * * * * *

Going north on I-85, after leaving school, we sang Christmas songs with Elvis. Sara Ann Powell, who was driving that day, turned the music down low and asked, "What's y'all's plans for Christmas?" I listened as the three of them talked about family gatherings at grandparents and about plans for New Year's Eve. When she asked me about my plans, I laughed and said I was taking one day at a time, and I planned to enjoy doing nothing. I knew that I wouldn't be "doing nothing." I'd be helping Mama clean, wash, iron, cook and bake for Christmas. There wouldn't be a big family holiday gathering at my grandparents. I couldn't recall my family ever having a holiday meal with my grandparents, who hated my daddy. There was no meal, period, to recall with my grandparents. None of us were allowed to ask my Grandmamma for even a cookie when we visited. Mama gave my oldest brother Claude the whipping of his life when he was seven and asked Grandmamma for a biscuit.

Some of my uncles, aunts, and cousins would come for Christmas dinner. My oldest sister and her husband Morgan, along with their two children, Rebecca and Miles, would come, bringing gifts and food. Also, my next-to-the-oldest sister, Bobbie Jo would bring her three-year old son Wayne, but not her husband, Grover, who was away in the Navy. My oldest brother Claude who lived in Maryland couldn't come this year. Richard, the brother who was two years older than I and lived in an apartment with a friend, would come. Most of the family would be together. We'd laugh and have fun, getting louder and louder, trying to over-talk one another. It would be a noisy beehive.

My boyfriend Winston Wesley Steele, whom I'd been dating for three years, would visit from college for several days. He'd stay at Mrs. Louise Edward's house. She rented him a bedroom, with a bath, each summer when he returned to lifeguard at the local pool.

Maybe, we'd talk about getting married in June, a topic that we'd recently begun to discuss. Nothing was definite, but if we planned to have a June wedding, we needed to start a conversation. My feelings were mixed. A part of me wanted to catch a fast train to New York City and pursue my dream of a career in fashion designing. The down-to-earth sensible me selected traditional marriage and security with someone I believed loved me deeply. The truth was somewhere in between both choices.

Deep down, I knew that I wanted to walk away and travel down unfamiliar roads, to be brave and to challenge myself. Lack of confidence would force me to accept marriage and the conventional life that was familiar to me. It was the first time in my life that I had to make a serious decision that could influence the rest of my life. I decided to pick a safe route for my life's journey, not knowing then that no routes are safe and not much is secure. What we think that we see or know at eighteen isn't always reality and the unknown might be better than the known.

One thing that I did know for sure, I didn't want to live any longer in a mill town. I wasn't going to work in any part of a cotton mill. The owner of the mills would never tell me how to vote or how to think, or own my soul. I had no intention of falling in line with the masses and thinking the same thing everyone else thought. No cookie cutter town with cookie cutter people for me.

Oh, I was fully aware of the fact that the mills provided my parents with jobs. Daddy and Mama worked long hours in the mills. Although they worked there, they didn't like anything about the mills or the owner, but there were no other jobs. The owner of the mills saw to that, by keeping labor unions and other industry out of the area for years. Then, Mama was laid off. Now, she was the cook at my sister Bobbie Jo's Midway Café, which opened at six each morning and closed at two in the afternoon.

I watched people who worked in the mills look old before their time. They were good people. Many of them suffered from lung disease, and the owner of the mills didn't care. The company dumped waste and dye from the mills into Osanippa Creek that ran below our house. The chemicals caused the creek to turn green and to smell of rot that suffocated the summer air. Dead fish, with shocked sticky glazed-over eyes, floated on the stagnant surface of the water. The environment was infected with the mill owner's neglect, indifference, abuse, and ignorance.

It wasn't that I thought of myself as being above mill folks. I certainly didn't. My parents were mill folks, but I sure didn't want to work in a mill for the rest of my life. It simply wasn't the cup of life from which I wanted to drink. Why pretend to embrace something that makes you nauseous?

Sometimes, I felt like living in Chambers County was like living in a foreign country. I didn't understand the language, and I didn't want to learn it. My ideas about life, politics, religion, race, or most anything, weren't the same as the majority of people I knew, not even the members of my family. I was a misplaced person in the only town that I'd ever known. We fit together like a square in a circle.

These things slowly rolled over my mind as I half listened to my friends talk and laugh. Jasmine Collins would marry at the end of the school term. Elizabeth Stone and Sara Ann were busy dating different guys. Mostly soldiers from Fort Benning, located in Columbus, Georgia. Neither was serious about any one guy. They were having fun. Marriage wasn't a part of their plans.

Before Sara Ann dropped Elizabeth off at her house, there was a brief discussion about who'd drive the first week after the holidays. Jasmine said that she would, if it didn't snow and school was cancelled. We all laughed. Sure, snow in Alabama. That didn't happen too often, but we couldn't help but glance out the windows at the sky or recall that the local weather station had made several comments about the possibility of snow, which was a wishful dream in the South. Just the threat of snow sent everyone rushing to the grocery store, grabbing whatever hadn't already flown off the shelves. It only took a few flakes for the parking lot at Piggy Wiggly to suddenly become packed with cars.

Chapter 2

By the time I got out of the car, the temperature had dropped. The cold crept through my thin gloves and nibbled at my fingers as I turned the chilly doorknob and walked into the warm kitchen that smelled of teacakes and cinnamon. I could hear the television in the living room and see Laura Faye and Johnny Lee sitting on the floor, facing the characters on the screen. Our television showed only black and white. The cedar tree, which had been cut from the woods behind our house, held skimpy decorations and sat in a corner of the room, with its multi-colored lights glowing. The only light in the room came from the lights on the tree and the television. The wood heater sat almost in the middle of the room and was so hot that I could see heat waves float to the ceiling. I reminded myself to check the wood box and to get more wood before dark.

I stood in the shadows and watched, feeling love for this family and a profound sadness for myself, for my uncertain future. A pity party was about to overtake me. I could not . . . I would not let that happen. One lesson that I learned at a very early age was not to feel pity for myself or to complain, but to be strong and never allow anyone to see my pain so that no one might see into my soul. No one told me that or taught me that. It was just something that I knew, like how my eyes change from green to blue.

Suddenly, I heard the news and was transported from a distant place in my mind to the present. Johnny Lee and Laura Faye got up from the floor and headed to the kitchen for teacakes that Mama and my sister Zelda had baked. As I walked into the living room, I heard the news anchor mention that Governor Wallace would soon appoint seven people to the Alabama Sovereignty Commission. Wallace and a group of people had created the ASC to fight the federal government's efforts to force integration. Wallace always used terms like "force" or "destroy" when he talked about the federal government, which was, according to him, an enemy of the American people. Sadly, too many people in Alabama agreed with him. I thought Wallace's new tactic was a waste of time and money. Things were changing in the South. And it was about time.

"Oh, for goodness sake!" I mumbled under my breath. "Why does he keep butting heads with Washington?" I didn't really need to ask that question. Anyone with any sense knew that he had plans to move to the city of power, to the White House on Pennsylvania Avenue, to the head of the government that he claimed to despise and insisted wanted to destroy our Christian way of life.

I adjusted the rabbit ears on top of the television. They were wrapped in tin foil and had tin foil flags on the metal poles. The tin foil helped get better reception. Someone constantly had to adjust the foil. Finally, I managed to rid the screen of so much snow. "Now, if we can just get that much snow!" I thought, directing the comment to the screen in front of me.

As I adjusted the rabbit ears, I thought about Wallace. He became governor in January, 1963, which was my senior year in high school. He was a short man, with a powerful voice that caught the listener's ear. He said things that many people in Alabama wanted to hear, regarding the white and black races. He preached "Separate but equal" and bad-mouthed the federal government every opportunity he got. Bad mouthing the Feds was a political win in most Southern states. The South had always hated the federal government, which I thought they saw as an extension of the Union soldiers and the North, telling the South how to live. One thing you had to say for Wallace. He knew his audience, and he knew how to pull their strings. He did the thinking for a whole lot of folks. Even I knew that.

Mama didn't like Wallace. She called him "that short little man with the ugly mouth." Naturally, most people who heard her say that just assumed she was talking about the shape of his mouth, because she'd also said many times, "I didn't like him the minute I saw his mouth. Something about his mouth's not right."

Everyone in my family knew that Mama often spoke in metaphors. What she really meant was that she didn't like the ugly things that came out of his mouth. She said many times, with anger, "That little man likes trouble. He's always starting something. I don't know if he hates black folks as much as he carries on, but he's using this whole race thing to be king."

I took it for granted that Daddy felt the same way. He never said, but he laughed when Mama put Wallace down. Mama was more outspoken than Daddy when it came to politics. She was a Democrat. "But not a Wallace kinda Democrat," she was quick to inform. "I'm more a President Kennedy kinda Democrat. All this race and hate stuff won't lead to nothing but more hate and trouble." I thought that she'd summed up Wallace pretty well.

It wasn't unusual for Mama to sum up a person's character in a matter of minutes, just by watching and listening. She had a quick wit and a deep insight into people and situations. No one thought for her. She never jumped on any bandwagons. I don't care how powerful or glamorous they appeared to be.

Although Chambers County hadn't seen racial confrontation in regards to desegregation, we heard about the racial troubles in Birmingham, Tuscaloosa, Huntsville, Montgomery, and Mobile. Somehow, I missed most of the news concerning Macon County, which was only about forty minutes or so south on I-85. I'd been to Birmingham and Tuscaloosa. I'd driven past the exit on I-85 that takes you to Tuskegee, but I'd never been there or to Mobile. We didn't get a newspaper. We lived in a bubble, untouched by racial issues that were happening in nearby counties.

On television, the weatherman talked about how much colder it was going to get in the coming days. Sure enough, by the next morning, temperatures had dropped. We hoped for snow and a delayed return to school. It wouldn't take much snow to keep people home for days, although no one would be caught dead inside. We'd seen some snow on December fourteenth, but not much. Just enough to tease. Getting snow was more exciting than Christmas. It would be the best present ever.

Normal Alabama temperatures are warm and humid, with hot scorching summers that bake the tar highways and make leaves droop. Last June thirteenth had been one of the hottest days in years and years. I could still feel the sticky heat on my skin, making it feel as if tiny insects were creeping beneath my clammy sun-parched arms. Just the thought of that hot June made me long for cold and snow that covered everything. The countryside would be one huge marshmallow, covered in sugar.

* * * * * * *

Winston came home from college on Thursday, bringing with him more cold and threatening clouds. He arrived at Mrs. Edward's house just before the snow started to fall. He'd stay until Saturday. Then, he'd go to his parents' home. His dad, who'd been a local Methodist minister, had been transferred to a town outside of Birmingham. Mr. Steele would give a Christmas sermon on Sunday at his new church. Then, Winston and his parents would travel to north Alabama to visit family for four or five days. On his return, after Christmas, we'd exchange gifts and spend some time together before we both returned to school. We had big plans to attend a New Year's Eve party at a friend's cabin on the lake. If Winston didn't get stuck in north Alabama.

The severe weather started with a low pressure system that moved northward through the eastern Gulf of Mexico, from the Mississippi River and Alabama, up east of the Appalachians and on into Tennessee. The South was getting lots of snow, coming just after Christmas.

By Tuesday, December thirty-first, I awoke to cold rain, mixed with sleet. At noon, the sleet began to turn to snow. Snow continued to fall throughout the day over much of the southern United States. By midnight, everything was covered in white. When the sun hit the snow the next morning, millions of diamonds blinded me when I opened the kitchen door and looked across the back yard. The cold and the moisture took my breath away, burning my exposed cheeks. But I couldn't turn away. I stood on the back porch and soaked in as much of the beauty as I could tolerate, before I began to shiver and shake.

My sisters, my brother, and I dressed in warm clothing and headed outside. We made a snowman, giving him a corncob for a nose, coal for eyes, and a long slender stick for a mouth. We wrapped him in an old scarf and placed torn mittens on the stick hands that hung from his skinny stick arms. We lay in the snow and made snow angels. We stayed in the house just long enough to make snow ice cream and listen to the weather report, wishing for more of the magical white stuff. We wanted a pristine glowing, blinding blanket of snow.

We got our wish. Strong, cloudy winds and cold air moved over the Deep South, as heavy snow fell into the twilight. The snow lit up the outside world like thousands of lights. Shadows danced over the snow as New Year's Eve began to approach. From twelve o' clock midnight to early morning, January first, a heavy layer of snow covered everything that hadn't been previously covered by the white mass. By that morning, we had thirteen inches of snow. Huntsville had seventeen inches and Mississippi had fifteen inches. It was the worst snowstorm since 1899. And we loved it.

Much of Alabama was locked down by a snowstorm on the morning of the New Year. Winston was stranded in north Alabama. There were traffic jams and hundreds of vehicles were abandoned on highways. Families were forced to remain in their cars, waiting to be rescued. Some cars plowed into snow banks. The snow crushed bushes and tore off sides of roofs and awnings. Travel throughout the South was restricted for several days, and all major roads were impassable. Flights in and out of Birmingham airport were cancelled. It didn't stop us from playing in the snow until past dark, when the snow cast a bright light against the black sky.

Since Winston's plans were to coach football, I kept up with as many teams as I could. The University of Alabama was scheduled to play Ole Miss in the Sugar Bowl in New Orleans, while Auburn University was to play Nebraska in the Orange Bowl in Miami. "The Crimson Tide," Coach Bear Bryant said, "can deal with anything but the snow." Governor Wallace informed everyone in the state that he'd be at the Sugar Bowl to see the game, snow or no snow. Everyone cheered and complimented him for being so brave and determined.

When Alabama played Ole Miss in Louisiana, Tulane Stadium was an open deep freezer, with snow banks along the sidelines of the field. Earlier, it'd been a true bowl of sugar. Snow had to be cleared from the bleachers, as well as the field. When the second-string quarterback Steve Sloan, who was filling in for the suspended Joe Namath, walked onto the field, the Alabama fans went crazy. The powerhouse Ole Miss, leading the nation in rushing defense, forced Bama to kick a thirty-one yard field goal. As always, Bama's quick-hitting offense took advantage, in spite of a field that looked like glass. They beat Ole Miss twelve to seven.

Jimmy Sidle, Auburn's All-American Quarterback, couldn't lead the Tigers to victory in the Orange Bowl, with a Miami temperature of sixty-eight. The national champion rushing team, the Nebraska Cornhuskers, defeated Auburn thirteen to seven. It was a grim, disappointing loss for us Auburn fans, but we were just happy that we'd been invited to the party. But, it meant that we'd have to listen to Bama fans brag for another year.

The first day of 1964 was another day of playing in the snow. Our seven friends—Shelby Jean, Eli, Hattie, Eddie, Samuel, Mae Bell, and Pearlie—who lived down the road, joined us in racing down the steep hill near our houses. The Smiths were the only black family on Hopewell Road, and we'd played together since we were children. I got Daddy's old rusty aluminum ladder out of the barn. Three of us would take turns sitting on the rungs, while two others gave a strong shove, sending us sliding down hill on the icy snow. When we grew tired of sailing on a mound of white, we made snowballs and played catch. Of course, it soon turned into target practice.

Three days after New Year's Eve, the ice and snow began to melt, bringing down limbs and knocking out power that hadn't previously been lost. School was delayed for a week, as we'd hoped. Winston and I had some time together, in spite of his being caught in north Alabama longer than he'd planned. It was now time to return to school.

I wasn't as worried about tuition as I'd been before Christmas. In addition to the gift of snow that Heaven sent us, Winston gave me two gifts. One was a thin fourteen-karat gold chain necklace, with a small glass heart filled with chips of thin gold. The second gift was enough money to cover the tuition for my second semester of school. He told Mama and Daddy before Christmas what he planned to give me so that they wouldn't give me money. Instead, they gave me new gloves and a box filled with school supplies that I badly needed for the next term. The box contained four shorthand tablets, a box of pencils, a box of pens, a carton of index cards, and a large black notebook filled with a ton of notebook paper. A simple gift, but so important. They were things that I needed, and money was tight after Christmas.

I cried when Winston gave me the Christmas card that contained money for my tuition. It meant my future, a job that offered survival and independence. It meant that Mama and Daddy hadn't spent so much money on me for Christmas.

More importantly, it sealed my loyalty to him for more decades than I'd be able to recall in my old age. I appreciated the gift more than I could say, but I felt that I owed him. How do you repay love, kindness, or loyalty? And how long do you repay the debt?

During one of the days that school was delayed, Winston and I planned a June wedding. He was almost guaranteed a coaching job in Clay County, where he'd played football and graduated from high school, and where his dad had preached for six years. I believed that our future looked as pure and bright as the snowy icy winter land that surrounded us.

I was eager to get back into a routine, to finish the school year, and to start a new life. As I planned my future, I had absolutely no idea how innocent I was to the world that revolved around me. My life was an example of ordinary. Nothing special. But, I was about to start a new life, without a clue as to the degree this new life would change me.

In spite of my unawareness of the world, I was becoming more aware of the fact that Alabama was a breeding ground for hate and racial tension. Terrible things were happening from one corner of the state to another, just as they were in other southern states, but Chambers County hadn't been touched by the violence. It was as if we saw the horrors through a tinted window that blurred the images.

This was true, in spite of the assassination of President Kennedy in November, 1963. I remember coming home from school and turning on the television to see the President collapsing from gunshots to his head. I watched in disbelief as the convertible in which he rode flew through the Dallas streets. I sat on the edge of the sofa, hearing but not believing the speaker's voice, telling the world that the President of the United States had been assassinated.

Even as a young woman, I knew what the assassination of the leader of the free world would mean to America and to the entire world. I was glued to the screen and watched as a sad-eyed Jackie stood beside Lyndon Johnson, while he took the oath of office, her pink suit stained red with her husband's blood. The world was in shock. The horror unfolded over and over on the screen. That horror was unable to prevent other horrors, to stop other deaths. It seeped into my soul and left a desire for justice that never stopped burning.

Chapter 3

The first time that I heard of Notasulga was the day we returned to school from Christmas break. We left for classes on a cold morning, as the sun poked over the eastern sky. On the way to school, we shared stories about the snow and ice. Talk soon switched to the end of the school year. All of us were ready to wrap up the last semester and look for jobs. Jasmine and I would marry and move away before we located jobs. Although I was excited about my plans for a June wedding, I didn't mention it. I decided that I'd wait until the end of the semester to bring it up.

After my second class, which was speed typing, I took a break and walked into the students' lounge. Two girls, whom I hadn't seen before, because they weren't students the first semester, were laughing and boasting about ". . . burning the school . . . 'cause niggers were coming . . ." As they talked, pretty much to one another, most of us listened in shock. Someone asked where the school was located. One of the girls, who had a long, narrow face, thin pencil lips, and curly black hair that clung close to her head, said in a husky voice, "Notasulga. That's where we live. 'Bout thirty minutes from here. We're all so sick and tired of integration being forced down our throats. I can't understand why the niggers want to come to our school. We don't want 'em in our school. They need to stay where they're at. In their own schools."

I was certain that some of the girls in the room thought that the evil deed was a good deed. It was, after all, 1964 in the South. Racial conflict happened across Alabama, from Tuscaloosa to Mobile, from Huntsville to Birmingham. Those towns, in my mind, seemed so far away, so removed from my life. As I said earlier, racial issues hadn't become a problem where I lived. That would happen almost a decade later. There still wouldn't be any violence in Chambers County. Mostly, just some people who peacefully demonstrated.

I wasn't one of those girls who appreciated the conversation. I quickly left the room, never thinking to ask questions. I'd heard enough. In my mind, there was never justification for burning a school. Any school—black or white. Certainly not to prevent integration, which the biggest fool in the South should know was coming, sooner or later. The almighty Wallace wouldn't be able to stop it.

Something deep in my chest ached. My stomach was in a knot, and I felt sick. I thought that I might throw up, so I went into the bathroom and washed my face, feeling cold water sting my eyelids. Looking into the tiny mirror, I barely recognized the pale face staring back at me. Who was this person so upset about two silly girls' gossip that had nothing to do with her life?

Comprehension escaped me, but there was no denying that I was profoundly affected by the hateful, gleeful laughter of the two girls whom I didn't know or want to know. I wondered where such hate came from. I debated whether or not I should discuss it with my friends. Something told me "No." I was afraid that they might agree with the girls, and I wasn't ready to face that from my friends.

I left the bathroom and sat on the stairs that led to the front doors of the school. I looked through the long glass doors, at the melting snow that was turning to dirty slush on the curbs. I watched as cars moved down the street, as the muddy snow covered the tires and splashed onto the lower part of the cars. Life was returning to normal after the snowstorm; yet, I knew, in some faraway place in my mind, that life as I once knew it would never again be what most of the folks in the South called normal.

In a moment—a now, I began to change. I realized that I didn't live in an innocent world and that I couldn't escape racial hate and injustice. No one's life was that ordinary. Bits and pieces of two young girls' broken conversation would stick with me and alter me forever. Sadness swept over me, and I wanted to walk into the melting snow, to go far away from too many unspoken truths of hate and racism. I sighed, wishing that I could just board a bus and head to New York City, attend The Fashion Institute of Technology, and never look back.

Slowly, I got up and headed to my next class. Shorthand demanded all of my attention, as I listened to Mrs. Grace dictate in her soft voice. She talked and my pen flew over the tablet. At the end of class, I wondered, Would she understand? Are there many people who feel as I do?

On the ride home, I was quiet. Earlier that morning, I decided not to talk about the conversation that I half-heard during break. I hadn't been in the room long enough to get details. It'd be best not to discuss something that I really didn't know anything about. That was one reason I decided not to bring up the subject with my friends. Of course, too, I feared what they'd say. What if they laughed, like those girls had laughed, thinking that burning a school to stop or slow down integration was a good thing? I knew that I didn't want to know my friends' opinions about desegregation or about anything to do with race. School would end in four months. It'd be best to leave some things unspoken. I made up mind to stay away from the girls from Notasulga.

Notasulga. An odd name. Probably an Indian name, like so many Alabama towns. I'd never heard of that town, and I decided that I never wanted to know anything about it or its people.

April arrived full of awakening life. New beginnings were evident everywhere. Spring brought hope. One more month of school and another journey would begin for me. I was apprehensive and afraid, but not sure of the reasons. I kept those feelings to myself, as my friends and I sang along with the music on the car radio, coming home each day from school. We laughed and planned our futures, eager to be grownups.

Finally, the last day of class came. The four of us received certificates and ran down the stairs to the sidewalk and down the steep hill to the car for the last time. We passed the drugstore, forgetting about a Coke before heading home. A new life tugged, and we dashed toward it. In our hurry to embrace new beginnings, we soon left our friendships some place along I-85. In the months and years to follow, we went our separate ways and lost touch, quickly dropping out of one another's lives, like exhausted runners in a marathon.

Chapter 4

Our wedding took place on June 2, 1964, the day of my sister Zelda's birthday, and the day after Mama's birthday. We were married in Hopewell, as dusk began to fall on the small country wood-frame Methodist church that I'd attended since I was a young girl. It was a small wedding. The flowers on the altar were large bouquets of Queen Anne's Lace that lined the highways all over the county. A friend's mother made the simple wedding cake. My first cousin Jane was my Maid of Honor. She was the only attendant, and she was my best friend in the entire world. Winston's dad performed the ceremony. When he announced us husband and wife, I felt a fist in my belly. Just that quickly, I went from being Marley Jane Norrell to Mrs. Winston Wesley Steele.

Winston and I left the church in his red 1960 Chevrolet convertible, with its large fins and the top down. We drove to the rooming house where he'd lived for the past two summers when he returned to work as a lifeguard and swimming coach. For three months, we'd rent the same room and bath from Mrs. Edwards, with kitchen privileges, until we left for his job as assistant football coach at Edward High School in Clay County, Alabama. During those three months, he worked as a lifeguard, while I worked at being a housewife.

The plan was to get our suitcases and head to Florida for a four-day honeymoon. It'd be nearby and quick. I was getting a glimpse into my future as Winston's wife. No frills. No nonsense. No vacations. No money foolishly spent. Before leaving, I went into the bathroom to change clothes, while he changed in the bedroom. Marriage was still a new concept, and I wasn't comfortable dressing and undressing in front of him. After changing my clothes and combing my curly hair, I closed the lid of the commode and sat, staring at the wall in front of me. Tears came to my eyes. My stomach was in a tight knot. I could only think of one thing. I wanted to go home. To run out of that tiny bathroom, across the wooden floor of the large bedroom, onto the glassed-in front porch, and down the long seven mile road to my parents' house. I'd save time and miles if I took the dirt road toward my uncle's house, straight onto another paved road. Then, I'd be five minutes from my house.

"I've changed my mind," I planned to tell Mama and Daddy. "I don't know what I'm doing. This isn't what I want."

I inhaled and exhaled slowly, trying to shut off the conversation that was taking place inside my head, between my parents and myself. I never thought of Winston while the conversation continued. Realizing that I couldn't run away, I sucked in a large volume of air and released it slowly. I washed my face and looked at the sad-eyed girl-woman before me. "You bought this. Now, pay for it," I told her. I unlocked the door and walked into my new life.

* * * * * * *

At the end of the summer, Winston and I moved to Clay County and joined the United Methodist Church, where Winston's dad had once been a minister. Everyone who knew and loved his dad welcomed us. Many people recalled when Winston had been an outstanding running back on the high school football team. After graduation, he left to attend a small college in north Alabama. His parents moved to Chambers County, where I lived. During my sophomore year of high school, he and I met at a ballpark, where he was playing softball with a local league. He'd come full circle and returned to his roots.

We lived there for two years, and our son, Wesley, was born there, a little over a month after our first wedding anniversary. Soon after we settled in, I was hired as a secretary at a local telephone company, which was owned by a retired probate judge. We lived close enough to town that I walked back and forth to work each day. I still hadn't obtained my driver's license, and we had only one car.

It was a cold day near the end of February, and I was four months pregnant. When I walked to work that morning, the sky was gloomy and overcast. By three that afternoon, it began to snow. A thin, white layer of snow lay on the ground as I stepped out of the warm building, where I worked, and into the blowing wind and snow that rapidly fell. As I turned a corner and headed toward the eastern side of the courthouse, which sat in the center of town, the snow fell faster and thicker. Wrapping my coat tightly around my upper body and my stomach, I left town, headed home, hoping that I reached my front door before the snow blurred my vision. My head was covered with a wet crown of white. I heard a car horn. I turned to my left and saw Winston wave at me as he drove by.

"Stop!" I yelled into the wind. My voice was muffled by soft droplets of white that floated in front of me and by the wind that jerked the words from my mouth and sent them into silence.

When I walked into the house, Winston was reclining on the sofa, watching television. "Why didn't you stop?" I asked. "You do know I'm pregnant, or have you forgotten?"

"Dr. Perry told you to walk," he laughed.

I threw my coat at him.

As I grew larger, winter snaked across the calendar. I continued to walk back and forth to work each day. Soon, hints of spring began to appear, making my daily walk nicer. Although I was much heavier, I didn't mind walking as the season changed.

* * * * * *

In March, 1965, the Selma to Montgomery March, to remove voting restrictions on blacks, became the topic throughout the state. Three marchers died in an attempt to cross Selma's Edmund Pettus Bridge. When the third person was killed, the world took notice. Congress began to notice as well. Alabama became the topic of discussion throughout the world. Again, not for a good reason.

For days, I watched the horrific deeds of Jim Clark and his mounted posse unfold on television. I heard Wallace's negative speeches that incited his followers into a rage and sent hundreds flocking to Selma to defend the white Christian way of life. I've never understood the reason that so many people act like the Christian way of life means depriving others. They never comprehend the irony between what they say and do. During all of the madness, Dr. Martin Luther King, Jr., asked for peace and justice that he hoped could be gained through non-violence.

Congress passed the Voting Rights Act and President Johnson signed it into law on August 6, 1965, almost a month after our son was born.

Chapter 5

Wesley arrived on a steamy hot July night, after I'd been in labor for more than five hours, which Dr. Perry said wasn't bad. He credited the short labor time to the fact that I walked four to six miles every day. Regardless, the length of time was insignificant when I held my tiny son in my arms. He was five pounds of joy and perfection. I knew that he was worth the choice that I'd made.

For Wesley's sake, I could no longer delay getting my driver's license. No more excuses. No more waiting. John Yates, the policeman who gave the driver's test, wouldn't have to say to me every day of the week when I passed him on the street, "When are you gonna get your license? With that baby comin', you need to be able to drive."

Mr. Yates and I decided that I'd come to the courthouse on a Tuesday morning to get my license. The day that we'd agreed upon just happened to be a miserable day. It began to rain abundantly after midnight and was still soaking the ground when daylight appeared. Since it was too rainy to go fishing, Winston agreed to baby-sit. When I walked outside, I realized that God was squeezing every cloud to cause a downpour. Thunder roared and lightning cracked, zipping across acres of a wet heaven and lighting up the sky.

Driving about twenty miles per hour, I finally arrived in front of the red brick courthouse that sat in the middle of town. Not many cars surrounded the building. I was thankful. By the time I got inside the building, I was drenched. I located Mr. Yates and he administered the written part of the exam. Perfect score! This was gonna be a piece of cake.

Time for the driving part of the exam. I was apprehensive, but cool, confident. As we ran to my car, I fought the wind for my umbrella, while water again soaked through my sandals. Once I started the car, the nightmare began. Instead of putting the car in reverse, I put it in drive. It seemed to be its own driver as it shot over the curb and onto the soggy lawn of the courthouse. "Oh, my God! Stop!" my brain yelled. I managed to miss the veranda of the courthouse before I was able to stop the car. Mr. Yates, an elderly man with gray hair and a friendly face, was silent. "I'm sorry," I barely uttered.

I changed gears and bumped backwards over the curb, leaving tire tracks on the lawn. Without looking behind me, I stomped the gas and flew into the street. Realizing what I'd done, I slammed on the brakes. Mr. Yates' head just missed the windshield. He was silent, looking through rain and steam. "I'm sorry," I said, just above a whisper.

Determined to compose myself, I eased down the street as water sprayed away from the car and hit the door handles. I took a right as I was told to do. Damn! I forgot to give a signal. "I'm sorry." A hill was ahead. I'd been up that hill hundreds of times, with Winston driving. He and I walked up and down it almost every day that I was pregnant. Only, it seemed like a mountain that rose straight into a rain forest during the monsoon season. A light was at the top. Just as I got near, the light turned red. I slammed on the brakes. As I attempted to change gears, the car rolled all the way down the hill. The rain picked up intensity as if it'd decided to compete in some crazy competition with me. By the time the car slowed to a stop at the bottom of the hill, I was ready to call it quits. To further complicate matters, the car went dead. My first attempt to start it failed. "I'm sorry." I'd forgotten how many times I'd said those words. Mr. Yates was silent, as he looked out the window at the heavy strips of rain, whipped to a frenzy by the wind.

As we sat at the bottom of the hill, I glanced sideways at him. He scratched his head with the eraser end of the pencil. "You're doing okay. Let's try that again." I turned and looked at him in disbelief and total confusion.

The motor caught and I started the climb up the hill for the second time. Thank goodness the light stayed green, and I sailed right through it. The silent man beside me became a talking machine. "I'm gonna say, 'Stop,' and I want you to slang me through the window." That sounded easy enough. I could do that.

I drove for about a half a mile. "Stop!" I slowed down and stopped. Silence. Neither of us spoke. Finally, Mr. Yates said in a kind calm voice, "I'm gonna say it again, and I want you to slam on the brakes. Okay?" I nodded.

The second time I sent him to the windshield. "Good. That was good. Now, let's parallel park." I turned and stared at him like I didn't understand English. He ignored my look. "Go ahead. Right here's fine."

It was absolutely the worst parallel parking ever attempted. The front of the car faced the curb and the trunk of the car faced the street. Still, I managed to barely miss scraping the back end of another car. The owner would never know that it was his lucky day. The rain gods smiled on him.

"Okay. Let's head back to the courthouse."

I didn't need to back out too far because I was pretty much already in the street. I decided that I'd take it easy. Still, I managed to run a red light before we reached the courthouse. I pulled into a parking spot and cut off the motor. Rain pounded on the roof of the car and covered the windows so that nothing outside was visible. We sat in a confined muggy space as fog began to cover the world around us. We heard a pop of thunder and saw a flashing streak of lightning. There was the sound of rain and silence.

Mr. Yates looked into the foggy rain and seemed to slump in the seat. He scratched his head with the pencil. Then, he placed it in his mouth and chewed for a while. I didn't dare say a word. "I'm sorry" seemed a little bit worn out.

Finally, he looked at me and grinned. "I know what the problem is. The windshield is so dang dirty. Your husband should'a cleaned it before you came." Like a dummy, I nodded in agreement. He laughed as if he'd told a joke. I gave a sad little lop-sided grin.

"Well, I tell you what I'm gonna do. I'm gonna give you these licenses. 'Cause if I don't, you ain't never gonna learn how to drive. You got that baby now. You need them licenses so you'll learn how to drive." He slapped his left knee. "Come on. Let's make you legal."

I smiled from ear to ear and clapped my hands like a child. We opened the doors and dashed up the walkway to the courthouse. In my haste, I'd forgotten the umbrella. Minutes later, I practically danced out the door, into liquid gold. I was a licensed driver.

The rain gods smiled on me. God blessed me as well as everyone who'd been smart enough not to get within five hundred feet of my car during the driving exam. I rode on raindrops and sang all the way home, while thunder boomed and the sky lit up with streaks of zigging and zagging light.

* * * * * * *

Winston called me from school the following week. "I need you to drive to Talladega for me. I want you to pick up some supplies that I need at the sports store. Get Raylee Love to bring you to the school to get the car. Ask her if she'll ride to Talladega with you."

Since my mouth was hanging open while he was giving instructions, I wasn't able to interrupt. For several minutes neither of us spoke. "What? Are you serious? I don't know how to drive that far. I can't take Wesley with me and drive. Can't you do this?" I pleaded.

"No. I can't. I can't leave school. You're gonna have to do this. You'll be fine. And Raylee will be with you. She's a good driver. But don't let her drive. You do the driving." More instructions. I was getting upset with his bossiness, which wasn't helping my nervousness.

Another moment of silence. "I'll do it. Against my will. If I wreck the car, don't blame me."

"Good. See you. Just drive to the gym. I'll give you the keys there. I'll be waiting." He hung up before I could say anything else.

Raylee agreed to go with me. She placed her three-year-old daughter in the backseat, beside her eighteen-month-old son. I held Wesley in my lap. We drove to the gym and Winston gave me the keys. We transferred the kids from her car to my car. Raylee sat in the front seat and held Wesley in her lap.

It seemed to take hours to make a thirty-minute drive up and down one steep hill after another. The countryside was beautiful, but I didn't dare take my eyes off the road ahead of me. Cows and horses grazed on the rich green grass that went by us in slow motion. A pristine blue sky slept above our heads. Raylee understood that I was nervous, so she didn't do much talking.

I made it to the sports store without an accident. The salesman loaded up the trunk of the car and we headed home, climbing up hills and cruising down them. I began to feel confident and proud of myself as I released my fear into the hills around me. I knew that Winston had forced me to make the trip so that I'd overcome my fears. I'd conquered one small mountain.

I had no idea of the mountains that I'd confront in the coming years. That day gave me some much-needed confidence. Future mountains would consist of faces of evil and injustice that destroy lives and families. The world in which I lived was still innocent, to a degree, in spite of the horrible events that unfolded on the TV screen. So far, nothing had happened in my life that really tested me.

Chapter 6

The following year we moved to Shelby County, to a community outside of Birmingham. In January, I enrolled at a nearby college and signed up for three classes. I was excited. Finally, I was on the road to achieving my secret dream of attending college and obtaining a degree. I loved classes and learning new things. I didn't have a problem finding a babysitter for Wesley. Since we lived across the road from the Methodist minister of our church, the minister's wife agreed to babysit for me three days a week.

My world seemed complete. Wesley was a healthy, chubby delightful toddler who smiled and danced as the minister's teenage daughter strummed her guitar. He could count to fifty, say all of his ABCs, and loved to finger paint. The minister and his family adored him, and he returned their love. It was an ideal situation. My baby was taken care of in my absence by people who treasured him.

In late June, Winston received a call from the Superintendent of Education in Macon County. Notasulga High School needed a football coach. A sports salesman recommended that the superintendent contact Winston. The principal of the school had also been the football coach. Things weren't working out. The team hadn't won a game in two years, since the high school was rebuilt.

"Notasulga? That sounds familiar," I kept thinking. "What bothers me about that name?"

I mentioned my thoughts to Winston, and he dismissed them with, "Well, it's in Alabama. I'm sure you've heard the name. It doesn't mean anything."

Winston agreed to go for an interview. We drove down I-65 and exited onto I-85 at Montgomery. We headed north to Tuskegee, to the superintendent's office. John Watson met us at the front desk and showed us around the building, introducing us to the employees. Afterwards, we got into his car, headed to Notasulga High School. Winston sat up front. I rode in the back.

As we headed east, Mr. Watson began talking about Notasulga. He told us that the town, located in north-central Macon County and southwestern Lee County, in the east-central part of Alabama, was once called Moore's Cross Roads, which was settled by Amos Moore. No one in Macon County remembered anything about him.

"Camp Watts, now called Union Camp Road, was located there during the Civil War. It supported 2,000 to 3,000 Confederate soldiers and served as a training camp. It was also a place for picking up supplies that were brought in on the train and sent to other camps. At one time, there was a small Confederate graveyard, located some place near the railroad tracks. I understand that farmers plowed up the graveyard years ago. Now, there's no reminder left of Notasulga's part in the Civil War," he said, delivering history in a monotone.

It surprised me that a small rural Southern town wasn't embracing every scrap of Civil War history. Don't get me wrong. I like history, and I believe everyone should know some history. But, I'm not a fanatic about the Civil War. Nor am I a person who believes "the South will rise again." And, if it does, I damn sure hope it won't be a repeat of the days of slavery. So, no, I don't wave the Confederate flag or dress up to play pretend. That's gone. Time to move on.

Leaving the Civil War in the past, where it belongs, I turned my attention back to Mr. Watson, who was now giving a geography lesson. "Tuskegee National Park is three miles southwest of town. You can get to Phenix City—which, as you know, rests on the western bank of the Chattahoochee River—through the park. Auburn University, coming from Wire Road, almost backs up to the school. It's a ten or fifteen minute drive from Notasulga to Auburn, in any three directions. So, you'll be close to a bigger town. Actually, five roads lead into Notasulga. There are roads that intersect with Interstate I-85, which means a quick drive south to Montgomery or north to Atlanta."

"I like that," said Winston, with more enthusiasm than I believed. "Are there any good places to hunt or fish?"

"You bet!" Mr. Watson smiled. As he talked, I looked out the window, knowing Winston was headed to Heaven, in a place called Notasulga.

Mr. Watson finished naming places to hunt and fish in the area. Just before we came into the residential section of town, we crossed a high bridge that curved into the sky over a railroad track. As we drove into the business section of town, we slowed for a caution light. To the left was a two-story red brick building. Looking at the name on the building, a memory stirred in a closed file of my mind. We continued driving down Main Street and across a second bridge that curved high over the railroad tracks. I turned and looked at the building. My mind located the file. The name hit me as we crossed the bridge and headed to the school.

"Oh, no, I cannot live here!" my brain screamed, recalling the laughter of two young girls on a cold January morning in 1964. I recalled that the last name of one of them was the same name that appeared on the building.

From that moment on, it was difficult for me to focus on anything Mr. Watson said. Later, I could barely remember walking through the gym, the elementary school, the auditorium, the cafeteria, the high school, and the football field with the principal whom we met as soon as we entered the high school. But, I did remember his powerful personality and diverse stories.

Hunter Moore had been hired as principal for first through twelve grades, as well as football coach, when the new school was completed in the summer of 1965. It was his idea to be football coach. The idea, like many of his ideas, had been a bad one. The team hadn't won a game. As a matter of fact, they didn't simply lose. Each opponent stomped them to the point of embarrassment. It was amazing that Hunter could get anyone to play football. Lots of people in town said that the team enjoyed being whooped and humiliated. "Them players are plain weird," some folks said.

Before desegregation, the football team was the pride of the town. Notasulga had bragging rights over their rival Reeltown, which was in an adjoining county. Reeltown had crushed them for the past two years, with records so absurd that no one in Notasulga talked about them. Those games had been sad sights to witness. No one in town, even the Macon Academy crowd, wanted to discuss the past two seasons.

Since most people hated Hunter for everything that they considered was wrong, he got the full blame. Which didn't seem to faze him in the least. He didn't care what people thought. In his opinion, anyone who didn't support public education was a fool. If they supported public education and still blamed him, well, they were idiots when it came to football. Too, he'd forgotten more football than they could imagine. He'd been an outstanding tackle for the University of Alabama, but that failed to impress the townspeople who lost no hesitation in saying, "Just 'cause you were a big college football player don't mean you know shit 'bout how to coach football."

Hunter's opinion of how much football he remembered led to an arrogant and condescending attitude toward anyone who only graduated from high school in a small town in the middle of nowhere. But, his good old country-boy charm was showered on anyone in that small town in the middle of nowhere, as long as that someone supported the public schools.

There were two classes of people in Hunter's mind. One was the good people with enough sense to support integration and to send their kids to the public schools. The other was the stuck-up sons-of-bitches who were racists and supported that private school over in Tuskegee. He tolerated the first group, who saw him as compassionate, warm, friendly, and generous to a fault. This group knew the teddy bear beneath the rough exterior. He could be charming and funny. He hated the other group, who he considered the enemy that'd burned a school, threw eggs at little black children, and burned barns. And he made it clear to everyone which side of the fence he was on. God help you if you were foolish enough to question anything he did, especially when it came to race or to the schools in town.

The three of us walked into Hunter's office, which was beyond cluttered. There was no place to sit, because a large box of shoulder pads sat in one chair, and a bundle of dirty, smelly uniforms, socks, and jockey straps filled the other chair and spilled onto the floor, leaving little space to walk. The sweaty clothing made the office smell like a locker room. Papers and textbooks covered almost every space. Hanging from the bathroom door was an outfit of clean clothing. A starched white shirt hung with a red tie looped over the neck of a wire hanger. Looking closely at the tie, I recognized very tiny heads of The Bear, wearing his famous houndstooth hat. A pressed pair of navy blue pants was folded on another wire hanger. A white tee shirt was folded over the pants. I wondered if the bathroom had a shower, and I wondered where the undershorts were. Maybe under the tee shirt.

Placing the box on top of papers and slinging the dirty smelly football uniforms, socks, and jockey straps behind his desk, with some socks and jockey straps landing and hanging on the blinds, he invited us to sit down. I made no move. I preferred to stand, thank you kindly. If no one sat down, maybe we'd leave that much faster.

"Y'all have to excuse this damn mess," he said in a loud, demanding voice that echoed out into the halls. "We don't have a washer and a dryer in the gym, so I have to take everything home to wash," he stated, giving Mr. Watson a hard, cold stare.

I did some simple mental math. Spring football training was in April. It was now late June. Those uniforms had been sitting around for months. No wonder it smelled so bad. They were probably covered in mold and mildew.

"Been too busy to clean, and I don't ask my secretary to clean up my messes. By the way, I'm Hunter Moore," he said, offering his hand to Winston and nodding at me. I gave a weak smile, looking straight into his dark brown eyes, as he took his left hand and pushed a lock of black thick hair from his left eye.

He was a tall handsome man with an athletic build and high shoulders that were stiff and square like a high-ranking officer. His nut-brown eyes were hot and burning, containing a fire that probably never died down to embers. When he smiled, the fire lit up. Tiny wrinkles lived in the corners of his eyes and along the edges of his mouth. Each movement that he made was guided by passion. A person could easily become consumed by his magnetic, overbearing personality, which reached out in friendship or devoured a person with rage. Several people in Notasulga learned the hard way not to get in the path of his rage.

They shook hands, while Mr. Watson said, "Well, now that y'all have met, maybe, you can show us around the campus, Hunter. Tell Marley and Winston a bit about the school. Convince them to come here." He gave Hunter a look that wasn't a request. I sensed some negative feelings.

Hunter exchanged a cool look with the superintendent. Briefly, I felt tension fill the air. Looking at Hunter, I knew that this solid packed man who stood slightly over six feet three inches was not someone who catered to anyone or who kissed ass. Yet there was a twinkle in his brown eyes, which told me that he was enjoying this. Being in control.

As we left Hunter's office and started to the cafeteria to meet "the ladies who run things around here," I saw a very dark-skinned man standing near the water fountain that was next to the boys' bathroom. His face was full and his black eyes were large. When I met his eyes, I looked into a book of knowledge and wisdom that he didn't share with too many people. A worn denim cap sat on his head and he wore faded overalls. In his right hand, he carried a large bucket. His left hand held a wet mop.

"Well, hi there, Mose," Mr. Watson said, extending his hand. "How are things going 'round here? I hope Mr. Moore's not working you too hard and that you're keeping him straight."

The large man smiled and gently sat the bucket on the polished oak floor and shook Mr. Watson's hand. "I be just fine, Mr. John. Not workin' hard a' tall. Things been good. Been good," and he chuckled.

Hunter spoke, "Mose, I want you to meet Mr. and Mrs. Steele. Winston. Marley. This is Mose Hurston. Mose, we're hoping Winston here is gonna be the next football coach at Notasulga." Placing his hand on Mose's large left shoulder, Hunter faced us and continued, "Now, if you're about to meet the most important women at the school, you've just met the most important man. We couldn't get along without Mose. He's been here since before the school was burned." Then, he looked at Mose and nodded his head.

Winston shook Mose's hand, and I followed suit. "It's nice to meet you, Mose," I said. "I know you've got a job, taking care of everything."

He laughed. "Yes ma'am. It sho' is a job. But, somebody's gotta do it."

Mr. Watson talked about how much Mose meant to the school and to the students and how much he was appreciated. I sensed that he was sincere about everything that he said. When I looked at Mose, I saw his ebony eyes twinkling. He was a man who was secure in his own skin.

We waved to Mose and walked to the cafeteria, where Hunter introduced us to the three women who worked there. Mrs. Mattie West was the head cook, in charge of the cafeteria. She was a tiny woman who looked like someone's sweet grey-haired grandmother. Her pale brown eyes twinkled, as she grinned and tilted her head to one side, blushing from the compliments that Hunter generously gave to her.

The second lady, Ada Ray, was a tall, big-boned woman who looked to be in her forties. A few blond curls managed to escape the clear plastic cap that covered her head. Her blue eyes sat wide apart, and her mouth was thin, but it never stopped smiling. We learned that her daughter was in elementary school and that her son was the same age as Wesley.

"And this here's Willie Mae Hurston. She's married to Mose. I hired her last year. I don't know what we ever did without her. We need another person in the cafeteria, but somebody doesn't agree," he finished, looking at Mr. Watson.

"Now, Hunter, I've told you that you just need to send me a written rationale for hiring another person. You do that and I'll do my part." He pointed a firm finger at Hunter.

While they batted back and forth, I looked at Willie Mae. She was approximately five feet ten inches of elegance and grace. Although she had big bones, she was well built. A halo of white, naturally curly short hair, that was a version of a shag, fell in waves, surrounding her long face. I saw a high forehead and high cheekbones. The chin was square. The nose was wide and flat. White teeth flashed behind full lips when she smiled. Her large round brown eyes, with a touch of green, lit up beneath thin arched eyebrows. She wore steel-rimmed glasses. It was her voice that got your attention. It was lazy Southern Sundays and Golden Eagle syrup. It was creamy grits and sunny eggs. The sound made you relax as you waited to hear more.

While Hunter and Mr. Watson went back and forth, she threw back her head and laughed, a deep happy sound of joy. Looking at us, she said, "Who you think's gonna win that argument?"

I laughed and shrugged. "Why are y'all here so soon before school starts?"

Mrs. West answered, "We got lots of stuff to do before the children come. We'll be here two days a week 'til school starts."

We talked for about twenty minutes, waved goodbye, and walked out the back door of the kitchen, into the glaring sun. As we walked to the elementary school, Hunter answered Winston's questions that never seemed to end.

Hunter enjoyed being in charge, and he controlled the next two hours, leading us through the buildings and over the campus, to the football field that sat in a hollow. In the distance, we could see a lake. Most of the time, Mr. Watson trailed behind us, speaking occasionally. Now and then, he would grunt or chuckle when Hunter told how he'd handled someone in town who didn't appreciate his association with Head Start, where ninety percent of the children were black. Some of the children he brought to school and took home each day.

One afternoon, after taking several children home from Head Start, he returned to the school to make sure that everything was locked down for the day. A man in town who was known for being a racist and who liked telling others what to do, came flying up the large U-shaped drive and braked just before hitting Hunter's car. "Moore," he said, with a twisted mouth, "I wanna talk with you 'bout takin' 'em niggers back and forth to school. Some of us folks don't like it." Still sitting in his car, with the window down, he gave Hunter a defiant look. His eyes were squinted and his face was flaming red.

Hunter walked slowly to the front of the car, grabbed the bumper and lifted the car. "I don't give a damn what you don't like, you sorry piece of shit. If you get out of that car, I'll whip your sorry ass. Now, get off this property and don't you ever come back. If you want to come on school property and tell folks what to do, you better take your ass on over to Macon Academy. Understand?" With that, he dropped the front of the car and headed to the driver's door. Before he could reach the door, the man threw the car into reverse and began to speed backwards.

It was clear that Hunter Moore didn't suffer fools easily, and no one told him what to do, how to do, or when to do. There was only one way. His. He knew when to listen and when to back off. For example, he backed off when the superintendent and board called his bluff about coaching football. They told him in no uncertain terms that he wasn't going to continue coaching. A new coach would be hired, and he needed to get on board. Before long, it became Hunter's idea. He was overworked and underpaid, being principal and coach. When he took the job, he thought that he could do it all. After two years of not winning a football game, or even coming close, he, along with the superintendent and board members, decided that it was too much. Times were still hard in Notasulga. There were still a lot of angry people. Maybe, a winning football team would help to reunite the town. Maybe, it would even drum up some support for the school. No one believed it would draw students back from Macon Academy or nearby counties, but if it helped in some small way, it would be worth it. Most people were working hard to make the school successful. People in the town needed to work together as a community.

As Hunter told story after story, it became clear there was another reason he'd been told to stop coaching. His methods of dealing with parents might be funny stories, but they didn't make for positive relationships between the parents and the board members who were constantly caught in the middle of controversial situations. They were a bit tired of defending him to outrageous parents.

"Winston, if you take this job, you got to watch Stoney Pointer's daddy. He's one crazy son-of-a-bitch. Drinks like a sailor who hasn't stepped on land in a year. Hell, he's a damn drunk. I'll just call him what he is. A sorry drunk!" he said, shaking his head and rolling his eyes upward. "I really feel bad for his kid. An embarrassment to his boy is what he is. One Friday night, about the middle of the season last year, the old man shows up at the game. Drunk. Same as always. Walking the sidelines, cussing me. Demanding to know why his son wasn't playing more. I couldn't concentrate on the game for listening to his screaming at the top of his lungs. He was yelling louder than the cheerleaders. Speaking of which, you might need to talk with the cheerleader sponsor about them girls doing a better job of cheering. They spend too much time socializing. Too concerned 'bout looking all pretty and nice. Don't want to sweat.

"Anyways, I got a belly full of his crap. So, I called time out. Then, I picked up that skinny kid like he was a baby and handed him over the fence to his daddy. The old man looked like he'd seen a ghost. His red drunk face changed to ash. But, by God, he stopped talking.

"I said, 'Take your son home. Keep him there. And, you, go to hell.'

"'I don't want him,' his daddy said, backing off.

"'I. Do. Not. Give. A Shit!' I screamed in his face. 'Take him, and if you step on my football field again, I'll stomp your sorry ass into the ground.' For once that fat drunk didn't know what to say.

"Finally, he said, 'I don't want him. I just want him to play more.'

"'Take him or I drop him.' Fatso took his son and his mouth hung open."

I glanced at Mr. Watson. He was looking at the ground, slightly shaking his head. I got a feeling that Hunter never ceased to amaze or amuse Mr. Watson, although he didn't approve of all of Hunter's methods of solving a problem.

"The following Monday, Fatso came to school, begging me to let his son play ball. I agreed. Under one condition. That he'd never come to another game as long as his son played. He said that he wouldn't. And he didn't. I let Stoney play. You know what? After his daddy stopped coming to the games, walking the fence, and yelling, the boy did a good job. Just goes to prove that you can't let parents run the show."

Chapter 7

The early afternoon sun beat down on us as we walked back to the school. Hunter answered Winston's questions about records, players, and contracts that'd been signed for the next season. It sounded gloomy as hell. Not the type of situation or atmosphere anyone with any sense wanted. Winston would later say, "It's a great opportunity for someone to turn things around and make a name for himself. It might as well be me." To me, family meant more than building one's reputation. That one subject about family would one day be the final blow to knock a huge hole in our marriage. A hole that would never be mended.

"Watch your ego," I thought, as he talked about making a name for himself.

After we left the school, Mr. Watson took us to four businesses and introduced us. There weren't more than four businesses in town that I could see. The second that we walked into Davis Hardware I felt the ice. Davis was a huge man whose mouth lines fell down in a bitter droop. Heavy jowls hung around his thick neck. He wore dark glasses with thick frames. When Mr. Watson introduced us, Davis didn't extend his hand after Winston offered his. I stood back and said nothing. I wasn't offering him squat.

On the way back to Tuskegee, Mr. Watson gave us more details about Hunter's character. Also, he told us that no one else would take the job after the school was rebuilt in 1965, and whoever took the job had to be tough. There were too many bad ghosts to handle. The town was split down the middle. People took sides, even in the churches. Not many people interviewed for the principal's job. Everyone wanted something better, with fewer problems. He understood. The board members wanted the principal to live in town. That was a real negative. The few people who came for an interview took one look at the town, walked into a couple of businesses, and after a few hostile attitudes, decided, "No way!"

It was one thing to operate a school that was recovering from a tragic recent history, but it was another thing to bring a family into unfriendly territory, especially in churches, where hostility shouldn't exist.

Then, Mr. Watson remembered Hunter Moore, who'd worked with Mr. Watson in another county. He asked Hunter to apply for the position. By that time, the board members agreed that they needed a "bad ass," someone strong enough and bull-headed enough to not care what anyone in the town thought. That someone had to be totally focused on making the school survive. Everything else would have to take a backseat. Even family.

Hunter had become known for taking jobs that no one else would touch. Later, we learned that Hunter was known as the man to desegregate schools in Alabama. He came to Notasulga at a time when a man like him was needed, and he got the school through two rough years. We learned, too, that he was a tough, but kind soul. But as I listened to Hunter that day, I wasn't too impressed.

There was one catch when he accepted the job. With him, there was always a catch. He'd have complete control, as well as absolute support from the superintendent and the board members. His every decision couldn't be questioned or doubted. And he wanted to be the football coach.

Everyone reluctantly agreed, because they were also having trouble finding a football coach. Hunter was paid extra for coaching, but Mr. Watson believed that he would've coached for free. After all, he'd been an outstanding tackle for the University of Alabama, and no one else was chasing the job. Now it was time for a change. The team hadn't won a game since the school was rebuilt. The boys played like a bunch of neighborhood kids who got together on a Sunday afternoon for touch football in an empty cornfield.

"I'm telling you all of this so you'll know what to expect. It's not gonna be easy for anybody who takes the job. I won't lie about it. There'll be people in town who will dislike you because of where you work. Some won't speak to you," Mr. Watson stated with raw honesty.

Looking in the rearview mirror at me, he promised, "The board will buy a washer and a dryer so the coach won't have to haul dirty uniforms home."

I smiled at his eyes and nose in the rectangular mirror, like I gave a crap. There was no way in hell I was trashing my washer and dryer for every football player's dirty clothes and jock itch. That was the least of my worries. I needed some convincing about lack of racism and hate, which I wasn't hearing.

As they talked, I watched Winston closely. He was glowing and the words, "I'll take it now" hung unspoken in the confined space of the car. Me, I was not so sure. I couldn't forget those girls' voices, as they laughed about burning the school, so long ago in a stuffy room. It seemed like decades, not three years.

Suddenly, I realized that no one had talked about the burning of the school. Not when the fire occurred or why. The talk had been about rebuilding. Not just a school, but a town and relationships. For some reason, I didn't want to mention it. I hesitated to ask Mr. Watson any questions about the burning.

Mr. Watson pulled into the parking lot of the Macon County Board of Education. We got out of the car, entered the building, and went straight to his office. Winston and I sat in chairs across from the superintendent's desk. I watched closely as he tilted his chair back and crossed his hands over his belly. "Well, what do y'all think of the school?" Without waiting for a response, he continued, "I know Hunter's a tad rough around the edges, but he's done a hell of a lot to keep the school together. Winston, you don't have to worry about him interfering with your coaching. I can assure you of that."

Winston said something about being able to work with Hunter and how impressed he was with the new building and how much progress had been made in the last two years. I didn't say a word. Finally, Mr. Watson looked at me and said, "What are you thinking, Marley Jane?"

I looked down at my hands, which were folded in my lap. There seemed to be a long silence, and I could hear Winston's breathing. I was inside his head, listening to him, telling me to be careful about what I said. Looking Mr. Watson in the eyes, I said, "I'm really bothered about the burning of the school in December, 1963. I just don't understand how anyone could do such a horrible thing. And I don't understand how an entire town can become so divided over something that is fair and just, that treats everyone equally. I don't get it. And I'm not sure that I want to live among people who harbor that type of hate."

There, I'd said it. Although I didn't look, I knew that Winston was giving me the evil eye, warning me to hold my tongue.

"But, the school wasn't burned in December, 1963. It was burned in April, 1964, after the school was desegregated—"

"But," I interrupted, "I overheard two girls from Notasulga talking in January, 1964, at Opelika Business School, about burning the school in December. Are you telling me that I didn't hear about a done deed? I heard about a deed that was yet to be done, and it was so commonly known that two girls in the town knew about it? That makes the horrendous deed even more horrendous than I imagined. Those girls weren't talking about roasting marshmallows. I know what I heard." Then I explained to him the entire circumstances of that day.

"So, you walked in on a conversation that you didn't hear from the beginning? I understand why you've been under the impression that the school was burned in December. It might not matter which month. The terrible truth is that it was burned. I want to go forward, to put the past behind us. Not to forget, but to make something positive out of a negative. I'd like for Winston and you to help me . . . and others . . . do that. I'd like for y'all to be a part of the rebuilding process of Notasulga," he said, leaning across the desk.

Without realizing it, I was nodding my head. Still, I didn't want to say anything that sounded like a commitment to Winston or to him. Winston coughed, but I didn't look at him. My eyes were locked with Mr. Watson's eyes. Slowly, he sat back in his chair and said, "Let me tell you the story. How it all began. Now, I want you to remember that I was there. I talked with Fred Gray, Judge Johnson, Governor Wallace, Jim Clark, the plaintiffs of the Lee v. Macon County lawsuit that brought about desegregation, and the people of Tuskegee. And Notasulga.

"Also, I have a journal here. Some place," he said, opening desk drawers. "Here it is." He held up a black composition notebook. "One of the six plaintiffs who integrated Notasulga High School kept this journal. After the school year ended, his mother wanted me to have the journal. It takes you inside his head and lets you know how he felt. And, of course, I'll give you my version of what happened. I know the whole story. Have y'all got time to hear it?"

"Yes," Winston and I answered together.

"Well, This is the story."

Chapter 8

The only sound on the bus was the clicking of the camera, as the photographer walked up and down the aisle, from left to right, window to window, to the front of the bus and back. He snapped the world outside the bus, as well as the faces of those on the bus, while the six young people and the driver looked straight ahead. Everyone stopped talking as the bus approached the town, although there hadn't been too much talk since they boarded the bus. The photographer had slipped onto the bus unnoticed, while those in charge were giving last minute instructions to the young people and the bus driver, before they departed. He went to the last seat on the left-hand side of the bus and pushed himself into the corner, hoping that no one would notice him and order him off. The bus pulled out of the parking lot before the others noticed him. The driver didn't say anything. In his opinion, this needed to be recorded, and he liked the idea of another adult being on the bus. A white man would do one of two things. He'd either calm people or infuriate them. It would be a toss of the coin.

As the bus slowly rolled into the small rural town, they could hear the crowd. The tension was as thick as a heavy fog that covered everything. The sky was dark, with clouds that threatened more rain. The temperature was thirty-four, with a cold that scratched the bone. The wind was gusty and made tree limbs twist like washcloths being rung out. Not a drop of sun shone through the solid cloud that lay over the sky like a gigantic sheet, with wrinkles here and there. The sheet was a canopy as far as the eye could see in any direction. To make the day even gloomier, a light drizzle that looked like ice fell off and on.

The heater on the bus couldn't warm the cold hands and feet of the passengers. But, if the temperature had been ninety-nine, they would've still felt chilled. No amount of heat could eliminate the cold air in which they moved.

No one on board the bus spoke. No one looked out a window. All seven dark faces stared straight ahead. Suddenly, it felt as if all of the air vanished from the bus. It became suffocating on that bleak early Wednesday morning in February, 1964. In the silence, you could hear the deep breathing of the passengers, mentally preparing themselves, as they recalled all that they'd been told and instructed to do or not to do.

The loud voices of the people outside mingled with the soft click of the camera inside the bus, shooting into the angry crowd, recording the mad mob, capturing the twisted mouths and wild eyes, the pumping fists in the air. The white gang of men and women stood on the sidewalks and faced the passengers on the bus, as it headed down the main street to an assigned designation that would soon change laws, opportunities, social and cultural issues, voting, and politics in Alabama, sweeping into neighboring states and across the country. The people on board the bus had no idea of the impact that this bus ride would have on events in Macon County or across Alabama. They only knew they wanted things to change for themselves and for their people. In many ways, they were too young and too innocent to comprehend what was taking place. Some of them would be much older before they grasped the overwhelming effect that day's trip would have outside Macon County. But, those who'd begun the desegregation lawsuit in Macon County probably guessed how things would evolve.

The world outside the bus had gone crazy with rage and hate. The whites had brought their hate to town with them on this cold morning. Before today, the atmosphere in Macon County had been somewhat restrained about racial matters. Today, it was full blown racial hate and tension. The whites' anger had been bottling up inside for months, and it was making them mean with outraged indignation and fear. Fear is a powerful thing that can turn into a raging storm. It can make a man a coward or a hero. Today was a test.

A heavy-set young man with curly red hair, freckles, and dull watery blue eyes raised his pale left hand into the air, looking as if he was about to throw the last ball of the World Series. His body twisted a bit to the right, and he hauled an object at the bus. Others followed, as if a command had been given. Several eggs hit the sides of the bus. The camera clicked.

The seven dark faces didn't flinch, but continued to look straight ahead. No one spoke. The black bus driver, a huge big-boned man who had the physical qualifications to play for the NFL, squared his high shoulders and gave a frosty glare ahead. His eyes were black coals, with dots of light. His mouth was firm. His jaws were locked and tense, with determination, not fear. This man was chosen because he didn't chase after fights, but he also didn't run from fights. He had a cool head on his shoulders. He was not a foolish man. His job was to use caution, to make a safe delivery, there and back. He had lived his entire life in the South. He knew its human temperature and its history. Neither scared him.

The bus passed under the only light in town, which was a caution light, and headed toward the second bridge that curved high over the Montgomery-West Point Railroad tracks that snaked through West Point, Georgia, on to Atlanta. They'd earlier ridden over a larger curved bridge that arched high above the tracks, just before entering the residential section of town. Pine trees, farms, and houses were along the country road from Tuskegee. All of that ended when they crossed the first large bridge and were suddenly in the midst of houses that sat close together, but not crowding one another, on both sides of the road. The houses extended for approximately a mile before the bus came to the caution light.

Chapter 9

The young man on the bus had to look, to see the faces of hate, to absorb the unbelievable anger that rippled through the town and onto the bus, which seemed to shake from the loud, violent voices. He'd never felt anything like this. Never known such a force. He sat in church many Sundays and listened to the preacher warn the congregation about evil and its power, about the powerful Satan who claimed so many souls. And about the Supreme Being that gave Satan free will, but was the only force strong enough to tame him. The preacher talked a lot lately about how God used man to fight Satan and how man had to muster the courage to rise up and defeat the forces of evil that Satan scattered like seeds across the earth. The preacher talked about God choosing brave men and women to carry out His plans. He said that God didn't always move as fast as man wanted, but He moved in His own time, when the time was ripe to pluck the fruits of His labor and when His people were ready to stand up against evil. And the preacher said that when the chosen walked through the fires of evil, God would protect them and deliver them safely to a better place. So, the young man had to be brave enough to look into the faces of evil so that he would never forget, so that he would recognize it if he ever saw it again, so that he could stare it down and demolish its power, so that he would become stronger and more knowledgeable.

With those thoughts, he summoned up his courage and looked out the window, into Hell's fire. They were passing Davis' Hardware store. Ten or twelve angry men, young and old, stood in front of the large glass window. Their faces were red as they stared with open hostility and eyes that floated in hard-filled hatred. Their voices were loud and rough. One man stood out among the others. He was tall and thin, worn looking. His face wore a brutal look and a cigarette dangled loosely from his thin, dry lips. He slowly raised a shotgun and pointed it at the young man in the window of the bus. The universe paused. Waiting.

Still, the young man could not look away. He and the older man locked eyes. Both felt a raging fire as they briefly measured one another. The young man stared into the stone cold eyes of the man. He waited for the bullet, for death. He damn sure would not look away. He would not die a coward. He would die, defying the face of evil, looking into its lying eyes.

The man lowered the shotgun to his thigh. He inhaled deeply on the cigarette before taking it from his mouth with a farmer's knotted and strong hand. His head tilted back ever so slightly and he blew grey smoke into the cold morning air, as he gave a defiant look at the bus. He threw the cigarette to the sidewalk and stomped out its small glowing red light. Then, he laughed and yelled something that faded into the wind.

The young man grinned. More with his eyes than his mouth. At that moment, he knew some truth, some secret that only God can reveal. He exhaled silently and slowly. His body relaxed into the leather. White men wouldn't piss him off today, and they wouldn't scare him—ever. It would be a long time before he felt fear again. In some jungle in Vietnam. Not here. Not in Notasulga, Alabama, on his way to integrate a white public school in Macon County. He was one of thirteen who'd been chosen by the black community in Tuskegee and by the white superintendent of education and all of the white board members. "Maybe God has chosen me as well," he thought. And, damn it, he'd behave like he'd been chosen.

The bus crossed a second curved bridge and slowly moved down a tree-lined street, where the houses were nicer and the yards were well kept. The young man wondered if anyone on this street supported the cause. Looking in front of the bus, he saw a car, and he knew it contained four federal marshals. Two other cars followed the bus. They'd been told that more federal marshals would be at the school.

More of the angry mob waited on the lawn of the school. George Wallace wouldn't be blocking the schoolhouse door, but everyone knew his finger was in the pot, stirring up chaos and confusion, giving orders to local and state officials, staying in contact with Ku Klux Klan leaders. The older men, who talked with the young people and watched as they boarded the bus, suspected that Wallace would send some of his cronies and that he'd spoken with people in Notasulga, ordering and advising them what actions to take. The angry people would do whatever he told them. He was their savior, sent to save them from a social change sweeping the country, from a way of life that they didn't want and refused to accept. If anyone could stop the federal government, it was Wallace.

Some people said that Governor George Wallace had slept with the devil in order to become the governor of Alabama and that he was now the devil's harlot. Old Scratch would be Wallace's pimp for years, advising and aiding him in his efforts to gain political power. Of course, there were others for whom the devil pimped. In order to acquire power in the state, a long list of well-known men had made race the focus of Alabama politics. In some cases, others simply used race as a means to boost their egos.

There were enough "johns" in the South to keep those whores in power and business for years. The pimp provided Wallace and others with everything they needed, which, of course, was very willing clients. It was a time when the devil owned the souls of governors, judges, sheriffs, national guardsmen, state troopers, and ordinary unknown citizens who flocked to join the KKK or the Citizens' Council. All of them bullying and running over anyone who got in their way or disagreed with their opinions on race, politics, religion, or the amount of water used to boil an egg.

All the determined efforts of the pimp, his whores, and their clients couldn't stop forever the work of God, or so the young man's preacher said. He told the congregation that God had had enough. It was His time to move. The ball was in His court. He was captain of the team. The players had been chosen, and they were on a mission to win. The game would get rough, but never too rough for The Man who allowed all games to be played.

As the bus moved down the deserted street, everyone on board was aware that one Being knew exactly how the game would be played and who would win. Winning demanded a price. But then, it always did. Change does not come easy or without a price tag of some sort.

A segregated community ballpark and swimming pool came into view and disappeared as the bus made its way to the school. Not one black child played ball on that field or swam in that pool. And the white folks in Notasulga wanted it to stay that way. They had no intentions of ever allowing a black child to catch a fly ball or hit a home run on that field. No black child would swim on a hot Southern summer day in the cool blue waters of white territory.

The six black students on the bus saw the school ahead on the right, sitting off a distance from the highway, on top of a slight incline. The elementary school was to the east. The auditorium sat between the elementary and the high schools, while the gym was beyond the elementary school. No one discussed if anyone aboard the bus had previously been to the town. No one had. Blacks from Tuskegee didn't come too often to Notasulga, where they weren't welcome. If they wanted to go to Lee County, they took Interstate I-85 North.

It'd been obvious as the bus drove into town that it was entering the belly of a hungry mob that had become a beast, roaring with rage. People along the streets in town waved small Confederate flags and signs. One man, perhaps a sawmill worker, who appeared to be in his forties, had dark, greasy hair and wore a white tee shirt beneath a worn brown corduroy jacket and faded Levis. A skinny hand carried a large Confederate flag as he took large strides up and down the sidewalk. Twisting his mouth and making it look as if it would explode, he yelled things that the passengers on the bus couldn't hear.

A similar scene was taking place on the school lawn as the rain fell. Irate men and women raised signs that read: "Keep our schools white," "Judge Johnson has betrayed us," "Obey not Washington, D.C.," "We want private schools," and "No niggers allowed in Notasulga schools." People, waving flags and signs, stood on both sides of the drive that led to the entrance of the high school

The bus driver and some of the federal marshals recognized Jim Clark and his mounted posse from Selma, Alabama. Clark was the sheriff of Dallas County, where Selma is located. His posse, known as "the sheriff's posse," consisted of volunteers who were thrilled to ride horses and beat the shit out of every black, male or female, who dared be bold enough to stand up and demand justice. Clark and his mounted posse were more than happy to be invited outside of Dallas County, to put fear into anyone who gave a minute's thought to opposing their authority or Alabama's white way of life.

Clark's full name was James Garner Clark. He was 6'2" and built like a bull. He had a fleshy face, with a short neck and a chin that melted into it; his eyes were cold and dark. The corners of his mouth turned down. On his belt hung a billy club, a pistol, and an electric cattle prod. He was known for his acts of brutality, especially against blacks in Dallas County. He routinely ordered beatings with clubs and tear-gassing. His methods became well-known during the Jim Crow era, as he ordered and participated in violent actions against civil rights demonstrators who attempted to vote.

Two respected men would later confront Jim Clark and win on his own turf. By March 7, 1965, Fred Gray, a black civil rights attorney from Montgomery, filed a lawsuit in the federal district court of Judge Frank M. Johnson for the Selma to Montgomery March to take place and to demand removal of voting restrictions on blacks.

Wallace would again welcome Clark's explosive and shocking participation, as the first of three attempts to march from Selma to Montgomery began. Jim Clark and his mounted posse were among those who'd been ordered by Wallace to stop the march.

The first attempt to march from Selma to Montgomery was stopped by state and local officials, who attacked approximately six hundred people, as they crossed the Edmund Pettus Bridge in Selma. Pettus had been a leader in the KKK and a racist. When people marched across the bridge for voting rights, they walked on Pettus himself. One person would later die as a result of the attack. Another attempt to march would be stopped soon thereafter. At the end of two attempts, three people would be dead

Gray spoke with Judge Johnson, who told Gray to notify Martin Luther King, Jr., to delay the third march, until Judge Johnson could get an order from President Lyndon Johnson that would give the marchers federal protection. President Johnson federalized the Alabama National Guard. The date for the march from Selma to Montgomery was set for March 21, 1965. On that day, Martin Luther King, Jr., led thousands of marchers from Selma to Montgomery. Four days later, King gave a speech on the Alabama capitol steps. On August 6, 1965, President Lyndon B. Johnson signed the Voting Rights Act into law, which had been passed by Congress.

The Voting Rights Law changed politics in Alabama for decades, but soon the lawmakers in Montgomery began looking for any means possible to reverse the course of political voting.

* * * * * * *

Mr. Watson's story was fascinating, and I realized that I was sitting on the edge of my chair, clinging to every word and recalling what I'd heard about the Selma to Montgomery March. I'd never heard of Fred Gray, but already I admired him. The superintendent knew Fred Gray and other well-known people involved in the story; therefore, I trusted what he was saying.

Questions were swimming inside my head; yet, I didn't dare interrupt the story. I glanced over at Winston. He was as captivated as I was. I took a deep breath and exhaled, as Mr. Watson continued. "Let me tell you what Vernon Merritt told me. He's the photographer who sneaked onto the bus before it left Tuskegee. I also talked with the two federal agents who rescued him. The next part of the story is taken from conversations that I had with Vernon and the federal marshals."

Chapter 10

If tension was high on board the bus, it didn't show. The driver flipped on the right blinker and began a slow turn onto the circular drive that would take them to the steps of the high school. As the bus turned into the driveway and began to move toward the entrance, the voices of the men and women who were standing on the lawn and in front of the school were silent. Suddenly, the chanting began.

"Segregation is morally right. Segregation is morally right."

The photographer rolled down a window and began to capture the scene. The camera zoomed in so close to one dirty, skinny boy, who looked to be about seventeen, that the red acne covering his face looked like tiny volcanoes about to rupture. The camera protruding from the window infuriated the crowd. Clark and one of his men rushed the doors of the bus, forcing the driver to stop. If the bus hit one of the men, hell would break loose. The quick eye of the man with the camera saw them coming. He bent downward and moved to the front of the bus, away from the young passengers. As he did so, a stocky man, with a bulbous nose, a blood-red face, and close-set hazel eyes, pushed the doors open with one swift, savage movement, as he screamed at the photographer, "I'll fuckin' kill you. You goddamn nigger lover. I'll stomp yo' white ass!"

As the man stood on the first step of the bus and screamed, Clark took seven steps into the bus and grabbed the photographer's right arm, jerking him forward. Both men pulled him from the bus. Another man snatched the camera from the left hand of the photographer. He threw it to the ground, pounding it with his scuffed, dirty boot. Clark slung the photographer to the ground, striking his back and neck with an electrical cattle prod, which was his favorite weapon of choice. Truth be told, each use of the prod sent adrenaline rushing through Clark's body like a shot of heroin. The rush was addictive.

He stayed bent low over the photographer and mumbled near his ear, "Boy, we gonna beat all the black offa you. You hear me, boy?"

The man who'd pushed open the doors of the bus began to slam his fists into the photographer's face and body. Other men ran to join in the attack, hitting and kicking the photographer who was now on the ground. Clark moved back to allow the others to finish what he'd started. As they beat the photographer, they dragged him over to the curb.

Two or three men continued to pound the helpless man as he lay on the ground. The others chased after the bus that was moving to the steps of the school. The crowd was pumped. The bus driver was calm, but worried about his passengers who were frozen in their seats. They knew not to respond or to comment, but to remain calm. They'd been warned that violence could erupt. Federal marshals had begun to surround the bus as it crept closer to the entrance of the school. They stopped their cars, got out, and headed to the bus, each with a hand near a hip. Some remained outside the crowd, as others moved into the crowd.

A Notasulga police officer was in the process of arresting the photographer and hauling him off to the local jail. Before the officer could shove him into the police car, two federal marshals ran to the aid of the photographer and blocked the officer. Words were exchanged. The marshals lifted the limp photographer and half-drug him to their vehicle. They placed him in the backseat of the car and started the motor. The car flew down the street, back toward Tuskegee. As they headed out of town, the weak photographer was beginning to look almost unrecognizable. He reached into his left sock and pulled out a roll of film. He held it above his head that was swollen and bloated. His right eye was almost completely shut and was quickly turning a light shade of amber. A large lump had popped up on his forehead. Blood flowed down Vernon Merritt's face, but he laughed. He had the film to take back to the editor of the Black Star syndicate. The two marshals in the front seat turned around to see why he was laughing. They thought he might be in shock. Their eyes opened in surprise and they laughed with him.

"Lord, man," one of them said. "I hope that film's worth the ass-whipping you just got."

"You know some people back in Tuskegee are gonna be pissed that you were on that bus. Hell, we had no idea. We thought those mother fuckers were going on the bus to pull the kids off," the other man told Vernon. "We were getting ready for hell to open wide up. Then, we saw that son-of-a-bitch, Jim Clark, pulling your ass off the bus."

Vernon Merritt no longer looked like the same man who'd boarded the bus in Tuskegee. His long, slender face, with a prominent forehead and chiseled chin, looked like a pumpkin and his handlebar mustache was caked in blood. Steel-rimmed glasses sat cock-eyed on his lean nose. His lips were torn and puffed.

"Yeah," Vernon managed to croak, "I was worried for the kids and the position I'd put them in. But, once those white men saw me on that bus, their only thought was to kill me, if possible."

He was quiet for a moment, staring at the road ahead, coming up to meet them. His brown eyes, the color of dark coffee, had grown darker, and he spoke in a strained, low voice. "Somebody ought to stomp Clark and ram that damn electric cattle prod up his ass. Maybe, one day, that bastard will get what he deserves. And to think, a damn governor, of any state, allows a bastard like Clark to wander around the state, treating its citizens like pieces of shit, is beyond comprehension. Wallace is so hungry for power he'll allow anything to happen. If it means he gets to move up the political ladder and onto the world stage."

"We've seen you around since September. We know you work free-lance for the Black Star agency of Birmingham. But where are you from?"

"Born and raised a liberal rebel in the South. In Montgomery. My parents support desegregation, but my mama's dad is a racist. A family divided. Needless to say, my grandpaw's not too happy 'bout what I do, especially my reason for doing it." He laughed. "He'll probably be glad I got my ass whipped."

He turned and looked out of the window and watched blurred visions of the countryside rush pass. A soft sigh escaped his lips. "So, I'm a free-lance photo journalist, a graduate of the University of Alabama and the Art Center in Los Angeles. I came back home to record the changes taking place in the South. I've been threatened and jailed. Hell almost got jailed again. Would've, if not for you guys. By the way. Thanks."

"So, what are you going to do once this is over?" asked the marshal who was driving. "If it's ever over, that is."

"I'm going to Vietnam to capture the war and its effects on our soldiers, as well as the Vietnamese people . . . and country. Hell. Maybe, one day, my pictures will be in *Life* or *Newsweek*." He gave a hollow laugh. "If I live through all this shit in the South."

Silence rode with the three men for several minutes before Vernon spoke again in a tired, sad voice that made him sound older. "I've grown up here. In the South. Love it. All my life I've seen respectable, decent folks, like my grandpaw, live a lie that politicians, and preachers, and history tell over and over. These decent people believe the lie out of fear and ignorance. Too, they're afraid of change. Watching all of those people standing on the sidewalks, as we drove into town, and on the lawn at the school, made me realize that they don't want new beginnings that'll change life as they know it. Because change scares the hell out of folks. Southerners aren't called Conservatives for nothing. They want life to be the same as their parents and grandparents knew it. Everything they know or ever believed in is disappearing. And they're afraid they'll shrink to nothing, that they'll lose their values and beliefs." He seemed to be thinking. "Yeah, it's fear. Raw, ugly fear. It'll get really nasty, because men in Montgomery, in courthouses across the state, and even in churches, are in control. To accomplish their mission and to justify their causes, they use fear. Sadly, it works every single time. Not a damn one of those white bastards who're creating chaos gives a damn that the universe is shrinking into madness. Just as long as they're calling the shots and pulling the strings of people who trust others to do their thinking and who live in fear. As long as they're in power.

"Ironically, many poor whites, who don't have the power of money or position to speak for them, have the old Southern belief that they are better than black folks. It gives them a deep, false sense of power. So many rich and powerful people control almost every aspect of their lives. The divide between the races is the only power that they can personally and legally claim over another group of people who they consider to be on a lower social status. The psychology behind that idea is complex and brutally sad, but one's need to control with absolute and supreme power keeps the wheels of politics, families, and religion in the forefront of people's beliefs and values. It also keeps the prisons full and the devil happy. But never content."

The driver slightly turned his head to glance at Vernon and added, "Hell, I agree that the only people a poor man in the South can feel superior to are black people. You're right. So many white folks don't have any control or power, so they play 'follow-the-leader' with any white son-of-a-bitch who has what they want. I guess, somehow, it makes them feel connected to wealth and power. I've heard that some whites sell their votes or vote however the upper man tells them to vote, especially if he's writing that poor man's paycheck. How long you think that's gonna take to change?"

"Well, for sure, the South has more issues than desegregation. There's that. What you're talking 'bout. Then, there's the fact that blacks can't vote in Alabama, without answering some stupid question like 'How many bubbles in a bar of soap?' If I were asked that, I'd say, 'It depends on the size of the soap.' For that answer, I'd be called a smart-ass. Whereas, if a black man gave that answer, he might be beaten to death by a Klansman and thrown in a creek. It'd be called suicide. Even if he had a cement block tied around his waist, with his feet and hands bound with rope." He stopped talking for several minutes. "If you're a black person in Alabama, or most of the South, you're damned if you do and damned if you don't. But, hey, change is coming. I feel it. That keeps me going. Keeps me believing."

Silence filled the car as it sailed under I-85 and into Tuskegee. No one spoke as the car moved toward downtown. Each man was lost in deep thought about the events unraveling in that small rural county in Alabama.

* * * * * *

"I think Vernon's comments summed up what a whole lotta folks felt, but were simply too afraid to express. Vernon Merritt's a smart man. I've got a whole heap of respect for him."

I realized that I'd added another person to my "Respect List."

"So, let me tell you what was going on back at the school," Mr. Watson said.

Chapter 11

White students stood on the steps of the auditorium, on the sidewalk, and near the school building, watching as the drama unfolded. No one ordered them back into the building. Not many had stayed home. A few left before Christmas and enrolled at Macon Academy, a private school in Tuskegee that had opened in an old mansion in September, 1963. The new private school was across the road from the all-white school, Tuskegee High School, which federal district circuit Judge Frank M. Johnson ordered to be desegregated on September 2, 1963, after Fred Gray filed a lawsuit on January 28, 1963, against the Macon County Board of Education. When thirteen black students from Tuskegee attempted to desegregate Tuskegee High School, "white flight" was rapid, and Macon Academy sprung up overnight.

Detroit Lee was a founder of the Tuskegee NAACP chapter in 1944. In 1962, he approached Fred Gray, the attorney for the Tuskegee Civil Association, to help him desegregate Tuskegee High School. He wanted Gray to file a lawsuit against the Macon County School Board of Education. Gray agreed and filed the lawsuit, along with attorneys for the NAACP. The lawsuit became known as Lee v. Macon County Board of Education.

When discussion of the lawsuit began, the superintendent of Education and board members met with Fred Gray, Detroit Lee, local minsters, and others to peacefully desegregate Tuskegee High School. A committee selected the black students whom they thought would be the best students to send to the all-white school. The students were interviewed and tested. Students who did well on the tests and the interviews were chosen. The committee wanted smart students, but not so smart that they'd perform better academically than the white students, because everyone was well aware of the whites' attitudes toward blacks whom they considered to be "uppity."

Anthony and Henry Lee, who were Detroit Lee's sons, were named the lead plaintiffs in the lawsuit. Thirteen black students were plaintiffs, along with the NAACP. In an unusual, innovative, and bold move, Judge Johnson ordered the United States Justice Department as a "litigating amicus." This made the United States another plaintiff in the case. As a result, the plaintiffs would have full access to all evidence, arguments, briefs, etc., of the Justice Department, as well as the Department of Health, Education, and Welfare. The United States would participate as an active party in every legal aspect of the case and could ask for injunctions or for contempt of court, which would happen again and again.

The United States could maintain and preserve justice, as well as the judicial authority of the United States. Judge Johnson would have all resources of the Justice Department, as well as the Federal Bureau of Investigation, along with the Department of Health, Education and Welfare. The FBI would be involved many times with the desegregation of Macon County, as well as the horrific events that occurred as a result of Lee v. Macon. In the end, the bad would be changed to good, although many people would refuse to acknowledge that fact.

The hearing for Lee v. Macon took place in the old Opelika Courthouse in August, 1963. Later, Judge Johnson issued a desegregation order for Tuskegee High School, declaring that it be desegregated on September 2, 1963, when the new school year began. Some whites in Tuskegee were determined that Tuskegee High School wouldn't survive, and they contacted Governor George Wallace.

Wallace straightened his short stature into a stiff general's posture and dove into his legal texts, summoned his advisors and his very willing racist supporters, from the KKK to Jim Clark to Bull Conner, to all Southerners who were clinging to the old way of life, to all they'd ever known or cared to know. He polished his already shiny political rhetoric that appealed to both uneducated and educated people throughout Alabama. After all, a man can be well-educated and remain ignorant about many things that concern life, humanity, compassion, and justice.

Wallace was determined to use everything and everyone at his command to dispose of the forces that he said were against the southern, Christian way of life and the southern social structure. He began to issue executive orders left and right. The first order postponed the start of classes at Tuskegee High School.

The opening day, September 2, 1963, was delayed until Monday, September 9, a week from the day Judge Johnson's order was to go into effect, because Wallace issued an executive order to postpone classes for a week. He used the same excuse that he'd been using since he'd been elected governor. It was his duty to "maintain peace and order." Everyone in the know was aware that he was lying and that his only interest was political. If he could convince the people of Alabama that he was protecting them from a federal government that wanted absolute control over every aspect of their lives, as well as interfering in ways that involved their Christian beliefs, he would become a well-known figure on the political stage.

There was no end to his political possibilities. So, he did what he did well; he began to create double trouble. He sent several hundred state troopers to surround the school to enforce his executive order. Of course, why send only one force when you can send all branches of force? In addition to sending the state troopers, Wallace sent the sheriff of Macon County, the local police, Jim Clark from Selma and his posse, as well as the Alabama National Guard. If Jim Clark, with his billy club, pistol, electric cattle prod, and his mounted posse showed up, along with the KKK, they could instill enough fear to stop the desegregation process.

Still, many whites opposed their tactics and supported desegregation. Some spoke out, but many remained silent, afraid for themselves and for their families. Hundreds of white people throughout the state despised the tactics used by the state's bullies and leaders. They, along with many whites in Tuskegee, supported desegregation. Fear kept them quiet.

Judge Johnson's response was to issue a restraining order against Wallace, who was at the same time interfering with school desegregation in Birmingham, Huntsville, Tuscaloosa, and Mobile. He was behind, or approved, the extreme racial actions in those cities.

Federal marshals were sent to deliver Judge Johnson's order against Wallace, but they were told he wasn't in his office, while, in fact, he was there, thumbing through legal texts and writing more orders to place the National Guard at schools throughout the state so that black students couldn't enter white schools.

President John F. Kennedy stopped Wallace's plan by federalizing the Alabama National Guard, but Wallace had the local police, Jim Clark, Clark's mounted posse, the KKK, and angry white people to assist him.

* * * * * * *

By this time, I was leaning toward Mr. Watson, absorbing every word and wondering, "How could I not have heard or read about what was going on in Macon County? How could I have been that out of touch?" I was beyond fascinated.

"I know that I'm giving y'all a lot of information, but it's important that you understand the full story. I mean, the burning of the school didn't just pop up out of nowhere, for no reason. There's a reason, good or bad. You've got to know the thing—the lawsuit—that caused trouble in Notasulga. Understand me. I'm not saying that the lawsuit was trouble. Hell, no! It helped bring racism to light in the town. It was the cause that created the effect. Not many people outside of the county know that. To tell you the truth, there aren't too many people in the state who even know about Lee v. Macon."

"So, what happened next?" I asked.

"Well, it was like this . . ."

Chapter 12

By the time Tuskegee High School opened on September 9, 1963, thirteen black students and one hundred twenty-five whites showed up. Enrollment continued to drop throughout the week, until the only students in the building were the thirteen black students. "White flight" had occurred by the end of the first week of school. The white students who hadn't enrolled in the newly established Macon Academy had fled to public schools in surrounding areas or counties. They enrolled in Macon County High School in Notasulga, as well as public schools in nearby counties, such as Auburn, Reeltown, and Tallassee. Those who fled to Notasulga would, before long, find another place to flee, because six of the thirteen plaintiffs would soon head to Notasulga to desegregate Macon County High School.

Wallace was in control again, giving orders to the state superintendent that Tuskegee High School had to close, due to the fact that the Alabama Constitution stated that a public school couldn't function without a certain number of students. It was too costly. As a result, Tuskegee High School was closed by an order from the Alabama State Board of Education. The order was given on January 30, 1963. The state board ordered that the twelve black students return to Tuskegee Institute High, an all black school. By now, one of the plaintiffs had been dropped from the lawsuit, for whistling at a white girl.

Fred Gray asked Judge Johnson to stop the segregation of the school system in Macon County, by desegregating all public schools in the county and by allowing whites to transfer to other public schools in the system. Judge Johnson ordered that Shorter High School and Macon County High School be desegregated on February 3, 1964.

Six of the remaining plaintiffs would desegregate Shorter High School and six would be sent to Macon County High School, which would later be named Notasulga High School so that the whites of Notasulga could forever and a day say, "No blacks ever graduated from Macon County High School."

On Monday, February 3, 1964, Fred Gray filed an amended and supplemental complaint in Lee v. Macon. In the complaint, he stated that the State of Alabama controlled local boards of education. In their rush to control and manipulate the situation, with total disregard to state and federal laws, the Alabama State Board had given Gray and Judge Johnson a path of attack. The complaint further stated that the State of Alabama was operating the public school system on a racially segregated basis. Again, when the state ordered the students to return to Tuskegee Institute High, it was guilty of state interference and obstruction; the state was extending its limits of power. Gray asked the court to include the Alabama State Board of Education, its individual members, and the governor, as its president, as defendants in the case. He asked that they be barred from interfering in Macon County desegregation.

In addition, Gray did something that many people never knew, not then or now. He also asked Judge Johnson to go one step further and to add all public schools in Alabama, which hadn't already desegregated, as defendants in the Lee v. Macon case. Johnson didn't go that far, because he knew it'd be like dropping an eighteen-wheeler, loaded with gasoline, into the fires of hell. It wasn't the time.

Judge Johnson was aware that segregationists and Wallace hadn't given up on tuition grants or grant-in-aid to segregated private schools. Those grants had been given to whites in Macon County in 1963, in order that their children could attend the quickly established private school, Macon Academy. Not only were grants given and buses provided, but some people suspected that Wallace had state troopers transporting, in state owned vehicles, white students throughout Macon County to Macon Academy. By allowing grants and busing, Wallace slipped up and opened the door to statewide expansion of Lee v. Macon County. Thank you, Governor Wallace.

It was an opportunity that Fred Gray jumped on immediately, and he successfully argued that the state's public school system controlled education policy and sanctioned racial segregation. Wallace was a smart legal cookie, but history would prove that he was no match for the legal wits of Fred Gray and Judge Frank M. Johnson. It didn't hurt that they had right on their side. So, with Gray pushing and a three-judge panel listening, the court further ordered that no more public funds could be used for grants and given by any state employee to any private school or to anyone attending a private school.

Chapter 13

It was believed that the people in Notasulga were told that their school wouldn't be desegregated until the fall of 1964. Apparently, some parents in Tuskegee heard the same thing, so they sent their children to Notasulga in September. Things happened faster than they thought, thanks to Governor Wallace and his cohorts who were constantly interfering.

If the truth be known, the white people in Macon County were betting that desegregation of their schools wouldn't happen. After all, they had powerful, loud-mouthed Wallace and others firing them up, boosting their faith in a false prophet. They had confidence in "that little man," who had the courage to take on the federal government, even the President of the United States and the Attorney General. No other state had a governor who stood up to such power. Little did they know that Wallace, who knew the Constitution, was simply performing, an actor on stage, aware of the script and how the play would end. He was an actor with ambition, and he wanted to perform on a larger stage. Like any good performer, he knew his audience. He convinced them that they all shared the same beliefs and the same Christian values. So many people on the same page couldn't be wrong.

So, whites withdrew from Tuskegee High School to enroll in Macon Academy. At the same time, there were public school supporters who hoped tensions would settle down and the white students would return to public schools. Liberals in Tuskegee, who supported desegregation, wanted things to move smoothly; yet, they, too, withdrew their children from Tuskegee High School. Their children's welfare overrode their political views. These folks continued to support integration and public schools in Macon County.

* * * * * * *

I interrupted to ask, "But what about now? How many people support the new school?"

"I'll be honest with you," he spoke softly. "It's a divided town. But, the town needs new people, with new ideas and positive attitudes."

I nodded my head. "I'm sorry to interrupt. Please continue."

Winston was listening, but making no comments.

Chapter 14

The six students, who boarded that school bus in Tuskegee, on a cold, rainy February morning, and traveled approximately five miles on Highway 81, to desegregate the all white Macon County High School in Notasulga, had witnessed the first violent outbreak of a mob that didn't want them in their town or in their school. Oh, they hadn't been wanted at Tuskegee High School either, but there hadn't been this type of anger and hate, combined with violence. They were aware that violence might erupt, but it was the first time since the initial attempt to desegregate that they'd seen anything as violent as what they were seeing and hearing.

These students were the oldest of the twelve students who'd been divided between Shorter High School and Macon County High School. Since Macon County High was known for being a rough school, the older students were sent there. Now, they sat in silence on the bus, after watching the brutal beating of Vernon Merritt. Suddenly, they were aware they'd entered an environment that demanded they move cautiously and be aware of their surroundings. Perhaps, for the first time, some of them thought, "Do I really belong here? Is this where I want to be?"

When the bus stopped at the steps to the front of the school, the passengers on the bus saw a rotund man standing at the schoolhouse doors. It was a repeat of Wallace's attempt to block the doors of the University of Alabama to prevent Vivian Malone and James Hood from registering for classes as the first African-American students. The man, with his short legs spread apart and his hands clasped below his waist, was James N. "Kayo" Rea, the mayor of Notasulga. His looks were imposing. He had close-chopped brown hair, silver rim-less glasses, and a paunch that stuck out over his belt, which had a large silver buckle with the head of a lone star steer on it. His protruding belly pulled his starched white shirt across his barrel chest and several buttons looked as if they might pop right off. A spot of dried ketchup, the size of the end of a felt tipped pen, stained his lemon-colored tie. Several inches shy of six feet, his short arms and legs didn't match the rest of his body.

He had written two ordinances at the beginning of the week and had them approved by local officials. They were a "Civil Disturbance Ordinance" and a "Safety Ordinance," which gave the mayor the authority to close any public facility, if its operation might incite or result in violence. His office could determine the maximum capacities at any public facility. He, along with others, established that the maximum capacity for Macon County High School was one hundred and seventy-five, which just happened to be the enrollment at the school.

When he spoke, his accent, courtesy of the deep rural South, was slow and almost gentle. No college degrees could erase the accent that ran in a slow syrupy drip, but echoed across the school lawn to the opposite side of the road. "Six more students," he claimed to the bus driver, loud enough for those across the street to hear, "would violate a recently passed city fire ordinance that limits the number of students who can enroll. It would present a fire hazard to the school. I cannot allow that to happen."

One individual stood in the shadows of the school auditorium, watching the drama unfold and listening to the mayor's lies. He was as black as ebony. Tall, with slightly stooped shoulders, he had a full moon face and a wide nose. Faded overalls clung loosely on his tall frame. An old faded denim jacket hung below his waist. A beat-up blue hat covered his shiny bald head. A smile turned up the corners of his mouth, and his teary eyes sparkled as the yellow school bus, with its few passengers, turned into the driveway of the school.

He'd seen Clark and his posse ride in before dawn, because it was his responsibility to be at the school hours before the buses arrived. Three state trooper vehicles from Dallas County led the posse into town before daylight. The three lean, white cars were now parked along the street in front of the school, on the public road. Twelve state troopers stood on the grass behind the cars, with their hands behind their backs and their feet spread apart, staring at the bus as it entered the driveway.

The man's eyes opened wide in horror. He observed the young white photographer being pulled from the bus and beaten. It all happened so fast, but he didn't miss a second of the violence that the man endured as he fell to the ground into a fetal position to protect himself. The man's body jerked when Clark shocked him with his overused weapon of choice.

The onlooker's eyes followed the bus as it continued to the doors of the school, where "Kayo" Rea stood, looking like one of Queen Elizabeth's castle guards, with his hands behind his back. The man had overheard the mayor, the principal, some state troopers, Clark, and some local men talking earlier that morning before the buses unloaded the students. The men were in the principal's outer office with the door open. They talked freely. No need to whisper. Everyone was in total agreement. Except the man who had eavesdropped, and they weren't worried about him.

As the bus crept closer, he noticed that the federal marshals were beginning to surround the crowd that circled the bus, while other marshals stood outside the crowd. He realized they were preparing to open fire if the need arose. But, unlike the man who watched from the shadows, they had no idea that there were local men in a classroom overlooking the driveway. The men locked the door of the classroom early that morning so that no teacher or student could enter. The lights were off. They had guns. He overheard this fact just before the bus came into view. There hadn't been time to warn anyone. Even if he could have let someone know, he wasn't sure that he had the courage to do so. All he could do was silently pray and watch as his heart beat a fast irregular rhythm in his chest. His head began to throb from the tension.

He was proud. His people were taking a brave stand. He admired the six young people on the bus. In his youth, no black with any sense would have dared do what they were doing. Now, all he wanted was for them to stay alive, to live long enough to witness change, and to know the part they played in bringing about that change. He wasn't sure they knew or cared too much about that at the moment. And he didn't blame them, because they were facing an angry crowd, one whose anger could turn into serious trouble at any minute. The kind of trouble that could bring death with it.

Some white men might call him a "good ole nigger." It was a term that many Southerners used when they talked about a black man whom they trusted. He learned to portray that as a means of survival in a white man's world. "Being a good nigger who knows his place so's he can stay alive," he often told his wife Willie Mae, who resented that he acted humble and meek.

He'd worked at the school as a janitor since he was younger than any of those six passengers on the bus. He was a school dropout who went to work to help support his family. For years, he moved quietly in and out of the buildings on the school property, cleaning up behind spoiled white kids, working hard, staying quiet, smiling, and being polite. The students and teachers liked him. There'd been times when some smart-ass white boys teased him and played tricks on him. If they were discovered, they got a soft slap on their wrists. Otherwise, he hadn't been mistreated. For the most part, everyone liked and respected him. No one gave too much thought to comments they made in his presence, as he looked down and away from them. They had no reason to fear Mose. He wasn't a threat.

Rea's loud slow voice carried to Mose, and he heard several students who stood on the sidewalk snigger. He saw some of their parents in the crowd applaud and heard their cheers. He heard the bus driver crank the bus. Mose crossed to the shadows of the high school so that he could better see its departure and the crowd across the road.

The chairman of the board had told the bus driver not to argue if they were turned away, but to return to Tuskegee. The driver drove off the school property and headed back to Tuskegee. For the second time, the bus passed the flagpole that stood in the middle of the circular driveway. The Alabama state flag and the Confederate battle flag blew back and forth in the chilly rain, as if waving goodbye. As the bus turned left onto the main road, the driver looked again to his right at the group of journalists and photographers who weren't being allowed to take pictures. The state troopers stood in front of the news media, to prevent them from viewing what was happening across the street. It was clear that no one who disapproved of the six students being in Notasulga wanted documentation of the event.

The state troopers had been at the school since dawn, selecting the locations they believed gave them an opportunity to interfere if necessary. Wallace sent them to Shorter and to Notasulga. Although Mayor Rea claimed to have invited Dallas County Sheriff Jim Clark to Notasulga, many believed that Wallace sent the invitation and told Rea that Clark would be there. Clark traveled ninety miles, coming through Montgomery, to arrive at Macon County High in the early morning hours, before the morning light washed through the chilling rain that fell gently off and on throughout the day. The horses had been transported in trailers that were parked behind the police station. The men rode the horses from the station to the school, which impressed everyone who stood and cheered in front of the school as the mounted posse trotted up the U-shaped drive.

Again, Wallace, a defiant little rooster, was using his segregationist contacts to create disorder so that he could have an excuse to close a school, in order "to maintain law and order, to protect the whites' peace and tranquility, as well as their property," which just happened to be all-white public schools. He had another opportunity to tell people how much the federal government was interfering in their lives. He was an attorney and he knew that federal law overrode state law. Basically, he was whistling "Dixie." He could huff and puff, but he couldn't blow the house down.

Mose watched until the bus disappeared, while the crowd cheered louder and louder, as if they were at a football game. He sighed, but he knew they'd be back. He worked in a white man's world, but he lived in a black man's world. He was aware of the people's determination that public schools in Macon County would be desegregated. Fred Gray was well-known in the black communities of Macon County. Like Joe Lewis from Chambers County, Alabama, he was a fighter. Just a different kind of fighter, one who fought for different reasons. The whites had their fighters—lots of them. But they were about to reckon with a black man who, like Joe Lewis, kept getting up every time he took a blow. Fred Gray wasn't just any fighter. He was a highly intelligent fighter who used his wits and the law to win. He didn't like to lose, and he was unaccustomed to losing.

"You white folks just don't know you got a tiger," Mose thought. He walked away from the laughing crowd, from the racist talk, and went further back into the shadows, away from the eyes of the crowd. An unknown, silent man who walked among them.

* * * * * * *

Mr. Watson stopped talking and looked out the window. Silence filled the room as Winston and I waited for him to speak. Finally, he said, "Mose is a quiet man. We all like and respect him. I talked with him about that day, and he was very open about his feelings. He had a lotta respect for the young people who were on that bus."

* * * * * * *

As the bus drove over the bridge and into town for the second time in less than an hour, people on the sidewalks stood silent. Each face wore a satisfied, insulting look. They had won a battle. They had stood up for their beliefs and had won. No federal judge was going to tell them what to do.

"You won this battle," the young man thought.

He was told there might be resistance. Everyone on the bus knew that they might be turned away. The night before, he and his parents had talked for hours about this day, and the tone of his parents' voices revealed deep concern. They spoke about "the movement," as they often did. He showed interest in "the movement" when it was frequently discussed as his family gathered at the table; he'd heard of its goals; he'd also heard of the dangers and the complications involved in voting rights and desegregation. Politics was an open subject among his family. He was aware that he and the other plaintiffs in the lawsuit were tests and that they had to be courageous. That's often a hard horse to ride when you're still in high school, dealing with explosive issues in a country, not just a small town. But, the young never think of dying. They think they can tie water in knots or sail too near the wind.

He was now on the opposite side of town as the bus headed west, back to Tuskegee. He looked out the window to his left. He sensed the man with the shotgun on the other side of the street, but the young man didn't turn his head to the right to look out the window. That man would stay in his brain forever, a symbol of who and what not to fear. The man was a weak enemy whose only control came with a weapon in his hand, not in his mind.

No one on the bus spoke until they were out of town. The six young people saw that the federal marshals were again in front of and behind the bus. They began to laugh, nervously at first, and joke about the physical characteristics of the people in the crowd along the streets and at the school. Then, there was a silence that spoke louder than any words could about their innermost feelings and what they'd experienced. They'd gone through a storm and survived. They all knew they'd go back—again and again, if necessary.

* * * * * * *

I interrupted, "I've never heard that expression before. 'Tie water in knots.' But, some people did just that . . . the impossible. Or what, then, seemed to be almost impossible."

"You're right, Marley Jane," said Mr. Watson. "It was a time of adversity. That's for sure." He glanced at the far wall and continued the story.

Chapter 15

People were concerned about the changes taking place in their society. The whites believed that their values and way of life would no longer be preserved. Many people had the opinion that a great deal was at stake: racial purity for the white race, segregation in every area of society, the evils of segregation, inferior education for both races, Christian beliefs and their interpretations of the Bible. There was the one thing that no one talked about in mixed company and was discussed only among those who shared the same opinion, which was the loss of white political power throughout the state and beyond. It made an outsider wonder how much of the concern was about Christian values and how much was about power. Holding the rein of power has been the desire of man since the beginning of time. Man doesn't relinquish power willingly. Power is more seductive than money. Sometimes.

Many shuddered to think what blacks would do with the right to vote. This was a time when blacks were denied opportunities to vote by any underhanded means that the white men in the South could dream up. Politicians knew who had the power of the vote, and they used that knowledge to maintain the status quo. A black man with the power to vote was a force that could defeat the power of a multitude of privileged white men.

Some people in Macon County would say that desegregation of schools and other places didn't influence their communities, their society, their way of life. Either they were blind or refused to acknowledge what happened around them. Outsiders who moved into Macon County didn't ignore or pretend not to see overt bitterness, harassment, and social ostracism. Many incidents were toned down, but they didn't disappear.

Crosses were burned on people's property. Barns were burned. The Ku Klux Klan made their presence known by leaving leaflets on doors or marching in their white robes. Mischief happened to people who were supporters of integration. People received threatening phone calls or no one would speak when someone answered a phone. Some people avoided others, because they didn't agree with their opinions or because of where they worked. Some whites were refused service in places of business. Some white people were called "nigger lover." These things happened on the streets, in stores, and in churches. Of course, there was the other side of the coin. Many people who didn't support private schools, which were organized because of racial issues, disliked those who fled to private schools. Neighbor turned against neighbor. Families became divided over differing opinions. Social institutions were places where racial issues were handled in cruel and nasty ways. Law officials became violent offenders. Towns were torn apart, and whites abandoned the towns in which they'd grown up and planned to raise their families. People lost their homes, their farms, their jobs, their schools, their churches, and, in some cases, their families.

Many white people in Macon County believed that Wallace had saved them from the control and power of blacks, as well as the evil federal government. They believed that Wallace helped them fight the forces that would ultimately destroy the way of life they wanted. He gave them a false sense of power to control their futures and the futures of their children. He helped give them Macon Academy, a new place for their children, a safe haven where they could continue to express their values, their beliefs, and their prejudices.

But, they knew the day was coming. Things were changing. Elections were coming. The Voting Rights Act would be passed by Congress and signed into law by President Lyndon B. Johnson. Whites were losing control. Their powers would be limited. Blacks and some whites would see it as a positive thing. Most of the Southern whites would see it as a negative thing. Regardless, change was coming. Like a violent storm, it wouldn't be stopped.

It seemed that every force was determined to delay or stop the desegregation of Macon County's all-white public high schools. Wallace, Mayor Rea, Jim Clark, the state board of education, the local people, and others were hell bent on interference and with maintaining white supremacy in Alabama.

As strong and powerful as the forces were, they wouldn't be as powerful as some of man's laws and God's laws. Fred Gray, Judge Johnson, and Washington, D.C. would use laws and wits as their weapons. They refused to surrender. They kept coming back and coming back, like rushing waves on a rocky beach in the moonlight.

Just as quickly as the six students had been denied enrollment at Macon County High School, Gray, along with other civil rights attorneys, immediately filed a complaint against James Rea, regarding any further interference with desegregation.

Judge Johnson responded rapidly to Mayor Rea's ordinances, which he referred to as a ruse, a "devious means of interfering with" Johnson's order to admit the six black students to the all-white school in Notasulga. He went on to say that Rea's intentions were to interfere with and to obstruct the Court's order and Rea's actions "illegally deprived" the six plaintiffs of "their constitutional rights to attend the public schools in Macon County . . . because of their race or color." The judge issued a restraining order on James Rea to stop interfering in the desegregation process.

Meanwhile, Rea was busy closing the schools in Notasulga. He told anyone who was willing to listen that a suspicious fire at Notasulga's water system plant had led to a shortage of water. This was a fire hazard. It would later be proof that some fires couldn't be controlled, and Rea gave an early excuse.

Approximately a week later, Macon County High School's name was changed to Notasulga High School. White students fled. Those who left went to Macon Academy, to other segregated white schools in nearby counties, or moved away. The white students in the elementary school remained.

A few loose cannons in Macon County still claimed they were "ready to kill some niggers." For the most part, they did their talking among themselves and discussed options that had been hashed back and forth since Tuskegee High School had been desegregated. One plan had been on the table for discussion for months. The groundwork had been laid. The game was on, but everyone agreed to "wait and let's see how things turn out."

Now Mayor Rea had played his weak card. Wallace had played his aces, but still bluffed his way through the game. Jim Clark had thrown in his hand on Macon County and was focusing on black demonstrations that were about to take place in Selma in Dallas County. He was gearing up for a new game, where he would be top dog, head of the food chain, and in control. A perfect opportunity was coming for him to "show 'em niggers a thing or two" and to "put 'em in their place." There was talk that Martin Luther King, Jr., "the black sumbitch," as Clark called him, was coming to Selma to lead a march to the capitol steps in Montgomery, to push for voting rights for blacks. The first attempted march from Selma to Montgomery hadn't taken place, but rumors were floating like summer dust on a dirt road.

"Hell, this's gonna be big time. Martin L. King, Jr., thinks he's comin to Selma to interfere." Clark took it personally. "No black sumbitch is gonna piss on my territory. King ain't king in Dallas County," Clark said, time and again. "By God, it's time that nigger finds out who controls Dallas County. I cannot wait to let him know who's in charge." Clark often wondered aloud why King didn't "keep his black ass in Atlanta." We got our own way of doin' things in Alabama. Ain't no outsider gonna come in here and tell us what to do." As far as Clark was concerned, King was a boil on the white man's ass, and it needed to be gone. For good.

* * * * * * *

Mr. Watson paused and looked out a window to his left. I could hear Winston, breathing beside me, and a bird chirping loudly in a tree. Finally, Mr. Watson spoke. "I hope I'm not giving y'all too much information. But, it's part of the story. And it got some outsiders away from the situation. We needed that. So, I'll pick up nine days after the bus left Notasulga."

Chapter 16

The students were on their way back to Notasulga nine days after being denied entrance to the school. As the bus traveled east along Highway 81, the sky was clear. The sun jumped over a hill, blinding the driver with its brilliance. It was a cold day, but there were no dark clouds and rain as before. U. S. Justice Department officials and federal marshals were ahead of and behind the bus. The same driver navigated the bus. One passenger was missing, the white photographer.

Everyone was serious, silently wondering if they'd face anything like the last time. The young people talked in low, soft voices among themselves and watched the rural countryside pass by. The bus passed cotton fields that lay empty, but would soon be filled with low green plants, bursting with white balls of cotton. Cattle stood in large open fields, eating on bales of hay that farmers had laid on the frozen brown ground. Suddenly, to the right, they saw what was once a large barn. Now, it was a pile of black ashes, a confirmation of rumors in the last week of barns being burned by the KKK. The barns belonged to whites who were members of the county board of education or to whites who expressed their disgust with the segregationists and their bullying tactics.

The young man turned his head and looked at the burned barn until it was no longer in his vision. Burning something was symbolic of many things. His preacher talked about the burning bush. In his mind's eye, he saw the large, energetic preacher, who constantly mopped sweat from his forehead and paced the pulpit, telling them how fire could cleanse one's sins. He talked about the fire of hell and how, like the sun, it burned everything to nothing, if things got too close. The young man didn't believe burning that barn had anything to do with cleansing one from sin, and he thought the preacher would agree with him. That burning was a sinful, hate-filled act done by cowards and bullies.

Seeing the smouldering ashes made him feel like he was returning to the gates of hell, where a fire-breathing dragon waited to destroy his people and all of their dreams. It was almost impossible to dream of peace and equality when you were being consumed by those fires. He knew there was no other way to reach the Promised Land without walking through the fires of hell, which would cleanse his people and set them free.

As the bus entered the town, everything was quiet. A few people stood on the sidewalks, but no one carried posters, yelled, or threw things. Here and there were state trooper cars and one local police car. No one stood in front of Davis' Hardware. Old man Davis stood inside, in front of the big window, wearing a frown and a sour face, probably gritting his teeth until his jaws ached.

When the school came into view, the young man saw Mayor Rea, standing beside his vehicle across the road from the school, watching. There was one state trooper parked next to Rea's car. The bus turned into the U-shaped driveway for the second time. At every door were federal marshals. They stood on the lawn. State troopers stood with them or sat in their cars.

There were no white students standing around outside or looking out the windows as they did the last time. The whites boycotted the high school. A few teachers stayed, but most fled with the white students. The teachers who remained were Coach Threadgill who taught history and P.E., Mr. Carroll, the principal who taught physics and chemistry, Mr. Shealey who taught English, Mr. Arnold who taught vocational agriculture, and Mrs. Justiss who taught math.

Mose stood inside the front doors with a broom in his left hand. Without realizing it, he'd unconsciously removed his old ragged cap and was holding it in his big, calloused right hand as the six students slowly stepped off the bus. Mr. Carroll stood at the top of the steps, telling them to go inside and wait for him.

Entering the building together, the six students huddled in a tight group, holding their breath; expecting, God knows what. They'd always heard that the white schools were nicer than the black schools and had everything they needed—books, indoor toilets, toilet paper, desks, and the list went on. Everything they had heard was true. Compared to their school's appearance, this school ranked high. They'd been told many times in the last week that they'd be safe, but no one really knew that for sure. First, their eyes fell on federal marshals who were standing inside the front door. As their eyes moved left to right, they saw other marshals. The quiet was a deafening silence in an enemy's camp.

Finally, their eyes located Mose who stood almost humbled to their right; his bare head slightly bowed and his cap in his tight fist. They nodded at one another, glad that someone with the same skin color was there.

Mose knew that he was different from the six young people who locked eyes with him. His world wasn't as comfortable as theirs, but they shared things that were deep and profound. They felt an immediate kinship and were united by their race, by the abuse and hatred of a white society, by the things that they weren't allowed to share with that society. Within themselves, they shared the sufferings endured in a South that refused to let go of yesterday or to practice the Christian values they loudly claimed to treasure.

The principal came through the doors. "Okay, boys," he said. "Let's enroll y'all. Come with me."

They followed him down the hall and into a warm classroom, filled with sunbeams, catching morning dust bunnies. In the room were four teachers who enrolled them, gave each a schedule, and became their first white teachers. Most of the morning was spent filling out forms and discussing classes. The teachers did all of the talking. None of the six young people asked questions. At noon, they went to lunch in the bright empty cafeteria. The elementary students had eaten and returned to their classrooms. The meal consisted of fried chicken, mashed potatoes, gravy, green beans, rolls, milk, and peach cobbler. They talked quietly to one another. No teacher sat with them. They ate alone. The students weren't offended. The teachers at their old school, Tuskegee Institute High, did the same thing. Everyone knew only elementary teachers ate at the same table with their students.

After lunch, they returned to the classroom. The rest of the day moved rapidly. The teachers and the principal talked to them, telling them the rules and explaining the schedule. They were shown the rooms where classes would be held. Then, they walked over to the school gym, which was in a separate building, beyond the elementary school. Coach Threadgill took them through the gym and told them what they'd be doing during P.E. classes. It didn't sound as if they'd be outside. Federal marshals followed, wherever they went. Two sat in the classroom with them, looking out the windows.

It was soon three o'clock. Time to board the bus and return to Tuskegee. The marshals once again, as they'd do every day until the school year ended, drove in front of and behind the bus.

When the bus moved slowly through town, no one could be seen. The streets were deserted. It was like a ghost town. All it needed was a tumbleweed blowing down main street and a salon door flapping back and forth in the cold wind to resemble a set in a Western movie. It represented the loneliness that the six students felt when they rode down the streets of Notasulga or sat in the classrooms, where, just a little over a week earlier, white students sat, laughed, and completed assignments, as they talked about sports and other school events, about the ongoing basketball season and the coming baseball season.

Regardless of how lonely they got or how much they didn't want to return to the white man's town or school, they knew they would. No one would drop out or refuse to participate in "the movement." It meant too much for too many, and they couldn't forget the pride in Mose's eyes. In his eyes, they saw a glimpse of how powerful their presence in that school was for their people and their place in American society, especially in the South. They were doing what had to be done. There would be no turning back.

Chapter 17

One day moved into another. One week into a month. A month became two. Each day was a routine that no one dared venture too far from. You walked carefully, putting one foot in front of the other, like walking over a raging river on a thin rotten pine tree. No one let down his guard for a minute, because each one knew that he still walked through a dark forest. Things could happen quickly and without warning.

It was a Friday, the second week of April. The weekend, just one day away, would be a break from the tension. Spring was arriving. The mornings were cool, but the days got warm by noon. Trees were putting forth tiny brown-gold buds. Jonquils were blooming along Highway 81. It looked as if God finished painting the morning sun and gave His paintbrush a shake, covering the shoulders of the road with gold. Cows chewed grass that was turning green. Birds tweeted as they built nests for soon-to-be newborns.

The bus drove through the morning, covered in a thin sheet of dew. Visibility was down to a few hundred feet in parts of the countryside because of dense fog. In some areas, the bus slowed to a crawl. When the fog lifted, it would be a clear day that spoke of spring, new birth, and new beginnings. The young people on the bus had hopes. Things had gone smoothly at the school, but not so much at home for most of the six students. Some of their parents had received threats, which were handled by federal agents. The KKK had recently burned more barns and crosses in people's yards. Everyone knew the KKK was probably plotting more evil doings. If not in Macon County, some other county. The devil's work was never done.

Soon school would end. The seniors had already made plans to enroll in nearby colleges. The young man and his friend would leave Notasulga High School for Auburn University. They'd be among the first blacks to desegregate the university, which had decided at the beginning to support desegregation. Once Auburn's administration made that decision, it never wavered from it.

As the bus cut through the dense fog, the young man and his friend discussed their plans to attend Auburn, which was close to Tuskegee. The two would get onto I-85 a few miles from their homes, pass one exit to Wire Road, and make a left at the second exit. It'd be about a fifteen-minute drive. They'd ride together. The future looked bright, and they had the rest of their lives ahead of them. Both were optimistic and hopeful, looking forward to a future in a country that included them.

The fog began to scatter a bit here and there as the bus rolled into town and drove over the bridge. It seemed unusually quiet for the small town. A hush fell over the bus. Each person became aware of the silence, as it slid along the road with them. There was no fear, only a warning that beat in time with their heartbeats. They knew the enemy was near, and they were alert.

The U-shaped driveway was outlined and the school was a light charcoal etching in the fog. When the bus made a complete turn into the drive and moved toward the school, the six students gaped. The driver only looked hard as he tightened his grip on the steering wheel. His knuckles popped up. "I knew them damn fools hadn't finished," he thought to himself. "These folks too damn mean to stop." His next thoughts concerned the safety of his passengers. No way was he going to open the doors to the bus and unload those kids. Not, by God, until he saw some decent white faces.

He noticed in the fog the federal marshals everywhere, along with state troopers, and three local police cars. He saw Mr. Carroll at the bottom of the steps, waiting for the bus. The teachers stood on the steps. No one from the town stood on the lawn or across the road to watch. There was no indication of parents dropping their children off at the elementary school.

Everyone on the bus gasped and covered his mouth, with eyes wide-open. They hoped someone had contacted their parents and Fred Gray. There was no way they could have been warned before leaving Tuskegee. Perhaps, someone called just as they left. Surely, someone in Tuskegee knew, because there seemed to be more marshals and state troopers than usual.

The bus pulled to the steps and stopped. The bus driver told the students to remain seated. He opened the door to the bus as Mr. Carroll walked forward. "What's goin on?" the driver asked.

"Had some mischief here last night," Mr. Carroll replied, waving his hands behind him. "Otherwise, everything's okay. The building's been checked already. Appears to be safe."

"'Appears to be ain't good enough," said the driver in a low, cool voice. "Let me speak to the marshal in charge 'fore I let my passengers off this here bus." Then, he added, "And I wanna know someone's done contacted Fred Gray and Mr. Watson. And the board members."

"They know. Mr. Watson, some of the board members, the sheriff, and more feds are comin," Carroll assured him. "I'll get Mr. Lomas." He walked away and began to talk with a husky bald-headed man who wore thick glasses. He nodded while Carroll talked and pointed. Then, they walked toward the bus as the driver re-opened the doors.

"Are things safe? Can I let these kids off so's nothin's gonna happen to them?"

"We've checked every inch of both schools, the gym, and the auditorium, as well as the entire grounds. Everything looks fine, as far as we can tell. If you want to keep the kids on the bus until the superintendent and others get here, that'll be fine. The teachers can wait inside."

"I'm gonna keep 'em on the bus, since it's all the same to you, 'til Mr. Watson gets here," he told the stocky man with the steel blue eyes.

"No problem."

The students listened to the conversation. They were glad to remain on the bus. If necessary, the driver could whisk them away in a flash. Again, they looked at the enormous writing on the entire side of the white stucco building of the high school and realized the anger and hate that ran deep in this town, an extension of the anger and hate that coursed throughout the South.

Mose stood inside the school, looking out the windows of the front doors. He'd arrived at school that morning at five forty-five, in his F-1, six cylinder 1949 two-door Ford pickup truck, which Emmitt Jenkins, the chairman of the Macon County Board, had sold him for one hundred and fifty dollars. Mose and his wife worked for the Jenkins on Saturdays. Mose helped with farm chores, repaired buildings or machinery, or whatever was needed to make the farm run smoothly. His wife helped Eva Jewell Jenkins in the house and garden.

He'd driven the truck around the school, as he did every morning, before getting out and starting the workday. Slowly, he came from the west, made a right at the school, down the drive by the gym. The school had two U-shaped driveways. One came beside the gym and circled the back of the elementary school, the auditorium, and the high school. It was used for buses, as well as for trucks that made deliveries to the cafeteria, which was located behind the high school. A smaller U-shaped drive was in front of the schools and auditorium. Faculty, guests, and parents used the smaller driveway.

What Mose saw might have been for real or the fog could be playing tricks on him, so he completed the big U-shaped drive and turned into the smaller drive. He stopped the truck in front of the steps to the high school, in order to make sure he saw what he thought he'd seen. He opened the door and stood on the running board of the truck. Yeah. No trick. Time to call the principal and get him to the school early this morning.

Mose dropped out of school after finishing the ninth grade. He loved to read, but there were not many books at home when he was a child. Through the years, working at the school, he'd taken his time sweeping the halls, so that he could overhear the teachers' lessons. He learned a lot by listening. He certainly read well enough that there was no mistaking those bold red letters, even in the fog.

As the bus driver waited for instructions to groan the bus to life, the six students saw clearly the bloody words. "Judge Johnson's and Robert Kennedy's School" and "Godfathers of niggers" screamed in red paint, burning into the morning sunlight through the fog. Here and there, the paint dripped down the wall of the building and made the building appear to be bleeding. Drops of red lay on the ground.

All eyes on the bus observed federal marshals, state troopers, local police, and the principal as they talked to one another and walked up and down the side of the building. Occasionally, one would nod or shake his head or point to the building or to some other location. The sheriff's car came up the drive and stopped thirty or forty feet ahead of the bus. A deputy followed and pulled onto the grass within the driveway. The sheriff and three deputies joined the group of men. Within minutes, the superintendent arrived, with three board members.

Mr. Watson talked to the federal marshal in charge. Afterwards, they walked over to the bus. Seeing them approaching, the driver opened the doors and stepped outside. All six passengers got quiet to eavesdrop so that they could take talk back to their parents who'd want to know every detail. And they wondered again if their parents knew what had happened. Although no one said it, they wondered if the local police, teachers, or any of the state troopers knew before it'd happened. Had there been any rumors?

After ten or more minutes of talking, the bus driver climbed the steps of the bus and sat down. The superintendent followed him and addressed the six students. "I know y'all are upset, 'cause I'm upset myself. I'm deeply sorry this happened and y'all saw it. Rest assured that it'll be cleaned up before y'all return to school on Monday. But, today, I'm sending y'all home. Your parents have been notified 'bout what's happened here, and they'll be waiting for y'all in Tuskegee when the bus arrives. Let your families know that I'll be in touch with each of them by tomorrow morning," he drawled.

He looked at each one and turned to the bus driver. "Take them home, Mr. Pollard. I'll be in touch with you later." He bobbed his head at no one in particular and stepped off the bus, back into the crowd of men.

Everything was more poignant in the glare of the morning sun. Fog was no longer a shade to block out the day. As the bus headed slowly down the driveway toward the main road, the six students turned and looked at the stark white building that appeared to be bleeding to death. It looked like a scary poster for Halloween. An early, cruel, Halloween trick. The townspeople hadn't gotten the early treat that they wanted from Judge Johnson and the Attorney General, so they played a trick.

Out of nowhere, they saw a slender man, riding a black motorcycle, sweep into the driveway behind them and stop. A local police officer and a state trooper talked briefly to the man, while he continued to gun the motor of the machine. Few words were exchanged. A federal investigator walked up and told the man to leave. Quickly, his motorcycle ripped up and he roared around the bus. Everyone aboard felt a chill, as if he'd stirred a wind around the bus.

* * * * * * *

Mr. Watson looked at the journal in front of him. When he raised his eyes, I couldn't tell if he was sad or angry. Both, I decided.

"Well, that was a warning for sure. We should've known something really bad was about to happen. Of course, we anticipated a lotta stuff happening. I guess our minds just couldn't grasp the type of evil that was coming. There's not much more to tell. But it's the worst of the story."

I had a strong gut feeling that I knew the rest of the story. I'd been carrying it around with me for years, trying to comprehend that kind of anger, that kind of insanity, that kind of hate.

Chapter 18

When the students arrived in Tuskegee, their parents were waiting with concerned faces and questions that had no answers. Fear squeezed their hearts, and they wondered if it was really worth it to endanger the lives of their children on a daily basis. Hate was an emotion that they learned long ago existed amongst some whites toward blacks, and, yes, amongst some blacks toward whites. It was an unwanted companion in their lives; yet, they didn't want that for their children, and, yet, they believed in "the movement." The possible death of a child? That went too far.

No one had a good feeling. No one wanted to think, "What next?" They were too afraid of the answer.

The following morning, Saturday, April 19, 1964, would answer that question for them. Each set of parents received a phone call from the superintendent, asking them to come to his office at two o' clock that afternoon. Mr. Watson gave each a very brief report and told them that they all needed to meet with Fred Gray and some others. All agreed to come to the meeting, and by ten minutes to two o' clock everyone had arrived. They were shown into the conference room.

Mr. Watson sat at the end of the long table, with his large hands folded in front of him on the table. Fred Gray sat to his right. Standing along the walls of the room were several federal marshals, the Macon County sheriff, and all of the board members. Each parent felt a tightness in the chest as they glanced at the solemn faces around the room. Of course, they knew this wasn't a social call to report a positive progress of events. They hadn't been summoned to hear good news. Another repulsive event had unexpectedly arrived, although they knew nothing should be considered unexpected.

Then, they were given details. An unknown person or persons had burned Notasulga High School to the ground. There was only one witness to the burning, and she'd not been able to see or hear much. No one else admitted to seeing or hearing anyone at the school in the early Saturday morning hours of April 19, 1964, as darkness lay over the town.

None of the parents were given the news regarding the burning of the school during the morning phone calls from Mr. Watson. Some of the women opened their mouths in shock. One woman put a hand to her mouth, while another covered her ears and closed her eyes, mumbling,

"Praise you, Jesus," thankful that the fire hadn't occurred while the children were there. The men's eyes turned hard and dark like the smoldering ashes that lay on the ground in a town they despised for its hate and anger.

As the story unfolded, they learned that Ellie Sue Cotney, who lived next door on the west side of the school, told the federal investigators that she got up about three o' clock in the morning when she heard the back-firing of a vehicle and the sound of cars behind the school. When she looked out of her bedroom window, she saw a figure on a dark motorcycle race down the driveway on the west side of the high school. He wore a helmet; therefore, she wasn't able to see his face. Plus, it was too dark. Two cars followed the motorcycle. She couldn't tell how many people were in the cars or much about the cars.

After she returned to bed, she estimated it was about ten minutes later, or less, that she heard a boom, which lit up her bedroom. It was sudden and shocking and scared her to death. When she got to the window, she saw the fire. That's when she called the fire department, "because that's who you call when there's a fire." By the time they got to the school, which was almost thirty minutes later, the school was consumed in flames, filling the night with orange and red lights that leaped and danced toward the stars, swaying back and forth like crazy dancers across the sky.

Ellie Sue described the beginning of the fire, as yellow flames, which became pulsating gray-blue, and reached to touch the darkness. In the center of each flame was a white glow. The tongues of fire licked and devoured every inch of the blazing building. It was a line of burning hell, from east to west, embracing as much of the north and south as it could reach. The wind rode the fire, making ripping sounds that tore through the air, like the tearing or crumbling of thick paper. The flames split, and Ellie Sue saw the dark, smoky heaven peeping through.

Ashes and sparks of fire shot in every direction. It looked like fireworks on the Fourth of July that'd gone terribly wrong, intent on demolishing and removing by force anything that stood in its path. An overwhelming sense of hopelessness surrounded the school grounds and Ellie Sue, while the fire, which seemed alive, primal, and maleficent, commanded attention and wrapped itself around everything within its reach.

The crackling and popping of the fire sounded like the moaning of thousands dying, as the roof timbers gave way. The fire grew hotter, making the fresh dew evaporate from the scorching earth. It produced intense, dry heat, so hot that Ellie Sue could feel it through her window. Sparks continuously shot across the lawn of the school and into the atmosphere. It was like some crazy celebration.

At last, the fire was on the ground, but still sending wild twisting flames upward, licking the darkness. Ellie Sue saw the west end of the building start to collapse as the supporting wood gave itself to the grabbing arms of the fire, a lover surrendering in total submission. Just as the other end of the building began to cave toward the earth, the fire department arrived. Awfully slow, it seemed to Ellie Sue, as she watched the monster fire.

There was a wall of smoke, filled with the scent of books, polished oak floors, melting plastic, and rot. The smoldering, stinging, acrid fragrance stung her eyes and clung to the insides of her nostrils. The smell bombarded her, creating more panic and making her lightheaded.

Driven smoke was energized and pressurized with force behind it, as the fire pushed through the building. Finally, free floating smoke—formerly driven smoke, which had lost its energy—was seen and would eventually settle, but it'd be weeks before the smoke disappeared. It'd also be a long time before the fire completely dissipated, even after the fire department arrived, too late to do anything. For days, the heavy smothering ashes would give off pungent smells that intruded on the senses and in every nearby house. The woodsy, acrid odor would eventually travel downtown, hover over the railroad tracks, and not leave.

When federal marshals and state investigators arrived a couple of hours after the dawn, all that remained of the school was rubble and the lingering smoke. Several small fires still burned and hot coals lay scattered here and there, across the blackened earth. Soot was everywhere among charred timbers and slush. Once water had hit the fire, it gave off a wet, decaying smell.

The fire was determined to be arson, but, unless someone came forward and gave names, it appeared doubtful that anyone would ever be arrested. The word "arson" often implies that someone started the fire to collect insurance, but that wasn't the reason that gasoline and a match became weapons in the early morning hours on a spring day in 1964. It was race. It was hate. It was discrimination. Plain and simple. People could call it anything that they wanted, but the truth was the truth.

Ellie Sue told the investigators, "I just can't understand why it took so long for the fire truck to get here. After all, it's only a mile or less from the school. It shouldn't have taken more than five minutes."

Later that day, she received a threatening phone call. According to what she told the investigators, the caller, in a low voice, said, "You best keep yo' mouth shut if you know what's good for you. Keep talkin' and yo' house might be next. You didn't see nothin'. Got it?" After taking her statement, the lead investigator told her to call her daughter who lived in Dothan. The daughter arrived as the sun was setting and, within an hour, Ellie Sue and her daughter were headed to Dothan. She sold her house as quickly as she could and never returned to Notasulga.

The feds flocked into Montgomery and Macon County after the school was burned. That didn't surprise anyone. It was 1964, and segregation in the public schools in the South was going to become a thing of the past. This'd been determined in Washington, D.C., and Robert Kennedy was enforcing the laws. The feds were sticking their noses in the South's business, making them do things against their will, butting into Southerners' lives. Same old federal government. It never occurred to anyone that if you're doing what you should be doing, the government might not be telling you what to do. It's a shame that Big Daddy has to keep such a tight rein on people, has to watch them like a cat playing with a mouse. It's a fact that lacks comprehension by a large portion of the population.

Many knew the people who were responsible for the fire, but they refused to reveal that information to just anyone. Those names were kept close to the chests of those who knew. People who knew about the fire or who helped in some way stayed quiet. The bragging stopped. Some people behaved out of fear of being exposed for who they really were or for the part they played in the fire. Directly or indirectly. Even an asinine person knew that the much-hated feds could fry you. Not many were so out of touch that they didn't understand the power of the federal government, the power that bothered so many in the South. Not too many stopped to think if it hadn't been for that power, many more people would be discriminated against.

To many people, it was a closed chapter, never to be discussed or reread. "Let the past go," they'd say. "Things are good now, and we don't want to remember. We don't want no trouble."

But, one supporter of desegregation would say, "In my opinion, we need to re-examine some things that no one wants to talk about. Only if people are willing to trouble the ashes, to closely examine and admit what happened and why, can they come out whole on the other side.

"For a lotta folks, it ain't a fairy tale, nor fiction. It's a burning truth that they recall with acute memories. It's the story of a town that suffered the wicked deeds of a handful of men and their followers, who took grossification and hate to the ultimate level. The story is about ugly racism in the South, where it still lingers in closets, under beds, and inside the mind. Yet, no one admits to being racist.

"Denying racism doesn't make it less true. Today, if one listens carefully and observes, it can almost be seen, heard, touched, tasted, and smelled. Censored talk and actions cannot cover up racism. It cannot tell a lie."

* * * * * * *

No one knew exactly where the students would finish out the school year. Gray spoke often with Judge Johnson before a decision was made. After the meeting with the parents of the six students, he and another attorney met with the superintendent and the board members. Someone from the FBI arrived to give an up-to-date report of the incident. One of the board members thought, "An incident? What the hell! Call it what it is."

Before the meeting with the parents ended, the superintendent said as soon as he knew something, a decision would be made about the remaining school year, and the parents would be called back for another meeting. "Until then, keep your children home. The teachers will send assignments to my office. I'll get them to the kids. Then, I'll send someone to get the completed work and return it to the teachers," he told them.

Then, he asked Fred Gray to speak. Gray talked for about thirty minutes, informing the parents about his conversation with Judge Johnson. When he finished, he asked for questions. There were plenty of questions, but there weren't any answers to what type of individuals would burn down a school. Theirs was a race of people who knew the value of a school, its place in a community, its symbol for upward mobility. In their world, you didn't burn a school. Oh, they knew the "Why?" They'd lived with the "Why?" all of their lives. And it looked like their children might have to live with the same "Why?" for the rest of their lives. But, not, by God, if they could help it.

After the last question had been answered, Gray had a question for the parents. "Do you want to continue what we've started in Macon County, to desegregate all public schools?"

"Yes sir!" the parents echoed in unison.

* * * * * *

When the parents, marshals, and sheriff left the meeting, those remaining discussed where to send the six displaced students. Several people suggested sending them back to Tuskegee Institute High. Fred Gray, along with others, vetoed that idea, because it would put everything back to square one. Nothing would have been accomplished. Too, the parents answered Gray's question and made it clear that they wanted to move forward. Gray told the superintendent that he'd be in contact with him as soon as he spoke again with Judge Johnson. Then, a date would be set for the next meeting with the parents.

After listening to all of the arguments the following week, Judge Johnson made a decision that the six students would return to Notasulga as quickly as possible. Makeshift classrooms would be set up in the school auditorium so that the students could complete the school year.

Two weeks later, the students returned to Notasulga High School. On a hot Friday in mid-May, the principal walked into the auditorium, handed the seniors their diplomas, and told the students not to return to school. The school year was over. There wouldn't be a graduation ceremony.

Chapter 19

When Mr. Watson finished his story, he looked at the ceiling. For a long moment, he sat there, staring upward, deep in thought. Then, he gave a sigh and looked from Winston to me. It was the first time that I'd ever heard about the desegregation lawsuit, Lee v. Macon. It was the first time that I'd heard about many of the things and people he talked about in his story. The courage of those involved was overpowering. I felt humble and ordinary.

"That's the end of the story. And it's been three years. It was a dark period in the history of Alabama, but it was the beginning of a light in the darkness. Many people in Macon County believed in the cause, believed in desegregation of the schools. Whites as well as blacks. I'm proud of Macon County. And I'm proud of the people in Notauslga who stood up for what was right and who supported the schools. We fight for Notasulga, because it represents a reason why mankind should fight for the rights of others. It represents that a school and society should stand up and fight for justice."

All I could say was, "I believe in justice for all. And troubling the ashes." I felt a bit silly, but it was sincere and from the heart.

"Me, too, Marley Jane," Mr. Watson replied. "And that's one reason I want Winston and you to come to Notasulga. We need more people who believe in justice for all." He stood up and shook our hands. As he walked to the door with us, he said, "Think about it and get in touch with me. It's been a pleasure meeting both of you, and I hope that you'll soon be moving to Notasulga."

* * * * * * *

During the drive home, Winston and I had a heated argument. "Did you notice that no one we met today talked about the burning of the school by people in the town? Why? Are they trying to hide something?" I asked, tilting my head toward him.

"No. I don't think so. My goodness, Marley Jane, they just met us. People aren't gonna talk about something like that to strangers. Why bring it up? It's over and done with. I don't think that we should let it influence my decision."

"Your decision?" I started to ask, but rejected it.

I looked out the window and didn't respond. Why bring it up, indeed. Why not? I wondered if Winston noticed how cool some people in town had been. Sure, some were friendly and nice, but there was a feeling that a river ran deep below the surface. You just knew not to go there, not to ask questions. I felt as if sharp blades of ice were poking my flesh.

"I don't want to live there. Too much negative energy. Too many ghosts that won't die," I said, as I watched the landscape flash by.

Winston laughed and patted my knee. He gave a low, long sigh. "I've got to take this job. You know that. I need to take advantage of this offer. You've got to forget about hearing two silly girls talk. That's what young girls do. They talk about nonsense. We're all older now."

"They were not talking about nonsense. Do you really call burning down a school to prevent integration nonsense? That's an absurd statement. And a lousy rationale to win an argument," I said in anger.

"Okay. So, you might be right. It's really beside the point. This is about my career." Then, after a brief hesitation, "About taking care of my family. Providing for you and Wesley."

"So, all of a sudden, it's about me and Wesley? I've always gone with you, wherever you've wanted to go, and I've never questioned the move. I am now. This isn't just about football, Winston. It's about something a lot bigger. A lot more important. And you don't seem to get it," I said in a tired voice. "It isn't really about Wesley or me. Don't play your mind games with me."

Glancing at my face, he replied, "Yeah. I think I do get it, but I can't let it matter. I need this opportunity, and I need you to support me. Let's give it two or three years. If it isn't working by then, we'll leave. I promise. Okay?"

I turned away to stare out the window at the fading day, at the sinking sun that was dropping too fast into its nightly bed. I felt hopeless, tired and old, without any will. Without any choice. Without a voice. I breathed in deeply and closed my eyes to the vanishing sun. There was no reason for more talk. The deed was done.

* * * * * * *

Well, Winston took the job. It was a great opportunity and all of that. I began to pack between classes and taking care of Wesley. I was tired of moving. I wanted to settle, to nest some place, to finish college. That dream would have to be shelved for a while, and I had no idea how long a while would be. I was able to complete the first of two short terms that the college offered during the summer months. My plans didn't include a town with a history of hate and violence. I didn't want my son to be raised in an atmosphere of prejudice and racial conflict, although I knew that it'd be difficult to completely escape those things as long as I lived in the South. I swore to myself that I'd do whatever it took to give him an open-mind, with a tolerant attitude of the world and to all of the people who lived in it.

Again, I thought, "I bought it. Now I've got to pay for it."

To Winston, I whispered in my head, "Your ego brought us here. Watch your ego."

We moved to Notasulga the weekend of the third week of July, into a huge old wooden house that badly needed painting. It became our home for one month. The walls were thin, with no insulation, and the front of the house sloped downhill as you went from the long front hall to the kitchen, which hadn't been remodeled in thirty years or more. The stove didn't work. The refrigerator was short and squatty and I was certain it was an antique. There were only two cabinets, and the sink was stained yellow, with chipped places here and there.

As I wandered through the house, I grew depressed. The heat inside was unbearable. The only cool breeze drifted slowly across the long front porch. Fans would be the first purchase. Maybe one or two window air conditioners. Even as I thought about asking the landlord to purchase window units, I knew that it'd be a useless request.

Wesley walked over the rough wooden floors, made of two by fours. His reddish-blond hair was plastered to his head and sweat was dripping past his ears. It was hot and muggy. Winters would be brutal in the house. We'd all be sick the entire time. My main concern was Wesley who had asthma. He needed cool air for hot summer days so that he could breathe well. Cool air in the winter would make his breathing easier, but he couldn't be exposed to bitter cold. There had to be some other house we could rent. Until we found it, I decided to unpack only what we needed. We'd eat something that didn't require cooking. Tomorrow I would start looking for another place to live.

One month later we moved into a nice brick home that had three bedrooms and one bath. It was located two miles outside of town, in the country. It had an air conditioner and an up-dated kitchen. We purchased kitchen appliances and began to settle down. The front and back yards were large and open.

That Christmas, we got Wesley a swing set, and he soon climbed the poles, rather than swing. I'd look out the kitchen window and see him hanging from the bars that helped to brace the legs of the swing. When he wasn't swinging, he was playing with his daddy's bird dog. Blue was his best friend. As he got older, he never considered Winston's bird dogs to be hunting dogs. They were his pets, not partners that assisted in a kill.

Winston was gone from daylight to dark, getting ready for football season, looking at a pre-planned schedule and contracts. At night, he watched film after film. Stopping. Pausing. He assigned me tasks as we watched the films. One time I might be instructed to keep my eyes on a tackle. The next time I might watch a running back. We seldom saw one another during the day, but, by now, I was used to that. When Winston wasn't at the school or at the football field, he was fishing or hunting on the weekends. He lost no time in finding friends who shared his passion for fishing and hunting. He'd be gone all day on Saturdays and every Sunday afternoon. He'd leave as soon as we finished Sunday dinner. In four years of marriage, it'd become a routine that no amount of complaining or arguing resolved. Finally, I just said, "To hell with it."

The weekends were long because I didn't have a car. Wesley and I were left alone, without the means to go anywhere; therefore, we were forced to stay home, unless someone came by and took us wherever I needed to go. I didn't know anyone well enough to ask for a favor, so I spent most Saturdays making and hanging curtains for the house, while Wesley played on the floor, colored in coloring books, or watched cartoons on television. Later, we'd go outside for him to play.

One Saturday morning, thirty minutes before lunch, an old blue Plymouth station wagon drove into the driveway and stopped with a jerk. I watched out of the picture window in the living room. A head of fuzzy short dark brown hair could barely be seen over the steering wheel, and the woman seemed to be struggling with the door. The short, stocky woman appeared to be having a hard time of it, climbing out of the car. She moved slowly and deliberately, as her round face turned to look at me. Her eyes were small and dark. I could tell she sighed heavily as she walked across the yard to the door. In her hands, she carried a dish with a cloth over it.

"Hey, open up. It's me. Bertha Joyce Brooks. Brought you some rabbit stew," she hollered through the closed door.

Rabbit stew? I'd eaten rabbit stew that my daddy made, but it'd been a long time. Opening the door, I said, "Come in, Bertha. I'm Marley Jane Steele. Let me take that and sit it on the table. Thank you."

She passed the dish to me like it was a hot potato. And it was hot. While I walked across the room to the table, she flopped into a wing back chair, with her arms and legs spread. Slumped into the chair, she rolled her eyes toward the ceiling. Then, she closed them and let out an enormous breath of air. I hoped that she wasn't about to die in my living room.

"Are you okay?" I asked. "Can I get you something to drink?"

"No. I just need to catch my breath. This heat kills me. I been rushing 'round all morning, cooking and trying to sew. Lord, I never get through with everthing. Whew! That AC sho' does feel good. It's nice and cool in here. My house is hot as blazes, even with the window unit going full blast all the time. I keep two more fans going in the room where the unit is 'cause of the babies I keep. You know? Too hot to take them outside. Well, I didn't have any kids to keep this morning so I thought I'd come see you. Meet you and welcome you to Notasulga, which you're gonna find *real* interesting. I can tell you that. But, it's a good town." She finished with another deep sigh and rolling of her eyes to the ceiling, after which, she gave me a long, level stare.

Wesley stood there and watched, moving closer as she completed her last sentence. He laid a toy in her lap and propped his arms across her chubby right leg, looking up at her face. Then, he smiled and said, "Hi. Me name is Wesley."

"Well, hello, honey babe. You sho' are cute. How old are you?'

"Me three. How old are you?"

I caught myself editing Wesley's use of the word "me." We'd been hopelessly trying to get him to say "I" when it was grammatically proper. "And I am three," I corrected.

"Me, too," he quickly replied, which was his usual response. I suspected that he knew what we were attempting to do and chose to ignore us.

"Wesley, you don't ask people how old they are. It's not polite," I told him, continuing to correct.

"Why?"

"Because it's not polite," I repeated. Then, to Bertha Joyce, I said, "'Why' is his favorite word."

"Well, that's okay," she said to me. Looking at Wesley, she said, "I'm ten. She reached and pulled him onto her plump lap. He looked at me and smiled.

He looked up at her with his daddy's brown, almost black, eyes and asked, "What's your name?"

"Bertha Joyce."

"Miss Bertha to you, Wesley," I told him.

Laughing and hugging him, she completely destroyed any control I had, which, apparently, wasn't much. "Just Bertha Joyce. Tell Mama not to be an old fuddy duddy. Say, 'Don't be an old fuddy duddy, Mama.'"

Pointing a tiny finger at me, he said, "Don't be an old fud doodoo."

"Well, he makes it sound like I'm full of it," I said, laughing.

"What'cha making?" she asked, looking at the sewing machine and material on the table.

"I'm making curtains for the house. I've been at it all morning, plus several days, and I'm ready to take a break. Let's have a glass of tea," I said, walking into the kitchen. "Come and sit at the table. Wesley, come to the table and eat lunch. Bertha, would you like a sandwich?" I placed the large dictionary on a chair and sat Wesley on top of it. "There you go," I said, kissing his forehead.

"No, honey. I got a roast in the oven at home. Sid, that's my husband, will come looking for me if I'm gone too long." After a pause, she said, "That's a lie. I could stay gone all day and all night, and he wouldn't notice, until he got ready to eat."

She fingered the material and asked how many curtains I planned to make. I told her that I'd completed curtains for the master bedroom and Wesley's room. "I'm working on curtains for the living room, and they're a pain. Ruffles, you know. Then, I'll start on the third bedroom. And end with the kitchen and bath," I told her, sitting a tall glass of sweet tea in front of her.

She took a long swallow, smacked her lips, and said, "Uhmmm. That's some good tea. I ain't done nothing but sweat all day long. I needed a refreshment. Let me see what design them curtains for the living room's gonna be." She examined my drawings of the curtains and the patterns that I'd cut from newspapers.

"I'll take these patterns and the material for the living room curtains home with me and finish them. Have them back to you in a couple of days," she said in a tone that left no room for contradiction.

"Oh, I can't let you do that." I was shocked that a woman whom I'd just met wanted to help me make curtains.

She leaned towards me and raised her small dark eyes to my face. "Yes, you can. Just consider it a housewarming gift, or whatever. Sewing is one of the things I do to make money. I'm good at it. Heck, I can have these things done before you get started. Don't say nothing. I'm doing it. So, I gotta go. Enjoy the stew. I'll see you in a few days."

We walked to the front door. In her arms, she held the material and patterns for my living room curtains. On the porch, she stopped and turned to me. "A bunch of us are gonna give you and Coach Win—Oh, we're calling him that 'cause we expect him to be our lucky charm and win lots of games—a little welcome party in ten days or so. I'll let you know more later. The people who'll be there support the school. You won't have no problems with them, but I can't promise you the same 'bout some other folks. After awhile, you'll know who you can and can't trust. There's some good and some bad folks here. Like everywheres, I guess. Anyways, don't worry 'bout it. I'll be in touch. Bye."

"Bye." I watched, as she turned sideways to walk slowly down the steps to her car. She opened the back door on the driver's side and placed the material on the car seat. As she slowly got into the driver's seat, she waved with one small, chubby hand. I waved back. The car jerked forward. Then, it suddenly flew backwards, out of the drive. She changed from reverse to drive, and after a few jerks, the car jumped forward and took off.

Five days later Bertha returned with the curtains. We hung them and stood back to admire her work. We sat at the kitchen table, drinking tea and talking. She told me about the party and who'd be there. We didn't talk about the burning of the school. That subject seemed to be off limits, and I wanted to concentrate on the positive. I had plenty of time to gather facts about the burning.

She left with the material for the kitchen and bathroom windows. "You've got enough to do without making curtains," she told me. "Consider it a gift." I was learning that it was hard to argue with her. She was tiny, but very determined. It seemed as if everyone I'd met so far had a strong personality.

Chapter 20

The party was a few days later at Viola and Clyde Owens' home. The Owens were an older couple whose son and daughter were both grown, married, and lived in other states. It was a beautiful late sunny afternoon, not a cloud in the sky. Seven o'clock was approaching when we arrived. Along with about forty other people, we gathered on the Owens' well-manicured back lawn for a barbeque. Most of the men stood around a large grill. Tables were covered in bright tablecloths, and lanterns sat on each table. Lights were strung throughout the branches of the trees. Flowers bloomed everywhere. Soft music played in the background. Ice buckets, filled with sodas, wine, and beer, sat on a long table that held trays of food. I saw Bertha arranging more food on the table, and I waved. She waved back, yelling something that I couldn't hear. The mood was festive. Laughter floated through the air like chimes that vibrated when the wind blew.

Viola introduced us to people as they arrived. After greeting the Owens, Hunter and his tall, slender wife, Reba, who looked like a model, headed straight for our table. Hunter had introduced Reba to us the day after we moved to town. They came by the old wooden framed house late that afternoon. I wasn't surprised that I immediately liked her. She was graceful and friendly, nothing superficial about her. She was one of the most beautiful women I'd ever met. She adored Hunter, and he felt the same way about her, though I'd soon learn that didn't stop him from disappearing for days at a time, without telling her where he was going.

Reba sat beside me and asked how I was adjusting. I told her about meeting Bertha. She said that I'd see lots of Bertha, because she was in charge of the concession stand at the home football games, which meant that she stopped by the school frequently. Everyone knew and loved her. "She's here some place. I'm sure. Because she doesn't miss an opportunity to welcome anyone. You'll meet people like her. Then, there'll be some who you'll be happy not to meet. The town's divided. Between the public school and Macon Academy. I'll say that things are better than they were when we first came here. God, how I hated it! Now, I know some really great people. Just give it time. It won't be like any place you've ever lived before. So, don't expect it to be." The last advice ended with laughter.

I nodded and listened, hoping to learn something, to gain some wisdom. We were here, and as long as we knew people like the crowd who'd gathered tonight, I could learn to accept things and to know what couldn't be changed. As she talked, I knew that forces were at work in my life, and those forces would influence my thinking about many things, as well as about people.

Viola interrupted our conversation to introduce me to the Jenkins, a couple who owned hundreds of acres of land in Macon County. I'd heard of Emmitt Jenkins, who'd served on the Macon County Board of Education for the past six years. He was a member of the board in 1962 when the superintendent and board members worked with the black community in Tuskegee to desegregate Tuskegee High School, which would've been successful, if Wallace hadn't gotten involved. Just prior to the burning of the school, the KKK burned a cross on his front lawn. Several days later, they returned after midnight and burned one of his barns. He received threatening letters that were left on his front door and phone calls that awoke him in the early morning hours, only to hear faint breathing.

I'd heard from Hunter that Emmitt, a wealthy, well-known, well-respected, and fearless man of God, was in his middle forties before he married a woman who was twenty-one and who'd just begun working as a teller at the Macon County Bank in Tuskegee, where he did some of his banking. Her uncle owned the bank, and after she received a business degree from Birmingham Southern College, he talked her into coming to work for him. His plan was to promote her, until she was first vice-president of the bank. She lived with her aunt and uncle, and she'd been at the bank for two weeks when she met Emmitt Jenkins.

The morning that he met Eva Jewel Scott, his family had been kidding him about finding a wife. When he walked into the bank that morning, he was upset about his family "sticking their noses" in his private affairs. He took one look at Eva Jewel and fell in love. It didn't take long before everyone who worked at the bank knew that he had it bad. He came to the bank every day for two weeks, until he got the courage to ask her for a date.

Although his family worried that he might never marry, they were surprised when he informed them the day he met Eva Jewel that he intended to marry her. "He's losing his marbles," they said, shaking their heads sadly. "He just met her. He doesn't know anything about her. A man shouldn't up and marry the first woman he meets, only hours after being teased about not being married. For gracious sake!"

Within five months they were married. Before their first anniversary, she was pregnant. A daughter was born, and within seven years, three other children arrived, two boys and another girl. By the time the three oldest were in sixth, fourth, and second grades, Notasulga High School was integrated. It never occurred to the Jenkins that their children would attend any school but public schools. So, when desegregation became a topic of discussion, Emmitt Jenkins supported it. As he'd say many times, "You've got to weigh important issues. Think them through. You can't play follow the leader. Sometimes, you've got to lead. You've got to get the facts, look into the future, and make decisions that are best for the majority of people. Social change needs cool heads and people who're not selfish, not thinking about their own wants." He didn't speak much, but when he did, he had a calm voice and a quiet manner about him.

As we were introduced, I looked into Emmitt's piercing blue eyes. There were small smile wrinkles at the corner of each eye. A square chin told me that he was firmly authentic. He stood approximately five feet ten inches, with a slender, solid build. He knew what it was to work for hours, farming land and taking care of cattle. His voice was soft-spoken and low. When he smiled, I saw even white teeth. Later, as I watched people interact with him, I realized that he was sharp, intelligent, and incredibly observant. I knew from the things I'd heard about him that he was good at leading and that people tended to follow him, because he was trustworthy. Others admired him, but he never got caught up in the praise.

Jewel was a slender captivating woman, with glimmering emerald eyes that caught the light of the fading sun. When I looked at those eyes, I thought of a forest after a rain, at sunset, and I thought how appropriate the name Jewel was for her. She had fair skin, the color of milk, and I wondered if she ever worked outside. Later, I learned that she did and could drive a tractor as well as her husband. Her face was heart-shaped. Her lips were full and wide. A smile covered her entire face. Copper, burning bright hair, framed her face. Her hair was the same style, only shorter, as that worn by Anne Bancoft in *The Graduate*. She wore a blue shirtwaist dress that had white polka dots and a white lace Peter Pan collar. A white, thin patent leather belt was around her slim waist, and she had on white patent leather sandals that showed off her slender feet. She radiated a force of energy.

Like her husband, she was quiet, intelligent, and devoted to family. Both were committed to their church and to making Notasulga public schools successful. Desegregation had split the schools and the churches, important institutions that acted like glue to hold the community together. The Jenkins were determined that those two important social connections in the community would survive and make the town stronger, in spite of the differences of opinions that divided it.

As the evening fell into darkness, and everyone was full of good food and drink, we pulled our chairs into a large circle. A full yellow moon hung low in the east, slowly working its way south. Stars winked off and on like white Christmas lights, while flowers sent intoxicating odors over the plush lawn. A train roared loudly by, on its way to West Point, Georgia, then on beyond to Atlanta. Everyone stopped talking until it disappeared out of sight, listening to the mournful whistle that could break a heart.

Wesley and six other children played hide and seek. When they tired of that game, they chased lightning bugs and put them in fruit jars that Viola gave them. Later, as the adults talked and the children became sleepy, she made pallets for them on the floor of her den. They slept until the gathering ended, just before midnight.

Story after story was told, with each person taking his or her turn. Winston and I listened, absorbing the character of these people, as well as the character of the town. As the stories unfolded, we learned that passions in Notasulga were still strong. Memories were still fresh. People talked about the "school trouble" as though it happened months ago, instead of three years ago. We listened and learned, not asking too many questions. We felt the anger and the pain, as we began to bond with some of those in the group who'd suffered. We doubted if we'd ever be given an opportunity to bond with the other group who'd suffered. We were told that we'd most likely be ignored by some people, especially by those who believed that we chose sides, simply by coming to work at the school. If we hadn't chosen sides that night, we'd have done so within a short period of time.

Then, Victor Alexander, who'd grown up in Notasulga and had given up a career at Red Stone Arsenal in Huntsville to teach math at the high school, began to tell about one of Hunter's episodes, which occurred during Hunter's first year at Notasulga. Hunter picked up the story and finished it. We gained additional insight into how he handled problems. In his straightforward, honest way, he told us things that'd occurred. Knowing him, we knew that none of what he said was fabricated. The crowd laughed. Some just shook their heads. I laughed, while in a state of shock. It was like reading Flannery O'Conner. You didn't want to laugh, but you couldn't stop.

Two incidents stood out in my mind. Hunter met with the faculty several days before the students arrived for the first day of school. After everything on the agenda had been discussed, one female teacher raised her hand. With her head cocked to one side, she asked him, "What are you gonna do when Billy Joe Meadows comes flying down the hall on his motorcycle? And he will. He's already bragging about how he's gonna do it."

The entire faculty began to talk at once about Billy Joe and how he disrupted class any time that he took a notion to the year before the school burned. They told how he came to the school after all of the white students left, planning to race down the halls, but the federal marshals, who were posted at each door, stopped him. Then, they began to talk about other things that Billy Joe had done. They got louder and louder and madder and madder.

Finally, Hunter hollered, "Wow! Wait a minute! Everybody stop talking. I can't hear no damn body! You, back there in the green shirt, tell me who in the hell is Billy Joe Meadows. Okay, I'm listening." Looking around the room at everyone else, he continued, "And don't nobody else say a word 'til I ask you to speak. Understood? Now. You. Go ahead," he instructed Lamar Phillips. "Talk to me."

"Well," the short older man said, in a slow drawl that suggested Hunter might have picked the wrong person to speak, since the story might take forever and a day. "He's a young man. Maybe in his twenties or early thirties. I don't rightly know. A skinny runt of a fellow who doesn't like black people. He likes to think that he associates with the upper crust. People with money and power. 'Cause he doesn't have any. If an uppity person spit on a wall and told him to lick it off, he'd do it. Just because of who told him to. He'll do whatever those people tell him to do.

"You know," he continued slowly, "there's always been a rumor that he was involved in the burning of the school, along with others. A lot of folks think he was used. He ain't got a lick of sense, not one thought of his own in his head. Anyways, before the school burned, he paid the school a visit on his motorcycle any time he wanted the thrill of zooming around the buildings. But, then, he never drove down the halls. It was his idea of a fun thing to do back before the school burned. Thank goodness no one got hurt. But, mark my words, he's coming. He's already spreading the word about it. Everybody in town's heard him brag about how he's going to stir things up over here. And it will not do any good to call the police. They will not come." He spoke the last two sentences with conviction. The others nodded.

One person spoke at a time, and it appeared that most of them knew Billy Joe and had heard all about his intentions. They believed that someone in town was putting him up to his old tricks, just to make trouble. Apparently, Billy Joe, for whatever reason, didn't fear the law. He freely revealed his plans to "stir things up at that school." One teacher said that people were placing bets on how many times he'd drive down the halls. The rumor was that someone or several people offered him fifty dollars for each time that he rode through the school. It was getting out of hand.

Hunter told them to keep the students in the classroom, not to allow anyone to go to the bathroom, if they heard the sound of a motorcycle approaching the school. "And don't get all upset if I don't do something the first time he comes through. If he comes through. And don't let none of your students go running to the doors or windows. Make them stay in their seats. And stay quiet."

The first week of school no skinny man on a motorcycle zoomed down the hall. The second week came and went. No man on a motorcycle. The Wednesday of the third week came, and it was halfway into first period when the distant sound of a motorcycle drifted into the classrooms and into Hunter's office. He listened for a minute and walked into the outer office. His secretary sat listening, wondering if Billy Joe would dare come into the building, and if so, which door he would enter.

The general layout of the halls, inside most schools that were built in the sixties and earlier, looks like a cross. There were doors that opened to the south, north, east, and west. In the 60s, there was no air-conditioning and no fans; therefore, all of the exterior doors were left open by necessity. No one could have dreamed that in the future someone would enter and shoot anyone within pointing range.

The sound got closer, just outside the west entrance to the school. Billy Joe opened the throttle and accelerated. He roared up the steps, into the school and down the hall, stopping in the middle of the building, gunning the motor as loudly as he could. He raced the engine one final time and soared down the hall on one wheel, toward the office. The front end of the motorcycle was suspended in the air, as if invisible strings kept it up on its rear wheel. Near the door on the east side of the building, he dropped onto two wheels, flew out the door and down the steps. Hunter remained standing in the outer office. Then, he walked into his office. He listened for the sound of the gunned engine to fade, as the motorcycle neared the end of the driveway. Then, he looked out the window, watching the motorcycle head back toward town.

The next day, after each class started, Hunter cut off the hall lights. Just before each class ended, he cut them back on. It was third period when Billy Joe returned, gunning the motorcycle. Hunter stood in his secretary's office, watching the pattern. He now knew when Billy Joe would slow down before coming to a stop in the middle of the hall. The teachers wondered what he could possibly do to stop the idiots in this town? They didn't yet know Hunter.

The following day was a hot Friday. Everyone suffered the heat and waited for the sound of the motorcycle. Hunter was ready. He came to school an hour earlier that morning, and he was tense, waiting. He had a plan. The clock ticked slowly. He repeated the pattern of the day before, of cutting off the hall lights. Sure enough, during third period, everyone heard the dreaded sound of the engine being gunned, just before Billy Joe shot up the steps from the west entrance, into the building and down the hall toward the east entrance. Hunter was enveloped in the shadows of the hall and blended into the wall, at the point where he figured Billy Joe would stop. Just as Billy Joe came to a stop, Hunter stepped in front of the motorcycle, took hold of the handlebars, and gave a quick, hard, upward jerk. Billy Joe's skinny ass fell off the motorcycle. His face was a picture of shock.

While the motor was still running, Hunter dragged the machine to the east door and slung it out of the building. Billy Joe got up quickly; he wasn't happy. Using some strong language, he moved toward Hunter. Big mistake. They came face-to-face. Billy Joe began to tell Hunter how he was going to whip his ass. Hunter grabbed him by the shirtfront, reached behind Billy Joe and got a good grip on his belt. Billy Joe was off the floor, as level as a sitting plane. Hunter carried him to the open door and threw him onto the sidewalk.

"If you ever put one foot inside my school again, I'll shove that goddamn motorcycle up your redneck ass!" Hunter warned him. "Now, I'm going to give you one shake of a horse's ass to get off this property before I seriously hurt you."

The entire school was quiet. You could hear a gnat pissing on cotton ten miles away. Every word that Hunter said echoed down the halls and through the closed doors of the classrooms. Then the clapping started. It became a roar. Doors opened as teachers and students filled the halls. Some of the dread and fear of returning to a new school disappeared that day, and it never returned. Teachers who had hesitations about working there now felt a calmness and security that'd evaded them. Hopefully, they could get on with the job of teaching.

The second incident involved two white students and a dad. Not long after the event with the motorcycle, and soon enough for tempers to be tested, the fighting started among some of the male students. It was mostly white on white. Not too many black students wanted to come to Notasulga, and even the ones who should've been coming were not doing so. No one made an issue of it. The black students who did come stayed out of fights and kept a low profile. Soon, most of every day was taken up dealing with fights. Not much teaching or learning was taking place in some classes. It became apparent that two white boys, John Earl Talley and Rusty White, were the biggest problem. By the end of the day, during P.E., they became more edgy.

The P.E. teacher, Avery Bond, would bring the boys to the office every day for fighting. They didn't really fight, just poking, shoving, and mouthing off. Finally, Hunter was tired of it. He'd grown up in a real bad environment, where fighting was a means of survival. In his world, you didn't play at fighting. Fighting was serious. Bond walked into the office, with the two boys behind him. They were dragging their feet, still mumbling at one another under their breaths. Hunter listened again, for more times than he cared to remember. After he'd heard out Bond and the boys, he said, "Let's go. Follow me."

Out of the office they all marched—Hunter, Rusty, John Earl, and Bond. Hunter led them to the gym and into the dressing room. When they got there, he turned around, faced the two boys, and ordered, "Fight!"

"What?" both boys asked together, with shock written all over their faces.

"I said, 'Fight!' I'm sick of this," he told them. "You're gonna fight today. Fight!"

They began their routine. Rusty softly pushed John Earl's shoulder. John Earl returned a soft lick. Rusty pushed John Earl a bit harder, and a harder push was returned. This continued back and forth for a while. Suddenly, Hunter took off his belt. He slapped each boy on his butt and said, "Fight!" They fought until they were exhausted and both were crying. At the end, each had bruises and small cuts. John Earl sat on a bench and hung his head. Rusty sat on the floor, glad that it was over.

Dobbie Talley was at school early the next morning, storming through the offices. Hunter was sitting behind his desk. Dobbie slammed his hands on the desk and got close to Hunter's face. "For an excuse, Moore, I'll stomp yo' ass through this here floor. Just give me one good reason!" he yelled, sending spit on Hunter's chin. Dobbie eyed the glistening tiny crystal that hung on the cliff of Hunter's square chin. The man's weather-beaten face was so close that Hunter could see the broken blood vessels and the large pores that fell across Dobbie's big nose. Frosty looks of outraged indignation filled his pale blue eyes.

Without speaking, Hunter reached out and thumped Dobbie's nose. Blood filled the lower part of the man's astonished face; it hit the desk; it slapped Hunter in the face. As it began to soak into the papers on the desk, Hunter stood up. "Is that a good enough reason? Get the hell out of my office and talk to your boy about wanting to fight all the time, because I'm not gonna have him fighting in my school. Get out!"

"You ain't heard the last of this, Moore. That's a promise. You hear me? Who the hell you thank you are, comin' here, actin' like a bad-ass? We don't want your kind in this town. Just watch your back," he said, pointing a finger at Hunter and moving toward the door. "My boy is gonna be gone from this school, but you just better watch out."

"Take him out. I don't give a damn. We don't want your kind at this school. Take your boy some place that doesn't mind fighting. And I'm not telling you to leave again," he warned, moving around his desk.

Dobbie didn't wait for another warning. He practically ran down the steps of the school, jumped into his truck, and almost lost control of the vehicle when it took the slight curve and leaned too far to the right. John Earl stayed at home that day. As a matter of fact, his mother was enrolling him in Macon Academy while his daddy's nose was shooting blood everywhere.

A man of Hunter's character couldn't last long in future schools, once desegregation swept through Alabama and became a part of the environment of the public schools. Future private and public schools would cater to every whim and whine of a parent or a child, stroking them to prevent an unhappy situation. But, only a strong individual could handle the demanding problems of desegregation. During the early days of desegregation, being a teacher or an administrator in the public schools wasn't a profession for the weak or the bigoted.

* * * * * * *

After Hunter told his stories, which everyone but Winston and I had heard before, Clyde Owens talked about the burning of the school. He mentioned that a week before the school was burned Emmitt Jenkins' barn had been destroyed by fire, along with five other barns in the county.

Very quietly, Emmitt said, "The superintendent and board members were afraid that something bad was going to happen. We'd heard the rumors for months about burning the school. We'd even heard rumors of who the ringleaders were, but we couldn't get proof. Although we knew it was useless, we asked the Notasulga Police Department to keep a close watch on the school every night. Well, y'all know that was a failure." He paused and bent forward in his chair, his hands clasped between his legs. He looked at the ground and continued. "I felt so guilty after the school burned. Like I could've done more. You know? The afternoon it happened, I went to the church. I sat in a pew for a long time. Then, I went to the altar and knelt. I prayed, 'God, give me strength. Bring to justice anyone who was in the middle of this horrible tragedy.' This calm washed over me, and I heard a voice in my head say, 'I'll take care of it. Each guilty person will be punished.' I stayed on my knees for a while longer. When I walked out of the church, I knew that it was in God's hands, and His will would be done."

Everyone remained silent, looking at his bent head. He raised his head and looked around the circle of people. "You know, within two years, five men were dead. I won't call any names, but most of you know the men. You've heard this before. One committed suicide. One died of a heart attack. One was killed in an awful automobile accident, coming home from a bar. Another man fell off his roof, while he was repairing it. An enraged, jealous husband murdered the last man. The husband accused him of having an affair with his wife. Those were the five men—and, like I said, some of you know them—who were suspected of being the ringleaders who burned the school."

"Was Billy Joe Meadows involved?" someone asked.

Clyde said, "That's the rumor. If you recall, Ellie Sue Cotney, who lived next door to the school, said she saw a dark motorcycle leave from behind the school that night. Just before the school caught on fire."

After a moment of quiet, Nelson Judd said, "Rumors were that Wallace knew about the burning of the school. That he sent an eighteen-wheeler to the school to be loaded with textbooks, desks, chairs, and anything else that could be useful. Everything was taken to Macon Academy. So, the rumors go."

His wife, Patti, spoke up, "But, that was never proven. And Mrs. Cotney didn't say a word about seeing or hearing an eighteen-wheeler the night of the fire."

Hunter said, "Nothing was proven. We still don't know, today, who started that fire, for sure. As far as desks, chairs, books, or anything else in the classrooms go, they could've been taken a little bit at a time."

No one spoke. Each person seemed to be deep in thought. Then, Lester Horn stood up, stretched, and said, "Hopefully, we can move forward and put the past behind us. I, for one, don't wanna keep rememberin' all that bad stuff. At some point, we gotta let go and forget, in order to accomplish what Emmitt and all of us want, which is to unite this town."

Decades after we left, Winston and Lester would remain friends and fishing buddies. I was never convinced that the best idea was to bury the past and not deal with it. It's okay to move on. After you come to terms with a problem and resolve it. After you look the devil in the eye and demand the truth. I don't think that Lester and I interpreted "letting go" and "moving on" in the same way.

"Well, it's been great. It's getting to be bedtime. Marley. Winston. Let's do this again real soon. Welcome to Notasulga," Clyde said.

It was around midnight, and people prepared to go home. Winston lifted our sleeping son from the pallet and carried him to the car, placing him on my lap. As we drove home, Wesley barely stirred. He opened his eyes briefly as I sponged his face, arms, hands, and feet with a wet washcloth. Before I had his pajamas on, he'd fallen back into a deep sleep. I kissed his forehead and left on the night light beside his bed.

I took a bath and put on my nightgown. Then, I went into the kitchen. Winston was at the kitchen table, going over his playbook. We sat and talked for thirty or thirty-five minutes about the people we'd met and the stories that we'd heard. I went to bed, leaving him drawing circles and X's on typing paper. I knew that he'd be up for at least two hours or more, toiling over offensive and defensive plays. I didn't encourage him to put things away and come to bed. He had too much on his mind. For one thing, he didn't have an assistant football coach, and he wouldn't have one for two more years.

Chapter 21

Although Hunter had been convinced to hire a new coach, he wasn't so willing to stop being totally involved. He didn't have any bitterness about someone else being coach, but he couldn't stop being himself, which was controlling. On Friday nights, he stalked the sidelines and yelled at the players, telling them what to do, even if it meant the opposite of what Winston told them to do. The team was absolutely confused. A new coach, whom they didn't know, and the principal were both telling them what to do. They didn't know whom to obey. I had a front row seat, at home and at school, to watch the drama unfold between Hunter and Winston.

After the third game, and the third loss, Winston went into Hunter's office the following Monday. He asked with a slight smirk, "Do you want me to coach?"

Hunter looked at him like he'd lost his mind. "Hell, Winston, why do you think I wanted to hire you?" he barked, as if he'd been insulted. "If I really wanted to be coaching, I'd be on that field." Winston hesitateded, because that wasn't exactly the way things had been presented to him when he came for an interview and was later hired. As we were quickly learning, Hunter was always saying something that made you pause for a moment. Too often, he seemed to be in contradiction with himself.

"Well, the problem, Hunter, is that you're on the field. Telling my boys what to do," Winston replied with his familiar lopsided grin, "and it's got to stop. The players have got to know that there's only one head coach. And no assistant. It's affecting them. In a bad way. We're never going to win, if they're confused."

"Damn! I didn't know you didn't want me on the field. I thought I'd be there for you. For support. You know? Let this town know I'm behind you all the way," he said in a tone that suggested any fool would know the obvious.

"I appreciate that Hunter. Really, I do. But. I'd rather you support me from the stands. Can we agree that you'll stay off the field during a game?"

With his brown eyes wide with wonder, Hunter said in a tone that he used when he was being nice, "Hell, yeah, man! I want to win, too."

"Wow! Thank goodness that's solved," Winston thought, while doubting that it was going to be that easy to stop Hunter Moore from doing anything.

A man of his word, Hunter stayed in the stands or outside the fence. He no longer yelled instructions to the players. Soon, he found something better with which to occupy himself. When he heard anyone say anything negative about the game, the players, or Winston, he immediately defended them, and, often, he didn't bother to use polite language. If anyone wanted to express a negative opinion, he or she made certain that Hunter couldn't overhear the comment. Of course, he never stopped giving Winston advice when they were alone.

Hunter became one of Winston's biggest fans. He wasn't about being jealous or about not wanting someone else to get credit. Winston's success didn't threaten him. After all, he'd come to Notasulga to fight a war against segregation, not to win a game. The real battle was in the community itself, not what was happening on the football field. Anyway, he'd much rather be stomping badass men than coaching football. He'd earned his glory on the football field at the University of Alabama. He didn't need strokes for football anymore, but he did want the school to succeed in everything, and he didn't want to block the way for any progress or success.

The first year that we were there, Notasulga won one game, and the crowd went crazy. You'd have thought they'd won the Super Bowl. For weeks, when the players went anywhere in town, people hugged them and slapped them on their backs. When townspeople who supported Macon Academy praised them, they were pleased. They couldn't stop smiling, until the following week when they lost. An important lesson had been learned. They could win. Since they'd tasted victory, they wanted more. That team, as well as future teams, would never be the same. From that time, until we left, Notasulga High School football teams believed that they were winners. They thought of themselves as winners, and they played the game like winners. Faith in winning football games gave them faith to believe that they could do other things, that they could be good students, and that they could have a better life.

Often, Winston would comment that everyone didn't fully comprehend the importance of sports in a young person's life, especially if that was just about all a person had. "Many don't get it. I know they sometimes make cruel remarks about athletes and coaches," he'd say. He believed there was no need to respond. It was like spitting in the wind. What they didn't know didn't matter. "I understand people well enough to know that, too often, people's thoughts are based on opinions, with no facts or stats to support those opinions. Sadly, they generally don't care to learn the facts. Doing so might mean that they'd have to change their minds," he'd say and laugh.

Then, he'd continue, "I've got a completely different reaction to an educator who makes nasty remarks about sports. I figure that person should have enough ground sense to know that there must be important reasons why superintendents and board members agree to spend thousands of dollars for sports activities. I don't waste my time enlightening them bout the positive qualities of sports. Usually, it's best to let ignorance slide past like thin snot." It was just another unpleasant inconvenience that caused him to wrinkle his nose in disgust, while smiling.

* * * * * * *

The Tuesday, following the party at the Owens, Hunter came by the house late one afternoon to talk with me. His secretary was leaving at the end of the week, due to the fact that her husband had been transferred by Alabama Power Company to Dothan. Friday was to be her last day, and Hunter wanted me to take the job as his secretary.

"You can come in Wednesday, Thursday, and Friday mornings so that she can go over everything with you. What she won't have time to cover, Bo Oliver can help you with. He works over at the central office and is in charge of most of the monthly reports. So, just come in tomorrow morning 'bout nine. I'll tell her that you're coming," he instructed me, without pausing.

"Wait! Just wait a minute, Hunter," I said. "I don't have anyone to take care of Wesley. I can't just up and start working in the morning."

"Oh, I forgot to mention that I've already talked with the superintendent. Bo will get you on the payroll before the end of the week. Oh, hell, don't worry about Wesley. I've already taken care of him. I talked with Bertha Joyce this morning, and she's going to keep him until school starts. Then, he's going to Head Start. And, I've already talked with Fran Weaver, who's in charge of Head Start. I spoke with her yesterday. So, …"

"Wait. Wesley is only two years old. He's not old enough to go to Head Start," I interrupted. I was beginning to doubt that he'd actually spoken with Fran, whom I'd met briefly one afternoon when I picked Winston up at the gym. They were talking about sports. Her son, who was in junior high, played basketball, which Hunter continued to coach.

Fran was an attractive, slim woman who was about five feet six inches of poise. The afternoon sun caught the golden lights in her chestnut hair, making tiny gold winks. A sparkle lived in her hazel eyes. Winston introduced us and walked away to lock up the gym. She told me that she worked at Head Start and that Hunter had hired her the first year that he was in Notasulga. As she talked about the children in the program, I knew that she was a woman with a selfless heart, caring and nurturing.

She wasn't at the Owens' party. She and Viola weren't friends. I'd soon realize that she didn't appear where the Owens' appeared together. Many years later, Viola would tell me the reason, as we drove to Montgomery to do some Christmas shopping. It'd be the last time that we talked about Fran, and, afterwards, I never spoke to one about the other. I grew to deeply respect and like both women. Both became my friends. I never allowed their feelings for one another to interfere with my friendship with either one. That type of behavior from grown women disgusted me. It was too much like the behavior of teenage girls.

Sighing and looking up to his right, he continued in a drawn out voice, "As I was saying. It's taken care of. You don't have to worry about anything." He turned to me, all smug and satisfied with himself.

"Did it ever occur to you to talk with me before you made all of those plans?" I asked in a mean tone. He and I needed to come to an understanding. Real fast.

"Well, hell! I figured that you'd jump at this." He began to count off the reasons on his fingers, leaning down to look me in the eyes. "The hours are good. The pay's good. You can't ask for anybody any better than Bertha Joyce or Fran to take care of Wesley. You need to work, and I need a secretary. I've been told that Opelika Business School can't be beat. What do you say?"

I looked down at the floor. Then, I looked at Hunter. He was slowly nodding his head. It was true that I needed to work. We could use the extra money, and this gave me the opportunity to work in town. I wouldn't have to travel to Auburn, Opelika, or Tuskegee. I'd be nearby, if Wesley needed me. And I'd have the same holidays as Winston. It was an unexpected opportunity. One I couldn't resist. "Okay, but I can't start tomorrow morning. I'll start early Thursday, and work all day Thursday and Friday. Tomorrow, I want to talk with Bertha and Fran. I want Wesley to meet Fran, and I want her to spend some time with him," I said, standing my ground. "Bo can help me, if I have any questions."

"Good. That's settled. Geez, Louise!" He shook his head and rolled his eyes. "I'll see you Thursday morning. Oh, here're the keys to the school and to the office. Stella will be there by eight. I'll tell her that you're not coming tomorrow. I'm easy to work for. We'll get along just fine."

He lifted his huge solid frame from the sofa and headed to the front door. Turning to face me, he said, "It's good that you'll be working at the school. It'll show people in this town that y'all came prepared to support the school one hundred percent. Your entire family will be a part of the school. It's important that as many people as possible in this town support public education and integration. The school has got to survive. Without the school, there'll be nothing here.

"Plus, you and I both know it's just a matter of time before every public school in this state's going to be desegregated—before every one of those schools has to follow federal guidelines. I want to be ready for it when it comes. I don't intend for no damn fool rednecks in this town to get in the way when it happens. They've messed with this school for the last time. If I've anything to say or to do about it, their asses will be the ones burning, not the school. We've come too far to turn back now. I want you and Winston to help make it work. You both have a lot to offer the school and the town. Bye. See you Thursday."

I watched him walk to his car. After he cranked the motor, he turned and waved. I waved back. Wesley stayed by my side while we talked, listening to every word, as if he understood what was being said. "Bye, Hunter," he yelled as the car began backing out of the driveway. Again, he'd totally disregarded my instructions on how to address adults.

"Wesley, don't call people by their names, without saying 'Mr.' or 'Ms,'" I reminded him again, knowing that he'd ignore me.

"Me know. It be okay, Mama," he said, moving toward his Radio Flyer Bounce Horse that sat on rods, which went from the front legs to the back legs. The horse was light brown leather, with a dark brown saddle and two positions for stirrups. He climbed aboard the rocking horse, but he didn't rock. In fact, he'd never rocked back and forth on that horse. Instead, he lifted up on the handles near the horse's ears and took off, bouncing down the hall. At the end of the hall, he turned the horse around and headed back. I couldn't figure out how he managed to turn that big horse around at the end of the hall. Heck, I didn't know how he turned it period; yet, he maneuvered it around as if it were a tricycle.

When he came back, I said, "Let's go visit Miss Bertha, 'cause you're going to be staying with her during the day for a few weeks. Next, we'll visit

Mrs. Weaver. She'll be your teacher when school starts. You have to call her Mrs. Weaver. Okay?"

I'd kept the car that day so that I could go grocery shopping, at a store located about five miles in the country, at a crossroads near Reeltown. Before shopping, I wanted to visit with Fran. Then Bertha. I knew that I'd stay longer at Bertha's, because she loved to talk. I enjoyed listening and getting the low-down on everybody.

* * * * * * *

After the first visit to my house, Bertha stopped by often, bringing baked goods or vegetables. When I didn't have the use of the car, she picked Wesley and me up for trips to Opelika or Auburn. She finished the curtains for the house. Since she sewed for the public, I knew that I'd often be bringing material to her. I was small, which meant that it wasn't easy for me to purchase clothes off the racks. Sometimes she put two or three patterns together to create what I wanted. She learned what I liked, and often she'd say, "Now, that's you."

Bertha and I remained friends long after I left—to the day she died. We laughed together and shared secrets. As friends, we argued in a good-hearted manner and teased one another. She probably understood me better than anyone in the town, and I knew that she cared about the person that I am.

I learned that she'd been in a previous marriage that was abusive, with extreme violence. Cooter Williams had a worthless reputation, but he managed to charm a sixteen-year-old into marrying him. She was a child who had no idea how to defend herself or how to deal with an explosive husband, who isolated her from her family. He was a fiend who lashed out at a helpless young girl. If she did anything to displease him, which was almost everything, she had the devil to pay. They lived with his parents and three siblings, two sisters and a brother. None of them defended her, because they, too, took delight in tormenting her. Wanting to avoid the abuse of the daddy and the two brothers, the sisters played along. As long as Bertha was there to be tormented, they were out of the firing line. It seemed that the entire family consisted of seething savages who enjoyed the misery of anyone who was suffering.

In the early morning hours of a steamy summer Saturday night, Cooter came home drunk. Bertha had fallen asleep on the sofa. When she asked where he'd been, he went into a rage, almost beating her to death, pounding her small body with blow after blow, punching her in the face and in her stomach, screaming at her, "I will kill you! You sorry bitch! You whore! You don't ask me no questions or tell me what to do. I do the askin'! I do the tellin'! You're my property, and, by God, I'll do with you what the hell I please."

As she lay on the floor, he kicked her again and again with his steel-toed boots. Suddenly, she was in a pool of blood that ran like a small red creek between her legs and began to outline the lower section of her body. Pain shot through her like arrows, and she could barely breathe. "Look at you! You look like a bleedin' pig. Git your ass up and clean up that damn mess." He bent and yelled into her swollen bloody face. "Hey! Do you hear me, gal? Git up!" Then he slapped her so hard that her neck rotated and slammed onto the other side of the floor.

At that moment, his older sister, Amy Lou, appeared. She stood between him and Bertha. Although the others heard the yelling and beating, they stayed in their beds. The brother opened one eye. "What the hell?" Instantly, he went back to sleep. The younger sister, Mary Lee, sat up in bed and covered her ears, while giggling softly. A shiver ran over her body, and she trembled slightly.

The parents cocked their heads and listened. The old man mumbled to his wife, "That there ain't none of our business. A man's gotta a right to tame his woman. 'Specially a young thing like her. Mind your own business is what I always say. Let other folks be."

"That's enough. You hear me? You gonna kill her! Git outta here! Now!" Amy Lou screamed. He saw a look in her eyes that he'd never seen before. Her anger surprised him, and he stormed out of the room, into the bedroom that he shared with Bertha. He fell onto the bed, fully clothed. Soon, the house was quiet, except for the loud snoring of the three men.

While everyone, but Mary Lee, slept, the older sister helped Bertha into the bathroom. She gently washed Bertha's face. "He gits all likkered up so's he can hardly stand. Then, he's gotta whip everbody." She looked down and saw blood running down the insides of Bertha's legs. Handing Bertha a folded face towel, she said, "Stick this in yer panties. Lean on me. I'm takin' you to the hospital. The bleedin's bad. It won't stop."

"We can't. You know he'll kill us both. I'm afraid of him, Amy Lou," Bertha whispered in a quivering voice, filled with fear.

"It don't make no difference now. If you don't git to the hospital, you are gonna die anyways. Where you wanna die? Here, with him beatin' the shit outta you? Or somewheres people can help you? Bertha, we gotta go now," she said in a low strong, soft, voice. "You gotta trust me. There might never be another chance to save you. Do you know what I'm tellin you? Let's git outta here."

Bertha looked into the teary eyes of a woman whom she thought hated her and knew that this might be her last opportunity to save herself. "What about you? What will they do to you for helping me?"

"We ain't got no time to be thinkin' 'bout me. I'll take care of me. Don't you worry. I been livin' in this for a long time." Then, gently, she said, "Let's git the hell outta here."

No one awoke as the car roared to life and headed to safety. Mary Lee lay in bed, listening as best she could, unable to piece together all of the conversation. As the headlights of the car swept across the walls of her room, she crept deeper under the covers, with her hand over her mouth. She'd protect her sister. They had no one but each other and had been abused in many ways by their daddy and their two brothers. The mother ignored their pleas, while she favored her sons and feared her husband.

Bertha managed to escape in the wee hours of the morning, with the help of Amy Lou, while Cooter Williams snored, drunk, in their miserable bed. After they arrived at the hospital, Amy Lou talked with the nurse and doctor, not telling them everything, just that her brother got drunk, became real mean, and started beating his wife. Then, she left Bertha and drove to Bertha's parents' home. She woke them up and told them what'd happened. When they arrived at the hospital, they learned from the doctor that Bertha was three months pregnant and had lost the baby. The beating was so brutal that she'd never be able to have a child. As she told me stories of the abuse and the loss of her child, she cried and I held her in my arms.

I asked her what happened to the sister-in-law who'd taken her to the hospital. "She went back to her house and got Mary Lee. They stuffed some clothes in pillowcases, took their mom's secret money that was hidden in the kitchen, and sneaked out of the house. Several days later, the car was located two miles from the bus stop in Opelika," Bertha answered, and she continued to tell me what little she knew about the two sisters who, at one time, had been her enemies. Seventeen months afterwards, Amy Lou called Bertha and told her that they were in a safe place, but wouldn't tell her where. Off and on throughout the years, Bertha would receive a Christmas card or a brief note, letting her know that they were doing well and that they had new lives, far away. The first cards were stamped from Atlanta, Georgia.

The cards that'd been sent in the last four years had been stamped from a small town in Florida.

After leaving the hospital, Bertha returned to her parents' home. Several weeks later, Cooter showed up in the front yard, cursing and demanding, "You git yore ass out here, gal. You hear what I say! Git out here! Now!"

Bertha's dad went to the door, holding a shotgun. He pointed it at Cooter and shot just over his sorry head. In a voice as cold as steel, he said, "That weren't no accident. The next bullet's goin' 'tween your eyes. Get the hell off my property 'fore I kill you. Don't ever come back. Don't ever again bother my daughter or you gonna be one dead son-of-a-bitch." Saying that, he walked to the edge of the porch, pulled the shotgun to his shoulder, looked down the barrel, and took aim.

Cooter jumped into his dusty old truck and flew out of the driveway, screaming out the window, "Go straight t'hell in a jet, ol' man!" Tires squealed and gravel scattered across the yard. As he pulled onto the highway, he stuck his left hand out the window and above the top of the truck. His long, knotty middle finger shot Bertha's dad a bird.

"Good riddance. Just a goddamn no-good son-of-a-bitch." Reuben Madison mumbled under his breath as he lowered the shotgun.

Four years later, Bertha married Sid Brooks, and they built a house next door to her parents' home. She was determined that she'd never again be too far away from the safety net of her mama and daddy. Her daddy passed away eleven years before we came to town, but Maud Madison was still living when we left.

Sid had a daughter who came to live with them when she was in elementary school. That took place several years after we moved to town. I was informed of every step of the procedure that they took to get legal custody of Dallas. Finally, the court awarded them custody.

Dallas had long legs and arms. She was a beauty, with blond hair that was almost white. Her bright blue eyes twinkled. Adults thought she was enchanting. They were impressed with her polite behavior and soft voice.

Bertha and Sid fought a long battle to keep their daughter. So many of us who worked at the school helped them fight that battle, to protect Dallas when her mother came from California to unsuccessfully kidnap her. That day her mom stood in my office and cursed me to hell and back, demanding that I tell her where Dallas was so that she could take her. Dianne Ridgeway, Dallas' fourth grade teacher, had stopped by my office earlier. She was holding Dallas' hand, and she told me that the mother was on campus.

Dianne stated, "I'm hiding Dallas, until Bertha can get here." Then she asked me to call Bertha. I immediately made the call.

As the thin, angry woman screamed, I calmly said, "I don't give a tinker's damn what you say. You're not taking her off this campus today without a court order. Get your court order and come back. But for now, the only court order that we're going to follow at this school is the court order that Sid and Bertha have been issued. Please, leave or I'm calling the police." I picked up the phone and began to dial. She left the building, screaming at me, calling me every ugly name that she knew. Soon after she drove off, Bertha came running into my office. We located Dianne and Dallas. Bertha took Dallas home and kept her there for several days, until the court was notified of what'd taken place.

Dallas graduated several years after I began teaching, married her high school sweetheart, and followed him when he joined the military. They traveled extensively, and I assume were happy. I saw her many years after she left town, and she was more beautiful than she'd been in high school. She had one of those faces with great bones, which allows a person to age gracefully. Bertha and I were always delighted when she came for a visit, but she seldom returned. Her heart wasn't there. She'd let go and moved on.

Chapter 22

Fran was at Head Start, and I introduced Wesley to her. I got the feeling that they fell in love with one another right off the bat. It made me feel good. I watched as she walked with him around the room, showing him one thing, then another. He knew his colors and his alphabet, which he proudly said for her. He counted to fifty, before telling her that he liked to color. She asked him to color a picture for her, and he did, staying within the lines most of the time. I sat down on one of the small chairs and listened to their conversation. When he climbed onto her lap for her to read him a story, I knew that she'd take care of my baby and that he knew enough to attend Head Start. After the story, he asked a dozen questions, and she patiently answered each one. When we left, he hugged her and planted a wet kiss on her cheek. "Bye, Miss Fran. See you later," he said, waving goodbye.

"I'm so proud of you. You did so good. And you were so nice to say, 'Miss Fran,'" I told him, while stroking his head. He nodded and smiled.

Next, I stopped by Bertha's and asked her to ride with us to the grocery store. Along the way, she pointed out who lived where and told me something about each family. Wesley sat in her lap, looking left and right at each house that she pointed to as we passed. I learned who along the highway sent their kids to Notasulga and who sent their kids to Macon Academy or to Reeltown.

I trusted Bertha and listened carefully when she spoke about the town and its people. She'd grown up there, and she knew everyone. Her friends included those who supported Macon Academy. She was a steadfast supporter of public schools. Although she was a talker, she knew when to stay silent and listen. Bertha seemed to be one of few people who hadn't allowed desegregation of the high school in 1964 to determine with whom she associated.

When the discussion came up, she made it clear that she supported public schools, which meant that she supported desegregation and that she thought the burning of the school was a coward's way of dealing with the situation. Soon, those who took issue with her opinions stopped speaking their minds in her presence. This sort of mutual respect for one another's opinions made it possible for her to move back and forth in the two social worlds that existed when we arrived.

After shopping, I dropped her off at her house and told her that I'd bring Wesley by before eight the next morning. Hunter told her that Wesley would go to Head Start when the school year began at the end of August. Any uneasiness that I had about leaving him with Bertha or Fran disappeared that day. He'd be safe with those two women. When the school year ended, and while I worked throughout the summer, he stayed with Bertha. After our daughter, Katherine, was born, Bertha kept her year-round, until she, too, began Head Start.

Soon after coming to town, I'd been told that Bertha operated the concession stands at the football and basketball games; therefore, she dropped by the school office often with her three or four little ones, whose parents might or might not support the public schools in town. The ones who could walk would wander behind her like chicks, following a mother hen. Usually, she had the smallest child on a hip or in a stroller. I never saw a child who didn't love her and cling to her.

* * * * * * *

It didn't take me long to understand the sound of relief that I heard in Stella's voice when she spoke about quitting her job as secretary at the school and moving away to Dothan. As we went over the bookkeeping, the monthly attendance reports, and the cafeteria account and reports, it was evident that the financial situation at the school was a train wreck on a large scale. How in heaven's name it got that way in two short years was beyond my comprehension.

After I'd worked one month at the school, I understood. Handling money was most definitely not one of Hunter's strong points, personally or professionally.

In the first month that I worked, I looked carefully at the books and followed the money trail. Well, let me tell you, the money ran out long before the trail ran out. The books were a mess, and they told a lie. In fact, they told several lies. The entire bank account had about five hundred dollars; yet, the Home Economics account alone was supposed to have two thousand dollars. Every account on the books was in the same financial mess.

There was a large ledger for the school's many accounts, except for the cafeteria, which had its own set of books. The elementary school operated out of the general fund account. The accounts were broken down in the ledger. For example, each club had an account, and there were accounts for the junior and senior classes, the cheerleaders, various clubs, the athletic program, and the general fund. But the bank had only one account for all of those accounts that were in the ledger. In other words, the bank didn't recognize or care about what was written in the ledger. As far as the bank was concerned, the school had only one account.

I could only wonder why no one was worried. It worried me. I thought that some people at the central office must be aware of the finances at the school, but, perhaps, Hunter was given free rein. It seemed that he could do as he pleased with the funds. It was another one of those issues that you didn't question in too much depth. Maybe, after the school was rebuilt, it was all about making the school survive. Other things could wait, but I hadn't been trained to make books lie. If I was off a penny, I found that penny. I didn't like lying books.

I soon learned where the money was going. Hunter spent whatever he wanted, as if the school had unlimited funds. In October, he took the football team to Tuscaloosa to attend an Alabama game. He informed me after the plans were made. The trip involved taking a bus, several cars, and four or five grown men. Naturally, Winston was included and didn't seem to hear my complaints about money. They left town before dawn. Hunter planned for them to eat two meals each day. It was a blessing that Hunter managed to get free tickets to the game for everyone. Still, we were talking about spending lots of money. The athletic department didn't have the money, so it was coming from the Home Economics account, which told another lie about its balance.

My question to Hunter was, "Why didn't you just take the team to see an Auburn game? It's just down the road. Less than fifteen minutes. And everyone could eat at McDonald's."

"Marley Jane, are you serious? I wanted those boys to see a real game," he replied, as if I didn't have a lick of football sense. Maybe not, but I knew money.

"Did it help them win last Friday's game?" I asked.

"You're a real smarty pants. You know that?" he jabbed back at me.

Near the end of the school year, Hunter decided that the faculty had worked really hard, and they needed to be rewarded. I can tell you that there isn't one teacher, anywhere, who doesn't think that he or she deserves a reward for hard work. Even the lazy ones. Also, everyone was so totally in the dark. No one had a clue about who would be paying for those steak dinners. The Beta Club didn't know that they'd be footing the bill.

I worried constantly about the books. "Isn't it against the law? Could Hunter go to jail?" I asked myself. I pictured the two of us, being led away in handcuffs, in balls and chains. One chain going from Hunter's left ankle to my tiny little right ankle. I didn't want to go to prison. I didn't believe that I was the prison type. I probably wouldn't do too well there, but I knew that I wouldn't cry too often. I've also never walked away from a problem that seemed to repress someone or some positive idea. Since I come from a family of eight kids, I know how to fight, how to survive. My siblings and I learned that lesson at an early age. Still, prison is full of people who know how to fight and survive a hell of a lot better than I.

I repeatedly expressed my concerns about the financial situation to Winston, who dismissed me with a laugh, saying, "Well, you know how Hunter is. Just learn to work with it. Do the best that you can. That's all anybody expects." It was clear that he didn't grasp the problem, possibly due to a lack of comprehension about money, or that he just didn't want to listen.

"Work with it? How am I supposed to work with it when funds are being misused, short of going to the authorities?" I asked, with agitation. "I've got to find another job." Winston just sighed and shrugged his shoulders. It was "Winston speak," which meant the subject was closed to further discussion.

It was the third week of July when I told Winston that I was going to tell Hunter the following week that I could no longer work for him. I planned to make up some excuse. Winston sighed and shrugged his shoulders, like he always did when he disagreed with me or didn't want to talk about the subject. He knew not to argue, and I think by then, he was beginning to realize the full gist of the problem.

Chapter 23

I began to plan the speech that I'd give to Hunter on Monday. On Sunday afternoon, he pulled into our driveway. Before I closed the door behind him, he told us that he had some news. We gathered around the kitchen table, and I poured coffee. Hunter took a long sip and let out a sigh. We waited for him to speak, but we weren't prepared for what he told us.

He was leaving, going further south. "I'm taking a school, near the Mississippi line, with lots of problems. There's a constant teacher and principal turnover. The board members feel like they're flipping pancakes. They told me they need someone who's not afraid of a challenge," he said, as he twirled the cup in his big hands. "It's time for me to move on. I've been talking to the superintendent there for months. It looks like a really good deal, and we'll be close to the Alabama campus. I'll be able to attend more Bama games." In my head, I saw a map of Alabama and the town. It didn't appear to be too close to the University of Alabama campus, but I didn't mention it.

"Man, this is sudden," Winston said in a sad tone. "We're sure going to miss you. You've done a lot for the school. When are you leaving?"

"I'll be gone by Saturday. One of the board members there has already found a job for Reba. She starts work in two weeks," he said, getting to his feet and hugging Winston. Then he hugged me. "You've done a damn good job, Marley. I drove you crazy 'bout the money sometimes. But, hell, the next principal is going to need you. I know things are in a mess, but someone new can straighten it out better than I can. As you know by now, I'm no good at that stuff." We both knew what he meant by "that stuff." There was nothing that I could say, so I said nothing.

"Take care of yourself," I whispered in his ear as he hugged me goodbye.

We followed him to the door, each of us making promises to stay in touch. We watched as he drove away. After he was gone, we sat down at the table and talked about how tough Hunter was and how, many times, he was too raw. In those days, the public schools in Alabama were a treat for someone like Hunter. The topic of desegregation had become his oxygen. Wherever he went, he wasn't going to allow racism to win. He'd found his calling.

We had no idea that he'd been fired on Friday. It'd be decades before I was told that truth. The individual who cut Hunter's final check that Friday told me almost forty years later.

Hunter and Reba were gone by the next Saturday.

The following week, Mr. Watson brought Nathan S. Bridges into my office and told me that he'd be my new boss. By appearances, Mr. Bridges wasn't a Hunter. I smiled at a rotund, short man, who wore thick, dark-rimmed glasses. His hair was the color of pure snow and his clear blue eyes were bottomless sparkling pools. His hair grew back from his forehead and lay in curls on his neck. His rosy fat cheeks reminded me of Santa Claus, and he appeared to be as jolly.

He was very talkative and told me that he was also a Baptist preacher, with a church in Auburn. I learned immediately that he'd continue to live in Auburn, not move to Notasulga. Those two things told me something about him. This man was used to getting his way. I sensed that he knew how to talk and how to bargain. I thought, "Don't we need someone who lives in Notasulga to be hands on? I'm surprised he's allowed to stay in Auburn." It wasn't my call.

As they prepared to leave, Mr. Bridges turned to me, "Mrs. Steele, I'll be here at seven-thirty in the morning. Be here early. We're going over the books."

Now, I knew three things about him. "Oh, Lord!" I whispered to myself.

There are days that you know the winds of time are blowing in change. You give a sigh of relief and prepare yourself to embrace the change. You release everything to a power that is beyond your mere human understanding. You let go and breathe in the freshness and newness of change. It's naural to fear the unknown, but the universe is no one's to control.

I felt that way the day I met Mr. Bridges. I liked that his blue eyes twinkled and that he appeared to be older than my daddy. Also, I believed that he was a different kind of tough than Hunter. I figured that he was tough or John Watson would never have hired him. I knew that many people at school and in town would underestimate him because of his appearance. Too, I knew that his appearance was an advantage. I was right. I doubt if too many people in the town, even today, realize what he accomplished.

Mr. Bridges took the job with the knowledge that Judge Frank Johnson had finally done what Fred Gray had asked him to do in 1964. He added every public school in Alabama that wasn't already under a court order, as defendants in the Lee v. Macon lawsuit. Every public school in the state would begin immediate desegregation. The schools had until 1972 to meet the federal guidelines for total integration. The order could possibly reopen old wounds in the town, and so many of us were tense, fearing the worst. Instead, we learned that time does, in fact, heal and take care of many things.

The date of the deadline would become one of Mr. Bridges' most important roles in education at Notasulga, making it clear that God knows whom to send at the right time. He sent one of His own, a man, like Martin L. King, Jr., who believed that God's laws came before man's laws. Mr. Bridges told me once, "You don't break God's laws to honor man's laws, and you must have a deep understanding of what God wants." Before long, I'd meet another man, my new preacher, who believed the same thing.

One day, Mr. Bridges said to me, "It isn't discrimination or hate of any kind, in any form, in any size, that God wants. A man can't claim to comprehend the mind of God and deny those basic truths. If he denies them, he fails to know God." This wasn't just any man talking about God. This was a man of God, a man who studied and preached God's word.

He was at school when I arrived the next morning at seven-thirty. He'd made a big pot of coffee, and the air conditioner was humming. I watched as he poured me a strong cup of coffee, while we exchanged small talk. We weren't really interested in tea and cookie talk, just enough to become comfortable. In less than fifteen minutes, he asked to see the ledger. "Okay, here we go," I thought to myself. "After this eye-opener, he might regret taking the job. If he can't face reality and handle it, it's best we all know now. It's too late for him to run, and the financial situation at this school is going to be a hard horse for him to ride."

The school was so badly in debt that, percentage-wise, it made the national debt seem like pennies. Think of bad. Now. Think of worse. I had no faith that it could get any worse. "Let me give you some background and bring you up-to-date so that you'll know what you're seeing," I said, hoping to soften the blow.

"Sure," he said, leaning back in his chair. "Go ahead."

I began by naming all of the organizations that were at the school. I explained how each account was broken down on the ledger and how there was only one account at the bank. Then, I got to the ugly part. Some individual accounts in the ledger indicated a high balance, but it wasn't true. At that point, he interrupted me to ask the reason. I wanted to be honest, but I also wanted to be loyal to Hunter. By now, I figured that wherever

Hunter was working, the local superintendent and board had given him absolute control. Hunter had been given a free pass, and he was using it to spend whoever's money however he chose. It was left up to Mr. Bridges to tell the sponsors of the organizations that they didn't have any funds. No money. He asked, "How much are we in debt?"

"Close to one hundred thousand," I stated in a calm tone. Close was between fifteen and twenty thousand. It was 1968, and that was a hell of a lot of money. I told him without emotion. There was an elephant in the room. Mr. Bridges needed to know the truth. "That doesn't include the cafeteria," I said, throwing more gasoline on the fire.

He got up from his chair, put his hands in his pockets, which I'd learn was a habit of his when he was thinking or talking. I watched as he walked into my office. He looked out the glass panes into the hallway. Slowly, he turned around and came back into his office. He walked to the window behind his desk and looked out for what seemed like a long time. It was a beautiful, sweaty July day, without a cloud in the sky. It wasn't eight o'clock, and the heat waves floated up from the pavement. In the distance I heard a bird singing. Mose was mowing the grass in front of the school, and I knew if I went outside, the world would smell like a freshly cut watermelon. The train whistled a drawn-out sadness in the distance. And, yet, the sound of silence was insufferable.

I didn't speak. He needed time to digest the news and time to make decisions. Finally, he turned from the window. I couldn't read his face. In a calm voice, he asked, "Do you believe in miracles?"

"Yes," was simple and truthful enough.

"So do I," he said. "I believe that God sent me here for a reason. Now, I think I know what one of the reasons is. Are you with me, Marley Jane? Because I'm going to need support. A lot of people aren't going to like how I'm about to do things."

"I'm with you. What's the plan?"

"I want a list of all our vendors. How much we owe each one. The last payment we paid each. The dates, the check numbers, the names and phone numbers. How soon can you have that ready?'

"Let's aim for lunch."

"Good, I'll go to the cafeteria and tell Mrs. West to fix us a couple of sandwiches. While you do that, I'm taking another tour."

By one o'clock, he began to call vendors. I sat in front of his desk, taking notes. His wheeling and dealing amazed me. I'd never seen anything like it, and I was soaking it all in. No one had taught me this at Opelika Business School. I was learning and loving it.

He'd call a vendor, ask to speak to the manager or owner, introduce himself, and before the person on the other end of the phone had too much time to think, he'd ask that the debt be erased. "Well, write it off as a tax deduction. That way, you'll get some money back. If you wait for us to pay the debt, you might not get much of anything. I'll be honest with you. We're broke."

If that didn't work, he'd ask that the debt be reduced. If that didn't work, he'd say, "Listen, I didn't make that debt. I'm not responsible for it. You should've known better than to keep dealing with someone who wasn't paying the bills. So, I'm not paying it. Take me to court." Then, he'd hang up the phone and wink at me. "He'll come around." There were some who didn't come around. To those vendors, we sent a letter, stating that Mr. Bridges wasn't responsible for creating the debt; therefore, he refused to pay it. They'd have to sue. No one did.

These phone calls continued for days. He kept calling the owners or managers until they were exhausted. It worked! The vendor from whom we purchased athletic equipment wrote off over thirty thousand dollars of debt. We never stopped dealing with that company. Everything that we purchased from them during Mr. Bridges' first year was paid in full by the end of the following June.

At the first faculty meeting of the school year, he explained in simple language that there was no money. Of course, all of the teachers were thinking that there was no money in the general fund. Then, he told them that he and I would meet with each sponsor and go over the account. "Meetings will start immediately after the faculty meeting. I'll call each of the sponsors into my office, one by one," he informed them, before moving on to another topic. I looked around the room at all of the teachers. No one seemed puzzled or worried. After all, they had no idea of their account's true balance. They were about to get a wake-up call, and they weren't going to be happy.

Mr. Bridges and I wanted the meetings to happen quickly. We didn't want much time between each meeting. That would allow for too much gossip. Make it quick and finish it. I warned him not to bad-mouth Hunter. The faculty loved him, and any negative comments would cause them to turn on Mr. Bridges.

One by one, we met with the sponsors and broke the bad news. A few of the women cried. A few of the men cursed and made demands. "Hey," I'm thinking, "it's a rung bell. It is what it is. No one's happy."

Mr. Bridges promised that he'd have each sponsor's money replaced by the end of the year. I prayed that he was right, but, to tell the truth, I wasn't so sure I believed that, in spite of the fact that I told him I believed in miracles. After all, God doesn't expect us to be stupid and make outlandish promises that we might not be able to keep.

Even today, I can't believe Mr. Bridges was able to keep his promise. At the end of the year, the books were in the black for the first time since the school had been rebuilt. Vendors were being paid, and they knew that they'd better have a purchase order, signed by Mr. Bridges, before they let a staff member at the school have anything.

Mr. Bridges told me to send a letter to all of the vendors, informing them that the school wouldn't be responsible for any invoices, unless they had a purchase order, signed by the principal. The letters were mailed.

The only person with whom we had trouble in regard to a purchase order was John Davis. Two months after the letters went out, I was paying bills, and I noticed that the local hardware store didn't have three purchase orders for invoices the store had sent to us. I called Mr. Davis and asked him if he had purchase orders, signed by Mr. Bridges.

"Yeah. I got the letter. Honey, I don't keep those damn things. I throw 'em in the trash," he told me, in a cold, condescending voice.

I was mad. Really mad. When I get really mad, I get really calm and my voice gets low. I'll then dance with the devil. He might beat me, but he'll know that he's been in a fight. "I don't give a damn if you strike a match to them. Understand? But I'm telling you. Today. If you and I don't have a purchase order, signed by the principal, for every invoice that you send to me, you will not be paid. And you will not be paid for the three invoices that I recently received. Do I make myself clear?" Then, I hung up the phone and told Mr. Bridges about the conversation.

"Good. No way are we paying. That's the reason I sent out the letters. I guess now he'll pay attention, when I send him a letter," he said, shaking his head. "You did what I want you to do. Don't worry about it."

"This man is the same man who told Winston that he wouldn't piss on this school if it was on fire. And his daughter-in-law is one of the third grade teachers. I don't know why we've ever done business with him," I said, still angry and upset. Mr. Bridges nodded his head. It was obvious that no one had pissed on the old school when it was burning. In some people's opinion, no one from the fire department had made much of an attempt to put out the fire. Let alone piss on it. It was one more way of someone in the town saying they didn't care if the new school burned to the ground. Division still existed, and some attitudes toward the school were the same.

Chapter 24

The first semester flew by. The football season improved. We won five games, and people were excited. Winston was on cloud nine. He believed that football taught lessons about life, hardships, and how to deal with conflict. He believed that leadership and teamwork were ingredients for the success of a school and in every aspect of life. In spite of the divisions, the team united the town. Some of the men who sent their children to Macon Academy were at the home football games when Macon Academy wasn't playing.

The football season wasn't the only thing that pleased me. When Mr. Bridges came, I'd recently learned that I was pregnant. In December, I told him that I was resigning after the baby was born. My plans were to stay home for two years. He didn't like the idea, but he began searching for a new secretary. The second week in January, he hired an older woman, Lucy Barfield, who'd worked at the Jefferson County Board of Education in Birmingham. After her husband passed away, she moved in with her daughter and son-in-law who lived in town. Mr. Bridges was thrilled, because she had just the type of experience that was needed. He was lucky. I felt good, knowing that he was no longer worried. She began working my last week on the job. I went over the books with her, introduced her to everyone, and covered as much territory as I could. At the end of the week, I reminded her that I'd be only a phone call away. Mr. Bridges was beaming when I left that Friday afternoon, near the end of January

My beautiful bald-headed daughter, whose large blue eyes looked into mine the second that she was placed in my arms, was born the next day. She barely weighed five pounds. A fragile bundle that stretched and yawned, falling asleep before she drank two ounces of milk. She slept and ate when I held her, so I had no reason to be concerned.

During my four-day stay in the hospital, Winston was only in the room once when the nurse brought Katherine to me. I shared a room with a woman whose husband seldom left. When he'd go to get food that his wife was craving, he'd ask me if I wanted anything. My answer was always, "No, thank you." I was embarrassed that Winston came late in the afternoons and stayed for only ten or fifteen minutes. When he left, there was a thick silence in the room, and I sensed their pity.

On the fourth day, the doctor told me that he was dismissing me, but Katherine would be staying. "What are you talking about? Why?" I asked in shocked. "What's wrong?" Winston wasn't there, and I called the school to tell him to pick me up. I didn't tell him that I'd be going home alone. When he arrived, I informed him that we couldn't take Katherine home because she wasn't keeping her formula down, and the doctors were still trying to determine the reason.

I went home without my baby. It was the hardest thing that I'd ever done. My feelings were so mixed that I didn't have time to get angry with Dr. Cofield for not telling me from the beginning that there was a problem. Two days later, we brought her home. I'd hold her for long periods of time or stand over the crib to watch her sleep. Unlike Wesley who loved waking up at two in the morning and being entertained for two or three hours, she slept night and day, waking up only long enough to drink two or three ounces of formula.

When she was three weeks old, Winston told me that Scarlett Redd, the new biology teacher at the high school, had invited us to dinner for the coming Saturday, along with Victor Alexander. Since they were both single, I assumed that she and Victor might be dating. I wasn't excited about taking a three-week-old baby into the cold night air, but I agreed. Victor rode with us, and I was surprised to learn that Scarlett's apartment building was next door to the hospital where I'd given birth three weeks earlier. A feeling rose up in my stomach, like I'd eaten too much greasy food.

Victor and Winston were sitting in the front seat. I was in the back, with Katherine and Wesley, who was excited about the trip. In the dark car, Winston didn't see the cold look that I gave the back of his head as we pulled into the parking lot. Thoughts ran through my head, and I tried to shut them off before we entered the apartment. As soon as we got inside, Scarlett asked Winston to help her in the kitchen, which was a strange request, considering that most women would've asked me to help. I looked at Victor's face, which gave nothing away. "What's going on?" I asked myself. "And how much does Victor know?"

As if reading my mind, he turned to me and said, "Let me hold Katherine. Is she a good baby?" I handed her to him. He began to bounce her in his arms and make goo-goo noises at her.

"Yes, she is," I said. "I've never seen you hold a baby before." Without checking myself or second-guessing, I asked, "Are you dating Scarlett?"

"No," he said in the way he had of letting someone know that he wasn't talking. When he looked at me, I saw pity in his fawn eyes. And I knew. In that moment, Scarlett told us to come to the table. Once we were seated and had begun to eat, Scarlett and Winston did all of the talking. Victor kept his head down, deeply concentrating on his food. Wesley asked one question after another that Scarlett thought was so cute. I watched closely every glance, every eye movement, and the body language of the two people sitting across the table from me. I listened for tones in their voices. I heard what I didn't want to hear, and I saw what I didn't want to see.

"It was hard for me to decide what to cook tonight," Scarlett said, with a nervous laugh, realizing that I wasn't saying much of anything. "Marley Jane, Winston ate dinner here every night that you were in the hospital. It's so close, you know. I knew he wasn't eating well at home. I hope you don't mind."

"That was so kind of you," I said, with a weak smile, wanting to tell her not to call me Marley Jane, only Marley to her. "It's just too bad that you couldn't have cooked for Wesley *and* Winston. Or did you send Wesley a doggie bag?"

Too quickly, Winston responded, "Oh, she did send food. And I appreciate what you did," he added, turning to Scarlett and flashing her a charming smile.

At that moment, Katherine began to scream. I picked her up, but she wouldn't stop. "I'm sorry, but we've got to go," I said, smiling sweetly at Scarlet. "I'm sure you understand." I gathered up bags and blankets, swaying Katherine in my right arm.

"She'll be okay in a minute. We don't want to leave the dishes and all for Scarlett," I heard Winston say, as I headed to the front door

I turned and faced him. Cold contempt and anger were written all over my face, and I knew it, but I didn't care. "We are going home. It's late. Katherine's cranky. And I'm losing my patience," I made it clear by the tone of my voice that he didn't want to continue to resist. "Victor, would you please get Wesley's coat and help him with it? Thank you, Scarlet, for an enlightening dinner." I waited by the door, watching the table.

Slowly, Winston pushed his chair back and sighed loudly. He turned to Scarlett, and said, "I'm so sorry. Can you handle the dishes?" At that moment, I wanted to ask him why he never offered to help me with the dishes. I managed to keep my mouth closed.

"Of course," she said, locking eyes with him. She felt sorry for poor Winston whose wife was a bitch. I wanted to slap the holy hell out of both of their smug faces as they were drowning in each other's eyes.

"Thank you," he said. By that time, Victor had helped Wesley with his coat and had joined me at the door. He opened the door, and we walked into the cold pitch-black night. A few stars hung loosely above our heads and a drifting silver cloud got caught on the lower hook of a slice of butter moon. We were at the car before we heard the door close behind Winston. No one spoke during the entire drive back, except for Wesley's endless chatter about the moon and stars.

After we arrived home, I got Katherine and Wesley ready for bed. Then, I stood in the hallway for a long time before I went into the living room, where Winston reclined on the sofa, watching television. I turned it off and said, "We need to talk. Where was Wesley while you were having dinner with Scarlett?"

"Listen. I think that you're overreacting to this whole thing. You've embarrassed me tonight. Someone invites you to dinner and you insult her? How cheap is that? I want you to apologize to Scarlett on Monday morning. She's alone, away from all of her family and friends. Why can't you have some sympathy for people?"

"First, of all, kiss my ass. Second, of all, where was my son, while you were spending hours with your friendless friend? Third, of all, hell will freeze over before I apologize. So don't hold your breath. Furthermore, I'm the one who should be getting an apology. And your behavior isn't cheap? You stop by to visit with me for ten minutes and run next door to be entertained by Miss Scarlett. Who's the cheap one? So, stop playing games with me. Now, where was my son?" I said in a voice so calm it scared me. "I don't give a damn why you were at Scarlett's, but I care a whole lot about where you left Wesley." That wasn't exactly true. I did care about the reason he was at her house for four nights in a row. And I wanted to know if he'd ever been there before, but I didn't ask. The jealous monster that I rarely allowed to visit me was making itself at home in my aching heart. The unexpected rage that I'd been fighting all of my life was a demon that I kept hogtied in my soul.

"I took him to Sylvia Sellers. You know the woman who lives about two houses down, on the left," he sighed, like he was exhausted. I knew that he hated to tell me. She and I didn't know one another, except to wave in passing. I'd heard too many rumors that she was addicted to legal drugs. Not someone whom I wanted to babysit my child.

"You're kidding. Right?" I asked in disbelief. "Did you just knock on her door and ask her to keep him? How do you know her?"

"I don't really know her. Yes, I did. I knocked on her door and asked her to keep him for a couple of hours. Are you satisfied? Look. He was okay."

"Why didn't you ask Bertha or someone we know?" I questioned, but I knew the answer. He didn't want any of the people whom we knew to know that he was staying out late, having dinner, after a brief visit to the hospital, with a pretty young single teacher.

"If you ever leave one of our kids alone with someone like that again, I'll leave you. And I mean it," I said, my voice so low and still that I barely heard it. I turned to leave the room. Then, I stopped and turned around to face him. "If you want to have dinner with other women, don't do it while I'm lying in a hospital bed, after having your baby. Yet, I suppose it's a step up from having a high school senior posing as your secretary." The last remark was a cheap shot, but I needed to remind him that this wasn't the first time he'd played me for a fool.

"Hey! Wait just one minute! You know that girl was older than the other seniors at Shelby High School. She was a nineteen-year-old dropout who returned to get a diploma. You know that she needed one more credit, so the principal and I agreed to let her act as my secretary. Nothing ever happened between us," he quickly shot back at me.

"No lust? Except in your heart?" I asked in a chilled sardonic tone. "Forget it, Winston. You know what? I'm beginning to reach the point where I don't care. You're never home. I understand the reasons that you're gone during the late afternoons. But what about the late nights and the weekends? You're up and gone by five o'clock on Saturdays and most Sundays you don't go to church. You don't return 'til after dark. Half of the time, I don't even know where you are or who you're with.

"I don't have a car, if anything happens." I paused for a moment and looked at the far wall in front of me. "But, that's going to change. We've got two kids now. I'm getting a car. You're not leaving us alone, stranded, any longer. I'm tired of the fact that you don't spend time with your family, that you put everyone ahead of us. It's getting worse. You use football as an excuse, but you're not coaching a football game on the weekends. And it doesn't take preparing for Friday's game until eleven o'clock, or later, four nights of the week. What about the nights when it's not football season?"

"Look, I don't need a lecture tonight. Okay? I'm tired. You're tired, too. And under lots of stress. I understand that," he said, with his head hanging and a sad, misunderstood expression on his face. He kept his head down for several minutes, thinking. He looked up, tilted his head to the right, and smiled. "We'll go next week and get you a car. You're right. You need one. What with two kids and all. Decide the day that you want to go look at cars." He walked over and hugged me. "Go on to bed. We'll talk more about the car tomorrow."

Winston kept his word, and we went the following Saturday to look at cars. I wanted a new car, but a cheap one that got good gas mileage. Off and on, throughout the months of October, November, and December, I'd looked at a 1968 Chevrolet Impala. It was a powder blue six-cylinder, four-door hardtop sedan, with lots of chrome inside and out. It had pleated tufted upholstery and door panels, with simulated walnut trim for the lower instrument panel. Since the new cars began arriving in October, the car that I liked was on sale. We drove straight to the dealership. Satisfied with the price, I drove off the lot with a car and freedom.

The days were long and slow. My comments hadn't put a dent in Winston's routine. He continued to work late at nights. Katherine slept most of the time, and Wesley was at Head Start. There was no nursery or kindergarten at that time in town. Head Start, a program that was started by Bank Street College, was the only place that young children could go to learn the basics.

Bank Street College, located in Manhattan, New York, was a tremendous influence on the policies of the federal Head Start program. The college worked closely with the federal government to make the program available to communities that needed a kindergarten or some type of educational program for preschoolers, as well as provide an atmosphere of learning for those who lived on or near the poverty level.

It seemed as if someone from Bank Street was in Macon County every month. They'd observe, evaluate, talk with educators, and document. Later, they'd be back, to improve or to make suggestions. They were interesting, well-informed people from another world. They knew their subject, and they knew the history of the county.

* * * * * * *

Mr. Bridges called me the second week of February. "You've got to come back to work. This woman doesn't know anything. Every monthly report—the attendance report, the financial report, and the cafeteria report—that she sent to Tuskegee was wrong. Bo sent all of them back. She doesn't know how to deduct Social Security from the cafeteria workers' paychecks. It's a mess in this office."

I said, "Mr. Bridges, I can't come back. Katherine isn't even a month old. I won't leave her. She's too young for me to leave her."

He got quiet. "Okay. How about you do the books at home? I'll bring everything to you, every day. You can pay the bills, too. I tell you what. Think about it tonight. Marley Jane, don't let me down. I'm depending on you."

"I'll think about it," I meekly responded. The conversation wore me out. The pay that he offered was good, and we needed the money. Katherine was a good baby, and I did have lots of time on my hands. Still . . . I was enjoying being home with her. I'd check on her every two hours to make certain that she was breathing. She'd sleep for hours, wake up and drink very little milk. Without any fuss, she'd go back to sleep.

So, I decided that I had enough time to do the school's books at home. When Mr. Bridges called to get my answer, I said, "Yes," and we agreed how it'd best work for both of us. I told him that I'd only keep the books until the end of the school year. By that time, he could find someone else. He said, "We'll see." Well, that should've been my warning.

As it turned out, I was back as school secretary at the beginning of the next school term. It'd be a month before Bertha could begin taking care of Katherine. "Don't worry bout it, Marley Jane," Mr. Bridges told me. "You bring Katherine to school with you. When she's not sleeping, I'll take care of her while you work."

I thought, "Is this man for real? It's a school, where anything can happen at any time." True, we didn't have many fights or serious issues at the school, but you never knew what an angry kid or an angry parent would do.

Guess who won that round? Mr. Bridges had a habit of getting his way. He never took "No" for an answer. In his own way, he was just as determined as Hunter to make things work. He saved the school from a financial disaster, and he returned every dime to every account. The company that delivered milk was no longer threatening to stop delivery. They were paid monthly. Everyone was being paid, thanks to vendors who'd reduced debts or erased them, and thanks to Mr. Bridges' good financial sense.

* * * * * * *

The cafeteria workers didn't make much money. By the time that social security was deducted, their checks were small. Willie Mae, in addition to working in the school cafeteria, took in laundry. Each Monday, I'd bring her a washed load of laundry to iron. The next day she'd return the sweet smelling clothes to me before the first bell rang. On Saturdays, she'd often go with Mose to the Jenkins, to help Jewel with washing and ironing. During the summer months, she'd help with the vegetable garden. She and Jewel would pick them, shell them, and can them. Sometimes, Bertha and I would stop for a visit. The four of us would sit in rockers on the back porch, sipping tart lemonade from tall sweaty glasses, while we shelled and talked, as the sun traveled from the East and around the side of the house to the West, where we sat.

We covered almost every topic under the sun. We talked about our children, about life in general. And we talked about our school and community. Often, Jewel and Willie Mae would talk about the year that the school desegregated. Usually, I listened, not asking many questions. I told them that I'd overheard two young women, years back, talking about the burning of the school. They were the only ones in town whom I ever told about that awful conversation so long ago. Sometimes, we gossiped about the townspeople, but we always discussed what was happening at the schools. Politics was another favorite topic.

Most of our talk in 1968 concerned the recent ruling that'd been handed down from the District Circuit Court. Most people in the state had heard of Judge Frank Johnson's ruling, regarding desegregation of all public schools in the state. The deadline for compliance with the federal guidelines would be 1972.

Two years after Lee v. Macon was issued, Alabama had made little progress toward integrating all public institutions of education, but the seed that Fred Gray planted in Judge Johnson's mind in 1963 was beginning to mature into a very strong, robust plant. Johnson knew that state officials were controlling public schools; therefore, on March 22, 1967, he issued a ruling that expanded Lee v. Macon to include every public school system in the state that wasn't already under court order. There were approximately ninety-six school districts named in the ruling. Johnson ordered the Alabama governor and educational officials to "take affirmative action to disestablish all state enforced or encouraged public school segregation."

The ruling consisted of twenty-eight pages and stated that former state superintendent Austin Meadows and Governor George Wallace had made attempts to "flout every effort to make the 14th Amendment a meaningful reality to Negro school children in Alabama." Johnson went on to state that they had used their influence to prevent desegregation and to maintain a dual school system. He stated that the State of Alabama and the defendant state officials were under "an affirmative Constitutional duty to take whatever corrective action is necessary." He instructed state superintendent Ernest Stone to notify all school districts in the State of Alabama of the order and to comply with all submitted plans for desegregation, in a reasonable period of time, and submit that to the court.

Those of us affiliated with the Notasulga schools were already having meetings with parents and discussing means of meeting the guidelines. This would continue through the deadline and beyond, in hopes that we wouldn't lose a single white student. Perhaps, we'd get some white students who lived in the Lee County portion of Notasulga, within a five-mile radius of the schools. We knew that the Auburn City School System would allow them to attend Notasulga, if they chose to do so.

Chapter 25

The beginning of the next school year was a test of how far the school had progressed and how much some people in the town had changed. A positive tone was needed in order for us to comply with Judge Johnson's 1967 order. When Fred Gray asked Judge Johnson to rule on total desegregation in 1963, Judge Johnson delayed it, giving Gray only the public schools in Macon County. Considering the violence that occurred the following two years, Judge Johnson was probably wise in delaying the order.

In 1964, the year following Gray's request, violence erupted in Birmingham, and four young girls were killed at the 16th Street Baptist Church. One man who was involved in the violence was Bull Connor, the Commissioner of Public Safety in Birmingham. He was a slightly heavy-set man who had a full, fleshy face, thin tight lips, and a smirking mouth. His cold eyes looked through dark-rimmed glasses. He was another face of racism in Alabama. He used fire hoses and allowed police to use dogs to attack peaceful demonstrators. Connor did nothing to stop the brutal beatings and violence used against the marchers. He allowed the KKK to roam the streets, creating mayhem. His outrageous tactics were shown on television throughout the nation and played a large part in the passage by Congress of the Civil Rights Act of 1964.

One year later, when hell broke loose in March, 1965, during the Selma to Montgomery March, many would agree that Judge Johnson had made a wise decision in delaying complete desegregation. Where race was concerned, the state was a hotbed, and Judge Johnson knew it. Many times I questioned if Alabama would ever throw off its negative image and become a state that treated everyone with dignity and respect. Time would tell.

* * * * * * *

In the early part of 1969, John Watson was preparing Notasulga for the order that Judge Johnson had signed into law. He called Mr. Bridges in July and told him that Josephine Jacobs had been hired to teach English at Notasulga High School. She would be the first black female high school teacher. "She's the right one," he told Mr. Bridges. "She's fearless. And she's more than qualified. She's well-spoken and knows her profession." He went on to tell Mr. Bridges that she had three educated sons who were high-ranking officers in various branches of the military.

When word got out that Mrs. Jacobs would be teaching English, some people in town expressed the opinion that they didn't want a black person teaching English to their children. "For goodness sake! We're talking about teaching English. Has the superintendent lost his mind? The first black teacher at the high school should be teaching PE."

Many changes had taken place at the school and in the town, but it takes time to lose years of bias. Decades later, bias would still be a part of the culture of the South, and people would still make the same comments about blacks teaching English to white students. These people would declare that they weren't racist, that it simply was a fact that they were stating, and, after all, a fact is a fact.

So, Mrs. Jacobs began teaching high school English, and I returned to work, pushing a stroller. When one of my office aides or I wasn't taking care of Katherine, or she wasn't sleeping, Mr. Bridges was holding her, walking around school, taking care of business. It was a common sight to see rotund Mr. Bridges, carrying a bald-headed baby who had a pacifier in her mouth. A kind heart lived in that man. A load of folks in town and at the school never knew or acknowledged his kindness.

Mr. Bridges' kindness and concern for students, regardless of their race, led to an unwritten school policy. Years before there were federal programs to assist, he saw that hungry students ate. It was a tightly kept secret. Only a few of us knew the help that he gave to students who came to school hungry. At the time he became principal, the Free and Reduced Lunch Program didn't exist at our schools. Macon County was, and still is, one of the poorest counties in Alabama. A large percentage of the population, then and now, lives in poverty. So it was no surprise to us that hundreds of students in the county went to school hungry every day.

Mr. Bridges quickly identified those students who came to school with empty stomachs. He didn't care, and I didn't care, if they had so-called lazy, parents. They needed food. He expressed his belief that any educator worth a grain of salt knows that kids learn better if they're not hungry. Mr. Bridges told Mrs. West and each child's teacher that the student would go through the cafeteria line each day and receive a lunch at no cost. The school would pay. It was made clear to Mrs. West and to the teachers that nothing would be done to call attention to the fact that the students were receiving free lunches. They wouldn't be washing or drying dishes or sweeping the cafeteria floor.

One day, Winston came to Mr. Bridges and told him about one of his best football players, Johnny Ballard, who was having a hard time at home. He was an only child whose parents were both alcoholics. It was common for them to get drunk, almost daily, start fighting, and run Johnny out of the house. Regardless of the weather, he'd be forced to spend the night in the barn. His parents would be on a binge for weeks, while he lived in the barn.

Johnny was one of the nicest, best-behaved students I knew at the school. The other students loved him and protected him, but they didn't have complete knowledge of his home life. The football team knew, to some extent, and they were concerned for him. All of the teachers were concerned.

Winston and Mr. Bridges decided that Johnny would spend the night in the gym when he needed to do so or wanted to do so. A cot was placed in a corner of the boys' dressing room. Depending on the season, the gym was warm or cool. He had a television and a phone. The team knew and was supportive. Outside of those people, and myself, few others knew of Johnny's living arrangements.

The next issue was food. Johnny often came to school hungry. He wasn't allowed inside of his house to get food when his parents were drinking, unless he slipped in, late at night, while they slept. Most of the time, there wasn't any food. Mr. Bridges went to Mrs. West and told her the story. He asked her to prepare breakfast for Johnny each morning, which he'd eat at the table in the kitchen so that none of the other students would see him. After lunches were served, Mrs. West bagged food for him to take to the gym or to his house, depending on where he was staying at the time.

On the weekends, he'd come to our house or he'd go to Mose's house. He'd often go hunting or fishing with Winston. Wesley and Katherine thought they had a big brother, and he was good with both of them. One day Katherine sat on Johnny's lap, with her head on his chest and her pacifier in her mouth, as he read to them. As Johnny turned a page, Wesley placed his tiny hand on top of Johnny's large hand, with its long slender fingers. Wesley asked, "Why are you more dark than me?" Katherine removed her pacifier and looked at Johnny.

I smiled at Johnny's answer, "God had a taste for brown sugar when he made me. And He had a taste for white sugar when He made you."

Wesley gave him a careful look and said, "Oh. Read." Then, Katherine stuck her pacifier back into her mouth, looking from Wesley to Johnny.

His parents came to his graduation, proud as punch. The day after graduation, Winston and I drove him to the bus station in Tuskegee, where he boarded a bus for basic training at Fort Jackson, South Carolina. In August, he was sent to Vietnam. Five months later, he was killed in action at Laos, in wet jungle terrain, with temperatures up to one hundred twenty degrees. When we learned of his death, Winston and I cried in one another's arms. I recalled what President Johnson had said, ". . . there ain't no daylight in Vietnam. There's not a bit."

Too late for Johnny, just a week after his death, on January 15, 1973, President Nixon announced a ceasefire, and the war ended on March 29, 1973. Rather, that's when the United States ended its military involvement, no longer giving South Vietnam assistance. The war lasted almost ten years and took thousands of lives, including our Johnny's. I often thought, "Oh, if he'd just waited a while longer," but I knew that he believed he had no choice but to join the military, that it was the only door he could open for a better life that would provide him with more opportunities.

During those five months that Johnny was in Vietnam, we received letters from him. Seldom did he write about the conditions in Vietnam or about the horrors of war. Instead, they were filled with what he planned to do when he completed his tour of duty. Then, one day, we got Johnny's body, instead of a letter.

His parents asked Mr. Bridges to preach the funeral. On a windy January morning, as a gelid, piercing drizzle fell on the flag that covered the casket, ex-teachers and ex-classmates of Johnny's gathered near his grave, under a large oak tree that had naked, twisted limbs reaching toward heaven. Mr. Ballard stood tall and quiet beside the casket, holding his wife in a firm grip that kept her from succumbing to the ground, as she cried and screamed to the cloudy sky overhead, "Why? Why *my* baby? Oh! My boy. My baby boy. *Why*?" The wind carried her grief across the motionless tombstones. And refused to answer.

"Why, indeed?" I asked myself. There *was* no answer.

It was a Saturday, and after the funeral, we all returned to the school cafeteria for food, prepared by Mrs. West and Willie Mae. We honored Johnny with our memories. We laughed and cried, as Winston showed old football films of him, as the star running back. In my mind, I whispered to him, as he raced across the field to the goal post, a black and white image in a lost yesterday, "You can stop running, now, Johnny. You can rest in peace."

Chapter 26

In the late summer, just as Johnny had been getting ready to go to Vietnam, the telephone company sent a new employee, Lee Roy Wright, to service its Notasulga customers. Actually, he was the only employee of the telephone company who worked there. We were told that he'd been transferred from Butler County, near the Mississippi line. Winston and I met him at a social gathering and thought he seemed to be a nice guy. Soon, we heard the gossip that he was a member of the KKK. We didn't give too much thought to that because many of the men in town belonged to the KKK. By the early 70s, not too many people in town feared them. Most people in Macon County learned in 1963 not to hide in fear, but to come face-to-face with evil and with evil men who hid their faces. My mama once suggested, "Do they believe that the hoods will hide them from the eyes of God?"

We'd not had any problems with anyone who belonged to that ancient old boys' ego-boosting club. We didn't intend to have any problems, because we weren't going to play dead to a group of fourteen carat gold sons-of-bitches who wore dresses and didn't have the balls to uncover their faces while they carried out their evil deeds.

All of my life, growing up in Hopewell, I'd heard those dreadful words, KKK, spoken almost in a whisper. The words came out of one's mouth, laced with fear. As a child, I heard the tales of their deeds, just up the road from my house.

Many of the men in my community belonged to the club. It was a tight knot of nobodies wanting to be somebodies. Their only means of ever achieving any type of notoriety were by wearing dresses and masks, with holes for the eyes. They wanted power and control; yet, they lacked the intelligence or ambition to obtain it other than by bullying and creating fear. They wanted to be infamous among their buddies in their secret world. We've all met people like this. They're everywhere, in every organization and every work place. They're always stirring the pot, for reasons of anger, hate, or self-righteousness.

Like most bullies, they assume no one's going to dare to challenge them. They're under the mistaken notion that no one else has courage. As bullies, they expect a tough individual to be as loud and obnoxious as they are; therefore, they mistake a quiet man for a coward and are fixated on the idea that silence symbolizes fear. They mistake calmness in the midst of a storm as meekness. Sometimes, a bully is just stupid and ignorant. Daddy often said, "There's a lotta difference between stupid and ignorant. Stupid might be dumb or misguided. Ignorance can tell you something different about a person. It might be from being misinformed or uneducated in some things. It's almost as if a person can't help being stupid. Sometimes. But, he can choose not to be ignorant. Ignorance can be cured. There ain't no cure for stupid." I recalled Mama laughing.

The KKK was probably made up of men who met all of these definitions. Many of them were so-called leaders in the community. With leadership like that, many people in the communities didn't have a prayer.

As long as I'd heard stories of the KKK, I considered them to be bullies and hypocrites, doing the same thing that they were burning crosses in another man's yard for doing. I recalled when I was in grammar school, there was a family who lived about two miles west of us. The man had a mistress whom he openly saw and took frequently to his home to dine with his wife and children. The affair had been going on for years. In the darkness of night, the local KKK decided to teach the man a lesson. So, they went to his house and pulled him outside, where they beat him almost to death, in front of his wife and children.

The absolute irony of this is the fact that the leader of that local KKK was running around on his wife and had been for years. That sorry jackass didn't have just one woman—he had many. As I got older, I learned that people who behave this way are not uncommon. You begin to think they decided that by telling others how to live, giving opinions about everything under God's sun, were the surest ways to cover their own sins and convince those around them that they're the most sincere Christians who ever bowed their heads.

I agreed with Daddy, when he said, "They're just loud and deceptive. They've fine-tuned the art of lyin' and misinformin'. Their talent is playin' on the emotions of others who are often too lazy to analyze a thought, an action, or an idea."

I came to believe that those good ole boys can smell the scent of those who don't have the wherewithal to lead or who're too unintelligent or too unwilling to be an individual. They always recognize those who need to join the crowd, who can't have an independent thought, and need to follow the leader. The desire to be a part of the "in crowd" or to be accepted causes them to surrender themselves to the whim of others.

* * * * * * *

A year after Lee Roy came to town, I learned how quickly the mind can flashback to a dim memory and draw light into darkness. I came to know the true character of Lee Roy and how deceptive a person can be.

So much was happening at the high school that I didn't have too much time to question anyone's character in great detail. It seemed as if the school was constantly given a grant for one thing or another, though whatever we received came from the federal government, not from the state of Alabama. After the desegregation of the Macon County schools and after Wallace's loud proclamation that there would be no desegregation, the only real friend we had was the federal government and the programs it offered. The state didn't care if we failed. Macon County could ride to hell on top of a missile. If we failed, it'd just be further proof that Wallace and all of his followers were right. Desegregation of schools wouldn't work.

As the 1970-71 school year was coming to an end, the entire faculty at the elementary and high schools were working together to meet the 1972 deadline. Many townspeople who were concerned about a smooth transition worked with us. The issue of desegregation had once again become a part of people's dialogue in Notasulga. I believe that was one of the reasons Lee Roy began his prank calls. To tell the truth, I was so involved with the 1972 deadline that the calls didn't upset me too much, at the beginning.

Everyone was concentrating on the students who didn't attend Notasulga schools. This included many black students who were going to Tuskegee or to Loachapoka. According to the federal guidelines that'd been issued, soon they would no longer be allowed to attend a school outside of the zone in which they lived. We prepared for them, which would mean an increase in enrollment at our schools, and the majority of the new students would be black. We were hoping that "white flight" wouldn't happen as it had in the past. We did know one thing for sure. We'd not be getting any white students back from Macon Academy.

We didn't know what to expect from the people in town who didn't support the school, because if things progressed as they should, we'd have a larger percentage of black students than we'd ever had before. It'd been seven years since the school was burned. Those who wanted no part of integration had put their kids in Macon Academy or had gone to another school. By this time, many of those students who left in 1963 had graduated from high school. Some of them had younger brothers or sisters who still attended the private school. We knew that none of those students would return to Notasulga.

In our preparations, we weren't anticipating any violence or demonstrations. The school and the town were slowly coming to accept one another's position on integration of the public schools. If a few eyes batted, we weren't worried. At least, we told ourselves not to worry. Throughout the years, as the football team began to win game after game, there seemed to be an unspoken unity among those who supported the public schools and those who supported the private school. With each football victory, we saw a man or two on the sidelines who'd enrolled his kids in Macon Academy. Those men had played football at Notasulga High School, known then as Macon County High School. They were proud of their old school and the team, but they'd never bring their kids back.

In spite of the small steps toward progress, one man was going to make it evident to me that racism was alive and well, just in hiding, like the well-kept secret that it was.

Chapter 27

The year 1972 rushed in, bringing changes. Events happened during that year to make me more aware of my surroundings and my future. For the first time, I possessed the courage to take risks and to venture out, pursuing my dreams. I dared to dare, though knowing each decision required a purchase price that had nothing to do with dollars and cents.

In that year, Jimmy Carter was sworn in as Georgia's new governor. He made it clear to everyone in his state that he supported desegregation of the public schools. More and more voices from the South were echoing Carter's commitment, although many still resisted with anger. Those who exemplified anger would find other means to channel their contempt. They began to use a different language to express their disagreement and their bigotry. Others silently joined them and learned the racist language. But, once you see the face of racism, you can recognize it anywhere, at anytime, on anyone.

In the summer before Carter was sworn into office, Mr. Bridges asked Winston and Victor to help with a survey among people in the black community who were sending their children to Tuskegee schools, where the enrollment was one hundred percent black. In addition, the survey was given to people in the white community who were sending their children to Auburn public schools. No surveys, to my knowledge, were given to those who sent their children to Macon Academy. It would've been a waste of time.

The three of them spent days driving throughout the school district, talking with people, taking surveys, and encouraging people to comply with the federal guidelines and to send their children to the Notasulga public schools.

While they visited every home that had children attending schools outside of the district, others in the community, along with Winston, Mr. Bridges, and Victor, were meeting people and talking with them in their homes, in the churches, or at social events. Victor was an important factor in communicating with families within the district. They knew him and his parents. Everyone respected the Alexander family. Many listened to Victor when they wouldn't listen to anyone else.

As a result, the school year began smoothly. No fires. No rocks. No demonstrations. No violence. Maybe those who once cared no longer did.

Whatever the reason, those of us who worked at the schools, as well as everyone who supported the schools, gave a huge sigh of relief. We didn't lose one single white student. We gained those white students who lived in the Lee County area of Notasulga. All of the black students in our district who'd attended the public schools in Tuskegee enrolled at Notasulga.

Winston and I, along with the supporters of the schools, were a united team. We'd chosen a path that we believed was the right one to take and that would make a difference. What would be changed forever would be our lives, our reaction to racism, our opinions of mankind, our goals and dreams, and our children's lives.

Many years later, when Katherine was a grown woman, someone would ask her, with sarcasm, "Aren't you prejudiced about anything?"

My intelligent daughter responded in a bat of an eye, "Yeah. I'm prejudiced against anyone who's prejudiced." I knew then that Winston and I had taught our daughter an important lesson when she was a child, living in a town that was divided by racism. She absorbed the environment in which she lived and decided to take the road of equality and opportunities for all.

Let me be clear, it wasn't because everything or everyone in Notasulga was negative. It was because of the divide that'd existed at one point in time and had slowly melted into respect and tolerance by the time that we left. Once you respect someone and tolerate the fact that they think and live differently from you, you can begin to live together in peace. My children learned that valuable lesson early in their lives, as they absorbed life around them.

Time was a friend to the public schools in Notasulga. Anger faded and wounds healed. People were nicer to one another. They seemed to be more compassionate and tolerant when they socialized. The darkness slipped into light, and some people tended to forget that the darkness in some men's hearts never goes away. So, even in times of peace and tolerance, one must use caution, without anger and hate.

Sadly, I've learned that people often play pretend, because it's no longer politically correct to reveal the darkness in one's soul. One must learn to play the game. As the years rolled by, I listened and watched people; I became well-tuned to what they didn't say. A whole lot of people weren't being honest, which is probably a good thing. In the South, we call it being polite, having manners. But there's a line between being polite and lying.

The only problem with having the talent to fool others is that the deceiver begins to believe that he or she can fool anyone at any time. That's okay with me, since sooner or later that person's going to make a big mistake and step right into it.

On the surface, things were better. People were nicer. The students felt safer. Everyone interested in the survival of the public schools in town wanted integration to work. We wanted it to work in Macon County, in all of Alabama, and throughout the South. It had to work.

"Public education for the masses in America is an intricate process that is necessary for a successful democracy," Winston, who taught history, told me. "A man who believes in the Constitution accepts and practices the principles of equality of rights, opportunity, and treatment of others. The common man's voice should be as loud as the wealthy man's voice. Our voices should become clear and equal when we vote. We should be able to vote with clearness and a sense of equality, especially when we're educated and know the facts." Of course, I knew that didn't always happen. Too often, emotions make decisions.

I learned soon enough that too many people don't want to know the facts or the truth. I recalled a conversation that I'd had with Clyde Owens. He said, "The facts or the truth could change some folks' entire world-view. Everything and everyone in their world of knowledge might be turned upside down. Some people fear change like they fear a raging madman. We've seen so many examples of that fear. Fear of the unknown has always presented a dilemma for many people."

When I thought of change, I recalled a sermon I once heard. The minister said that his response to change and the unknown was that God didn't put us on earth to live in darkness and ignorance, to judge, to walk narrow paths, or to hide ourselves inside our limited visions. He preached about embracing changes that were positive, and he demonstrated Christian beliefs.

Going to Notasulga forced Winston and me to deal with a truth that had America in turmoil. We had a choice to embrace the truth, or to allow racism to darken our souls. We chose truth. We accepted change and walked into the unknown, trusting in God and His righteousness. Although I must admit, I wasn't eager to walk into that unknown. God was watching, and I hoped we didn't fail Him. The change that came to Notasulga prepared the two of us for many changes that would influence our later lives and how we accepted that change. Our experiences in Notasulga prepared us to embrace what was right in regard to many topics that before we'd not given much thought to or that we didn't completely comprehend.

* * * * * * *

The summer of 1972 was flying on a weak wing, headed to its end. Football practice had begun. The mysterious phone calls, which Winston and I had been receiving for almost a year, were still coming, twenty-four-seven. They came most often when I was alone with the kids. I told Winston that whoever was making the calls had to have access to a phone every hour of every day.

Winston was at football practice, which was coming to an end for the day, and I was at home with the kids when the phone rang. I knew it was another one of those calls. When I spoke, there was the usual silence. Whoever was calling never hung up the phone before I did. Many times the receiver at the caller's end would stay off the hook for long periods of time, meaning that I couldn't call out.

No response. I hung up the phone. In a few minutes, I picked up the receiver. The line was still open, and I heard a sound that I'd heard long ago and had never forgotten. I can duplicate it to this day. It's a soft sound that you can make by placing your tongue on the left side of the roof of your mouth, just behind, and slightly above, your back teeth. The steady clicks vibrated in my ear.

Click.click.click..clickclick..click..clickclickclick.

Just like that I knew the man who was making the calls. He was the only person in town who had a key to the building that he was in at the moment. There was only one building of its kind in town. I had a flashback and could see what was inside the building. It served only one purpose, and the telephone company owned it.

Not long after Winston and I moved to Ashland, I went to work for Judge Wilbur Farr, who owned the telephone company that serviced Clay, Cleburne, and Randolph counties. One day, the office staff was sitting around talking, and I said how amazing it was that the company could gather so much information from one phone call.

Judge Farr said to one of the men, "Hoyt, take Marley Jane over to the building and show her how it all works."

We drove to a block building that I saw each day as I walked to work. I knew that the building belonged to Judge Farr, but I had no idea what was inside. The door was steel. There were no windows. Hoyt told me that only certain people had a key to the building. He opened the door, and it was like something out of a movie. There were wires on every wall, from floor to ceiling. Wires were even on the ceiling. Little lights like fireflies were running along all of the wires. In places, it looked like a picture of the Earth, taken at night from outer space.

The only sound was clickclickclick...clickclick...click...clickclickclick. The soft sound filled the room and vibrated in the open space, while thousands of tiny lights danced across the room and over the ceiling. I was looking at a dark heaven filled with flying stars.

Hoyt said, "I'm going to point here at this light, and I want you to watch it as it moves along the wire." I watched in amazement as the blinking light traveled along the wire, until it stopped.

"What you just saw was a phone call, being made from here to here," he told me, pointing at one location, then another. "I can now find out who made the call and who they called. I can find out how long they talked by standing here and watching or I can look up the record." Next, he told me how the data was collected and how they could trace a call. It was one of the most interesting field trips that I ever took.

The sights and sounds in that room never left my memory, and I had the flashback as I listened now and uncovered the secret of the man whom the telephone company had sent to our town a little more than a year ago. I didn't hang up the phone until he hung up. I called Winston. When he answered the phone, I said, "I know who's making the calls. We'll talk when you come home." After I hung up the phone, I wondered if the man had watched the light travel from my phone to the phone at the gym.

Winston and I talked late into the night and decided what we'd do. There was a possibility that our home phone was bugged, that the school phones were bugged, or that many phones in town were bugged. We couldn't talk openly over the phone with anyone, but there'd be three important parties that Winston would call, and it wouldn't matter if the phone was bugged and the devil was listening to what he had to say.

The next day, Winston called the Interstate Telephone Commissioner and gave the details of the phone calls that we'd been receiving for months. He explained how I recognized the sound in the background. After taking notes and telling Winston that action would be taken, the person on the other end advised him to call the FBI. The third phone call was made to the telephone company. Lee Roy was fired immediately. He left town, and we never heard where he went or what he did.

We will never know if he learned a lesson or just become meaner and more clever.

Chapter 28

In the four years that we'd lived in the town, the First United Methodist Church still had issues. One outstanding memory about the town took root at the church. It started in July of 1971, and it ended two years later. I can't say for sure that the entire episode revolved around race, but race played a part.

A new, young, handsome minister, Stuart Jackson White, just out of Emory University, came with his wife, Rachel, his nine-year-old daughter, Crystal, and their dog. They were the ideal family. He was tall and slim, knowledgeable, and friendly. His azure eyes and blond hair reminded me of Robert Redford. Crystal had blonde hair that she wore in pigtails. Freckles frolicked across her turned-up nose and beneath her brown eyes. Rachel was a petite brunette with shoulder-length straight hair, bangs, and large almond eyes. She worked diligently in the church and had a voice like an angel.

Some of us laughed as we spoke about the trouble that her beautiful voice was going to create with Daisy Marie Champion, who sang in the choir and also had a beautiful voice. She was an attractive tall woman who came from a prominent family. Her daddy, Woodrow Shaw, had been a leader in the church and town for decades. Some of us referred to her as "Solo Number One," because no one in the choir ever sang a solo but her. That didn't last long after Rachel arrived.

First mistake. They enrolled Crystal in Notasulga Elementary School. The Baptist church was overflowing with children who attended the public schools, but at that time, the only children in the Methodist church who attended the public schools in town were Wesley and Katherine. All of the other kids who went to the Methodist church went to Macon Academy. Wesley and Katherine were the recipients of a great deal of cruel teasing by the other children. It was still a divided town, with divided churches.

Many people in the church expressed how displeased they were with Jackson's decision to send Crystal to the public school, but he refused to change his mind, even when several people offered to pay the tuition for her to attend Macon Academy. The members of the church pressed their lips together in tight, straight lines and let it be known in a quiet manner from then on how disappointed they were with the new minister who had a mind of his own. They weren't racist—or so they said—but a man had to be crazy to send his only child, a female, into a tar pit. Plus, she'd never get a quality education. After all, everyone said that the standards had been lowered once blacks were allowed to desegregate the schools. To top it off, a black woman had been hired to teach English at the high school. People talked about how subject matter had to be watered down so that the black students could comprehend and pass, grade after grade. It was another type of racist language.

If anyone had bothered to ask, I could've told him or her that Wesley learned grammar from Mrs. Louisa Hamby, a black teacher, in first grade. She taught the students about action and linking verbs, as well as adjectives and adverbs. Wesley knew all about the different types of sentences. Math was advanced beyond the first grade. When we left Notasugla, I was afraid that rumors about the decline of pubic education after desegregation might ring with some truth, but I quickly learned just how false that rumor was. Wesley and Katherine didn't lag behind. As far as socializing in a mixed environment, they did extremely well and had a deeper understanding and respect of other races.

Second mistake. Solo Number One was no longer the only shining star in the choir. Rachel began singing solos, while Jackson played the guitar. Winston and I loved it, as much as we dreaded the drama that was taking place behind the scenes. Trouble was in the air.

It seemed that God got stuck on I-85, coming to church on Sundays. I'd think, "Hey. It's time for the sermon. Has anyone seen or heard God?" Then, I'd answer myself. "Yeah. He had a difficult time walking down the aisle through all the bad attitude."

Have you ever been in church and wondered if God just didn't want to show up, that it was simply a place He didn't want to be, but knew He had to go? I thought about that many times while I sat in church and looked around at the sour faces, wearing frowns, and tight lips, as they silently expressed disapproval of Jackson and his family. The congregation just couldn't keep their negative attitudes away from church, so they attended every Sunday, being the good Christian souls that they were, and gave a whole lot of negative attitude.

Jackson and Rachel enthusiastically supported the school. They became involved in following the federal guidelines for complete desegregation and joined committees that were formed to carry out plans to ensure success.

They were open with their beliefs, and, from the pulpit, Jackson spoke of Jesus' love and acceptance of all of mankind, of his compassion and his caring, of his belief that all men are equal in the eyes of God. He preached that God loved justice and truth, that He rejected the darkness in men's souls, and demanded that they seek the light. Jackson stepped on some toes and pissed off some important people in the church. In spite of that, he continued as if he wasn't aware of their anger or the bitter expressions painted across their faces.

Jackson, Rachel, and Crystal were invited to the social events that Winston and I attended. As the year progressed, I noticed that they were being included less and less in events that were held outside of the church, by those who supported Macon Academy. I began to overhear negative comments about Rachel singing and Jackson playing the guitar. Some people thought that it didn't reflect the beliefs of the Methodist Church and that it was too innovative. Near the end of April, several members of the church were talking about "letting him go." Others used the argument that it'd look bad for the church if they let a minister go who'd only been there for one year. That group won the argument, but they weren't really happy about the decision.

A small group of men paid Jackson and Rachel a visit in May and suggested strongly that they stop singing and playing the guitar during Sunday morning services. If not, they should include Solo Number One when they sang. Jackson smiled and told them that he'd consider it. And, he did, in fact, ask Solo Number One to sing with them on several occasions. I thought it was a nice gesture and eased some hard feelings. Solo Number One began singing more, and the tension toned down.

Chapter 29

On Friday, May 28, in the late afternoon, Crystal had her tenth birthday party on the front lawn of the parsonage. Huge balloons and ribbons were tied to tree limbs, as well as to the lamppost. A large banner with the words "Happy Birthday" was strung across the front of the porch. Two tables were brightly decorated. One held the birthday cake and the other held the birthday gifts. All of Crystal's classmates were there, as well as the kids from her Sunday school class. Everyone who'd received an invitation came, and all of the girls were invited to remain afterwards for a spend-the-night party.

Willie Mae and I helped with the party, so we arrived early to decorate. Sweet, who was Willie Mae's granddaughter and one of Crystal's classmates, as well as her best friend, jumped out of the car as soon as they arrived. She rushed to hug Crystal. As they embraced, they jumped up and down, squealing with delight. Soon, they disappeared into the house, laughing and holding hands. Crystal carried Sweet's small overnight bag.

Sweet was the only black girl in Crystal's class and one of only four black students in the fifth grade. Two of the black male students arrived by the time the first student who attended Macon Academy got there. I noticed the look of shock on Mary Lou Miler's face as she walked with her blond-haired, blue-eyed daughter up the path to the porch. Sara Grace's blond curls bounced on her back, and she carried a large gift that was wrapped in an enormous pink ribbon, while her mother carried a pink overnight bag. In my head, I gave Mary Lou a thumb's up for remaining classy and calm. She greeted everyone with enthusiasm, as she shoved the bag under the table that held the gifts. Then, she declared that she'd just love to stay and help.

In addition to Sara Grace, the three other kids from Crystal's Sunday school class were rough and tumble boys. They hung around in a tight little group as the party progressed. During a game of tag, I saw John Henry McKoon trip one of the black boys. His friends, Scotty Cole and Jimmy Lee Lewis, sniggered. I pulled John Henry, who was the ringleader and a bully, off to the side and said in a soft voice, "We're not having any of that."

"Whatcha talkin' 'bout?" he asked, with big innocent marble blue eyes that couldn't hide a twinkle.

"Tripping. Bad behavior. It's not going to happen. Do you understand?" I asked in a polite, but firm voice.

His lips stuck out. "Yeah." He walked over to his friends. They talked in low tones. Then, they began to walk away. I watched as they stepped onto the sidewalk and headed toward town, looking back over their shoulders. I was surprised that they didn't demand back the gifts they'd brought. Willie Mae came up and stood beside me, shaking her head. As I turned around, I saw Mary Lou watching the boys disappear.

When Willie Mae and I stepped onto the porch, Mary Lou asked, "Why are Scotty, John Henry, and Jimmy Lee leaving? Is something wrong? Marley Jane, don't tell me that you told those little boys to go home!"

"No," I replied in an insulted tone. "They don't want to play nice. No one told them to go home." I rolled my eyes slightly at her ridiculous suggestion.

As the sun began its descent, the kids sat on the steps, the railing, or the floor and ate cake. They watched as Crystal opened her gifts. Sara Grace was draped over her mama's left shoulder. When she placed her blond curls against her mama's perfectly styled raven waves, Mary Lou said in a soft voice to Rachel, "I'm so sorry, Rachel. But Sara Grace isn't feelin' well. I think all of the food, along with the runnin' around, has made her sick. I'm takin' her home. She's gonna hate to miss the spend-the-night party. Perhaps, next time." She stroked Sara Grace's curls and gave a sad look.

Rachel, who remained classy, said in a sugarcoated voice, "I totally understand. Don't worry, Mary Lou. I'm sure that she'll feel much better soon. We sure are going to miss her. But, we don't want the other children to catch something she might have." Looking at Crystal, she said, "Honey, carry Sara Grace's bag to the car and thank her for coming. And for the lovely gift."

Willie Mae, Rachel, and I waved as Mary Lou backed her large, shiny black station wagon out of the driveway. "I'll just bet she's sick," mumbled Willie Mae. "She ain't sick from no tummy ache. I'll tell you that."

In my most dripping Southern voice, I said, "Well, we sho' don't want the other children to catch somethin' her mama might have. Like racism. Lord, help us all and keep us Christians safe from the sin of mixed races." Willie Mae and Rachel laughed at my sarcasm.

I touched Willie Mae's arm and turned away, changing my tone. "Of course not. Just let it go. I'm surprised she stayed as long as she did." By that time, Jackson had gotten his guitar and had begun to entertain the kids with songs. Soon, they were all singing. Everyone stayed until the streetlights came on and parents came to pick up their sons. When Willie Mae and I left, the girls, happy and giggling, were discussing where they'd sleep.

The next day, Wesley and his two sidekicks, Jacob and Terri, rode their bikes out of our yard, headed to the pool. They'd had a light lunch of grilled cheese sandwiches and potato salad. It was approximately one o'clock when they rode away, wearing their bathing suits, and waving, "See you 'bout five." Katherine was on her tricycle, and we watched as they pedaled up the street, laughing and talking. The sun hung like a large halo over their heads and beat down on their already tanned bodies. I stood at the end of the driveway and watched them until they came to the end of the street and took a right. In my mind's eye, I saw them go several hundred yards, then cross the street at the caution light and take a left. When they were out of sight, we turned away and Katherine peddled as fast as she could down the driveway.

I walked halfway up the street and back, while Katherine rode her tricycle. When she was exhausted, I put her to bed for a nap. I was taking clothes out of the dryer when the kids returned about two hours later, still dripping wet.

"Y'all are back early. Did the pool dry up or did you get sent home?" I asked in a teasing manner. No one laughed. Each one of them gave me a "that ain't funny" look and walked past me, without saying a word.

They all flopped down at the kitchen table, reaching for cookies that I'd recently taken out of the oven. Terri rolled her large brown eyes and sighed, "Noooo. They closed it." She bit into a peanut butter cookie, leaving less than half in her chubby tanned hand and dropping crumbs onto the floor. Then, she shook her head, making her long pigtails sway back and forth, sending droplets of pool water over the floor.

"Okay. I give up. Why?" I asked, playing the game and reaching for a cookie.

Wesley stopped chewing and mumbled, "Crystal came to the pool and brought Sweet. And Toot Baker . . . you know who lets you in the pool . . . said, 'Can't no coloreds come in this here pool, gal. You ought to know that. Now, git.' Then, she told Crystal, 'Take yo' little colored friend and go home.' And Crystal said, 'Why can't she come in? We wanna swim.' Then, Toot said, 'Gal, didn't you hear me just tell you why? Now, git!' Then, the lifeguard came over to talk with Toot. He called the police." Wesley paused long enough to take two big bites from a cookie and continued. "I know. 'cause I stood at the counter and listened. He told me to leave. But I wouldn't. After he hung up the phone, he came and told everybody to get out of the pool. That it was closing. People started asking, 'Why?' He said, 'We got something in the pool that needs to be gotten out. And because I said so.' Everybody was mad. But I don't think everybody saw Crystal and Sweet."

Terri quickly injected, "But they saw 'em when they got outside. And some of the people was mad at 'em. That mean Toot called Sweet a colored and a gal. I mean, jeez, what's the problem? Then, the police came and told everybody to get out of the pool and go home. So, we did. We got on our bikes. Sweet was riding on the handlebars of Crystal's bike. And we was gonna go with 'em. Back to Crystal's house."

Jacob who hadn't spoken, turned his dark brown eyes to me and said, "That awful John Henry rode up beside Crystal, and reached out and shoved Sweet. And she almost fell. And he was saying nasty things to all of us, but, mostly, to Sweet."

"Yeah! When he pushed Sweet, we all got offa our bikes, and I grabbed his arm, and I twisted it behind his back 'til he begged me to stop. And I said to him, 'Boy, I'll wipe yo' butt right here on this here bridge and throw you in front of that train when it comes by. I think you better just shut yo' ugly mouth 'fore I shut it for ya.' Then, him and his buddy—that stupid Scotty Cole, who does everything that idiot John Henry tells him to do—started swinging their arms and poking their fists in the air." Terri demonstrated how she grabbed John Henry's arm and how John Henry and Scotty were swinging their arms.

Wesley added, "But the two of 'em shot us birds and called us 'nigger lovers.' And we said, 'So what? It ain't none of y'all's business.' We looked for rocks to throw at 'em, but we couldn't find none."

"Well, I'm glad of that. I don't want y'all throwing rocks at anybody," I interjected. "Or throwing anyone over a bridge."

"Jeez. I wadn't really gonna throw that idiot John Henry over the bridge," Terri said in an exhausted tone, while rolling her brown eyes to the ceiling and giggling. Which made me know that she wasn't serious. "I just wanted to scare him to death." She laughed harder, as if the idea of scaring him to death was a comedy.

"Anyway, 'bout that time, Mr. Owens came out and asked what was going on, and we told him we had to leave the pool . . ." said Wesley, who'd claimed the talking floor back from Terri.

"Yeah! And that ole Scotty Cole said, 'We had ta leave 'cause Crystal wanted to bring a nigger to the pool. And she knows ain't no niggers allowed in that there pool!' Mr. Owens told him to stop talking like that. 'I'll talk anyways I wanta talk,' said Scotty," Terri commented, with a smirk and sarcastic emphasis on each word, while she cut her eyes sideways at Wesley.

Wesley, who didn't like to be interrupted, added, "He sho' did. And Mr. Owens told 'em that they just better go on home. He made 'em leave. Then, he put Crystal's bike in the trunk of his car and told her and Sweet he was taking 'em home. Then, he told us to go straight home. And we did. Here we are."

Jacob added, "The policeman said that the pool will be closed 'til further notice and that some business had to be taken care of. I don't know what that means. Looks like we can't go swimming. But, I'm not mad at Crystal or Sweet, 'cause they just wanted to go swimming. Like everybody else."

Silence surrounded the table, as we all munched cookies. "Well, I tell you what. You all get on some dry clothes. I'll try to find out what this is all about," I said, like I didn't know. There wasn't any need to upset them further. I watched as they ran to change into dry clothes. Amidst their shoving as they rushed down the hall, trying to out talk one another, Katherine woke up. She came into the kitchen, rubbing her eyes with two small fists. Soon, the three wild ones were out the door and headed for their bikes.

"Do not go back to that pool. And I mean it!" I yelled as they headed in the direction away from town.

I heard "We're not," as they rode out of sight, singing silly songs, and weaving their bikes back and forth across the road.

As soon as they disappeared from sight, I gave Katherine a cookie and a small glass of milk. While she chewed on a cookie and sang a cartoon song, I called Rachel. The line was busy. I finished folding the clothes and putting them away.

I tried calling again. Rachel picked up the phone on the fifth ring, "Don't call this number again! Do you hear me?" I watched Katherine as she pushed a toy lawnmower in the back yard.

Before she could hang up, I said, "It's me, Marley Jane. What's going on? The kids came home from the pool and told me that the police came and closed it."

"It's a nightmare. I never should've let them go to the pool. I wasn't thinking, but it's Crystal's birthday and that was what she really wanted. I made a serious mistake by allowing her to take Sweet to the pool. Willie Mae just picked Sweet up. Clyde brought them home. He called Viola and told her that he was staying here 'til Willie Mae got Sweet. I feel so bad. It's all my fault. As you know, most all of the people in the church are already mad at us because Sweet was at the spend-the-night party."

I said, "Stop blaming yourself. What's done is done. Anyway, it's no one's business who your child chooses as friends. You can't start allowing people to make those decisions for you. Who's called you?"

"Everybody who's considered anybody in this town. One Christian lady just cursed me out. I got a threatening call from some man. The phone has been ringing for the last two hours. I'm taking it off the hook after we finish talking. How could I have been so stupid? I should've known better than to let Crystal take Sweet to that pool."

"Look, first, stop beating yourself up. Crystal is a child, without the prejudice of adults. Thank, God. You can't let her think that she's chosen the wrong friend because of the color of that friend's skin. Don't answer the phone. Would you like for me to come over?"

"No. We'll be okay. Surely no one will do anything violent," she said in an unconfident tone of voice. "Jackson called his parents. They're driving down from Birmingham in the morning to get Crystal. We're gonna let her stay with them 'til the third week in July. Then, we'll meet them at Gulf Shores and spend a week at the beach before getting ready for school. We can't take a chance on anything happening while Crystal's here. And Willie Mae's taking Sweet to her sister's house in Tuskegee."

I asked, "Will you call me, if you need us? Winston and I both will come over." Before we hung up, she assured me that she'd call, if we were needed. As I hung up the phone, I felt a wave of sickness wash over me. I stood at the sliding glass doors and watched Katherine push the lawnmower back and forth.

Next, I called Willie Mae. I heard the fear in her voice. She, better than I, knew the history of Notasulga. She wasn't upset with Rachel for allowing the girls to go to the pool. She was upset with the way things were, and she expressed her concern that things would never change. I had no way of knowing the things that she and her people had experienced, so I could only offer words of comfort and concern. She told me that Jewel called to make sure they were okay. I knew then that word had traveled like a streak of lightning and that the phone lines were as hot as blazes.

Just before we hung up, she told me that her sister was on the way from Tuskegee to get Sweet for the rest of the summer. "I don't want my baby to be here, if hell breaks loose. But she'll be close enough that I can see her.

Lord, what would I do if anything happens to my baby, my angel?" she said, and I could hear her crying softly. "I done lost her mama, Zoe, and her daddy's in the Army. You know he had to leave here after that beating Zoe and he took from those klansman when they were coming back from the Selma to Montgomery March. Oh, Jesus. When's all this mess gonna stop? I gotta keep my Sweet safe." I sensed her fear and recalled the details that she'd given me about Zoe's death.

* * * * * *

When Sweet was three, her parents, Zoe and Ash Zachery, marched from Selma to Montgomery, along with thousands of others. They drove to Montgomery and left their car at a friend's home. Then, along with others, they rode a bus to Selma. After Martin Luther King's speech at the steps of the Alabama capitol, they headed home, down I-85 to Shorter, which is a small community in Macon County. As Ash turned left, down a dirt road that'd take them the short distance to their home, they were ambushed by two truckloads of men, wearing white robes and hoods.

They had noticed that they were being followed, once they turned off I-85. Suddenly, the vehicle behind them turned its lights on bright. The lights flashed several times. Before they realized what was happening, a huge black truck flew around them and made a sharp turn, blocking Ash's car. He slammed on the brakes to keep from ramming into the truck. Men in white were packed in the bed of the truck. When the truck stopped, two of the men raised shotguns into the air and fired, while the others jumped over the sides.

Ash realized immediately that another truck, loaded with men dressed in white, was on his bumper. In the side mirror, he saw others leave the back of the truck. Soon, the car was completely surrounded with white sheets that moved ominously in the wind. At first, there'd been no sound, except the squealing of tires and the gunshots. All at once, bedlam broke out. The men began to shout, "Git outta that car, you niggers."

"We gonna teach y'all two a lesson."

"When we finish with y'all, there ain't gonna be no black left."

"Y'all won't be doin no more marchin."

Ash grabbed Zoe's hand and said in a low voice, "Stay calm. Don't talk back. I love you, Zoe." She nodded, and her large dark eyes flashed with fear.

As they looked into one another's eyes, the window beside Ash shattered and glass flew into the car. Before he could turn around, all of the other windows were being broken. Two men reached inside and unlocked the two front doors. Everything began to happen too quickly for Ash or Zoe to think. They held hands and clung to one another as they were pulled apart and out of the car. Both were dragged behind the car, in front of the burning lights of the second truck.

The beatings continued until Ash and Zoe could no longer move. Blood spilled onto the dirt road and trickled into the ditches. Terrified birds flew from the surrounding trees, looking for a safe haven.

When the full moon detached itself from a dark cloud and lit up the ground, the beatings stopped. The men stood in a circle around the young couple and joked. One man took off his hood and spit a stream of tobacco juice on each body. The others laughed. A short fat man hawked and spit up a wad of junk. Then, several other men began to spit. One large man drew back his muddy boot and kicked Ash's ribs. Five other men did the same to both bodies. To the surprise of several men, one man pulled out his pecker and pissed in Zoe's upturned face. "That bitch's mine, now," he laughed. Not too many laughed with him, and some of the men sensed that things could get even more ugly and evil.

A skinny man, who was missing several front teeth, made a cruel remark about "takin that nigger gal, just to see what that black stuff's like."

The leader stepped into the man's face and spoke in a voice of cutting steel. "We ain't that goddamn low down. You'll shut the fuck up or I'll stomp yo' ass to the center of hell. Right here on this dirt road." He turned to the men behind him and said, "Well, hell, boys, looks like the fun's over. We might as well leave." The other men turned away and headed to the trucks.

Ash was on his stomach and he lay perfectly still until he could no longer hear the trucks turning around in the middle of the road and, then, rumbling over the dirt. He lay there for five long minutes in the stillness, listening to the night sounds and feeling the cool air through his torn clothing. He hated the men and he hated himself for remaining silent while they treated his wife like trash. Although his eyes were swollen and almost completely closed, he slowly turned his painful neck to look for Zoe. She lay in a twisted position, about four feet away, on her back. Her head was turned in his direction and her right hand reached toward him. Blood formed an outline of her body.

Tears ran down Ash's cheeks, as he held out his hand. "Zoe. I'm here. Are you okay?" He waited for an answer. There was none. "Talk to me, Baby. Please. Answer me." He started to slowly crawl toward her. When he reached her side, he took her wet hand and he knew. He raised his head to heaven and screamed. The scream split the cool dark sky and wrapped itself around the cold yellow moon, as the sound echoed forever into space. Then, there was silence

Later, he couldn't recall how long he lay beside his wife, mindless of the blood beneath him. Finally, his neighbor, Joshua Huguley, who was returning home from the second shift at the Opelika cotton mill, suddenly stopped his car about seven feet from the bodies. Mr. Huguley was a man in his sixties. He'd seen a lot of beatings, but he'd never seen anything like what he saw in the road. Once he was out of the car and close to the bodies, he realized it was Ash and Zoe. He took one look at Zoe and knew she was gone.

As he bent down to Ash, he said, "Boy, it's me. Joshua Huguley. Can you hear me? We gotta git you two in the car and git outta here. Can you stand, if I help you?"

Ash's eyes were so badly swollen that he could only see the outline of Mr. Huguley. His mouth felt like cotton, and he didn't know if he'd ever be able to open it again, but he managed, "Yes, sir."

Somehow Mr. Huguley got Ash to his feet. Ash's legs wobbled and shook, but he didn't fall. With his right arm across Mr. Huguley's left shoulder, he leaned into the older man. It seemed as if it took forever to get Ash to the passenger's side of the front seat. When he bent to get into the car, he bit his lip from a pain that shot across his back. "We can't leave her. I won't leave her," he whispered to Mr. Huguley. His voice held notes of anger, sadness, and love.

"Boy, you think I'm stupid? Damn right, we ain't gonna leave her. I'm gittin' her in the back seat. Gonna take her home. Call her mama. After that, we'll decide what needs to be done." He closed Ash's door, opened the back door, and walked to the lifeless body. He gently lifted Zoe's body, carefully carried her to the car, and softly laid her on the back seat. "We going home now," he said to Zoe, as he pulled her dress down over her knees. To Ash, he said, "Lay yo' head back. Y'all be home soon."

When Mose told Willie Mae that their daughter had been beaten to death by klansmen, she fainted in his arms. The minute she came to, opened her eyes and saw his sad face, she knew it wasn't a dream. It was a nightmare that'd haunt her for the rest of her days. She screamed, "No! Mose! Don't lie to me! How dare you say my baby's dead," and tore at her flesh, leaving dots of blood in small trails on her arms and hands. Then, she began to pound Mose's chest. He held her as best he could and took the blows that rose from deep within her pain. At last, she fell into his lap, mourning like a whipped puppy. Her body jerked, and she couldn't stop the shaking. Mose stroked her head.

Somehow, they got through the ordeal of burying Zoe. Sweet watched with a bewildered expression on her face, asking over and over for her mama. "Yo' mama's an angel now, honey bunch. She's in heaven with God," Willie Mae would say to Sweet, holding her tightly against her chest. "And she ain't never again gonna be hurt by no crazy, mean white folks," she thought to herself.

Three weeks after Zoe was laid to rest in the cemetery of Shiloh Baptist Church, where she'd gone to church her entire life, Ash came to talk with Mose and Willie Mae about his and Sweet's future. His body was beginning to heal from the attack, but his heart hadn't healed and his anger hadn't died. He'd lost weight, and his shoulders slumped as if he was an old man.

"I gotta get away from this here place 'fore I'm killed or I kill somebody. There's just so much rage inside of me that I can't control it much longer. I've done the only thing I know to do to survive and to let go of some of this here anger. Yesterday, I joined the Army. I didn't wanta tell y'all before, 'cause I didn't wanta have to argue with y'all. I'd be obliged if y'all'd take care of Sweet for me 'til I can take care of her myself. She'll be better, for now, with y'all. Her mama would want y'all to keep her," he ended with a pleading tone in his voice and holding Willie Mae's hand.

No one spoke for some time. Everyone looked at the floor. Finally, Mose stood up and placed his hand on Ash's shoulder. He looked at Willie Mae who was watching him closely. In his quiet voice, he said, "You do what you feel you gotta do. Willie Mae and me understands. We got that same rage inside both of us. You go, take all our rage, and give it to the devil. In the mean time, we'll take care of Sweet. When you're ready, come git her. We'll understand."

The following week, Ash left for boot camp. He wrote letters to Sweet, Willie Mae, and Mose, wanting to know everything that Sweet did. He constantly sent money and gifts. When he could, he came to every important event in Sweet's life. Never once did he lose touch.

Willie Mae contacted him after the pool incident. He agreed for Sweet to stay with Precision Parsons, Willie Mae's sister. Fear rushed into his head and heart, an unforgotten fear that caused him to consider that, maybe, it was time for him to bring Sweet to live with him.

* * * * * * *

I could only say, "Willie Mae, she'll be fine. But. You're doing the right thing. Crystal and Sweet are just babies and, surely, no one's going crazy because two little girls wanted to go swimming. It's not like they actually got into the pool. Let me know, if I can help or if you just want to talk." We spoke for several minutes more and hung up.

I sat with my hand still on the phone and recalled the time that Willie Mae told me about the day Sweet was born. Willie Mae and Mose were with Zoe and Ash when the nurse placed the baby in Zoe's arms. Willie Mae recalled, "She held that tiny bundle in her arms, looked all serious at me, and said, 'She's the sweetest thing that ever happened to me, Mamma. That's why I'm calling her Sweet.'"

Chapter 30

For the next several days, it seemed that everyone was talking about the pool incident. I listened but didn't comment. The preacher's phone stayed off the hook, but I dropped by to check on the family. Jackson, Rachel, and I sat at the table, drinking coffee, recalling the events of the last few days. A group of women had come by to tell Rachel how wrong she was and how poor her judgment had been. She said that she acted meek, because it seemed to be the best thing to do, given the situation. Several men talked with Jackson and warned him to "rein in his wife." They were taking a beating, but they firmly believed that there was nothing wrong with two little girls, black or white, swimming in a public pool.

It wasn't a week before the board members of the church met with Jackson, and they had a mouthful to say to him. They demanded to know what possessed him to think that he could give a birthday party on the front lawn of the parsonage, for the world to see, and invite a bunch of little colored children. If that wasn't bad enough, he had the nerve to allow a black girl to spend the night in the parsonage. That'd never happened before, and, they didn't want it to ever happen again. On top of all that, three boys, whose families were faithful members of the church, had been insulted, causing them to leave the party and walk home. It didn't matter that they lived within walking distance of the parsonage or that no one had insulted them. They questioned his ability to reason and to think rationally. They informed him that they wanted a minister who understood the values and the desires of that church. He'd overstepped his bounds, and he wouldn't be allowed to make another mistake of that magnitude.

Jackson didn't sit quietly and take a whipping. He gave as good as he got. They were told that they didn't comprehend the meaning of being a Christian and that they had absolutely no idea who Jesus Christ was. He advised them to go home and read their Bibles, with more open-mindedness, especially the New Testament. Pulling *Webster's Dictionary* off the shelf in his study, he read the definitions of tolerance to them. Next, he quoted books and verses of the Bible, which should've put them to shame, but failed to do so. It only made them more angry and more determined to "teach him a lesson."

By the end of the meeting, a war had begun. Several men in the group vowed that night to destroy that "nigger-loving preacher." It would be another year before their plan to destroy his career in the church was put into motion.

The pool stayed closed for two weeks. When it reopened, there was a large sign at the gate that read: "This is a private pool. Only those who are invited can swim in this pool." I don't know how the pool went from being public to being private. Or maybe it'd always been a private pool. I really didn't know. If it was public, I'm sure some strings were pulled and some legal action was taken. Although my kids and their friends were happy to spend the remaining days of summer swimming under the hot sun, I felt a sadness that I tried to ignore and didn't want to question in depth. I was hiding. No, I was running. Again. I was a coward, blending into the crowd, accepting the unacceptable.

* * * * * *

Several weeks after Jackson met with the leaders of the church, about forty of us gathered for an open house at our new home, which we'd purchased several months prior to the pool incident. We were located within walking distance of downtown. I'd quickly made friends with a neighbor, Sherry Stroud, who had met and married her husband while they were both serving in the Army in California. They'd moved to town one month earlier. Sherry was from upstate New York, and she brought a Yankee accent with her to Alabama.

On the day that we moved into the house, I was headed to the front door with two lamps. I almost bumped into a tall woman who stood up straight, with squared shoulders. "Here, give me those lamps. I'll sit them on the floor. Then, I'll be back to help with something else." The voice was kind, but commanding. I looked up into a round face, devoid of make-up. First, I noticed the twinkling eyes and a smile. Then I saw short straight hair that had lost its curl. "Oh, by the way. I'm Sherry Stroud."

"Thanks. I'm Marley Jane Steele. I'm glad to know you. And I promise you we'll take a break soon . . . and have a glass of tea. Is that okay?" I smiled at eyes that smiled back at me.

"Sounds good to me." She took the lamps from me and headed into the house, while I stood watching her back.

Before an hour had passed, her son and daughter, Holly and Wade, were at my house. Wesley was older than they were, so he didn't act too impressed to be meeting new neighbors, but Katherine was happy.

That was the beginning of a long friendship with one of the nicest women I've ever known. When she and I weren't working, we had coffee together almost every morning. We discussed everything from our kids to politics and beyond. Sherry was extremely intelligent.

I invited her family to the open house party. I wanted her to meet Hunter and Reba, who were spending the weekend with us. The day of the open house, Winston and Hunter took charge of setting up the tables on the lawn and hanging stings of lights from the pecan tree, while Reba and I finished making desserts. Later, we put cloths on the long table and placed candles down the middle.

People began arriving at seven. The sun was still high in the sky, moving slowly to the West, as the huge pecan tree in the backyard threw an umbrella of shade across the yard. Music played from a record player in the den and floated through the open doors into the yard, mellowing the sounds of a summer afternoon. I introduced Sherry and her family to everyone, and I was pleased that they were comfortable with the crowd.

The men grilled hamburgers, while the women prepared food in the kitchen. Once that was done, the women strolled outside and sat in a circle on the lawn, talking amongst themselves. Kids were inside and outside of the house, playing games. Bees buzzed around the rose bushes near the fence, and the sound of a dog barking several streets over interrupted the laughter now and then.

After eating, the adults remained seated at the long table, made of sawhorses and plough board, covered with a mixture of tablecloths. We discussed the upcoming school year and the impact that Judge Johnson's ruling would have on the school, as well as the community. Sherry asked several questions, and the answers made her aware of the school situation. While we talked, some of the kids jumped on the trampoline. Some hung over all parts of the swing set, while some played hide and seek. A few sat on the floor in the den, watching television.

"Well, I hope all goes well," Jackson said, looking into the neighbor's back yard. "If the meeting I had with the church board members is any indication of how things will go, it's gonna be bad."

"I've been hearing things," Clyde replied, "and I wondered how much was true. What happened in that meeting? If you don't mind talking about it."

"No, I don't mind. As a matter of fact, I think people need to know. It gives you an insight into how some of the people in this town still think," he responded. After a long pause, he told us what'd taken place and all that'd been said.

Victor spoke up, "Well, I can tell you that the people who talked with you in that meeting aren't going to change. I've lived here all of my life, and they've always been that way. It's not an easy church to deal with. Not many of the people in that church are open to new ideas. Take my word for it."

"I don't go around telling this, but I was involved in the marches in Birmingham and Selma. I saw some awful things. When you see the things that I've seen, you do one of three things. You do nothing, you become a part of the evil, or you fight against it. Rachel and I decided to fight against that type of evil. I'm not going to allow a group of old angry self-righteous white men make me act differently," Jackson said, looking around the table at each of us. His blue eyes were icy with determination.

Hunter, who'd been sitting quietly, spoke, "I wish I'd been in that meeting. I'd have cleaned the church floors with their sorry asses. I know one member of that church who was a pain in my side the whole time we lived here." He looked across the table at Clyde and said, "I had to put him in his place a couple of times. He soon learned not to mess with me." Turning to Jackson, he said, "And I bet you he was in your meeting. He never misses an opportunity to flex his muscles. Yeah. Wish I'd been in that meeting."

Winston laughed and spoke up, "Hunter, I don't think God would want you to clean His house that way. It was a good thing you weren't there."

Jackson continued, as if no one had interrupted. "If they think that they're going to tell me who my daughter can invite to her party, they better think again. Or who she can ask to stay overnight." Everyone agreed and told him that they supported him. Winking in the direction of me and Winston, he added with a smile, "Don't miss my sermon on Sunday. You're invited, Hunter. Just don't take a notion to clean the church.

"But, hey, enough about that. Let's sing," he said, standing up and walking toward his guitar, which was on a lounge chair. Returning to his chair, he strummed a few chords before he began to sing. We all joined in, clapping our hands to the gospel song that he'd chosen.

Chapter 31

Hunter and Reba left before seven o'clock Sunday morning, so they didn't hear Jackson preach a doozy of a sermon. He hit every nail on the head, and then did so again. Backs begin to stiffen as he warmed up to his sermon. I smiled to myself, as I listened and watched the faces of those around me.

The sermon began with justice, the difference between man's justice and God's justice. Pointing his finger at the congregation, Jackson bellowed from the pulpit, "No man's justice ever overrides the justice of God! Make no mistake! God's justice does not include acts of violence against others. He does not embrace racism or hate. Where there is love and justice, racism does not exist. God will not condone deeds done in His name for the selfishness of mankind. We need to make Him proud and convince Him that we are good people. That we can right a wrong! That His laws are more powerful than any of man's laws. And that His laws will always override the unjust laws of man."

As he continued, there were no "Amens," which wasn't surprising. After all, we were in a Methodist church. Clearly, Jackson wasn't being moved by his audience, but by the power of God. "Changes have taken place in Macon County and Notasulga. Across Alabama. Our ugly history is becoming a history that no one should ever forget. Yet, we need to let it go and move into the future. Letting it go means that we let go of injustice, racism, and hate. But, we should not forget the scars left on an entire nation, that revealed the most brutal side of mankind, that showed the world the evil forces of a country's people, with their bias, their hatred, their racist attitudes, their discriminating behavior. Their corrupt judicial system that consisted of judicial bias, witness perjury, and social bigotry, and their outdated laws that caused a President, a Congress, and a Senate to create and enact a Civil Rights Law, which, to this day, is resented in many parts of this state—in the entire South and in states beyond.

"Friends, that was not the first concern for civil rights. Jesus Christ talked about civil rights. About human rights. He might not have used the words 'civil rights,' but he meant the same thing. Don't believe me? Look it up in the Bible. The United States Constitution also speaks of civil rights. Yes, Jesus and the Constitution both speak of equal rights, civil rights.

"Proverbs 31:8-9 states '. . . *open your mouth, judge righteously, defend the rights of the poor and the needy.*' Isaiah 1:17 states '. . . *learn to do good; seek justice, correct oppression.*' God lives where there is justice. If you do not have justice in your hearts, you must ask yourself if God lives there. He wants us to stand up for justice and for truth. If you have denied anyone justice, you are part of the problem. If this church has ever been a part of leading the effort to deny justice or to discriminate, this church is a part of the problem. Do not allow your foolishness to tell you that the poor, the misfits, and the weak are beyond God's grace. Do not allow your self-centered image of your own holiness to think that you are above anyone or that you can look down on others and think that you walk with Christ. Remember, Christ was not bound by cultural prejudices. He fought for the oppressed. He expects you to do the same. For your own sake.

"Presidents, from both political parties, believed in the teachings of Christ. They have wanted, and signed into law, various civil rights documents. Do you really want anyone for President—or for governor—who does not want equal rights for everyone in America? If not, what does that say about you? When I say that this state has elected, again and again, leaders who did not fight for equality, it is the truth. You *know* it is the truth. That is a problem! Anyone who supported men who fought to deprive others of the same rights that they themselves enjoy is part of the problem. That is not the will of God. *No!* It is *not* the will of God!

"I'm sure that there are some—maybe in this church, right now—who do not want equal rights and justice for all, because they believe that they are a better race or group of people. I ask you to take a look at your soul and ask yourself, 'Does God like what He sees?' Christianity and equal rights go hand-in-hand. God wants fair and equal treatment for all. Any action against this is not God's way. James 2:1-7 forbids unfair treatment of anyone. To recognize the importance of civil rights is to recognize the equality of all mankind. To see God's image.

"Many in America—and in this very county—have faced poverty and injustice for years. America is not and has not always been a country that behaved as if it believed in human rights and justice for all. She is the country we love, but we should not be blinded by her faults or weaknesses or evil doings. If we do that, we cannot teach her to be or to do better. We need to work on getting it right. Getting it right for God! That means that we get it right with all of mankind. With the poor, with the weak, with those whose skins are a different color, with those who do not believe as we believe, with our neighbors . . . regardless of how close or how far, with the sinner, with our enemies. With all of God's children."

As I heard those words, I thought, "It makes me proud when we get it right. Notasulga has done better at getting it right. There's still a distance to go." I knew that racism still lived in the town. It showed itself off and on, just as it had when the men of the church met with Jackson and when people got upset about Sweet going to the pool. Yet, it no longer dominated an entire town. Racism had won a battle when the school was burned, but it'd lost the war. The burning of the school didn't prevent desegregation in the public schools. It didn't destroy an entire community's school system. God had proven that He didn't like mean.

I brought my attention back to the sermon and heard Jackson say, "Each individual's character determines events. Life is about cause and effect. It is about growth that requires faith and healing. It is about understanding one another. Understanding the man whom we call Jesus Christ. I hope that one day all of us will come to a true awareness of God's beliefs that were laid deep in our souls on the days that we were born. When that happens, we will reach a higher state of being, with awareness that we are one with God. Until we understand the reasons for our beliefs, our opinions, and our behaviors, we cannot change and move toward reaching a state of higher being, of self-actualization. It is true that few people, like Christ, reach that state. So, do not flatter yourself that you are there! Most of us have not arrived and, most likely, never will; yet, we should strive to be and to do better. We can try. Yes, we can certainly try.

"Many people will never achieve that higher level. Do you know why? My thoughts are as follows: We do not care about anyone who does not think like we think. We sort of like who we are and how we believe. We believe that we are right and the other person is wrong. We believe that we are smarter; therefore, we are right. We have never had any type of experience like the person whom we do not like, with whom we disagree, or whom we believe is lazy or sorry. We are bigots, wearing the full definition of the word like a crown. We are racists who might deny it until the cows come home, but our words and our actions tell the truth. We are overwhelmed with fear for what we do not understand, and we are too afraid to attempt to understand. We are plainly and simply ignorant. Too many people enjoy that state of being. We are narrow-minded. And I'll just say it in plain language. We're as mean as a tormented bull dog and we don't want to change.

"But. Change will come! Change will come when God wills it to do so. There is nothing that man can do to stop His force. We have seen God's will work in this very state. In this very town. We have seen improvements and positive changes. Those changes will continue, in spite of those who want things to remain forever as they were. There are more changes to come. Prepare yourselves. Bury your heads in the sand, and we will move forward without you. Stay stuck in a time warp, and you will be left behind.

"Too many allow their environments to constrain them; therefore, they cannot thrive and accept change. Flexibility is a word in a foreign language for many who are constrained by the borders of a narrow mind, by the inability to move outside the box of their comfort zones. The universe is a threat, if they are not surrounded with the people, the ideas, the bias, the anger, the whatever that has been part of their environments for their entire lives. Some people believe that comprehension of anyone or anything that is different must be eliminated from their world view. They believe if something or someone is different, it is bad or wrong. We must stop being negative and intolerant.

"Friends, the eleven reasons that I gave for not obtaining a higher level of being are not the attitudes and opinions of a real Christian. Seriously, they are not. Think about it. If you know Christ, you know he would disapprove of those things. I wish that every individual would acknowledge the evil deep within his soul for another person, for another race or culture, or for another religion. Once those are acknowledged, we can begin to change for the better—if we care about doing what is right. We do not have to become something to understand it or to love it. We just have to behave like the Christians we think we are.

"Luke 6:24-26 speaks of the beatitudes and the woes. You may think that you fall under the beatitudes, but I am here to tell you that all of you fall under the woes. Do not flatter yourself that you have arrived." He paused and stepped forward, raising his hands above his head. "Let us pray."

As he finished, I thought, "Holy moley! That talk about beatitudes and woes was a powerful weapon. I think we all got hit."

After the service, I noticed that all of the men who'd been in the meeting with Jackson left without saying a word to him. Their wives, with straight, stiff shoulders and firm jaws, followed behind them. Not a one of them looked pleased with the message they'd just heard. It was my opinion that Jackson's sermon made them madder. I could smell the odor of bitterness in the church, and I knew that a battle was about to begin.

Winston and I spoke briefly with Jackson, telling him that we enjoyed the sermon and that he'd spoken words of truth. I added, "I think it made some people angry. A minister must speak the word of God and what He wants us to do. You might not have pleased some people in church this morning, but, I think, you pleased God."

Over roast, carrots, potatoes, green beans, sweet tea, and lemon pie, Winston and I discussed Jackson's sermon. We knew that he'd lit a stick of dynamite. It'd just be a matter of time before a serious attack would be mounted against him. We didn't have any idea how serious it'd be.

The following Thursday afternoon, Jewel, Willie Mae, Bertha, Rachel, and I sat in rockers on Jewel's back porch, shelling peas. Katherine played with toys on a pallet nearby. We watched Wesley, Ernest, the youngest Jenkins boy, Crystal, and Sweet, playing near the cotton field that was approximately three hundred yards from the back porch. We could hear the tractors in the distance, as Moses and Emmitt worked in the fields. Mose had mowed the lawn that morning and the fresh smell of cut grass filled the air.

Willie Mae had spent the morning ironing for Jewel. She'd gone to Tuskegee early that morning, as the sun rose, and gotten Sweet so that she could visit with her best friend, who was home for a short visit. Willie Mae would take Sweet back to Tuskegee at the end of the day, and Crystal would return to her grandparent's home on Saturday. As we watched, they held hands, running back and forth across the yard, occasionally rolling in the grass. Looking at them, Willie Mae said, "It's so good to see those two young'uns enjoying emselves." No one spoke. We just nodded.

Rachel spoke up. "Willie Mae, I'm so sorry for what's happened. Y'all have no idea how much we've suffered . . . as well as Mose and you, Willie Mae . . . because of my poor judgment. If I could turn back the clock . . ."

"Stop!" Jewel interrupted, putting her hand under Rachel's chin and turning her face toward her. "It's over. You did what was right. There was nothing wrong in your decision. Some attitudes around here are wrong. I can tell you this. One day it'll be different. And I believe that with all of my heart. We live in the now, but things will change. One day."

I noticed that Willie Mae dropped her head, and I knew that she doubted those words. She'd waited a long time and some changes had come, but she knew there was a long road ahead. Traveling that road wouldn't be easy for some. "I just pray to the Lord that I live to see attitudes change. If I don't, maybe, Sweet will. We all just want what's best for our children. Want 'em to be happy and safe. Especially safe." She sighed and began to hum "We Shall Overcome."

Rachel joined her, singing the words to the old gospel hymn that'd been Dr. Martin Luther King's theme song. Soon, Jewel and I sang along with them. Crystal and Sweet took Katherine's hands, and they danced in a circle, trying to catch the words of the song. When we finished, we all laughed and couldn't stop laughing. The kids stopped playing and looked at us. We waved them over, and Jewel told them to come get lemonade and cookies.

They sat at our feet on the porch, as we continued to shell peas. Sweat glistened on their innocent faces. They teased one another and ate until I thought that they'd pop. Full of cookies and lemonade, they chased one another across the yard, headed to the fields to take refreshments to Mose and Emmitt.

Chapter 32

At the end of the 1972 school year, Mr. Bridges retired from education to spend more time with his wife, who wasn't well, and to become a full-time minister. No one would ever know or acknowledge the many positive changes that he helped to bring about at Notasulga. Often, I'd think that I alone really knew how much he'd done for the schools and the students. Neither he nor I ever talked about it. It was enough for both of us to know the good that he'd done.

Victor, the hometown boy, who gave up a career at Red Stone Arsenal in Huntsville, became the next principal. The new school year began and, in many ways, he was a completely different leader than Hunter or Mr. Bridges had been; yet, in some ways, he showed many of the same personality traits—determination, strong-will, and stubbornness. A sense of justice and fairness helped him make decisions. He was much quieter than the two men who'd come before him. He was more relaxed, less prone to react to his emotions, but make no mistake. React he would, if action was required.

Hunter faced an entirely different situation than the one Victor inherited. Hunter had to iron out the wrinkles and go one-on-one with the bad guys. Being a follower wasn't in his character. If he followed rules, it was because they were rules that applied equally to all races. Otherwise, he made new rules that he thought were fair and just to everyone. A person might not like the way that he enforced the rules, but he was effective. On reflection, I'd say that all Hunter, Mr. Bridges, or Victor wanted was equality and justice for everyone.

Mr. Bridges saved the school from financial ruin. The welfare of every student was his main concern. If he saw that a child had a need not being met at home or at school, he took care of it as best he could. He was there when the court order came down for full integration, and he saw that things went smoothly. Many would say that things went smoothly because no one cared anymore about those damn schools. The reason or reasons didn't matter to those of us who worked there or who supported the schools. We wanted the schools and the students to succeed. It was important that they learn to live together in a society that wasn't going to be like the one in which we'd grown up.

Now, it was up to Victor to maintain and to improve on what the other men had done before him. It'd be easier for him for many reasons. One, the worst of times had passed. Sure, many people in the town were still racists, but they were less vocal about it. The KKK was hiding, not only behind hoods, but in secret tight groups. Too, Victor was a hometown boy. People in the town had grown up with him and had gone to school with him. They knew his parents who owned a local five and dime store. The Alexanders were good people who were admired and respected by everyone, both private and public school supporters.

Those of us who'd worked at the schools for years knew how important Victor was for continued success. He'd worked hard, along with many others, to prepare for the 1972 deadline for complete desegregation. Long before he became principal, we knew that he'd given up another career in order to stay in Notasulga and support desegregation of the schools. Although he was quiet and soft-spoken, his influence was felt in every major decision. His love for the schools and for the town was apparent to all who knew him. We knew that he was concerned with every aspect of the schools and the effects that each would have on the community. He wanted the people with whom he'd grown up to accept the schools, although they might never embrace them. He didn't want divided schools in a divided town. Most of us understood that he was the right person to make that happen.

When school started in 1972, more black students enrolled, and we didn't lose one single white student. As a matter of fact, we enrolled nine new white students. No one returned from Macon Academy. That was a given, which would never change. We accepted that fact and respected people's decisions to send their children to whatever school they chose. Our schools had survived. Now, the town had to mend. That could only begin with respecting one another's decisions. We wanted the war and hostility to end.

Whatever we did at the schools, we knew that we were being watched by the townspeople, by the county, and by others. But we really were more concerned about following Judge Johnson's court order, which we believed was justice for people throughout the South.

With all of the hard work and the right attitude, we were prepared for a new school year, for a new beginning. When the first day of school arrived, no one was standing on the sidewalks throwing eggs at the buses as they drove through town. No one was talking about burning a cross in someone's yard or burning down a barn. No one was yelling obscene words at black students as they walked downtown.

There hadn't been any racial incidents at the schools since the high school was rebuilt in 1965. The faculty and students fully understood what others had fought to achieve. We valued our peaceful progression into a new era and toward a positive change in society. We wanted to move forward. We didn't want to look back in anger or fear, but we didn't want to ever forget. Many people went through the fire and survived.

Several of the women who sent their kids to Macon Academy were playing bridge once a week with those of us who worked at or supported the public schools. Once a month, four or five cars, filled with women, would leave Notasulga. We went to dinner at some restaurant out of town, in Montgomery, Auburn, Opelika, or Columbus, Georgia.

The women had reached a silent agreement. Over bridge and dinner, we came into one another's worlds. We listened and shared. We laughed at one another's jokes and stories. We showed pictures of our kids and talked about their achievements. We felt one another's sadness. Some issues, such as race, weren't often discussed. When they were, everyone was polite and respected the other person's opinion. There weren't any yelling matches or arguments. We learned what we could and couldn't discuss.

In spite of this, the people of the town were still divided into the same two groups—pro-public school or pro-private. Everyone instinctively knew to which group he or she belonged. The "other group" had gatherings or parties, and we weren't invited. The group that I moved in did the same. Still, the women in both groups shared more with one another.

The two women whom I'd overheard at Opelika Business School in 1964 played bridge and went to dinner with the rest of us. I never mentioned to either one of them what I'd overhead so long ago. We never even acknowledged that we'd attended Opelika Business School at the same time. If they remembered me, I never knew it. It was one of many things that I'd realize decades later had never been discussed, hadn't been brought into the light. Like the topic of the school burning, some other things were also off limits. When people in town talked about the burned school, they'd say, "When the school burned," not "When the school was burned," which would apply blame to the individual or individuals who set the fire and address the reasons it was set.

* * * * * * *

In the summer of 1972, I made up my mind to begin college. Winston and I talked about it for some time. I'd start Southern Union Junior College that summer quarter. I chose SUJC for several reasons. It was less expensive than Auburn University, and I could work as school secretary during the day and attend classes there at night. At that time, Auburn University, which was only a fifteen-minute drive from our home, closed shop about one-thirty or two-thirty every day. Forget Saturday classes. Thank goodness, all of that changed at Auburn. Today, you can attend a night class, a Saturday class, or an afternoon class.

I talked with Victor. He thought it was a great idea and offered to help me in any way that he could. I couldn't go to college if I didn't work. It never occurred to me to get financial aid or to get a loan at the local bank. We'd manage some way, if Victor worked with us. And he always did. While I was enrolled at SUJC, I didn't take one class that Auburn wouldn't accept. I didn't have the time or the money to waste. Each class I took had to count toward my degree when I transferred to Auburn. Two years later, I took that same determination with me to Auburn.

Chapter 33

It was near the end of October and all of the houses on our street were decorated for Halloween. Wesley loved Halloween better than Christmas, so every Halloween our front yard was the most over-decorated one on the street. Each year he tried to outdo himself, drawing his designs on notebook paper and spending weeks getting ready. I must admit that during Halloween my yard and carport sometimes looked tacky, but we let Wesley have free rein.

The days were cool, promising a bitter winter. Brightly colored leaves covered the ground and crunched as you walked across the yard. The days were shorter and several frosts had already fallen as the temperatures dropped at the peak of darkness. The wind whistled day and night through the pecan tree in the backyard.

It was after we had eaten supper on a brisk Saturday, and I had cleared the table, when Woodrow Shaw knocked on our front door. When Winston opened the door, I heard Woodrow say, "Winston, I'd like to talk with you about something."

"Sure. Come on in," I heard Winston say as he opened the door wide. "Marley Jane, would you bring us some coffee?"

I stuck my head into the room. "Hi, Woodrow. How're you doing? I'll be with y'all in a minute. How do you like your coffee?" I asked Woodrow.

"I take mine black and strong," he instructed me. I poured two cups of hot, steaming coffee, sat the cups on a tray and walked into the living room. I handed Woodrow his cup of strong coffee and turned to leave the room. "Marley Jane, don't leave," he said. "I want to talk with both of you." I got myself a cup of coffee and sat down.

After some small talk, he got to the point. George Wallace was making plans to run again for President. A great deal had happened to Wallace since 1968, when he ran for President as the American Independent Party candidate.

* * * * * * *

After listening to Woodrow for a while, I recalled a recent gathering at the Owens. Clyde and Emmitt talked about the impact that Wallace's campaign had on millions of alienated white voters. Emmitt said that it wasn't lost on GOP strategists. Clyde predicted that many politicians would adopt toned-down versions of Wallace's anti-busing, anti-federal government rhetoric, in order to get low and middle-income whites to vote Republican. Those who had issues with the federal government could be potential voters for the GOP.

Those of us who were listening agreed that it'd be one obvious factor in the South that'd change the voting pattern from Democratic to Republican. If you listened to the rhetoric, it was evident that it was already happening.

Emmitt claimed that it might take years, but the two parties in the South would switch rhetoric and guidelines that'd appeal to a majority of white Southerners or anyone outside of the South who played on the same team. "Mark my word," he said. "The Republicans will begin to sound like old Southern Democrats, during the time Wallace was a young governor. Those who were once proud to call themselves Republicans, who were against segregation, will almost disappear from the South. It'll no longer be the Party of Lincoln. That'll be a memory, and, most likely, the Southern Democratic Party will sound more like the old Republican Party."

Clyde added, "It should be an interesting switch-a-roo that'll fascinate political historians for years. Hell, I find it interesting." Clyde went on to note that in the election year of 1968, Wallace carried five Southern states and won millions of popular votes.

Emmitt, who knew a thing or two about politics, nodded and added, "Wallace didn't win the election, but he's had a huge influence on future politics. Rhetoric, which was owned exclusively by Wallace and many Southerners, is now coming out of the mouths of leaders at the top of the Republican Party. It's gonna be an eye-opener for critics of both parties who analyze political talk."

A horrible event would change the course of Wallace's life and career. On May 15, 1972, Arthur Bremer shot him five times, while he was campaigning in Laurel, Maryland. One bullet hit his spinal column, causing him to be paralyzed from the waist down for the rest of his life. As a result, he'd spend his remaining days in a wheelchair and in constant pain.

Later, Wallace would announce that he was a born-again Christian and apologize to blacks for his actions as a segregationist. He asked for their forgiveness, and they gave it to him. We got a glimpse into his clever mind, when he persuasively declared, "The old South is gone. The New South is still opposed to government regulation of our lives."

"What?" I thought to myself. "If I believe his second sentence, I can't believe his first sentence. In two sentences, side-by-side, he appeals to different audiences. Wasn't part of racism anti-government?" Yes, clever.

The votes of Alabama blacks helped elect him to his final term as Alabama governor. Once elected, he kept his promise, appointing more blacks to state positions than any Alabama governor had done or has done since.

Was Wallace a changed man who felt remorse? Was he a clever politician who knew how to win? Or was he a man who recognized the winds of change and decided to again play politics for his own benefit? It'd be left to historians to answer those questions.

I don't know how many white people believed Wallace when he said, "I was wrong. Those days are over, and they ought to be over," but, apparently, most black people believed him. I admit that I, too, believed him. At least, I wanted to believe him, to think that he'd changed. After all, if Mose and Willie Mae could forgive him, why shouldn't I?

People who'd followed Wallace's political career knew that he'd spent the majority of his political life fighting to suppress the civil rights of those whom he now asked forgiveness. Surprisingly, it wasn't the people to whom he'd denied equality who doubted his sincerity. Perhaps, they'd seen so much evil and heard so many lies in their lives that they knew when a man spoke the truth. Or, perhaps, it was a means to cut a deal and to get positions filled with blacks. Whatever it was, it helped elect Wallace governor one last time. Some people said it was the same old Wallace, being a shrewd politician who played to his audience. He knew the power of the vote, and he knew math. Blacks could carry a large percentage of the votes. Some didn't care how or why change came. Just that change took place.

* * * * * *

Woodrow talked about Wallace and the people Wallace supported or didn't support. As we listened, we realized that Woodrow was one of those Southerners who were beginning to drift away from the Democratic Party. The old faithful crowd that'd supported Wallace and his segregationist ways was taking time to reflect and project into the future, concentrating on anti-government.

Soon, it became clear that Woodrow wanted us to vote for a certain candidate. We had no intentions of voting for the man who wasn't a candidate from our party and who didn't express ideas that we supported.

"I'm expecting your support and vote for this man," Woodrow said in a tone that revealed he felt like he was in control and had more knowledge than we had.

I felt my blood getting hot, as it rushed through my veins. I waited to hear what Winston would say. In case he didn't say the right thing, I was prepared to express a very strong opinion that'd send a loud and clear message to our neighbor.

Winston crossed his left leg over his right knee and locked his hands around his left knee. He bent slightly forward and gave a soft chuckle, looking down at the floor. Time stood still. He barely raised his head and looked Woodrow in the eye. "I appreciate your opinion of this man, but Marley Jane and I don't support him. Also, Woodrow, I don't like anyone coming into my house and telling me how to vote. I'm an educated man, with enough sense to make up my own mind."

The silence was awkward, but I wanted to jump up and hug Winston. Instead, I sat still and waited.

I watched as Woodrow nodded his head, staring at, but not seeing, the picture behind the sofa. "You're right, Winston. I shouldn't have used that approach. I apologize. This won't happen again," he said, slapping his thighs.

He quickly changed the subject to the World Series, and we enjoyed a nice visit from our new neighbor. We all had an understanding and had respectfully settled the matter of voting.

When we walked him to the door, he turned and said, "Welcome to the neighborhood. We're glad to have you on our street."

It's difficult not to like a man like that.

Chapter 34

It was a busy year for my family. I was working full-time and attending college. Winston was busy with the athletic department, and he now had an assistant football coach who was also the head basketball coach. Together, they began to rebuild the high school football and basketball teams to the "Glory Years," which existed before the school was burned.

Things weren't going well for Jackson and his family. After the birthday party and the pool incident, almost everyone in the church turned their backs on the young preacher. By the end of the school year, Jackson had been minister of the church for three years. It was time to consider whether or not to ask him back. Just as we expected, he wasn't asked to return. But, that's not the bad news. This happens frequently to Methodist ministers, who often move at least every four years. The powers that be in the local church didn't want him to ever again preach in a Methodist church, anywhere in the entire world. They wanted a pound of flesh—to brand him forever.

After I became aware of their intentions, my first thought was "Now, ain't they some lovely Christian folks, full of the Holy Ghost and the spirit of righteousness and love and compassion and understanding and tolerance and forgiveness and grace and mercy? They can't just send him to another church. They want to destroy him. This is the absolute ugly of the church." In my opinion, they'd cast shame on the Methodist church and on every church that ever allowed an injustice to take place.

Winston and I weren't aware of what'd taken place for several weeks. We weren't aware of the communication between the Bishop and the leaders of our church. We were surprised when Jackson called late one Saturday afternoon and asked if he could come by to talk with us. We had no idea what he wanted to say, since he'd told us that he didn't want to mention anything over the phone.

He arrived, looking haggard and exhausted. Circles were under his eyes. His shoulders were bent as he walked slowly into the house. We sat in the living room, away from the kids who were watching television in the den. I brought steaming cups of coffee and offered cake, which no one wanted.

"I hate to bother you, but I need your help. Something terrible is happening, and I think that I'm losing the fight. I'm going down, with all of my dreams and ambitions. The very church that I love is about to destroy me," he said, in a voice that lacked energy. Then, he began to tell his story. He explained what the leaders of the church were attempting to do. He said that it looked as if they were going to be successful. He ended the story by saying, "I can't believe the hate that's gone into destroying my family and my career."

Winston and I were shocked. Sure, we'd seen how badly some of the people of the church could behave. There were still members of the church who came face-to-face with us in church every Sunday and wouldn't speak because of where we worked. It was almost inconceivable that they'd strip a minister for minor infractions or for different opinions about race.

"What can I do?" Winston asked. "Just tell me."

"I'd like for you to write a letter to the Bishop, explaining the racial atmosphere in Notasulga and in the church. Just anything that's true that you think might help me. I need a solid recommendation of the work that I've done here. For goodness sakes! I gave up a career to become a Methodist minister. My wife and daughter had to sacrifice in order for me to go to Emory. The church and my family are my life." He bent forward and put his head in his hands, as he fought to gain control, to stop the tears from coming. Winston's right arm came across Jackson's bent shoulders, while I hugged him. We sat in silence, until Jackson raised his head.

Winston patted him on the back and said, "I'll be glad to help in any way that I can. What they're doing is wrong. I'll write the letter tonight."

"Thank you. I can't tell you how much I appreciate you doing this. Maybe it will help. Thanks, again." He stood up to leave and we walked him to the door.

"I'll let you read the letter before I send it," Winston said as we reached the door.

When Jackson drove away, I turned to Winston. "I cannot believe what I just heard. Maybe he made a mistake about some people wanting him totally out of the church as a minister. How low will these people go to destroy someone?"

"Believe me, Marley Jane, I've seen people in the church do some mean things through the years. I believe everything he said," he answered, "and I'm going to start writing that letter right now." He walked off to get paper and pencil, while I carried the cups to the kitchen.

Winston wrote long into the night and finished the letter in the early morning hours. He asked me to proofread it, but I was careful not to make many changes. I wanted his voice to be heard. It was a powerful eleven page handwritten letter. Winston told it straight. He began the letter by saying that he was the son of a Methodist minister, and, in all of his years in the church, he'd never seen a church as unchristian-like as the one in Notasugla. He wrote about its racism and told about its arrogant attitudes. He explained how jealous Solo One was of Rachel. He related the incident about the birthday party and the swimming pool. The letter went on and on, listing one sin after another of that church.

After the Sunday morning sermon, Winston handed Jackson a copy of the letter. "Read it. Then, call me and let me know what you think," he told Jackson as we stood on the steps of the church. Only a few people stopped to speak with Jackson. Everyone else hurried to their cars and drove away. One man walked out of church during the middle of the sermon. Actions were speaking louder than words.

On Monday morning, Winston mailed the letter to the Bishop. Several days later, the Bishop called him. It was close to seven o'clock, and we'd just finished eating supper. When Winston answered the phone, he looked at me, raised his eyebrows and shrugged his shoulders. Next, he motioned for me to send Wesley and Katherine into another room so that he'd not be interrupted. Later, he told me, almost word-for-word, what the Bishop had said, while he listened and said very little.

"I received your letter. First, your letter was deeply moving and convincing. Second, let me thank you for providing us with another side to the story. I'd like for you to know that a decision in regard to Reverend Jackson White has been made. Thanks in part to your letter, he'll remain in the Methodist church, but he will be transferred to another church that's more in touch with his attitudes and values. We're considering whether or not some action will be taken against the Notasulga church." At the end of the phone conversation, he said to Winston, "Your letter was powerful. It helped to convince us not to remove Reverend Jackson from the church. We weren't aware of the things that have happened at Notasulga Methodist Church. Thank you for opening our eyes."

As Winston related the conversation to me, I thought, "Really, Bishop? You were simply going to take the word of a bunch of mean Christians, without investigating? Just up and throw a man out of the church?" I didn't feel too good about being a Methodist at that point.

Of course, the powers that be in the church soon learned from the Bishop that Winston had written a letter on behalf of the minister whom they wanted to destroy. They weren't too happy about the letter, but they learned that the man who coached and taught at the local public school, which most of them didn't support, refused to play when it came to the church. He knew something about the cleansing fire of God and about the teachings of Jesus Christ.

Jackson, Rachel, Crystal, and their dog left at the end of the term. Jackson was sent to a church in Birmingham that reflected his beliefs. We stayed in touch with one another for years. Jackson and Rachel were always thankful that Winston stood up for justice.

Chapter 35

When I enrolled in Auburn University in the fall of 1974, I was still secretary at the school. I had three well-trained students who were office aides, and they operated the office each day until I finished my classes. I'd leave home in the early morning for a seven o'clock class and be back at work by eleven or twelve o'clock.

I received my degree after four years of college, two years at SUJC and two years at Auburn. My dream of earning a college degree had been realized through hard work, determination, and strength of will. I'd attained my goal. I was proud and thankful of the support that I'd received from Winston and Victor.

I began my internship in January, 1976, at Reeltown High School, in Tallapoosa County. The school was our biggest football rival, and I wondered how the students would accept me. My advisor, Dr. Avery Cornwell, pulled some strings to get me there, rather than sending me to a school further away. He considered the fact that I had two young children and needed to be close to home. And I didn't need to worry about being accepted. I had a wonderful internship, supervised by an excellent English teacher. I, perhaps more than some of the students, loved to listen to her teach literature.

Before I left my position as secretary in December, 1975, Victor called me into his office and offered me the position as English teacher for the upper three grades at the high school. Josephine Jacobs was retiring. Everyone had grown to love this strong pioneer. She was intelligent, funny, and kind-hearted. Those who opposed her at the beginning hated to see her leave.

* * * * * * *

But I'm getting ahead of the story. A lot would happen before I finished college and began teaching at Notasulga High School. Something happened in August, 1975, that shook the town to its core. By this time, Notasulga, barely large enough for a spot on a map, had settled into the heartbeat of a regular small Southern town. Racial conflict wasn't a concern when it came to the schools, though it still resided in the town. Some other things occurred that made me think of the Wild West. Those things reminded me that this town still had its own code of right and wrong and how to resolve a conflict. Also, many in the town didn't consider the solution to a family or neighbor problem any of the law's business.

Notasulga epitomized the belief that government—local, state, or federal—didn't have any right to interfere in one's personal business. What they thought was personal might not be the way the legal system thought about the matter. As I'd learned, the legal system often looked the other way in Macon County.

It was a hot day, near the end of summer, before school started. The sun had risen to its highest point in the sky. It beat onto the pavement and sucked the tar up into bubbles. Leaves drooped, exhausted and shriveled like bent-over old women. Small branches on bushes lost their vitality. Thin limbs on trees sagged from the heat. The grass was a languishing body of brown. Birds stopped singing from fatigue. Time dripped with sweat.

I walked up the street to visit a neighbor. Patsy Hadaway worked as an elementary school aide. We'd become fast friends. Wit and a sense of humor were two of her best characterists. Patsy was medium height, slim, and sexy. Men were attracted to her large brown eyes that appeared to be drowsy as they blinked and fluttered when she talked. With a square-shaped face, high cheekbones, and pouty lips, she caught a man's attention. Red lips sucked a cigarette, while her liquid eyes locked with the eyes of the person to whom she was speaking. When she exhaled smoke, she'd cock her head slightly upward, and glance sideways at the person. Low, throaty laughter would wrap itself around anyone in its path.

When I arrived, she was wearing very short white shorts and a sleeveless blue shirt that was tied in a knot at her waist. Large loop earrings dangled from her tiny earlobes. She was barefoot and her auburn hair was in a ponytail. We sat down on her porch. She stretched out her tanned legs and propped her feet on the porch railing. There was a thin gold band around her slender left ankle. She lit a cigarette. "Aaahh. It feels good to relax," she said as she closed her eyes and blew out a ring of smoke. Fascinated, I watched. I didn't smoke, but her talent for creating perfect round rings amazed me.

"You know, it's nice to rest and enjoy a smoke. If it just wasn't so hot." I agreed and neither of us spoke for several minutes. "The only good thing about this heat is sunbathing. I don't get to do that as much as I'd like 'cause every time I sunbathe in the backyard that creep, who lives behind me, watches from his bathroom window." She knocked ash from the cigarette with her middle finger. Pushing a loose strand of hair from her face, she laughed and said, "The creep's probably jerking off." We laughed at the not-so-pretty mental image of her fat, bald-headed elderly neighbor pleasuring himself at her expense.

She and I rocked slowly, fanning ourselves with copies of *Ladies Home Journal*, and watching an occasional car drive by with the windows down. Wesley and Katherine, Jacob, Terri, Holly and Wade, along with Patsy's four kids, were spending the afternoon at the pool. We were looking across the street at her neighbor's house and remarking how well Woodrow kept the yard and what a very ladylike wife he had. Everyone liked Vivian who was attractive and friendly. They were the perfect married couple.

Both had been nice to my family from the first time we attended the Methodist church. Their grandchildren attended Macon Academy, and, at the time, most people in the church who supported the private school weren't speaking to us because we worked at the public school. Woodrow and Vivian didn't allow others to dictate their thinking.

Patsy made a comment about how absolutely wonderful some people's lives appeared. I nodded in agreement and asked, "Do you think that we're just a tad bit jealous?"

Laughing, she replied, "You're damn right I'm jealous. I've cried on your shoulders enough for you to know that. I don't have to tell you who runs my house. Every detail of it. I'm so sick of it. Lord, it'd be nice to have a man treat me the way Woodrow treats Vivian. I'd think that I'd died and gone to heaven."

We sit there, deep in our thoughts, sipping iced tea and watching the house across the street. I was thinking about some of the things she'd told me about her husband Parker. According to Patsy, he wanted control from the bedroom to the grocery store.

Just as I was about to say something regarding what makes a perfect family, Woodrow's truck came flying into his driveway. He almost fell in his hurry to get out. We bent forward and stopped rocking to watch as he raced to the side door. We paused fanning, and the magazines flopped on our chests. A quiet settled over the porch, and we could hear the wind chimes as a slight breeze gently pushed them back and forth. Our total attention focused on the perfect house across the street. We watched and waited. We didn't know for what, but something was going to happen, and it was going to be important. The atmosphere had gotten heavier. Breathing was more labored. Both of us were tense as we waited, looking through waves of summer heat, into the window frame of others' lives.

We didn't have long to wait. Woodrow dashed out of the house. Vivian was behind him, reaching for his shirt, saying, "No! Woodrow. Don't!" She wasn't talking loud, but her voice easily carried across the road to us. He jerked away from her pleading hand and got into the truck. He slammed the truck into reverse, and it came flying backwards into the street, headed back the way it'd come. Back to town.

Vivian hung her head and walked slowly back into the house. Her shoulders dropped, and she looked like an old woman whose last bit of energy had suddenly disappeared. Patsy and I couldn't move, couldn't speak.

"Wonder what that was all about," Patsy quietly commented.

"I don't know, but it's not good. Whatever it is," I said solemnly.

We sat in silence for some time, thinking and watching the house across the street. We really didn't want to be a part of whatever had just happened. Something had taken place that would change lives, but we didn't know what, when, or how. We didn't realize it at the time, but we'd seen a decision made that could never be recalled. The deed would be done as we sat in deep thought. We knew that a horror lay dormant in the thick heat of summer, but we didn't know how it'd turn the heat into a chill.

Suddenly, the train made a long loud sound that was like a scream, going on and on, all the way to Loachapoka. It seemed like the whistle would never stop screaming. The sound just rested on the thick heat waves and wouldn't fade away or grow dim.

It must have been twenty minutes later when a car came flying into the driveway across the road. Daisy Marie jumped out and rushed into the house. Other cars began to pull into the driveway. Some of the cars we recognized. Woodrow's truck didn't return.

"My, Lord, what do you think's happened?" Patsy asked. I shook my head. "It's got to be bad," she added. "All of those cars flying up and people running into the house can't be good at all. And where's Woodrow?"

"I don't know," I finally spoke. "I've no idea, but I don't think it's a good thing. This isn't a time when you walk over to a neighbor's house to have coffee and get the latest news."

Midday had become the afternoon. It was time for me to go home. Winston had gone to the barbershop. He should've returned by now, but he never paid attention to time. I stood up and told Patsy that I'd talk with her later. Walking home, I felt a knot in my stomach. I felt sick, and I knew it wasn't from the heat. Wesley and Katherine would be home soon. I needed to start supper. Almost as soon as I walked into the house, Winston drove into the driveway. I took one look at his face, drained of color, and knew that something horrible had happened. "What's wrong?" I asked, afraid to hear the answer.

"Woodrow just killed his brother." He put his hand over his eyes. "He walked into the filling station and shot him." Winston sat down at the table and held his head in his hands. "We heard the shot in the barbershop and ran next door. Woodrow was standing, just inside the door. His brother, Lennie, was beside the counter. On the floor. Dead. It looked like he'd walked from behind the counter.

"Woodrow said, 'He pulled a knife on me, and I had to defend myself.' My God!" Winston raised his head and took a deep breath of air, exhaling slowly. "Blood was all over the floor. Woodrow was just standing there. Holding the gun." He was silent for a moment. "I don't believe it. They'd had an argument. Lennie was drunk. Woodrow said he told him to go home. To close the filling station. Woodrow didn't want him working drunk. Lennie wouldn't go."

I fixed two glasses of iced tea. We sat at the table, holding hands and talking. I told him what Patsy and I saw. It didn't take a genius to figure out how it all unfolded. We knew Woodrow had come home to get the gun, which made it more serious. It wasn't an accident, and we wondered if Woodrow really had to defend himself. He was mad, in a rage. He'd been the head of the family for years. When he spoke, his brothers listened.

It was all settled that night at city hall. The sheriff came. I'm sure that I was told who all was present, but, if so, I don't remember. There wouldn't be a grand jury to listen and to decide on a "yes" or a "no" vote. No investigation would ever take place. No one, but Woodrow, would ever be questioned. No one would gather evidence. Lennie's death was declared self-defense that night, in a small room, with Woodrow and a handful of men who formed a tight powerful group. Woodrow would never face his peers in a courtroom. He'd never stand before a judge. He'd never serve time in prison, nor even spend one night in the town jail. But, for the rest of his remaining five years on earth, he faced a higher power, the Judge who always makes the final decision.

His prison would be in his mind and in his heart, where his shame and guilt lived. We watched from Sunday to Sunday, as his face became tired, as sadness settled into the pores and lines of his skin. He seemed to age overnight and with every passing day. His shoulders were no longer proud and squared; his posture became bent. He no longer laughed and joked. Once a strong leader in the town, he was no longer involved.

I recalled what I'd heard about Woodrow. He was a wealthy farmer who worked hard and loved his family. He had three younger brothers, and he was the only one of them who'd long ago given up drinking. The rumor was that the four brothers had all been wild when they were teenagers. Woodrow made a complete turn and helped to make his brothers financially sound, but they, unlike him, never stopped drinking. They owned businesses and property, and each brother was responsible for some aspect of those businesses or property.

Woodrow wasn't the only one in Notasulga who took the law into his own hands. This sometimes seemed to be a pattern in the community. It appeared that some people were used to handling situations in an outlaw manner.

Several days after Woodrow killed his brother, Winston and I were discussing again the events of that fatal day. He recalled our ex-landlord, Hunky Sharp, who lived about eight hundred feet from our back door, when we lived in the country. He, like Woodrow, was a cattleman and a farmer. Some of his land on the other side of town was adjacent to land that Davis owned. Apparently, Hunky and Davis had been, for years, throwing rocks back and forth over the fence that divided their land. Davis started the rock throwing. Sailing large and small rocks across the fence onto Hunky's pasture. He told Davis several times to stop. Davis refused. Hunky would throw the rocks back over the fence. This went on for a couple of years. The same rocks flying back and forth.

The year before we purchased a house, Hunky told Winston how one night, about two-thirty in the early morning, he went to Davis' hardware store and poured acid all around the building and around all of the merchandise that was sitting outside. When he returned home, he waited about thirty minutes and called Davis. "If you wanna save all that goddamn stuff you got outside yo' store, you better git a hose and git yo' ass down there." He spoke slowly into the phone. "And don't ever throw no more damn rocks on my property, you sum bitch. I done told you. And I ain't tellin you no more!"

"How long ago was this?" Winston asked him. "And, will water stop acid?"

"Hell. A couple nights back. To tell you the truth, I don't rightly know. But, hey, it damn sho' got his attention." And he continued, "If he throws one more rock on my land, it's gonna be a helluva fight. He ain't saw nothin' yit." Hunky punctuated it by spitting on the ground between his boots.

I believed that ended the years of rock throwing, but the two men continued to hate one another. I don't believe that the school situation had anything to do with the way that they felt. Hunky supported the public schools. Although Davis' daughter-in-law worked at the public elementary school, he wasn't supportive. I don't know if he supported Macon Academy or not. I think that he was one of those men who is just naturally mean.

Good people can turn on a dime, given the right situation, at the right moment in time. I wondered how many people in Notasulga allowed their emotions to get out of control in 1964. I wondered if they had regrets. No one talked about those days or that year, except for brief moments during a conversation. You knew not to ask questions that were off limits.

I learned quickly when and when not to approach a topic. It depended a lot on to whom I was talking and what the topic was. Sometimes, I just knew that I needed to avoid certain things as if I was avoiding a bed of fire ants.

Chapter 36

By the time I received my degree from Auburn University, we'd become a part of the community. There was some division, but I'd come to accept the fact that might always be the case. People seemed to have accepted other's choices and to respect the decisions they'd made, at leasr in regard to public or private schools. There were wounds, but they'd healed, for the most part.

I don't think that many people, regardless of their chosen side, public or private, realized the mark that Notasulga had left on history, in regard to the desegregation of all the town's schools. It'd be a long, long time before I realized that. Decades after we left, an event occurred that brought the town together, as they fought again to save the high school.

In March, 1992, the Macon County Board of Education decided to build a new high school and to consolidate all of the high schools in the county. The State Department of Education was asked to conduct a survey of the Macon County school system. The state reported that high school enrollment in the school system had decreased. But, the enrollment at Notasulga had increased. It was the only school in the county where significant integration had occurred.

The Department of Education stated that Notasulga was the only truly integrated school in the county and suggested that it not be consolidated. Macon County could continue with the consolidation, which pretty much left the decision totally in Macon County's ballpark. The Macon County superintendent and board members decided to consolidate all the high schools. Based on this decision, a group of people from Notasulga filed a motion to intervene as plaintiffs in the case, alleging that the Macon County Board should not be permitted to eliminate the only integrated high school in the county.

Testimony revealed that Notasulga High School had held its racial composition, of almost equal representation of both blacks and whites for decades. The school, during all of those years, had provided integrated extracurricular activities, as well as integrated education.

After hearing the testimony of many educational leaders and people who'd been involved in the integration of Notasulga schools, the United States Court of Appeals Eleventh Circuit praised Victor's efforts. The court ruled that the consolidation of Notasulga High School would eventually lead to another "white flight," which would destroy the only integrated school in the county and would result in a single-race school system in Macon County; therefore, the court denied permission to close Notasulga High School.

The ruling made note that the school offered the only integrated educational experience in the county. The court recognized Notasulga as successful in its achievement of racial integration, in its ability to offer a quality curriculum, and in its exemplary involvement of parents. Victor was praised by Judge Clark and others for his efforts to achieve racial balance and harmony at Notasulga.

The court went even further and made a statement that I believe defines Notasulga and the entire desegregation process throughout the Unites States. It's the comment by the court that makes me proud to have lived in Notasulga and to have experienced one of the most amazing accomplishments in Alabama history. The court praised Notasulga for accomplishing the basic constitutional goals established by Brown v. Board of Education of 1954 and for fulfilling the objective of racial harmony. Now, how many school systems throughout this country have been given that written honor by a high court?

It was a perfect example of irony of the situation. Notasulga, once known for burning a school, in order to drive away black students, received praise from a high court. After the school burned and was rebuilt, educators and townspeople embraced desegregation and got it right. Notasulga was one of very few schools in the country to have those bragging rights. It spoke volumes about the path that leaders in the town had chosen. I was proud to have been a part of that choice, to be involved, on some level, with the successful desegregation of public schools. Notasulga, which fought against right, changed and became a model for desegregation.

A change was taking place, and I had the good fortune to witness it. I saw growth and forward movement. Change demands honesty. Lying to yourself or to others about racism or any serious subject isn't acceptable. Racism didn't die in Notasulga. No more than it died any other place in Alabama. Today, it's still alive and well. It just wears a different mask, but there's less of it than once existed, due, in a large degree, to laws being changed. Well, I decided that I'd take the change any way I could get it.

Most people in the town dealt with the changes and were honest with themselves. No, everyone didn't change their beliefs about race and integration, but they listened and respected the opinions of others, without the hate and anger. It proved that we can get along with one another, even with extreme points of view, regarding politics or religion, if we learn to communicate, minus the bitterness and hate.

I'd grown up in a family without judgment against others. The key word here is "against." Mama would say to us, "You don't have to be friends with everybody, but you can be nice and listen." She didn't just say those words. She enforced them. If she learned that we'd been mean or had mistreated someone for the fun of it or because we could, she'd use a thin limb from a bush and switch our legs. It'd sting like hundreds of bees. Of course, we'd hop around and around in a circle, hoping to avoid the switch, as it chewed into the skin. Mama would hold onto one of our arms, as we hopped and danced in a circle, so there was no getting away.

We had some wonderful friends in town. By now, Winston and I had friends who supported either the public schools or the private school. That was a big deal. The two school systems had been enemies for years. No one was denying that most private schools had begun as a means of avoiding desegregation. I'm sure some parents still send their children to private schools because of racism, but you won't hear many of them admit it. It's always, "They'll get a better education there." That can be true, but it can also be a lie. You've got the right to make that decision for your child. Just don't lie and expect me to believe it.

As the years came and went, we had many get-togethers. Often, it was a mixed crowd from both schools. Just as often, it was a racially mixed crowd, because teachers from the schools were invited to the different social gatherings. I don't believe that was the case in many towns in the South at that time. By then, many of us thought that we were different and, somehow, special.

A group of men from town went to Florida each summer to fish. They brought back large coolers of seafood. We'd have a huge seafood fry, broil, and grill at someone's house. Eighteen or twenty couples and their children would come. The party would begin about six o'clock on a hot summer day and go late into the night. After dark, two of the assistant coaches would get out their guitars to play and sing. Funny stories were told as we sat in a circle, while the smaller children slept inside on the den floor, with the television screen blinking at the little ones, curled into balls. The older children would play cards at the kitchen table. Those were wonderful times, with great friends.

Chapter 37

I started teaching at Notasulga High School in the fall of 1976. I'd worked hard to achieve my goals. Finally, I'd be a member of the profession that I loved. It had taken me a minute to get there, but I'd made it. When the first day of school started, I was nervous and excited, looking forward to implementing my yearly plans, and hoping to encourage awareness for literature and a love for the English language.

The night before my first day of teaching, Winston told me, "Marley Jane, you're small, so every smartass kid in class is gonna test you. Be tough. You can lighten up, but, once you lose control, it's hard to get it back. You can always ease up. If you start out loose, it'll be hard to whip everyone back into shape. Remember, your first responsibility is to teach, not to be friends with the students. I'm not saying don't be nice and kind. You can do that and be tough. Be the best teacher that you can be."

I'd recall those words for years, at the beginning of each new school term. My goals as a teacher were simple: teach students to think for themselves, to seek answers to all questions, and to know where to go to get answers. I wanted them to have open minds when it came to learning about everything. I wanted them to question and to evaluate every topic under the sun. I hoped to teach them that through literature. I was eager, and I wanted my students to be eager. I wanted them to love learning as much as I did. I'd soon discover that would be a hard horse for some students to ride. For some, it'd be a horse that they refused to ride.

One thing that I loved about teaching was the laughter. Regardless of how down I might be when I went to work each day, I knew two things would probably happen before the day was over. One, I'd want to chew nails. Two, some student would make me laugh. Lots of days, if I was lucky, learning and laughter occurred. If the students and I got really lucky, a wow, eye-opening moment would take place. I might be learning from my students. I could only hope they were learning a great deal from me.

Since Notasulga High School was a small school, the number of subjects taught had to be limited, so teachers had to be creative and incorporate subjects into their courses in order to expose the students to a wide variety of topics and ideas. The English Department didn't have the personnel to create a class just for poetry or for public speaking; therefore, I had to include those subjects as much as possible into my yearly calendar.

Several events that occurred the first year I taught stand out in my mind. Sadly, they happen so often in both private and public schools that it's a disgrace. This type of evil doesn't care about race or class. It's something that people want to keep secret. The actual incidents don't happen at school, but the children can't help but bring them to school. It's not something that they can leave at home and not think about. It influences their learning and behavior. It's a reality among educators who see it time and time again, year after year. Educators and schools should act quickly, as the law says they should. Some don't. In one incident, we didn't, and, for that, I'll forever carry a burden of shame.

The school year was rapidly approaching spring break. It was near the end of March, which, in the South, can be windy, cold, or warm. Each day, the weather tossed a five-sided coin. Like Southerners themselves, the weather can be unpredictable. But this was a perfect Friday. Not a cloud in the sky. The bell rang to dismiss school and by the next Friday, we'd all take a much-needed break for a week.

My classroom wasn't far from the office, and it was directly across from the media center. Many afternoons, several of us teachers would gather at the windows in the media center and watch the students get into their parents' cars. We gathered as usual that day and watched as each car pulled up, got students, and drove off. The last car pulled away, and we started to turn from the windows. Then, we saw him, walking down the steps. Puzzled, we turned back to the windows.

Something was about to happen. Victor never came to the front at the end of the school day. He always went to the buses, which loaded in the back of the school. He wasn't following his normal pattern. No one but Victor was at the front of the school. Further down, the elementary teachers who stood in front of the elementary school to help load their students into cars had gone back into the building. We waited.

Immediately, we saw the car, coming from town. It was a 1974 cranberry fire-mist Cadillac Fleetwood, with a front grille of four rows across and sixteen rows down, of large square "egg-crate" openings. The parking, turn signal, and cornering lights wrapped around the front corners of the car. The effect was a gigantic, red, grinning cat. It turned into the circular drive and eased to a stop beside Victor, who was now at the bottom of the steps. The motor purred. Victor reached out and opened the right side of the back passenger's door. As he did so, he turned to face the school. Not a word had been spoken. We heard the silence and felt the stillness. Time had gone into slow motion. Like a flash, a young girl, with long, swinging blond hair, flew down the steps, jumped into the back seat, and Victor firmly closed the door.

The car roared to life, flew down the drive and, without stopping at the end, made a sharp turn to the right. As soon as it made the turn, it leaped forward like a jungle cat. We, along with Victor, watched as it raced toward Wire Road, where we imagined it'd take a right turn toward I-85. What we didn't know was that from there it'd head toward California and freedom, coming as close to breaking the speed limit as it could without being stopped. It had to get to the Mississippi line.

By this time, we knew the young girl was Anna Clara Findley. Anna was approximately thirteen years old and a beauty. She enrolled in the fall, several months after school started. For a reason that I can't recall, her uncle had custody of her. His sister was her mother. When the teachers heard that she was staying with him, they were dumbfounded. Social Services, DHR, and the judge didn't know some things that we suspected or her piece-of-trash uncle would never have gotten her.

We watched as Victor came up the steps, combing his hair, and entered the building. He looked as cool as dewy grass after a summer drizzle. We knew that he'd not gone to his office and was waiting for something. No one spoke. The quiet settled in the air. We listened for his footsteps down the hall. Then, the quiet disappeared, and we heard a voice booming and echoing off the walls. His steps fell hard and fast. Screaming for Victor and calling him terrible names, he came nearer and nearer.

"Victor Alexander! I wanna talk to you! You sumbitch! You hear me? Git yo' ass out here. Now! I'm gonna kick yo' ass, boy," he thundered as he stormed down the hall, disturbing the silence that had hung like soft thin silk only seconds earlier.

We all moved as one toward the door and into the hall. If we had to, we'd take him down. Big Hatcher could sit on him and squash the air out of his lungs. The rest of us would beat the living hell out of him. Consequences of our actions be damned. We were dealing with a pure force of evil.

I took in every aspect of the tall, lanky man who walked with swift, rough, savage movements. His shoulders were hunched forward, as if a force of wind drove him. His body was agitated, filled with rage. Wavy brown hair came to the collar of his shirt and sideburns ran along his cheeks. There was a brutal look on his slender face, which appeared to be ready to explode at any moment. A look of raw hatred had settled on his face, and his hard hostile brown eyes held burning embers. His thin lips were tight and his mouth was twisted. Large pores covered his hawk nose. His temper was furious, and he appeared to be batshit crazy.

As he passed us, his total attention was focused on Victor, who was glancing at the floor, as if some secret of life lay in the wood. I looked closely and saw a tiny grin at the corners of his mouth. We fell in behind the man and made a semi-circle around him and Victor. I looked to my right and realized that Mose had joined the circle, with a shovel in his hand. The man was in Victor's face, almost nose-to-nose, screaming. He pointed a finger in the middle of Victor's face. Victor took out his comb, just as calm as you please, and began to comb his hair. You could sense the man's brief hesitation and imagine him thinking, "What the hell?"

It gave Victor time to calmly say, "Come in my office. We need to talk." Looking into the man's eyes, his lips in a tight line, he continued, "And I don't think you want to say, 'No.'"

It was as if Victor threw ice water in the man's face, which was still beet red, with veins popping at his temples. Victor turned and walked toward his office. The man stopped cursing and followed. Suddenly, it was like watching a fifth grade bully turn all meek and defeated.

No way were we going to leave this show. Plus, who knew, we might have to go to Victor's defense, although we'd just seen some of the anger leave the man. Victor's comb punched a hole in the man's hot air, like a pin had been stuck into a balloon. But it didn't pop; it just shriveled to nothing. We were aware of the rumor that the man carried a sawed-off shotgun in his car at all times. Most likely, he was carrying heat. Suddenly, I thought, "Is Victor crazy?"

We couldn't hear a word. Not a sound. Yet, we could imagine Victor explaining in his quiet way how things were going to be or the police would be contacted. Truth be known, he'd probably already spoken with some type of law officials. The Macon County sheriff was probably at I-85 to escort the get-away-car to the county line. With all of Victor's contacts, arrangements had probably been made for a police escort to the Mississippi line.

When they came out of Victor's office, the raging fire had left the man. He stormed past us and down the hall. We couldn't wait for Victor to bring us up-to-date, and he did.

Anna had gone to Victor a week before and told him what her uncle was doing to her. Since we'd not had much positive action from DHR before, Victor decided to handle it himself. He contacted her mother in California.

They decided on a date that she'd come to get Anna. It was a well-laid plan. Victor told Anna and no one else. We suspected that he'd told some officials, but we didn't ask. He wouldn't tell us what he'd said to the uncle, but we knew that our principal could be one tough cookie.

* * * * * * *

That should have been the end of that man, but let me tell you a truth. His kind of evil doesn't go gently into the night, it just keeps cropping back up.

Loretta Simms, his daughter, was a student of mine. She was a shy eleventh grader who seemed to make a special effort not to be attractive; yet, she possessed a natural beauty. Sadness lived in her hazel eyes. Long straight hair rested below her shoulders. She rarely spoke in class and sat in a position that suggested her desire to withdraw into herself. There was a rumor that her dad had sexually abused her for years. No one had proof, until she began to talk with Winston. After Anna was whisked away, Loretta went to Winston's office to talk about her secret life.

Winston had been appointed assistant principal and had a small office in the auditorium. Loretta continued to come to his office the following year. He and I discussed on two or more occasions her trips to talk. Those talks became more and more revealing. The story took a long time to come out, and, at first, things were ambiguous. As the year moved from one season to another, Loretta became more open and talked freely, revealing the horrible things that were happening at her house. I encouraged Winston to report what she was telling him to the authorities. I couldn't understand why he didn't.

Later, hell broke loose, and I became the target. I believed afterwards that one of Loretta's brothers discovered that she was talking to Winston and told their daddy. When he confronted her, she lied and told him that she'd been talking to me, rather than to Winston. Had he known that it was Winston, there's no telling what he would've done to her or to Winston. I believe that she lied out of fear. Still, I had no idea that the nut job would choose me as the focus of his next rage.

Winston's talks with Loretta weren't the first time that I was made aware of the strange relationship between this father and daughter. I first became aware when I overheard some students talking the previous year after Anna left. They were discussing the kiss he gave Loretta every morning when he dropped her off at school. I said, "Oh, you all need to be careful what you say. A lot of parents kiss their kids when they bring them to school."

They were emphatic, "This ain't no kiss a daddy gives his daughter, Mrs. Steele. It's a long tongue kiss!"

"That just can't be. Teachers are outside. Watching," I said, with total stupidity.

"Well, he does kiss her that way. No one says anything. Not even Coach Win." The tall, dark-haired girl blew a pink bubble that popped, covering her nose and cheeks. She scoffed at the idea that no adult had taken action. "Somebody ought to do something." I silently agreed.

Later that day, at home, I repeated what the students had said. I asked Winston if he'd seen the kiss. I was shocked when he said, "Yes. I've seen it. The kids are right."

"What did you do?" I demanded, pissed at him.

"Nothing."

"Are you crazy! I cannot believe that you stood there and watched that happen and did absolutely nothing!"

"Marley Jane, the man's crazy. He carries a sawed-off shotgun under the driver's seat."

"And, you know that . . . how? Even if it's true, so what?" I finally said, "I don't even want to speak to you right now," and I stormed out of the room, not knowing that the future would test how courageous I was.

* * * * * * *

It was the end of the school year, the beginning of the second semester, near the end of January. Cold winds and threatening clouds gave a hint of possible snow. My twelfth graders were more interested in looking out the windows and wishing for snow than about my instructions, regarding outline procedures for the research paper that would be due at the end of April. Suddenly, the door was jerked open. Every eye in the room flew to the door, including mine. A large slender frame filled the doorway and a harsh voice boomed, "I wanna see you! Now!"

It was the nut job who had confronted Victor almost a year ago in the hall, just outside the door of my classroom. His eyes were wild and his mouth was tight. His hands hung to his sides; his fists were knots of flesh and bone. Brown eyes burned with fire. I looked from him to Loretta, who sat on the first row, near the back of the room. Her head was bent and her long light brown hair fell across the profile of her face, which was drained of color. She was scared. One hand lay in her lap and the other held a strand of hair in her mouth. She chewed nervously on the strand of hair.

I knew that I had to handle this whirlwind as calmly as possible for Loretta's sake, although I was instantly mad, with an anger that'd been building for a long time. I was so calm that I wondered if I was breathing. I knew where my anger could take me. I'd spend a lifetime managing it.

I turned to the evil face in the doorway and said with the serenity of the Pope, "Wait outside, please. I'll be with you in a moment." Then, I took my time, explaining the outline that I wanted the students to follow in their research papers. I gave the class an assignment and asked if anyone had any questions. He'd been waiting outside my closed door for ten minutes or more. Twenty-one heads shook, "No." Their surprised faces were open books, showing a wide range of emotions. They all knew about the kiss, and most knew that Loretta had been making frequent trips to Winston's office.

I left the room and closed the door, oh so quietly, thinking, "Don't you feel my energy, you piece of shit? Don't you have any idea what's coming? Do you know the can of worms you just opened? You two-bit bastard."

Mose was slowly pushing the dust mop along the wall opposite my classroom door. His head was down, but he raised his eyes to look at me. I felt his presence as I walked toward the office, where the angry man stood at the door, his arms folded across his chest. I felt the heat of anger from his eyes as I approached.

"Follow me," I politely demanded. I opened the door to the office, which was less than thirty yards from my classroom. I asked the secretary if Victor was in. He wasn't, so I said to the stiff, fuming man, "Come in," and I opened the door into Victor's office. Then I slammed it, good and damn loud. I stepped further into the room. I was about to deliberately release the demon that I kept hogtied in my soul.

Suddenly, the man moved in front of the door and folded his arms across his chest. His legs were spread wide. "I got somethin' to say to you, missy," he hissed at me.

"Missy, my ass," I thought. I stepped into his chest. He was tall, and the top of my head barely hit his breastbone. I poked my right fist into his chest, hard, and pushed. "No, you goddamn son-of-a-bitch piece of shit. I got something to say to you," I said in a low, calm voice. "Don't you ever—come to my room again. Period. You piece of garbage. I'll hang your damn dirty laundry all over Macon County. Do you understand? Now. Get your ass away from that door, before I open your damn skull with a chair. Move! Now!"

His face was full of shock, and I watched as something replaced his anger. He didn't speak, but he did move away from the door. About that time, Victor came to the door and said, "Mrs. Steele, you can go back to class. I've got this."

"I don't know why she's so upset. I just wanted to ask Loretta if she's got my billfold," the lying jerk said.

I walked over to the phone and picked up the receiver. "Mr. Alexander, do you want me to call the police now and let everybody know what trash he is?"

"No. I've got it." He pointed to the man and said, "You. Sit down. It looks like I need to talk with you. Again. 'Cause you forgot our last conversation."

I left the office, walked to the door of my classroom, and stood in the hall at the door. I needed to regain my composure. Mose was suddenly beside me, pushing the dust mop. "You okay, Miss Marley?" he asked in a gentle tone.

"Yes," I replied. "Thank you, Mose." Then, I took a couple of deep breaths and exhaled slowly before I entered the room. "Where were we?" I asked the class. No one missed a beat, and class continued as if it'd never been interrupted.

When class ended, Loretta came to my desk. "I'm so sorry, Mrs. Steele. I didn't know he'd come here. I swear," she said, with tears in her eyes.

"Loretta, it's okay. It'll never happen again. Can I do something? Can I help in any way? Just say the word," I told her, as I took her right hand in mine.

"No. Please. Just leave it alone. Please," and her eyes held a world of pain and suffering. We locked eyes, and I'd never seen such sadness, such begging.

I couldn't say anything. At that moment, I honestly didn't know what to do. I turned it over to Victor and did nothing else. I was as guilty as Winston. One day I knew that I'd answer to God for that decision. I take the blame and I'll pay whatever He asks.

"God, forgive me. Forgive us all," I silently prayed, as I watched Loretta walk through the door, back to the only world she'd ever known, where there was no hope. I believed that everyone at the school had failed her.

After she left the room, I sat at my desk and looked out the window. I had time to catch a breather. There was a fifteen-minute break before the next class. I heard Willie Mae ask, "You all right, Marley Jane?" I turned and saw her holding a cup of coffee in one hand and a plate of cookies in the other.

"I'm fine. Other than I feel like I just took a beating," and I laughed. "Is that for me?"

"Mrs. West told me to bring these to you. We made peanut butter cookies this morning. She knows how much you like 'em cookies. We can't get used to you not coming by every morning for coffee. And cookies, when we make 'em. Thought you might need something, after that fool man showing hisself."

I laughed and sighed, "So, word travels fast. How did y'all know?"

"Mose told us. He saw that fool come to your door, and he waited to see what was gonna happen. When you went into Mr. A's office with that idiot, he got concerned. So, he got Mr. A. Told him what was happening. After you came out, he came and told us."

"Thank goodness for Mose," I said, laughing. "What would we do without him? Tell Mrs. West thanks for me. And thank you, Willie Mae."

"Well, you enjoy this," she said. "I gotta get back to work. We just wanta know you okay." When she got to the door, she turned around. "Oh, by the way, Mrs. West said to tell you that she's frying some chicken livers, 'specially for you. We're having fried chicken today. I'll put 'em on your plate when you come down the line."

"Thanks, Willie Mae." I smiled.

The remainder of the year zoomed by, without additional incidents from crazy parents, but that year never stopped haunting me.

Chapter 38

Victor had been married for several years to Iris, a beautiful woman with soulful dark almond eyes that gave her an Asian look. Her long straight raven hair hung down her slim back to her behind. She spoke in a low, soft Southern voice, a gift that she received from Louisiana. Since she was a professor at Auburn University, she understood education and the issues that the school system juggled.

Iris gave birth to a beautiful baby girl several months before school ended for the year. Victoria was their pride and joy. But, the delivery took its toll on Iris, leaving her in bad health. She was barely herself. It'd be some time before she returned to work at Auburn. When that school year ended, she was just beginning to speak clearly. The mend was a slow process. The entire staff at the elementary and high schools was concerned.

The teachers knew that Victor and Iris were expecting a visit from Robert Kennedy, Jr. The event had been planned for a long time and was scheduled for the second week in June. We knew people would be coming from long distances. Everyone wanted to meet the son of Robert Kennedy and the nephew of President Kennedy and Senator Ted Kennedy.

Ted Kennedy became friends with an attorney in Macon County, and Robert Kennedy, Jr., visited with the family many times. Victor also knew the family and had met the Kennedys there. He and Iris invited the young Kennedy to come to Notasulga the next time he came to Alabama. It was discussed, and numerous arrangements were made for a date after the birth of Victoria. In spite of the fact that Iris wasn't doing well, she didn't want to cancel the party.

The event took place on a sunny Saturday. The sky was an electric blue. A radiant sun hung loose and bright overhead. Since I lived on the street behind Victor and Iris, I planned to walk. Winston went almost an hour before I did. A baby-sitter took Wesley and Katherine to a movie in Auburn. I left the house and made the short walk around the block to the Alexander's house.

I heard voices and soft, drifting music. People were standing on the front lawn and spilling onto the sidewalk. Cars lined both sides of the entire street and into town. As I walked up the pathway to the front porch, I saw Victor, Robert Kennedy, Jr., and three men whom I didn't know. They were standing on the porch at the top of the steps.

As I started to climb the steps, Kennedy flashed a bright smile that revealed brilliant, white teeth. He walked toward me, raising his bushy eyebrows. "And who is this?" He had the Boston accent that all of the Kennedy men seemed to have and that I'd heard for years on television. He extended his large hand, as Victor introduced us.

I was glancing at a young man who was approximately twenty-four years old, brown from the sun, slender, and over six feet. He wore tan khaki pants and a white shirt, open at the neck. The sleeves were rolled to his elbows. Brown wavy hair hung on his neck in loose curls. His hair was just barely in need of a cut. A wave of hair kept falling into his sharp blue eyes, and he constantly pushed it to one side of his high forehead. His long, tanned face had high cheekbones, and a dimple winked in his chin. He was a handsome man, but not as handsome as his famous daddy.

He and I talked for approximately ten minutes about the town and the school—typical tea and cookie talk. I sensed in that brief conversation that the South intrigued him. It had certainly been important in the lives of his father and uncle. I didn't drool and gush about his famous relatives. Nor did I discuss the tragedies that seemed to hover over that well-known family. He'd lost his uncle, John F. Kennedy, the President of the United States, who died at the hands of an assassin in Dallas, in 1963. He was ten at that time, and he was fourteen when his own father, who was running for President, was assassinated in California.

In spite of his wide smile, I could almost hear a faraway sadness in the voice of this young Kennedy. I was nine years older than the man who stood before me, but his life experiences had already made him far older than me.

One of the men present touched Kennedy's arm. In a low voice, he said, "Bobby, someone wants to meet you. Can you take a moment?"

"Sure," the Boston accent answered. "Excuse me. Maybe we can talk again," the accent said to me, while the speaker flashed another brilliant smile.

"Maybe," I said, smiling back.

I made my way into the house, greeting people as I went. I located Iris who was seated in a comfortable chair in the den, looking pale. Her hair was cut to her shoulders. Her speech was strained, and she took time pronouncing each word. I thought how tired she must be. She sat in the chair like it was a throne and she was a queen.

After talking with her for several minutes, I made my way throughout the house, greeting people. I stopped and spoke at length with various friends. I walked onto the back porch, where a band performed in the far corner. Tables were scattered throughout the back yard. The crowd was so thick that you would've had a difficult time walking among them.

I glanced around the crowd and saw Winston, seated at one of the tables, deep in conversation. On his left was Lucy Dawson, the female trainer whom he'd hired the previous year. As far as we knew, she was the first female trainer to be hired for a high school football team in the South. To his right was one of his assistant coaches, and the basketball coach from Loachapoka sat across the table from him. Winston looked up and caught my eye. He waved at me and turned back around, before I could return his wave. My hand, which was in mid-air, dropped. I turned away.

As I walked across the porch to enter the den, my mind flashed back. The late, nightly phone calls from Lucy to Winston started the week before Kennedy's visit. The first call came on Monday night, after eleven-thirty. We'd just dozed when the sharp ringing of the phone cut through the darkness. Winston picked up the receiver on the third ring. "Hello. Oh, hi. Sure, I can talk. Are you okay?" He placed his hand over the receiver and told me that it was Lucy. I nodded and turned over, expecting a brief conversation. It lasted for over an hour. During that time, I drifted in and out of a light sleep.

On Tuesday night, the phone rang at about the same time. Winston answered and began another lengthy conversation with Lucy. I lay on my side, with my back to him, listening to his low voice and low laughter. I studied the tone of his voice and his language. Within twenty minutes or less, I knew that it was a call, meant to send me a message. I made no comment that night or the next day.

The third call came on Wednesday. Same time. Same low voice. Same low laughter. Again, I said nothing as unwanted questions occupied a foggy space in my brain. I wondered if this was becoming a nightly habit.

Thursday night the call came thirty minutes later than usual. I listened for ten minutes or less to the one-sided low conversation. Pushing myself to a sitting position, I turned on the bedside lamp and got out of bed. I walked around to Winston's side of the bed. By that time, he was sitting up in bed, frowning and giving me a "Huh?" expression.

I stood near the phone and placed my middle finger over the on/off button. "Hang up," I mouthed. He shook his head and gave me a mean look. "Hang up. Or I'll hang up for you," I mouthed.

"Look. I'm sorry. I've got to go. Yeah. I know. I'll talk to you in the morning. Nite." He placed the phone in its cradle. I could see the anger in his brown eyes and around the lines of his mouth that was pressed in a tight line. I walked to the other side of the bed.

"What's wrong with you? Lucy thinks you're nuts," he flung at me.

Pointing to my face, I flung back. "Look at my face. Do I look like I give a shit what Lucy thinks? You might. I sure as hell don't. When you talk to her in the morning, be sure you tell her not to call this house again after nine o'clock. If she does, I'll answer the phone. Neither she nor you will like what I say. That's a promise. No more midnight phone dates." I got into bed and turned off the light.

"You can be such a bitch. Why? We're just talking." I heard him flop down and exhale heavily.

"Bitch or no bitch, I'll be damned if I'll let you and some other bitch humiliate me in my own house at midnight. Every single night. How long were the two of you going to continue to 'just talk' after we were in bed?" I paused briefly. "Don't let it happen again. Talk at work. Goodnight." Winston responded by jerking the covers away from my side of the bed. There'd been no more phone calls from Lucy. Winston and I hadn't spoken about the calls since.

I went to the kitchen and took a plastic cup, filled with sweet iced tea. I sat on a stool to talk with Bertha and Willie Mae who were preparing food and supervising things in the kitchen. Willie Mae was beside herself. "Lordy, mercy, who'd ever thought in a million years I'd meet a Kennedy? I'm just so nervous I don't know what to do. Kiss him or shake his hand. Mr. A. said he's gonna introduce us."

"I'd start by shaking his hand," I told her, laughing at her nervousness.

"Well, he's sho' 'nuff good looking," she replied, unable to conceal her joy. She wiped a bead of sweat from her shiny forehead. "A Kennedy done come to town. Lord, Jesus!"

I laughed. "Willie Mae, he's just a man. No big deal. If one of his uncles hadn't been President of the United States and one a Senator—and his dad a United States Attorney General—we might not be making a fuss over him. But he is handsome."

Bertha added, "Yes, let's not forget his daddy. You know it was only ten years ago when he was assassinated. His son was only fourteen. I don't know how that family survives all that awful stuff." She shook her head and tears clouded her pale blue eyes.

Willie Mae and I nodded in agreement. Willie Mae looked up, holding a platter of cheese straws in the air, and said, "Lord. I remember how some white folks in this town cheered the day President Kennedy was killed. It was a crazy mess. Black folks knew they'd done lost a friend. Sad. Life's sad. Sometimes. But, today's a happy day. Well, let me get this to all these hungry folks. Bless 'em." She left the kitchen.

Changing subjects, Bertha asked, "Did you see Winston? He's sitting outside. With that woman he hired as trainer."

"Yes," I said, reaching for a carrot stick. "I saw him. Her name's Lucy." I felt her drilling stare, but I didn't look at her.

"Kennedy's gonna speak before long. You staying?" she asked.

Munching on the carrot stick, I answered, "Probably not."

I saw, rather than felt, her intense stare. She didn't say anything else, but I knew what she was thinking. "Well, I'm leaving," I announced, getting off the stool. "Bye. Talk to you later." She didn't reply. Just watched me leave.

I'd been there for almost ninety minutes, and I'd decided it was time to head home. Before I left, I wanted to see the baby. I went to the master bedroom, where Victor's mother told me that I'd find Victoria. I intended to peep in and leave. When I entered the room, I was surprised to see Kennedy. He was on the phone, talking softly to his mother, Ethel Kennedy. I learned later that he called her every day, regardless of where he was.

He waved at me. I waved back and bent over the baby, who was sleeping like an angel, in spite of the noise that drifted into the room. I touched one of her soft little hands that felt like velvet. As I left the room, I mouthed to Kennedy, "Bye. Nice meeting you." He nodded and pointed to himself, indicating, I assumed, "Me, too."

I slipped quietly out the side door and headed back home. Winston remained behind. As I entered the house, I could hear the sounds of the party. I changed into shorts and a tee shirt. Then, I sat on the patio, sipping ice water and listening to the DJ of a local radio station in Tuskegee. He talked about "a Kennedy in Macon County today." He reminisced about the Kennedy brothers and their contributions to the civil rights movement.

"Now it's time to stop talking and play some jazz," he declared in an upbeat voice.

I closed my eyes and listened to the sounds of soft jazz intermingle with the voices and the music from a distant street, where a young Kennedy shook hands with so many who believed in a dream and in a Kennedy's ability to make a dream a reality. Many in this country had been drawn to that dream and needed a warrior who'd fight the battle for them, who'd open doors of opportunity, and who'd give them hope.

"Does he acknowledge an assigned role, a responsibility? Does he care?" I silently asked myself. "To whom much is given, much is expected." I recalled Jesus saying something to that effect in Luke 12:48. And I remembered that President Kennedy had repeated those words years ago. I leaned back in the lounge chair, put on my dark shades, and looked up at the floating cotton clouds above me. I thought about how Jesus and the President probably weren't just talking about wealthy people, but how each of us should use our blessings to glorify God and to benefit others. It'd be a better world if we used whatever gift we had to serve others, to help mankind. The gift might be encouragement, and I thought of Bertha. Or it might be giving, and I thought of Willie Mae. Both women were, right now, in a kitchen, providing for hundreds who'd come to meet the son and nephew of men whom they admired and respected.

I closed my eyes and started to empty my head of any negative thought. I turned off the local radio station and allowed the music that drifted over my back fence to swim in the ocean of my mind, which was beginning to clear. I inhaled deeply and exhaled slowly. I knew that Kennedy would probably be on a flight back to Boston before Winston got home. I began to relax and allowed my mind to become one of those cotton clouds as I drifted into a state of relaxation where nothing mattered but the now.

Chapter 39

The first rape occurred in Tuskegee on the Halloween following Kennedy's visit to Notasulga. October brought its usual days of warmth, but the mornings and nights felt the bite of winter. Pumpkins sat on people's porches or steps. Wide cutout eyes gave off soft yellow glows from candles. Mouths were wide and carved differently. Some smiled, while others snarled, with snagged-teeth. Others pouted, with turned down mouths and droopy eyes.

Trick-or-treaters wandered the streets in various costumes, and their squeals lingered in the air as they ran from door to door, holding out brown paper sacks, plastic pumpkins, or sand pails for treats. Occasionally, there'd be large teenage boys who should've given up trick or treating long ago.

I sat in a straight-back chair, dressed in a full witch's outfit that Wesley had insisted I wear. The chair was near the front door, and on my right was an old black iron pot that'd been used many years ago to make soap or to boil water for killing hogs or washing clothes. My grandparents had used a similar pot many times for the same reasons. Half of the pot was filled with crumpled newspapers. On top of the papers was candy, filled to the rim of the pot. Each time I reached for a handful of candy the long straight black wig slipped and hid half of my face.

My next-door neighbor Sherry stood in the shadows of the carport, dressed as a ghost. Her tall frame made an impressive apparition. Blood dripped down her left cheek and out of hollow black eye sockets. She pounced out of the shadows, after I dropped candy into bags or pails. The kids would take off running, their screams shooting between the stars.

It was close to nine o'clock, and the crowd was beginning to thin. Wesley, Jacob, and Terri had left almost an hour earlier to trick or treat. For the first time, they'd allowed Katherine, Holly, and Wade to tag along. Up until they left, they'd all played a part in spooking the kids who were brave enough to come close and hold out their bags.

Sherry and I were getting ready to close up shop, but we decided to stay until the kids returned. We stood near the door, talking about the costumes that we'd seen and how well Wesley had decorated the carport and yard for this Halloween. Just as we expressed concern that they'd not returned, they rounded the corner about three hundred yards from the house. When they saw us, they began to run, holding up their bags and talking over one another.

When they walked onto the porch, I said, "Well, I hope y'all got lots of treats. And no tricks were played."

They all began to talk at once, showing me their treasures. I knew six kids who'd be on a sugar high for a week. Thank goodness Halloween came only once a year. Wesley and Jacob picked up the big pot and sat it, now almost empty, inside the front door. I made hot chocolate for everyone. As we drank the sweet stuff, Winston arrived home. Sherry, Holly, and Wade said their goodbyes and walked home next door. I asked Winston to take Terri and Jacob home. After they all left, Wesley and Katherine got ready for bed. As they slept from exhaustion, Winston and I stayed up to watch the Johnny Carson Show.

The next morning, Terri returned shortly after breakfast and joined Wesley, Katherine, Holly, and Wade on the trampoline. I'd just placed a load of bed linens in the washing machine, when the phone rang. I reached for the phone and turned to look out the sliding glass doors, watching five bodies bounce into the air and fall on butts or knees, to bounce back into the tree limbs. I just hoped no one tumbled off the trampoline and ended up with a broken leg or ankle.

"Hello," I said.

"You busy?" Bertha asked. "'Cause I got some news. I heard it on the radio. You got the radio on? I called my cousin Bubba Tatt, to verify it."

"No," I answered to both of her questions. "What's going on?"

"A black man broke into Mrs. Angel Smith's house last night. You know her. Don't you? She used to work at Carver's Grocery Store in Tuskegee. Well," she continued, not giving me time to respond, "anyways, you know she's bout eighty-seven or eight. I don't know for sure. But, she's old. Anyhow, she was raped and beat last night. Almost to death. She's in Lee County Hospital now. But, she can't talk."

I interrupted quickly enough to ask, "How do they know it was a black man?"

"She told 'em," Bertha answered, in a voice that suggested I was dim-witted and hadn't been paying attention.

"I thought you said she can't talk," I reminded her.

"Well, for goodness sake, Marley Jane! She talked enough to tell 'em that." I heard a tone of aggravation in her voice. She added, "The police haven't got a clue who did it. My first cousin Bubba . . . on my mama's side of the family. Is a policeman in Tuskegee. Did I ever tell you that?" she asked.

"Yes. You did," I replied. "About thirty times."

"You can be such a smarty pants. Have I ever told you *that*?"

"It's one of my many talents," I popped back at her.

"Well, it's a talent you need to get rid of," she informed me. "Anyhow, you know I can't remember things."

"Like hell, you can't," I thought to myself. Instead of making that comment, I asked, "And you've talked with your cousin?"

"Yes. I told you that. Right after you answered the phone. I swear, Marley Jane, you're forgetting a lot of stuff lately." She waited for me to respond. I didn't bite.

When she realized that I wasn't going to reply, she continued. "Of course, he can't say too much. But, he did tell me the rapist bit her on her chin and left breast. Whooping big red marks. Bubba said he ain't never seen nothing like it in his whole life. My Lord! The things a policeman has to put up with will just blow your mind. Beats all I've ever heard tell of. And they don't make enough money for doodly squat," she added, going in a whole different direction.

"Neither do I," I threw in. "So, what else did he not say much of?"

There was a pause, as if she was thinking about my response. I was afraid that I'd pissed her off and she might hang up. I heard a deep sigh.

"Well, he said she was not raped. You know. The normal way. The person used some type of object. In her behind. Don't you know that was painful?"

I quickly decided to completely disregard her comment about "the normal way." I wondered what was ever "normal" about being raped. Instead, I said, "Your cousin seems to know a lot. Do they have any idea who did it?"

"Nope. None. Just that it was a black man. And, let me tell you, white folks are gonna be real upset 'bout that. I mean him being black and all."

"Well, I hope people are enraged about the rape of an old woman. How did he get in?" I asked.

"Seems like he came through a kitchen window. For the life of me, I can't understand why folks don't lock their windows. The same as they lock their doors. Does that make any sense to you? The screen was torn off and was on the ground. And—"

"Was the window open or closed?" I interrupted.

"I don't know. My cousin didn't say anything 'bout that. Does it matter?" she asked, with just a hint of sarcasm.

"Well, maybe," I defended my question. "It might indicate whether or not he was in a hurry. Coming or going." I ended on a lame note.

"I didn't hear nothing 'bout that. But, I'm locking all my windows and doors. You do the same. Maybe you need to keep the kids inside for a while. 'Til they catch the rapist," she warned.

"Bertha, how can I keep the kids inside all of the time? Hopefully, he doesn't decide to rape children. But I'll make sure everything's double locked when night comes. After all, Winston doesn't get home 'til awful late most nights."

"I know. That's one reason I'm telling you 'bout this. Everything my cousin told me. Be careful. Call me, if you need anything. I gotta go. Got a sweet potato pie in the oven. Love you." I heard the click of the phone.

I stood for several minutes and watched the kids, as the sun filtered through the branches of the large pecan tree. I felt a shiver up my spine. "What type of monster rapes an old woman?" I thought to myself and added, "Or anyone for that matter." I heard a knock on the kitchen door. I looked out the window. Sherry had arrived for our morning coffee. I opened the door, saying, "Girl, I gotta tell you something. Did you know an elderly woman was raped in Tuskegee early this morning?"

Chapter 40

Weeks went by. Thanksgiving was around the corner, and the students and staff were ready for a break. Football season was over. The last three seasons had been good. Playoffs and championships were becoming common for the Notasulga Blue Devils.

On Thanksgiving Day, we went to my parents' home and spent the day with my family. It was a windy, cold, sunny day. We drove home under a dark sky and millions of twinkling lights. Wesley and Katherine fell asleep on the back seat of the car. When we got home, Winston led a zonked out Katherine into the house and put her to bed, fully clothed, minus her shoes. I gently shook Wesley awake and held his hand, while he stumbled through the door and down the hall to his bedroom.

The following morning, Winston left the house before dawn to go hunting. The kids slept late, while Sherry, Bertha, and I drank coffee at the kitchen table. The room was warm, and the aroma of a pound cake drifted through the house.

"He attacked another woman last night," Bertha said, suddenly changing the subject of her family's Thanksgiving gathering.

"Who was she?" I asked.

"Mrs. Pauline Monroe. Another older woman. She's 'bout seventy-eight. Lives by herself in Tuskegee. I don't know her," she said in a melancholy voice.

"Is she white?" Sherry asked.

"Yeah. He beat her pretty bad. Knocked out most of her teeth. Choked her and left bite marks on her chin and breast." After a moment, she added, "Or so Bubba said."

"Is she alive?" I asked, praying that she was.

"Barely. She's in Lee County Hospital. And she told the police it was a black man. She was sleeping, and he climbed in her bedroom window."

"Was it locked?" I wondered aloud.

"Apparently not. The screen was on the ground. Like before." She took a long sip of coffee and continued, "According to Bubba, this attack was worse than the last one." She stopped talking and added more sugar to her coffee—over stirring it. Looking up, she studied me for a moment and said, "I don't even want to go to Tuskegee during the day time. Let alone at night.

Everybody's scared. Especially older women. Older white women." She looked into her cup like she was trying to read tea leaves.

"I imagine older black women are scared, too," I added. "Everyone's talking. I've heard some nasty comments. It's opened up a whole new racial thing. We don't need that here. Of all places." I stood up and took the cake out of the oven. Leaving it to cool before I sat back down.

"Well, I don't know about the two of you, but it's scaring the holy shit outta me. I'll be glad when he's caught," Sherry said in her New York accent, as she poured herself another cup of coffee. When she sat down, she added, "I've heard lots of talk, too. I just hope the race thing doesn't get out of hand."

"That's for sure. I've heard things, as well. 'Bout what the men will do when they catch the rapist. Yeah. I'm worried 'bout lots of things. Things could get outta hand. Fast." Bertha watched the swirls that the stirring spoon created in her coffee. Without looking up, she said, "There's something else Bubba told me. The same night Mrs. Monroe was attacked, somebody broke into another old woman's house. She wasn't home. When she got home that morning, the kitchen window was open. It was freezing cold inside. Some furniture was knocked over. Of course, the police don't know if it was the same person, but they suspect that it was."

"So, she called the police?" I asked and felt stupid the second the question left my mouth. "Well, I guess if they came, somebody called them."

"Yep. She left that day to go stay with her son and his family in Montgomery. He came right away and got her." Bertha sipped her coffee.

We sat in silence for several minutes. Just as I was getting ready to offer them a slice of cake, Bertha stood up. "I gotta get going. I'm taking Mama to see her brother in Opelika." She got to the door and stopped with her hand on the doorknob. Turning to face us, she said, "My mama's seventy-four. This really bothers me. I'm gonna start spending the night with her. I don't want her to be by herself."

I heard the concern in her voice and knew how worried she was. "I don't blame you. That's a good idea." I walked over and hugged her.

"Well, bye," she said. "I'll call you later."

Sherry and I ate a slice of cake and discussed the rapes. After thirty minutes, she said, "Well, I've got to get home. The kids will be getting up soon. I'll talk with you later. Let me know if you hear anything."

As I placed our coffee cups in the sink, I thought about the terror that had seized women in Macon County. Fear resided in every house where there was a woman. People were becoming angry, and I worried that fear might overtake common sense, allowing the dreadful KKK to raise its ugly head, to demand justice on its terms.

Bertha, Sherry, and I certainly felt the terror. In my opinion, it wasn't just older white women. I'd talked with Willie Mae, and I knew it was black women as well. Young and old women. Regardless of where you went, that's all people were talking about. Everyone was getting antsy, and they were beginning to criticize the police.

* * * * * * *

Christmas came and went. The year ended without another rape incident. People were still on edge, as if they were waiting. There were so many unanswered questions.

After New Year's, the second semester of school began. As assistant principal, the second semester meant that Winston would have more administrative duties than he'd had the first semester. It also meant that he'd be at school every night that the doors were open, sports or otherwise. The kids and I would spend even more time alone, since he'd be hunting or fishing every Saturday and most Sundays, from before sunrise to after the sun vanished in the sky. I'd become used to that life and no longer bothered to get out of gear because he was so seldom home. The fight over that subject had long gone out of me. I was accustomed to being alone with the kids and making decisions without him.

It was the middle of January when the third attack happened. A light snow fell during the night, leaving a thin white blanket over everything. For once, Winston didn't get up early to go hunting. I eased out of bed, careful not to wake him. Wesley and Katherine slept, snuggled under quilts that my mama had made. I tiptoed down the hall to the kitchen and started a pot of coffee. As the coffee percolated, I stood at the sliding glass doors, admiring the sparkling snow. When the coffee was ready, I poured a cup and turned the radio on low so that it wouldn't disturb the sound sleepers.

I was thinking about the blistering cold Saturday morning. The sky was overcast, as daylight began to spread its wings across a bleak sky. I'd turned the heat up, but not enough to make it uncomfortable for the sleepy heads. Just enough that I wouldn't be cold.

The news caught my attention. I paused, with the cup halfway to my mouth, as I heard the announcer say that the rapist had assaulted another elderly woman in her home in Tuskegee. The attack occurred around four o'clock a.m. Just a little more than three hours earlier. It appeared that the rapist entered the house in the same manner that he'd done before. Through a window. The woman, whose name hadn't yet been released, was in intensive care at Lee County Hospital. The announcer ended with, "We have nothing further to report at this time. As soon as we get additional information, we'll let you know. Stay tuned to WJCM."

I leaned back against the kitchen counter and heard the beginning of "Three Times a Lady." The smooth voice of Lionel Richie, who was the lead vocalist for the Commodores, filled the warm kitchen. "Three ladies," I thought. "How many more?" I closed my eyes, but I couldn't concentrate on the magic of Richie's singing. Later, I heard the DJ say that Lionel Richie and the Commodores would be the featured singers throughout the day, and to stay tuned for the "fantastic music of Tuskegee's own amazing Commodores."

As I listened to the DJ praise Lionel Richie and the Commodores, I thought that no matter how much ugly you could find in Tuskegee, there was so much good. For every evil deed, Tuskegee had a history of strong, intellectual, talented, innovative thinking people who'd paved the way for so many positive things. I focused on that, in an attempt to stomp the recent evil deeds from my mind. One man can destroy so much.

By eight o'clock, Winston and the kids were up. I made pancakes and sausage. After breakfast, he took them outside to play in the snow. I washed dishes and watched them make snow angels. Soon, they came inside to tell me that they were headed for the school, to slide down the hill at the football field. Winston threw the tin tops of the two garbage cans into the back of the truck, and they left.

Bertha called soon after they drove off. She'd been in touch with Bubba, who was telling more than I was certain the police and the investigators wanted people to be told. He was a man in the know, and he was sharing what he knew to an attentive audience. I admit that I wanted to know just as much as Bertha did. Everyone wanted to know. I had no idea what was lost or gained in the line of gossip. People were upset, and they wanted an arrest to be made. The sooner the better.

I heard from Bertha, who heard from Bubba, that Mrs. Violet Rose, an eighty-year old woman who lived alone, just outside the city limits of

Tuskegee, was attacked in the early morning hours. The rapist had beaten, choked, and raped her with an object. Again, he'd left bite marks on her chin and left breast. He'd beaten her so violently in the face that she'd lost sight in one eye. She was near death when the maid entered the house at approximately six o'clock that morning.

Bubba also told Bertha that it appeared the rapist broke into another elderly woman's home earlier, about three o'clock. That woman, Mrs. Wilma Carson, had a daughter, Sally James who was visiting from New Site. Sally couldn't sleep and was watching an old movie on television, when she heard a noise that sounded like it came from the kitchen. She took the pistol that she always kept on a night table by her bed. Slowly, she got up and walked softly down the hall. As she walked into the kitchen, she flipped the switch and flooded the room with light.

The man was at the window, which he was holding just above his forehead. Sally fired a shot and hit the glass above the intruder's head. It shattered, sending slivers of glass in front of his face and into the sink. He dropped to the ground and began to run. She rushed to the window and looked out. He was running across the yard to the street. She fired a second shot. He kept running. When he ran under a streetlight, she got a good look at his size and build.

When the man darted across the street and under the light, she noticed that he was approximately six feet, lean, and well-built. He wore dark clothing and a dark toboggan that was pulled over his face. It had holes for the eyes. She was positive about that since she'd gotten a good look before she fired the first shot. He wore dark gloves, because she'd seen those as he held up the window. He carried some type of object in his left hand. She couldn't tell much about the man's face.

By the time the police arrived, there was no sign of the intruder. The darkness had swallowed him up. A search of the neighborhood gave up nothing. The police knocked on doors and asked if anyone had seen or heard anything, but no one had.

Later, the police were surprised to discover that the intruder had left and gone straight to find another victim. Some people wondered if the appearance of Mrs. Carson's daughter and the firing of the gun only enraged him, rather than scaring him. That would explain why the attack on the next victim had been so brutal.

Everyone felt some relief. At last, someone had seen the man and could identify him. Or some things about him. Now, he sort of had a face. A drawing of the man appeared later in papers that were published in nearby counties. As I looked at the drawing of the rapist, I was puzzled as to how Sally James gave such a thorough description, considering the fact that she never saw his face.

That day, shortly after lunch, Mrs. Carson and Sally were on their way to Sally's home in New Site, away from the rapist who'd terrorized an entire county. Mrs. Carson told the police that she wouldn't be returning home to stay until the rapist was caught.

Chapter 41

February crawled into March. New life began springing up. Buds clung to branches, ready to open into leaves that would fan the air and cast shade. Farmers plowed their fields and planted seeds. Cool mornings and nights still stayed around, but the days were getting warmer. Children took off their socks and shoes to run barefoot through fields and yards, as the first color of green rose from the ground.

It was near the end of March. The Girls Night Out crowd of twelve was seated around tables in Dianne Ridgeway's large dining area. There were four tables of bridge. My partner bid three spades. I bid four. After three passes, I exposed my cards and left the table to get a fresh cup of coffee. My partner took the game. Soon, we all stopped for refreshments and Dianne's delicious whoopee pies.

From the far table, Ruby Webb, who was one of the girls whom I'd heard talking about the fire at Notasulga High School years before, asked if anyone had heard the latest news about the rapist. Everyone answered, "No." All of us commented, worried that he'd never be caught and brought to justice. I found myself thinking about the many issues of justice that the people in the town had confronted, time and again. One could only hope that they chose the right side of justice and didn't allow fear to control them.

Some women repeated what their husbands were saying they'd do "to the black son-of-a-bitch," if they ever got their hands on him. One of the women said, "That nigger knows better than to come to Notasulga." That answered some questions that I'd been asking myself.

It was obvious that the terror had spread throughout the county and that it'd created racial unrest. If the rapes began to occur in Notasulga, the gates of hell would break wide open. The tension was thick as fog and blinded people, causing old fears to surface Fearing what could happen was understandable. A knot formed in my gut, just thinking about how things could get out-of-hand.

No sooner had the thought left my head, than Rose Jean Friman slightly tossed her long bleached curls, blew cigarette smoke through her nose, tapped the ashes of her half-smoked cigarette into an ash tray, and said in a firm voice, "Well, I can tell y'all right now, if he comes to Notasulga, there's gonna be a tarred nigger, hanging from a big ole tree. Mark my words."

Ruby laughed and smirked, "Honey, I know you're right 'bout that."

Several of the women laughed and agreed.

"Anyhow, this is what happens when the blacks get the right to vote. What do they do? Every blasted nigger in Macon County went and voted for that black sheriff. And he ain't done doodly squat to catch that rapist. He's probably glad white women are being raped and killed," Ruby continued, as she slammed a card on the table in front of her.

No one said a word. The only sound was the movement of cards as they hit the tables. I stood up and poured myself another cup of coffee. Anger was spreading through every vein. I turned slowly and looked at Ruby. She looked up at me and caught my cold, hard eyes. Years ago, I kept quiet, while she spewed racial venom, and I ran away. Not today.

"I voted for that black sheriff," I said in a low, calm voice that scared me, "and, personally, I think that you're wrong. He does care about the women. But, I have a question for you. Would you care if those women were black and being raped and killed by a black man?"

The cards were silent. I knew that everyone was looking down. I kept my eyes locked on Ruby. "Did anyone else in this room vote for the sheriff?" It was quiet, and I didn't think that anyone was going to answer. Ruby's eyes held anger. Her jaws were locked, but she didn't look away.

"I voted for him," Viola said.

"Me, too," Dianne acknowledged. Four others confirmed that they, too, had voted for the sheriff.

Ruby looked away. Surprising me, she said in a meek voice, "I did, too. Hey, y'all, I'm sorry. Hell, I'm just scared. We're all scared."

I walked over and hugged her. "Yeah. We all are, but we can't let our fears replace our common sense. Justice will triumph."

I stepped away from Ruby's chair. "Oh, by the way. Can everyone just stop using the 'N' word? Please."

Viola popped her hands together. "Okay. Enough. Let's play bridge."

As usual, we didn't stop playing bridge until around two o'clock. I, along with Dianne, who was a fourth grade teacher at the elementary school, would get little sleep before we reported for work. Although we had decided not to play bridge every week, when the rapist began attacking, we agreed to play once a month and to go out to dinner once a month at some restaurant outside of Macon County. Also, we paired up, agreeing to call a pal as soon as we were safely inside our homes. If a pal hadn't heard from her pal after thirty minutes of leaving for home, she was to notify the police.

As soon as I entered the house and locked the door, I dialed Viola's number to confirm that she was inside her house. She answered the phone on the first ring. We spoke briefly and hung up. I took a quick shower to wash the smell of cigarette smoke from my hair. I slipped into bed beside Winston and was asleep as soon as my head hit the pillow.

* * * * * *

Two weeks later, there was another attack. The rapist entered the home of two sisters who were in their late seventies. Each one was stabbed over twenty times. The oldest sister died during the brutal attack. Afterwards, the rapist turned his rage on the surviving sister. He beat, stabbed, raped, and bit her chin and left breast, as blood oozed from multiple stab wounds. When he finally left, she managed to dial the police. They arrived in time to rush her to the emergency room. She died two days later.

A week after the murders, on a Friday morning, Sally James brought her mother home to collect some items. A friend from New Site came with them. While the friend and Mrs. Carson gathered the needed items, Sally took her car to the local Ford dealership for an oil change and to have the tires rotated and balanced. After talking with the service manager, she walked to the lounge to wait.

He walked past her, just as she was pouring a steaming cup of coffee. She almost dropped the cup. "Stay calm. Stay calm," she told herself, while her hands trembled and the coffee rocked like a storm at sea. She considered asking the man a question, to determine if he gave any indication of recognizing her. Instead, she just watched him. He certainly looked like the man she shot at that night. Same build. Same height. If she could just see his eyes, which was about all that she'd seen of the man's face.

She studied his back. He was talking to a customer, and she realized that he was a car salesman. After a moment, he turned to point to several cars behind her on the showroom floor. He had a neat close-cut afro and thin sideburns ran down the sides of a lean, thin face, into a beard, which was trimmed neatly. A slender mustache covered his upper lip. The blue-green eyes, which were the color of teal, startled her. She'd never seen such a color, but she knew that many light skinned blacks had eyes similar to those.

She shook her head slightly to clear the cobwebs. Were those the same eyes that she'd stared into that night? It was dark. She might be confused about the eyes. Since she'd not seen anything but the man's eyes, I'd later say that I never could figure out how she gave a description of the man's face. But those eyes! How could anyone not recognize those eyes?

"No," she told herself. "I'm not confused. I know it's him."

The man turned away, giving no indication that he'd ever seen her. "Oh, he's cool," she whispered to herself. She left the lounge and wandered around the lot until her car was serviced. As soon as she got into the car, she drove straight to the police station, where she insisted that she knew the identity of the rapist.

That afternoon, the Tuskegee police arrested Donte Parsons, Willie Mae's nephew, for the rapes and murders of the elderly white women in Tuskegee. In absolute shock, he repeated over and over that he was innocent, that he'd never harmed anyone in his life.

Bertha called late that afternoon to tell me that an arrest had been made. I listened in shock, as she told me the name of the accused. "I don't believe it," I said, in disbelief. "He's a good man. I'm sure there's a mistake. Bertha, you know him, too. I'm having a hard time wrapping my head around this."

"Me, too. But, he's the one they've arrested. Sally James insisted that he was the man she saw at the kitchen window at her mama's house that night," she added, and I could almost see her shaking her head. "Bubba says that it was the only evidence they had, so they couldn't take no chance on letting him go until they investigate it further."

When we hung up, I called Willie Mae. She was completely devastated and in shock. "I know it ain't him," she kept repeating. "He wouldn't hurt no old women. That woman made a mistake. I tell you she made a mistake."

It was a long week. Rumors flew like leaves on a windy autumn day. Willie Mae and I didn't talk much about the arrest of her nephew while we were at school. No one mentioned it to her. Everyone respected her and didn't want to offend her. I'd ask her daily, "Are you okay?" or "How's your sister?"

"He didn't do it. I know he didn't do it," she'd say over and over. "My sister don't believe he did it. She's worried. Lord knows that."

Otherwise, she was quiet. Her face was tight and she looked tired. It seemed to me that she moved more slowly and that her shoulders were hunched. My heart broke for her.

Chapter 42

Before the week ended, a house of cards would fall. And another assault would take place, leaving an elderly white woman shaken, but determined to defend herself and not become a victim. She would later say that she had doubted that Donte was the rapist, because he just didn't fit the description Sally James had first given to authorities.

When Bertha, Willie Mae, and I met at Jewel's house on Saturday, Donte had been released from jail, and the rapist lay in a morgue. Events had unfolded rapidly, one layer at a time, until the truth was revealed.

Between Bertha's contact with her cousin, Bubba, and Willie Mae's contact with her sister, Precision Parsons, we got both stories. One story would never be completely known to the public.

As the kids watched a movie on television and stuffed themselves with popcorn, we took a break from baking and sat around the table, drinking coffee. Willie Mae told her story first, while we all leaned in toward her, not wanting to miss a comma.

Precision went every day to the jail, to visit Donte. The only thing that he'd say to her was, "I didn't rape those women. I swear to God. I've never killed anyone. I swear." Then, he'd sit with his head in his hands while she talked, begging him to talk to the sheriff and to get an attorney.

On the third visit, he raised his head, took both her hands in his, looked her in the eyes, and said, "Mama. I did not *do* those things." After several deep breaths, he continued. "I was with someone every time an attack happened. I was with someone. Do you hear me?"

"Just say so. Tell the sheriff who you was with. He can talk to that person," she pleaded, squeezing his hand.

"No, Mama. He can't. That person won't tell the truth. She can't tell the truth. Do you understand?" Pleading with her to understand, to comprehend what he couldn't tell her.

Taking her left hand from his right hand, she put it over her mouth. Her eyes opened wide. "Who was you with?" Silence was another occupant in the stuffy room. "Who? Tell me!" she demanded in a firm, but gentle voice that carried a touch of fear. "Tell me! Who?" Still, he didn't answer. He sat starring at the table. Slowly, he raised his eyes.

"Donte, this here is yo' life. Do you hear me, boy? Now, you tell me, son. Tell me. Now!" she demanded and slapped her right hand on the table.

Donte dropped his head. He looked defeated. Slowly, he raised his head. Tears floated in his blue-green eyes, and Precision, for more than a hundred times since she first held her son in her arms, thought how much those eyes looked like light turquoise. "I was with Virginia Wiggins. I was with her. Every time."

For a while, she couldn't speak. She was shocked. "That's the wife of the man who owns that dealership you work at," she whispered, just loud enough for him to hear.

The silence in that was room was the loudest that either had ever experienced, for it hung heavy with secrets and horror. Precision was trying to absorb what she'd heard. Leaning into her son, she asked, "Where?" She fought not to reveal her surprise and fear. This news was bad. Not as bad as rape and murder. But, after all, this *was* Alabama.

"At her house. In her bedroom."

"My, God! He would've killed you if he'd caught you together. He'd have killed you. And the State of Alabama wouldn't have done a damn thing to him," she stated in a flat tone, without mentioning who "he" was. There was no need.

Looking his mama in the eye, he confessed. "He knew, Mama. He was there."

"Where?" she asked, in a confused voice.

"There. In the bedroom. With us."

Shaking her head, to clear the confusion, she asked, "What was he doing?"

"Watching." He paused and cracked his knuckles. "He liked to watch."

All of the oxygen in the room was sucked up. Precision felt as if she'd faint. The image briefly strolled into her head, and she wanted to scream at him, "Don't put that in my head!" But, this was her son and he needed her. She was the first one to break the silence. "Do you have any proof?"

Donte looked at her in wonder, taking a long time to reply. He sighed and said, "Yes. He filmed us."

"You've got to tell the sheriff. Everything. Do you understand?" she asked. As she talked, she stood up. Before he could stop her, she opened the door.

"Deputy!" she yelled to a man who was standing guard not too far from the door. "Git the sheriff in here. My boy's gonna talk."

"Mama. No!" he pleaded.

Returning to the small table, she pointed a slender finger in his face. "You listen to me, boy. Hear me. I'll be damned if you gonna be put to death for raping and killing white women. For something you ain't done. No way in hell will I allow that to happen. Do you understand me?"

"Mama—," he begged, holding out his hands to her.

"No! It ain't happening. Now, you was man enough to screw that white woman. And you gonna be man enough to admit it."

The sheriff entered the room, chewing a toothpick. He was a large, tall black man who had a hard time believing that Donte Parsons was the rapist. But, when that white woman insisted it was so, he didn't have any choice but to make an arrest.

Precision turned to the sheriff and said, "Git yo' tape recorder, Sheriff. My son's got somethin' he wanna say. And I'm staying here while he says it."

The sheriff took his time, looking from Donte to Precision. "Yes, ma'am. Grover, bring that tape recorder in here to me."

Later that day, the sheriff went to the Wiggins' car lot. He asked to speak to Monty and Virginia Wiggins in private. He told them about Donte's alibi and about the films.

Monty Wiggins, who was a tall handsome man, slammed his heavy fist on the desk. "He's a damn lie. I'll stomp his black ass. What the hell, man? You takin' the word of a rapist? A black man?" He turned blood red.

In a slow Southern drawl, with a toothpick sticking from his lips, the sheriff gave Monty a cold stare and said, "An accused rapist. Accused. Now, unless you folks cooperate, I'm leavin' a deputy here and one at yo' house. Then, I'm marchin' down to the courthouse and gittin' a warrant to search both places—this dealership and yo' house—for films that you deny takin' of that lyin' nigger, screwin' yo' pretty wife here, while you watched. If they exist, them films are evidence in an ongoin' investigation. If there's evidence that he's not lyin', he's gonna be a free man."

I know that my mouth was dragging the floor when Willie Mae finished. "Well. I'll just be damned," I said. "He was watching." I'd almost forgotten about the rapes.

"That's right," she said, nodding and smiling. "They was never gonna tell. Of course, when the sheriff asked 'em, they denied it. At first. Finally, when he told 'em that he was gittin' a search warrant, Virginia Wiggins broke down and started cryin'. She admitted it was all true and had been goin' on for almost two years. Her husband got the films out of the big safe he kept in his office and gave 'em to the sheriff. But, he wasn't happy 'bout it."

We all sat. Stunned. Finally, Jewel said, "I'm a little shocked. I mean . . . I've heard about things like that. I just never—," and her voice stopped. We all nodded that we understood.

Looking at Bertha, I said, "It's your turn. Tell us what Bubba told you. Some of it we've heard on the news or read about."

"Well," she said, pursing her lips and looking sideways, "y'all know the last attack happened the night before they let Donte out of jail. Which was further proof that he didn't commit the rapes." We nodded and waited, knowing that Bertha liked to milk a cow.

She began to tell the story. The rapist had entered Mrs. Eugenia Pitts' home through the kitchen window. It was about three o'clock in the morning, and the eighty-six-year-old woman was sitting up in bed, reading. The bedside lamp threw light across her face and the book. She heard a noise and took her twenty-two pistol from the nightstand. She got quietly out of bed.

When the intruder walked through the door, he was surprised to see her standing beside the bed, holding a gun. She saw the shock on his face. 'Course she was as shocked to see him, as he was to see her. There was no mistaking the arched eyebrows like bird wings over black, shiny eyes that bulged from the sockets. "She sure 'nuff got those eyes wrong," she thought to herself.

He charged, swinging an object that was about twelve inches in length. She took a step back and struggled to maintain her balance. Filled with rage, he leaped toward her. She pulled the trigger. The bullet hit his left shoulder, and he twisted slightly from the impact. He kept coming and raised the pipe. The gun fired a second time, hitting him in the forehead, just above the eyes. She watched in amazement as a thick streak of red oozed from the small hole that now looked like a third eye. Drops of blood were splattered on her periwinkle cotton nightgown.

He fell at her feet, face down, his dead eyes staring into eternity. His legs were splayed apart; toes turned inward. She moved to her right and stepped over him, leaving the room to call the police. When they arrived, she was waiting at the front door, with the gun still in her right hand. She gave it to the first policeman who entered the house. In a calm voice, she said, "He's dead. I shot him dead. He's not gonna be raping or murdering no more women."

The second policeman led her to the sofa. She sat down slowly and took a deep breath. Looking at the policeman, who was about her grandson's age, she said, "I need a strong drink. In the kitchen cabinet, near the sink, is a bottle of whiskey. Bring it to me, please. Oh, and a glass." After a moment, "Hell, forget the glass. Just bring me the bottle."

She sat with her legs slightly apart, holding her hands between her knees. "Just yesterday, I made that bastard a fried bologna sandwich for lunch and gave him a slice of my apple pie. He sat right there at my kitchen table and ate ever mouthful of it. Being so nice and polite. Telling me how much he liked my apple pie. Did you know that I've won five blue ribbons for that apple pie? It's a damn good pie. If I do say so myself."

The policemen were shocked when they turned the dead man over and recognized Reuben Brewer. His shocked glazed-over eyes were focused on the far lower wall. He was a yardman around town, and he worked mainly for elderly white women. As a matter of fact, he'd worked for all of the victims. He was a hard worker who was in great demand. Everyone considered him to be a quiet, gentle young man, with good manners.

In his right back pants pocket, they found a black cap— the kind that could be pulled down over the face with holes for eyes. Bubba asked the other policemen who were in the room, "Wonder why he wasn't wearing that?"

"He didn't plan on Mrs. Pitts living to identify him. No need to cover his face," an older policeman answered. "This time, he picked the wrong old lady."

We were quiet after Bertha finished. The sound of the kids' laughter drifted into the room. Dust floated in sunbeams that streaked through the window. Then, Willie Mae said in a quiet voice, "My sister and nephew are moving to Chicago, to live with her daughter. You know she's a nurse there. They gonna try to start a new life. To move on."

Bertha added some new information, "And I heard that Monty Wiggins is selling the Ford dealership and moving away. They're not telling anybody where they're going. Bubba said the sheriff looked at those films. Wouldn't let nobody else see 'em. But he did say that it was just like Donte said. Only worse."

Few people would ever know that the films disappeared as evidence. Only one person watched them go up in smoke, and he later told Donte, "Don't worry 'bout them films no more. They don't exist. Somehow, they done gone and got lost. That's between us."

Chapter 43

Life returned to normal. The racial panic that held a county captive for months was gone. But, for Willie Mae, another tragedy was about to unfold. Throughout April, she was bubbly, always singing or humming softly as she worked in the school cafeteria. Summer was coming, and she was planning her annual July visit to see Sweet, who now lived in New Jersey with her daddy and stepmother. The summer after the swimming pool incident, Ash married a lovely woman who was a teacher. They wanted Sweet to come live with them and to make a new life, as far away from the South as they could get.

The first Thursday in May, Willie Mae awoke about five-thirty. She was surprised to find Mose still in bed, beside her. Shaking him, she said, "Mose. Git up. You gonna be late. Mr. A.'s gonna be at school 'fore you this mornin'. Git up." When he didn't respond, fear moved from her belly upward to her throat, and she began to yell his name and shake him. Throwing her body across his, she screamed and cried until she was exhausted. Finally, she called Victor. When he arrived ten minutes later, she was dressed, sitting in a rocker beside the bed, and looking into space. Victor made the necessary calls. Then, he called Sweet's daddy.

During homeroom, Winston spoke over the intercom and told the teachers to bring the students to the auditorium. As he gave the students and faculty the sad news of Mose's death, all of us wept for the man who'd been so devoted to the school and to its cause. There were no details about the funeral at that time. The elementary students and teachers weren't in the auditorium, but we learned that the teachers were told about Mose. Everyone agreed that it was best, for the time being, not to tell the younger students.

Mose was buried Saturday week, beside his daughter, Zoe, on a hill that overlooked Possum Run Creek, in the graveyard of Shiloh Baptist Church. The entire staff, elementary and high schools, was at the funeral, along with the superintendent of education and all of the board members. Many students came with their parents. There wasn't a cloud in the sky, and a gentle breeze blew across the casket before it was lowered into the ground. The choir from Mose's church sang and swayed, while their red robes moved back and forth. The sweet sound of their voices rocked through the pine trees and filled Possum Run Creek with ripples.

Victor stood with Wilie Mae, Sweet, her daddy, and her stepmother. Willie Mae locked arms with Victor and Sweet. Tears ran down the faces of all three and dripped off their chins. No one was ashamed to be seen crying for Mose. My throat was tight and tears slid down my face. Willie Mae mourned like a wounded animal. The sound tore through me and punched a hole in my heart.

After the funeral, most of us went to Willie Mae's. The school cafeteria staff had prepared massive amounts of food, on Victor's instructions. I talked with Sweet and her daddy. Each time that I attempted to speak with Willie Mae, she was speaking to someone. I managed to hug her before I left. We didn't speak, because the pain and sadness were too much for us.

It was two weeks before she returned to work. She came the last week of school to help clean the kitchen and put things away for the summer. On her first day back, I hugged her and whispered, "I've been thinking about you. I've missed you." She smiled and touched my hand, but said nothing.

The first Saturday in June, I met with Bertha and Willie Mae at Jewel's house after lunch. The kids were at the pool. It was just the four of us. We sat in rockers on the back porch, drinking sweet tea with lemon. After some chatter, there was a pause in the conversation. No one spoke for several minutes. There was no need. We were enjoying one another's company, as the sun wrapped us in its golden warmth and the sound of Emmitt's tractor came to us from a distance.

Suddenly, Willie Mae announced, "I'm leaving."

"What?" we all asked at once and stopped rocking.

"I'm leaving. Going to live with Sweet, her daddy, and his wife, who's expecting a baby in November. Sweet needs me, and I need her."

"When are you leaving?" Bertha asked.

"Just as soon as I gets packed. My brother and his wife are gonna live in my house. I mighta told y'all before that he's retired from the Army. He wants to do some farming. And raise a few cows and chickens. He's gonna take Mose's job. His wife's gonna take my job. We done all talked it over with Mr. A."

Bertha asked, "Why haven't you told us before now?"

"Didn't wanna tell nobody 'til everything was settled. No need for me to stay here any longer. My sister's done gone to Chicago. I need Sweet. And she needs me," she said, not realizing that she was repeating herself. "My mind's made up." There was an inner strength that covered her, protected her.

I got out of the rocker and knelt on the floor beside her chair. I took her right hand in both of mine and looked up at her. I felt hot tears fill my eyes. My vision blurred. "I don't want you to go," I whispered.

She ran her left hand down the side of my face and held my chin and tilted it up toward her. She smiled at me and said in a soothing tone, "Don't be sad. I want you to be happy for me. To know I'm doing what's best. Sometimes, you have to let go and move on.

"I'm letting go to get rid of all these painful feelings that done ripped apart my heart. I'm gonna let go of my bitter grudges and fears. And I'm gonna bury them ghosts that live in my head and cause too much heart-breaking disappointments that hold my spirit a prisoner.

"I'm gonna control my future. It's gonna be a struggle, but the Lord's with me." She let go of my chin and placed her hand on my head. "Don't look back in anger, sorrow, or regret. Learn from yesterday. Be strong and don't let nobody steal your joy. Forgive and move on. Be happy."

I lifted her hand and kissed the scar that a sharp knife had made when she was a young girl, learning to cook. I put my head in her lap and allowed the tears to soak her dress. She stroked my head. I sensed Bertha and Jewel surrounding us. I felt each one softly place a hand on my back. I knew they'd also placed a hand on Willie Mae's back. We became a circle of humanity, connected forever. I knew I'd not lost Willie Mae, my friend who'd taught me so much. I couldn't grieve for that.

The silence surrounded us.

Acknowledgements

The author wishes to acknowledge the following sources for information used in *Troubling the Ashes*:

Reference materials for Lee v. Macon County Board of Education including "970 F2d 767—Lee v. Macon County Board of Education," published online by OpenJurist, the home of legal info, lawyers, and the law; "Lee v. Macon County Board of Education," published online by Leagle, provider of primary case law from Federal and higher State courts; "Lee v. Macon County Board of Education," written by C. J. Schexnayder for the Encyclopedia of Alabama online © 2013, 25 February 2013.

Materials referred to for the racial history in Macon County, Alabama, and the State of Alabama, as well as other details include "School Desegregation, Law, and Order, and Litigating Social Justice in Alabama, 1954-1973" by Joseph Mark Bagley for dissertation at Georgia State University in 2014; *Reaping the Whirlwind: The Civil Rights Movement in Tuskegee* by Robert J. Norrell © 1985, published by Vintage Books.

Other sources include "Courage and Principal," published in *East Alabama Living* in the fall of 2012; "Macon County: The Rise of Black Run America" by Hunter Wallace, published online by Occidental Dissent on 29 June 2011; "Students Who Made History in 1960's Macon County, Alabama, to Speak May 23 in Tuskegee," published in the *Wire Eagle* on 8 May 2013, Auburn University's News Feed; "Wyatt, Other Students Faced Terrifying Events" by Melody Kitchens, published in *The Tuskegee News* on 16 February 2012.

The author would like to make special mention of the articles "Signs Painted on Notasulga Mixed School" on 17 April 1964; "Investigators Awaiting Cooling of Notasulga School Building" on 20 April 1964; "Motorbike Clue to Notasulga School Burning" on 21 April 1964; "Negro Students in Notasulga Reassigned" on 24 April 1964; "Notasulga Negro Students Take Plea to Federal Court" on 28 April 1964; "Negroes Ordered Back to Burned Notasulga High School Classes" on 29 April 1964; "Six Negro Students Return to Fire-Damaged Notasulga High" on 30 April 1964; "Six Negroes

Go Unnoticed at Notasulga High" on 1 May 1964; these articles appeared in the *Opelika Daily News* in 1964 and dealt with the desegregation and burning of Notasulga High School in Macon County, Alabama.

For help in researching the novel, the author wishes to give thanks to Willie B. Wyatt for phone interviews and e-mails regarding his experiences at Notasulga High School, as one of the plaintiffs in Lee v. Macon County Board of Education. He offered in-depth knowledge, based on his personal experiences. In the novel, he is the "young man" who rode the bus back and forth from Tuskegee; he saw Vernon Merritt beaten by Jim Clark and his followers. The author would like to thank Dr. Mark Wilson, of Auburn University, for interviews, e-mails, and guidance in suggesting sources that were extremely helpful.

The author would like to give special thanks to the following people who believed in equality, racial justice, desegregation, and the survival of the public school system in Macon County, Alabama: Fred Gray, a civil rights attorney from Montgomery, Alabama, who filed the desegregation lawsuit, Lee v. Macon County Board of Education; Federal District Judge Frank M. Johnson, who supported racial justice and upheld the Constitution; the plaintiffs in Lee v. Macon, who risked their lives for justice; Robert B. Anderson, principal of Notasulga High School, who stood up for his beliefs, regarding equality and desegregation.

The author expresses gratitude and thanks for the following people who supported and helped her in producing *Troubling the Ashes*: Tina Tatum, publisher at Woodson Knowles Publishing Group, who believed in the author and this novel; Judith Ballard, a friend who took the time to read, to edit, and to comment on the manuscript before it was submitted to the publisher; Bert Hitchcock, emeritus English professor at Auburn University, who made suggestions for tying the two sections of the novel together; Austin K. Sanderson and Della D. Sanderson, the author's son and daughter, who never stopped supporting their mother's "new" career; other family and friends, too numerous to name, who encouraged the author in her writing journey.

Book Group Discussion Questions

1. What is the historical significance of Lee v. Macon County Board of Education to Alabama's educational system? To Alabama's politics?

2. What point does the author wish to make about how the Notasulga schools implemented Judge Johnson's order in 1967, to completely desegregate by 1972?

3. Overall, how well does the author describe the atmosphere of a small Southern town facing desegregation in the 60s and 70s? Does the author present believable portrayals of the political and legal figures who played an active role in the fight for and against desegregation?

4. How does Mose contribute to the story? What is his role? What does he symbolize? Is the symbolism successful?

5. Discuss the contributions of Hunter Moore to the success of the new high school. Would he be an acceptable principal in today's schools?

6. What do the attitudes of the members of the Methodist Church reveal about the church? The young minister? The town?

7. What is the role of the church in the novel?

8. How active was the KKK in the novel? How active is it today?

9. Does Marley Jane's attitude toward the town change? How does the town change?

10. Compare and contrast the "young man," who is a plaintiff in Lee v. Macon, and Marley Jane.

11. What are the most significant relationships in this novel? How well does the author portray their significance and complexity?

12. What is the effect that the rapes have on the people of the county? What do they reveal? How did you, as a reader, react? Why has the author chosen to include this episode?

13. Is any of the violence in the novel justified?

14. Marley Jane says that her mother is a "Kennedy Democrat," not a "Wallace Democrat." What is the difference?

15. What is the importance of Robert Kennedy, Jr.'s visit to Notasulga?

16. Which characters impressed you as strong?

17. The arsonists who burned the school are never revealed. In your opinion, why? Who do you think was responsible?

18. How does this novel relate to today's issues in regard to race and discrimination? To Southern and national politics?

19. What does the inclusion of the photojournalist, Vernon Merrett, tell you about conflicting racial attitudes in the South, especially in Alabama, in 1964?

20. Voting rights is an important topic in the novel. How serious an issue is voting rights in America today? Does it remain a problem?

21. While playing bridge, Marley Jane confronts her peers in regards to voting rights. What does she learn during that scene?

About the Author

Shirley Aaron was born and raised in Valley, Alabama, the daughter of the late Bob C. Austin and Hazel S. Austin, of Hopewell Community. She is the widow of the late Charles O. Aaron, who was an attorney in Lanett, Alabama. She has two children—a son, Austin K. Sanderson, who lives in New Jersey, and a daughter, Della D. Sanderson, who lives in Huntsville, Alabama.

Shirley received a Bachelor of Science in Education degree in 1977 and a Master of Education degree in 1980 from Auburn University, where she also obtained certification as a media specialist.

She worked forty-two years as an educator, teaching English in grades 9-12, as well as teaching English 101 part-time at Southern Union State College. She retired in Alabama as an English teacher in 1996. Then, she began working in Georgia, where she retired in 2011 as a media specialist.

Shirley has enjoyed writing as a hobby for years, with a focus on poetry. She published a book of poetry, *Drops of Light*, in June, 2014. It was based on her life experiences and how she perceived those experiences. *Troubling the Ashes* is her first novel and is set in Notasulga, Alabama where she lived and worked for fourteen years.

Shirley is currently working on a second novel, tentatively titled *Sweet Tea with Lemon*. It is about three very funny women who have been friends for years and about one's battle with cancer. Cancer forces each woman to evaluate the true meaning of friendship, dying, and family. They realize that death cannot be stopped; therefore, they must embrace life in the process of dying. The story is set in two small Southern towns in the 1990s.

CPSIA information can be obtained at www.ICGtesting.com
Printed in the USA
BVOW05s0223200616

452701BV00033B/400/P